Jonathan Black is thf
Hungarian parents w
many years working
style of 'investigative
reputation. Inevitably
as many friends) and l
occasions. It was only .... one occasion by the
Army's insistence that he re-enlist – as they pointed out, he
was safer *in* than *out*. It is Black's nose for the truth behind
the façade and his unique ability to sniff out corruption that
informs his other highly successful novels, *The World Rapers*,
Oil, *Ride the Golden Tiger*, *Megacorp*, *The Plunderers* and *The
Carnage Merchants*.

By the same author

The World Rapers
Oil
Ride the Golden Tiger
Megacorp
The Plunderers
The Carnage Merchants

JONATHAN BLACK

The House on the Hill

GRAFTON BOOKS
A Division of the Collins Publishing Group

LONDON GLASGOW
TORONTO SYDNEY AUCKLAND

Grafton Books
A Division of the Collins Publishing Group
8 Grafton Street, London W1X 3LA

Published by Grafton Books 1978
Reprinted 1978, 1979, 1980, 1982, 1986, 1988

A Grafton Paperback Original

Copyright © Jonathan Black 1978

ISBN 0-583-12890-4

Printed and bound in Great Britain by
Collins, Glasgow

Set in Baskerville

To Page Cuddy – gratefully.

Author's Note

. . . Whole platoons of President Richard M Nixon's aides and advisers and men he appointed to high office are charged with committing criminal acts and in many cases found guilty.

. . . One of the most influential members of the House of Representatives is forced to resign after a squalid affair with a stripper and the revelation that he has long been a hopeless alcoholic.

. . . Another prominent legislator keeps a young woman on the public payroll at a five-figure salary. She is supposedly his secretary, but the only services she performs are sexual.

. . . Mystery still shrouds the truth about the handsome Senator who drove a car off a bridge and saved his own life while the girl with him drowned.

. . . Several of America's largest corporations admit making huge illegal contributions to US politicians of both major parties and giving astronomical bribes to foreign government officials and politicians.

. . . The Central Intelligence Agency is shown to have masterminded and financed bloody revolutions abroad – and planned and almost certainly carried out cold-blooded assassinations in various countries.

. . . A former Federal Bureau of Investigation Director was, for decades, a stridently self-avowed scourge of sexual deviates employed by the US Government and an implacable foe of crime and corruption in any form. Then the public learns that he himself was a homosexual and used Government funds to buy expensive gifts for his favorites.

. . . A new FBI Director pledges top-to-bottom reform and cleansing of the much-discredited Bureau. And then someone blows the whistle. His private home has been redecorated at the taxpayers' expense.

. . . A female newspaper publisher openly details her sexual relations with President Franklin D Roosevelt.

. . . Reliable accounts testify that President John F Kennedy virtually turned the White House into a brothel and a party-girl tells how she commuted between his bed and that of Mafia *capo* Sam Giancana . . .

The dismal recital is only a random quick-skim of Washington-centered scandals that have come to light in very recent years. There have been very many more, as news-media readers, viewers, and listeners have learned to their dismay, disgust, or sardonic amusement.

All this would seem to create almost insuperable problems for an author bent on writing a novel about Washington and those who hold, use – and abuse – power there. How can he hope to construct a fictional story that has not been far surpassed by published facts?

The solution is surprisingly simple. He needs but to dig deeper and uncover the even greater scandals that have not been reported and use them as a basis upon which his imagination can build a work of fiction.

True, Washington insiders are active, fulltime partners in a conspiracy of silence. They are politicians of both major parties, upper echelon military personnel, high-ranking civilian officials, lobbyists, bureaucrats, foreign diplomats, and representatives of the news media. They are determined to conceal the more bizarre – and often appalling – secrets about their own and each other's illicit activities, machinations, manipulations, excesses, and aberrations.

The mechanism of this mutual protection society works effectively save under certain exceptional conditions. These, for the most part, fall into one or another of three categories:

1. A large number of power-players unite in a decision to leak – or blow open – a story that will damage or destroy an individual or an entire Presidential Administration.

2. A member of the conspiratorial Establishment commits some act or creates an explosive situation before witnesses who cannot be controlled or in circumstances that make cover-up or whitewash impossible.

3. Vindictiveness – or simply momentary pique – motivates a politician, newsman, embittered wife, or discarded mistress to make sensational revelations too loudly and clearly for them to be concealed or suppressed.

In such instances, the luckless victims are abandoned to the mob by the Establishment, which concentrates on shoring up the protective wall around its survivors.

But those not bound by the unwritten law of Washington-style *omerta*, who do not belong to the tacit freemasonry, owe it no debts, and are willing to exert the necessary effort can find – or make – chinks and holes in the Establishment's wall. Through these the outsider can see, hear, observe. On occasion, he may even squeeze through to the inside and experience at first hand. It is thus that the novelist becomes familiar with the actual events and individuals that provide the ideas from which he manufactures a work of pure fiction.

Withal, I offer no apologies to any persons – or Personages – who might conceivably imagine themselves as being depicted among the fictional characters in this book. Any resemblances are – to use the hackneyed phrase – entirely coincidental. Or (and this is more likely) any who think they see resemblances to themselves will be having paranoid reactions – which are by no means uncommon among those ridden with guilt and fear.

JONATHAN BLACK
1977

I

Washington, D.C.: Tuesday, February 16. Early Morning.

The burly Secret Service agent on graveyard-shift foot-patrol of the White House grounds squeezed into the sentry box to make his scheduled 5:45 A.M. check with the uniformed East Gate guard.

'All quiet here,' the gate-guard reported. Bored, he wanted to talk. 'Everything peaceful in the palace?'

'Like halfway.' The Secret Service man was glad to break the monotony of his rounds with a little conversation. 'The Man came downstairs and went into the Oval Office at five.'

'He's been doing that for a week. Funny, he never did before.'

During the slightly more than two years since his inauguration President Charles Pendleton Talbot's White House day had begun regularly at eight-thirty. Recently, he had formed a new habit-pattern, arising long before dawn and closeting himself – alone – in the Oval Office.

'He never had so many headaches before, either,' the brawny plainclothes agent said. 'Christ, the economy stinks, people all over the country are raising hell – then there's the African mess. He probably wants to do some heavy thinking in private.' The agent paused, remembering. 'Phone the night security chief if you see the grey Jag coming in.'

'The Man's daughter AWOL again?'

'Uh-huh. Gave her security backup car the slip. Per usual – whenever she gets in the mood.'

The gate-guard scowled. 'The fucking government spends a fortune to protect that dame, and she thinks it's fun and games. She's a pain in the ass, if you ask me. Take that Jaguar she drives. It's imported – British – right? But we have a zillion people out of work because nobody's buying the cars they make in Detroit. If she was my kid . . .'

'She's not,' the Secret Service man broke in sharply. The sentry box might be bugged. President Talbot tolerated no criticisms of his daughter. Anyone on the White House staff heard – or overheard – passing uncomplimentary remarks about her was soon sent packing. 'She's Lexa Talbot – beautiful, whip-smart, and the public loves her.' It was true. 'Besides, friend, her father happens to be the President. With all that going for her, she can do damn near anything she pleases.'

Leaving the sentry box to resume his patrol, the agent glanced up at the sky. 'It's going to be a shitty day,' he muttered.

Washington seemed even more dismal and deserted than it usually does at 5:45 A.M. It had rained earlier; streets and sidewalks were still wet. Outdoor temperatures stood only a few degrees above freezing. Massed dark clouds guaranteed more foul weather later in the day.

Running die-straight from Kalorama Circle in Washington's Northwest quadrant to the Maryland state line, Upper Connecticut Avenue appeared especially empty and devoid of life. The thoroughfare is largely lined with densely populated apartment blocks. These were dark, the people in them asleep. During normal hours traffic along Upper Connecticut Avenue ranges from the congested to the chaotic. Now there was none – or almost none.

Coming from the direction of downtown Washington, a black Lincoln Continental sedan sped past the Bureau of Standards and onto the Brandywine Street intersection, where it slowed abruptly and pulled over to the curb on the far corner. Its lights went out, the engine continued to idle. There were two men in the front seat, two in back. The driver twisted his head around and spoke to a big, raw-boned man wearing a black overcoat who sat next to the curbside rear door. 'This okay?' he asked.

'Perfect. Don't want to attract attention driving up to the front entrance. Anyway, a walk'll do me good.' Thick-voiced and slurring his words, the big man got out, mumbled 'G'night – and thanks' and closed the door. The sedan remained where it was. He walked ahead, lurching slightly. Midway up the block he stepped off the sidewalk and started to cross Connecticut Avenue. Instantly headlights blazed and the Lincoln Continental leaped forward. Startled, the big man stared to his left and, blinded by the onrushing headlight beams, froze. For a split second the Continental's hood ornament was a cross-haired gunsight square on target. Then impact.

The car's weight and momentum were sufficient to hurl the black-overcoated target-figure thirty feet through the air. The sedan slowed but did not stop. Front and rear wheels bumped as tires crushed over the sprawled body. The Lincoln accelerated, drove on.

A drab Chevrolet materialized moments later, slowed to a low-gear crawl when it reached the Brandywine Street intersection and halted short of the mangled corpse. The driver and his companion stared through the windshield, shook their heads, and shrugged wearily. The Chevy made a tight U-turn and headed back toward the center of Washington.

Potomac Plaza is a vast hotel-apartment complex surpassing the nearby Watergate complex in luxury and astronomical rents without invoking memories of political scandals that destroyed a Presidential Administration and convulsed the nation.

Residents of Potomac Plaza are necessarily wealthy. Most are influential in one way or another. Many are prominent, some famous – few more so than Suzanne Loring, who occupied the $48,000-a-year Penthouse 'A' in Potomac Plaza's Lafayette Tower. At thirty-one, Suzanne Loring was rich, glamorous and a force in Washington. Her weekly 'Washington Inside Out' was America's highest-rated, politically oriented television talk-show. Each Tuesday night, twenty million coast-to-coast viewers watched her interrogate some public figure – and often demolish him – with scalpel-sharp questions, barbed wit, and wryly cynical comments.

Suzanne obtained scoops, disinterred long-buried bodies, and created innumerable sensations on her show. But she knew the tacit boundaries beyond which it was professionally fatal to venture. Certain capital scandals and facets of capital manners, mores, and behavior were sacrosanct. Touching upon them would unite all the disparate elements of the Washington Establishment, bring on its collective vengeance in the form of social ostracism, information blackouts, and retaliation by such Government bureaus and agencies as the FCC and IRS. Suzanne trod dangerously close to the limits but never overstepped them, yet consistently delighted her ever-growing audience. She received much praise and publicity and was the darling of her prime-time sponsors and her Continental Broadcasting Network chiefs.

Suzanne Loring – née Fournier – had reached her success plateau the hard way. The product of a stormy mixed marriage between a temperamental father of French descent and a possessive Jewish mother, she was born with an ability to cope with a claustrophobic home-atmosphere and even to see the humorous side of her parents' incessant squabbles. An intelligent, perceptive child, she was fascinated by all that went on in the world around her. She developed into a precocious, elfin child, later into a gangly adolescent, and finally into a beautiful young woman. Many people claimed that, in certain moods, she bore a striking resemblance to Jacqueline Kennedy – but, they agreed, Suzanne had more warmth and character, plus an elusive gamin-like quality all her own.

Eager to gain experience of Life – and have a life of her own – Suzanne left college at nineteen, at the start of her senior year. She talked herself into a job as Girl Friday with Anthony Loring, a second-string political columnist for a third-rate feature syndicate. Within a week he ended her virginity, and a month later she moved in with him to become his mistress, legwoman, whipping-boy, nursemaid, and housekeeper. Suddenly feeling grownup, free, independent and marvelously wicked, Suzanne somehow failed to realize that she had been trapped into servitude and was being used by Loring mercilessly.

Of course she was very much in love with him. Although lazy and much too glib, Loring did possess a great deal of worldly knowledge, and he taught her much. He was also good in bed – how good was something Suzanne did not fully appreciate until several years and several affairs later. Their relationship remained unchanged for about eighteen months, when Anthony Loring was offered a high-paying contract as a political columnist for a major Washington daily paper. By then Suzanne was doing most of his work – researching, interviewing, and even ghosting many items in his columns. He could not risk losing her and proposed marriage. She accepted without hesitation and thought herself blissfully happy.

Three years passed before she discovered that her husband had obtained – and was holding – his contract by sporadically bedding the middle-aged widow who owned the newspaper. 'God, but I was a slow study,' Suzanne was wont to remark afterward. Naively, she demanded he end the affair. He refused. She filed suit for divorce. Once the decree was granted, Loring married a skinny model from New York and went to Europe as a *Time* political correspondent. Suzanne nearly had a nervous breakdown but got fat instead. She did nothing but eat, sleep, and feel sorry for herself. Then, when the always infrequent alimony checks stopped coming altogether, she pulled herself together, went on a brutal diet and got a job as a researcher with the Continental Broadcasting Network's Washington television station.

Fiercely determined to be forever independent – emotionally as well as financially – Suzanne worked extremely hard and well. Soon she was doing fill-ins in local newscasts. When given a tryout as a local talk-show hostess, Suzanne transformed that dud morning program into one no housewife would miss, even if the breakfast dishes stayed unwashed.

Suzanne Loring's rise to her national 'Washington Inside Out' show and six-figure annual salary was swift. She dressed in offbeat clothes that made the most of her shapely bosom and shapelier legs. Her brains, wit, sauciness, and sex appeal delighted viewers, as did her inside Washington knowledge and caustic remarks. But although her show was a fixture with an eye-popping Nielsen, her ambition remained strong. There were higher peaks, and she had resolved to reach them.

At 5:45 A.M. the Lucite-cube digital clock in the bedroom of Suzanne Loring's penthouse sounded its early-warning purr. Russell Hatch stirred, awoke. Easing out of the warm tangle in which he and Suzanne had been sleeping, he leaned across her and pressed the glowing button that silenced the purr and turned on the bedside lamp. His hand slid under the Roman-striped sheet, gently caressing Suzanne's breasts. She made small, sleep-blurred noises. His easy grin formed. Head bent low, lips against her ear, Russell Hatch parodied the sounds.

Awake now behind still-closed eyes, Suzanne Loring feigned petulance. 'Go away, Senator. Hold yourself a quorum or something.' Turning toward him, she opened one brown eye. 'You know I'm a lousy lover in the morning.' Her other eye opened. 'Unless it's a special occasion.' Her right eyebrow arched hopefully. 'Is it?'

'Sort of, for you. But no sex. You don't have time.'

'Oh, God!' Suzanne groaned. 'You're right, Russ.' Her face, noted for being mobile and expressive, registered dejection. She sat up. The covers fell to her waist revealing a delectably proportioned torso, slender and firm-fleshed. 'Shit! I have to get up in the middle of the night. We can't make love. All because Daniel A. – for Asshole – Madigan won't tape his interview in the afternoon like everyone else. It has to be done at eight in the morning. At *eight*, for Christ's sake!'

They had met two years before when Russell Hatch began his first term as a junior senator from Oregon. Young, one of the more promising new legislators washed into office by Presidential candidate Charles Talbot's successful 'Renew America' campaign, Hatch was a natural for

Suzanne's show. She found him refreshing, practically unique. During the interview he came across as a realist who still retained ideals and as an intelligent, informed, and forthright man with a disarming sense of humor. She was instantly drawn to him. After taping the show they went to the Hay-Adams for cocktails, the ultra-In Jean-Pierre for dinner – and, later that night, to bed.

Their relationship had since grown into much more than an affair, yet considerably less than a Marriage Inevitable situation. A childless widower, Hatch had never quite got over his wife's death. Suzanne, understandably soured on the theory and practice of matrimony, valued her career and independent life-style. But they were good – very good – together, in bed and out. Suzanne obtained complete gratification from Russ's imaginative – yet always considerate – lovemaking. And he was genuine as a person, unlike the assortment of phonies, egomaniacs, and other creeps with whom she had had affairs before.

'I loathe Dan Madigan,' Suzy resumed her tirade. 'Your friend – or strawboss – is a . . .'

'Hey, come off the wall.' Russ ran fingers through his thick shock of red hair. 'Madigan does his job, and I wish he were my friend. It'd help me do mine.'

'Tell me how – I'm fascinated.'

'Honey, a Senate Majority Leader carries clout. A nod from Madigan and I might be able to do more than roost in a back row and read stupid sub-sub-committee reports.'

Hatch had come to the Senate eager to implement his Party's sweeping campaign promises. He soon learned that freshmen senators rank a bare notch above page boys and rate only condescending nods from more senior members of the Anointed One Hundred.

Russ looked at the clock. 'Go take your bath,' he said, slapping Suzanne's bare bottom lightly. She stretched her supple body, gave him an affectionate kiss and headed for the bathroom. He went into the kitchen. Moments later, he was leaning against a polished butcher-block countertop waiting for Suzanne's latest electronic gadget to transform water into coffee. His clear blue eyes scanned the familiar, spotless room and he smiled. The most elaborately equipped and least-used kitchen east of Palm Springs, he thought. The coffee machine gave a muted gurgle. He filled two bright red mugs and carried them into the bathroom.

'Your first fix of the day,' he announced, handing her a mug as she luxuriated in Givenchy bath-foam. He sat on a padded stool next to the huge, free-form sunken bathtub and sipped his coffee. Suzanne gazed at him over her coffee-mug rim and made a fond, oft-recurring appraisal. He's well muscled, well endowed, well put together, she mused, but it's that open boyish face, mop of red hair and those Goddamned freckles that make him so appealing. No wonder *Newsweek* called him 'an overgrown Tom Sawyer'. And no wonder I can't help feeling protective toward him.

'Suzy?'

'I'm on the line.'

'What size can opener are you going to use on Dan Madigan?'

Her right eyebrow arched. 'Who uses can openers on a pile of mush that drivels platitudes?' Her lips curved into a smile at once elfin and malicious. 'I'll go for his jugular, though.'

Russ brushed away a bit of bath foam that had somehow attached itself to her short, dark brown hair. 'Care to give me a preview?'

'A pleasure. I want his views – not quotations from the Bible or Bartlett's – on whether the economy will be given mouth-to-mouth resuscitation before it's stone-cold dead. What do he and dum-dum Talbot intend doing about the riots in Detroit and points east, west, north and south? Is Madigan supporting the Pentagon-CIA African safari?' Suzy chuckled. 'And that's just for openers.'

Russ winced. 'No mercy, huh?'

'Russ! The country's in lousy shape. People haven't only lost confidence. They've lost hope. And you're talking about *mercy*?'

'Honey, you're television's gorgeous, super-sexy Grand Inquisitor, and I'm your Number One fan. But you're exaggerating – and you'll be exacerbating. Thing's aren't good, but they can't improve unless Talbot and Congress get together and come up with solutions. Tearing Daniel Madigan apart won't help.'

'Spoken like a true Talbot Administration tightrope-walker.' Suzy climbed out of the bath, wrapped herself in a vast, brightly patterned terry cloth robe and gestured toward the tub. 'It's all yours.'

She took a step, stopped short, eyes narrowing. *'Wait a minute!* Did Madigan con you into asking me to pull my punches?' She studied him. 'He did, didn't he, Russ?'

His freckles seemed to fade as his face flushed. 'Suzy – everybody knows how close you and I are. Madigan stopped me yesterday in the cloakroom – the first time he's ever said more than a dozen words to me – and yes, he did mention the show . . .'

'I see.' Suzanne looked away, professional integrity and personal feelings unhappily colliding. She did loathe Madi-gad, considered him an oil-slick, grafting pol who deserved the full stab, chop, and slash treatment. And the public was entitled to see him and the rest of Talbot's feeble, inept administration exposed. Suzy chewed her lower lip. On the other hand Russ had never – but never – asked her for a favor. That's a miracle in this town, she reflected. Everyone in Washington is forever asking – or demanding – favors, using each other. God knows my husband, that bastard, used *me*. Most – maybe *all* – the other men I've been in-volved with sooner or later asked me to put in a word here, give them a plug, help them get this or that. Besides, didn't I just tell myself I couldn't help feeling protective about Russ?

Professional conscience died a painful death.

'All right, Russ,' she said at last. 'I won't play rough.' Despite herself, Suzanne could not keep a chill note out of her tone.

The sleek, silver-gray Jaguar J72 was unmistakable, as was the breathtakingly lovely blonde girl whose gloved hands held the steering wheel. The two armed guards posted at the AUTHORIZED WHITE HOUSE PERSONNEL ONLY entrance hastened to open the gates and saluted smartly.

'Good morning, Miss Talbot,' they chanted in unison and were rewarded with the fabled Lexa Talbot smile. Behind it she gloated, tingling with a familiar feeling of excitement. The guards were like dolls – like dolls that belonged to her, dolls she could make jump, open gates, stand at attention and salute, all with nothing more than a glance. And she had so many dolls – hundreds, thousands, even millions at her beck and call. Wonderful!

Lexa drove through the open gates. Except for her father, she was the only person in the world who could do so without showing a special pass, possibly undergoing a car – even a body – search.

White House security was stricter than under any previous Administration, having been greatly tightened some months before when the latest round of civil rioting began. Police, Secret Service, and Marine contingents were doubled and huge sums spent on new electrical surveillance and alarm devices. Regular staff members and employees displayed passes when entering the grounds, again when going into the buildings. Anyone else – Cabinet officer or deliveryman – was subject to yet more stringent ID checks before being allowed to enter.

Lexa Talbot was exempt from all these rules and accorded the treatment due a Princess Royal. The Night Security Chief personally held open the Presidential family entrance door for her. He took her coat, ceremoniously handing it to an attending Marine gunnery sergeant.

The coat was fake-fur. It had to be. Conservation and environmental protection had been major planks in the Talbot campaign platform, and Lexa was the Honorary Chairperson of the American Wildlife Preservation Society. Other organizations devoted to worthy causes had showered the President's charismatic twenty-five-year-old daughter with titles and positions customarily reserved for society dowagers and the middle-aged wives of men of very great wealth. Her involvement in humanitarian and philanthropic activities added weight to news media claims that Lexa Talbot was her father's most valuable political asset.

'The President said he would like to see you when you arrived, Miss Talbot,' the Night Security Chief – another doll, Lexa thought – told her. 'He's in the Oval Office.'

Lexa's delicately boned features and her eyes, smoky-gray like those of her father, registered concern. 'Poor Daddy, he should still be in bed, asleep – but thank you, I'll go right in to see him.' She hurried down the corridor, electrically controlled steel barriers swinging wide before her as the Marine sergeant manipulated switches. The Night Security Chief felt a twinge of envy. He had a daughter about the same age and wished she showed him a fraction of the love and affection that Lexa had for her father.

Charles Talbot admitted his daughter into the Oval Office and grinned when she hugged and kissed him. At fifty-four, Talbot retained traces of his college football player look. Five-feet-ten, he had a flat belly, but his broad face was lined and the crewcut hair was peppered with gray.

'You're getting in later and later, Puss,' he said indulgently. They went to a sofa opposite the Presidential desk, sat side-by-side.

'And you're getting up earlier and earlier,' Lexa chided. She noticed the stacks of folders on the desk. Neat stacks. Clearly, they hadn't been touched. 'You weren't working,' she said, sensing that he wished to talk.

'Been staring at the walls. You might call it thinking.' Talbot leaned back against the sofa cushions. 'The job's growing tougher and tougher, Baby. Too much piling up that I can't sort out.'

'Hilarious. This place crawls with advisers, aides, experts . . .'

Talbot snorted. 'They get their kicks contradicting each other.' His wide shoulders drooped. 'A thousand things are going wrong – then all of a sudden Basanda threatens to blow up in our faces.'

A large West African country enormously rich in oil and metal ores, Basanda gained independence from Britain in 1968. American multinational companies made heavy investments to exploit its natural resources and helped establish a reactionary authoritarian government which ruled for several years. Then dissidents began an armed revolt. CIA money and arms and U.S. military advisers aided the incumbent – and increasingly oppressive – native government, but the rebel forces were gaining the upper hand. Talbot was under increasing pressure to order full-scale American intervention.

'What are your options?' Lexa asked casually. The daughter of a professional politician, she had learned that politics were a game and a lucrative commercial enterprise. Candidates were – or were not – elected. Those who were In reveled in power. In or Out, politicians made deals, divided spoils, sent laundered profits to Swiss banks. She had gained her own profits by playing the game at her father's side. Lexa reveled, too – in her public role as America's Perfect Daughter symbol and Princess Royal surrogate. As for her private life – that was another exciting game, her very own and nobody else's business.

'Options?' President Talbot echoed. 'Well, Pearce thinks we should go in fast and hit hard. He says we can't let a friendly government go under without destroying what little is left of our credibility.'

MacDonald Pearce, the dour Secretary of State, was not one of Lexa's favorites. Her finely sculpted nose wrinkled. 'That's preacher Pearce at his sermonizing worst. What's the real reason?'

'American companies will lose billions if the rebels – Reds or whatever the hell they are – win and expropriate U.S. holdings over there.'

'There must be more to it.'

'Sure. The NAM, big business wheels like Jordan Rickhoven, and a slew of others argue that military intervention will get industry moving and cut unemployment.' Talbot curled a strand of Lexa's fair hair around a finger. 'Nothing like a small war to give the economy a boost.'

'Daddy, Korea wrecked Truman. Vietnam finished Johnson.'

'Different now. We have an all-volunteer military. The

men are professionals – mercenaries, if you want to be honest. They're paid damned good money to fight for God, country, and Mom's apple pie. No draftees the public might get worked up over if they're killed or wounded.'

'Sounds like a cut-and-dried consensus to me.'

'It isn't. The Chairman of the Joint Chiefs is a holdout. He's afraid the Russians will wade in if we sent combat troops. And we've got flocks of noisy doves in the Senate and House.' Talbot felt better already, as always when he talked to his daughter. They were very much alike, a team, and she was the one person who wanted nothing from him – nothing but love and affection, he reflected.

Lexa rested a hand on his thigh. 'Which way are you leaning?'

'Neither, yet. I'd like some advice from a couple of people whose instincts I trust. Avery Braithwaite for one. He's a wise old coot and shrewd.' Braithwaite had been Chief Justice of the Supreme Court for a decade. Like Talbot, he came from Illinois. They were old friends.

'Good idea. Who else?'

'I'd rather not say.'

'Not even to *me*?' Lexa blinked. Her father had never before refused to answer a question she put to him directly.

'Sorry, Puss. Not even to you.' He averted his eyes.

'Oh.' Lexa stood up. 'Well, I absolutely must get some sleep.' She started toward the door, stopped. 'I almost forgot, Daddy. I met a man at a party who'd be a terrific press aide or speechwriter . . .'

'Say no more. Tell whoever's in charge of those things to put your literary genius on the payroll.' That should make up for having dodged her question, Talbot thought.

'You're a love.' Lexa bent down and kissed him on the lips.

Alone once more, Oval Office doors locked, Talbot stretched out on the sofa. He guessed that Lexa had already been to bed with the man she mentioned. He long ago perceived that Lexa had inherited his own highly sexed nature. Thoughts marched on in methodical association. His own biggest personal problem was sex – or rather, lack of it. His wife, Evelyn – Lexa's mother – was a 'resident guest' in an upstate New York clinic that specialized in discreet, maximum-security care of Very Important problem patients suffering from 'nervous ailments'. Not that Evelyn could satisfy my needs, Talbot mused. She never did.

While a Congressman and later a Senator, Talbot enjoyed an endless succession of women. But the Presidency imposed severe restrictions. He could not bring a woman into the White House. There had been too many lurid revelations about his predecessors – Kennedy, Johnson, Nixon, others. Public opinion and Party bosses would condone no more scandals about what they piously called 'illicit sex' in the White House. As President, he was forced to obtain sexual outlet away from Washington. Arrangements for any liaison had to be made far in advance. And, wherever he went, the knowledge that Secret Service men lurked outside doors and windows was inhibiting, dulled his pleasure. Worse yet, recent developments required his full-time presence in the White House, precluding even such occasional forays.

Lexa's lucky, Talbot told himself. She's not caged in like I am. An unbidded image sprang into his mind. He visualized Lexa in bed, her cornsilk hair tangled, arms and legs locked around a faceless man, body thrusting against his. Talbot struggled to erase the picture, but jump-cut scenes of his own sexual encounters replaced it. He fought to stop them, but it was only the weight of history that kept the hand of the President of the United States away from his belt buckle.

Lexa Talbot was logged in by the White House gate-guards at 5:51 A.M. At precisely the same time, a police prowl car cruising Upper Connecticut Avenue reached the corner of Brandywine Street. Officer George Vreeland, the driver, saw the corpse, cursed, swung the car broadside and switched on the dome flasher. His partner, Ned Lattimer, vaulted out, ran to the body and bent down to examine it.

'Hit-run,' Lattimer said as Vreeland joined him. 'Must've

24

been boozed to the ears.' The reek of liquor cut through the stench of blood and pulped organic matter. 'Brace yourself and look at the face.'

The massive square jaw, bushy eyebrows, and ragged scar running diagonally across the high forehead were unmistakable.

'Son of a bitch!' Vreeland was stunned. 'General Weidener!'

'Yeah.' Lattimer examined documents he found on the body. These positively identified the victim as General Keith Weidener, winner of the Medal of Honor in Korea, gallant division commander in Vietnam, national folk hero, and more recently Chairman of the Joint Chiefs of Staff.

'A nine hundred – call it in,' Ned Lattimer muttered.

District of Columbia police provide Washington's elite with considerable insurance against embarrassment or scandal. If anyone of high rank in Government, the Military, or the Diplomatic Corps is found dead – or even in a compromising situation – the police make no initial record. Instead, the civilian police notify the Federal department or agency or the foreign embassy of which the individual is a member. Such notifications have the code-call-number 900. Later – frequently much later and sometimes never – District Police records are retroactively doctored to reflect whatever versions the appropriate authorities desire. Although clearly the victim of a hit-and-run accident, it was evident that General Weidener had been drunk – a fact the Army would most definitely want kept off the record.

Vreeland activated the prowl-car's radio. 'We have a nine-oh-oh, Army,' he reported. His radio transmission was promptly spliced into the Fort McNair Duty Officer's line. The Duty Officer answered, identifying himself as Captain something-or-other.

'One of yours nine-oh-oh at Upper Connecticut and Brandywine,' Vreeland said. 'Hit-run – but he was eight-six' – the code for drunk.

'What size?' the Captain asked, meaning how high in rank.

'Couldn't be any larger.'

'We'll have people there in minutes. Cover the body.'

'It's been done.'

Lattimer had already spread a canvas tarpaulin from the prowl car's trunk over the corpse, carefully shrowding the face of the gallant General Weidener.

2

Washington, D.C.: Tuesday, February 16. Midmorning.

Suzanne Loring had been increasingly withdrawn while she and Russell Hatch dressed and waited for the Central Broadcasting Network limousine that would take her to the studio. Hatch retrieved his Pontiac from the underground garage and drove home to his own Cleveland Park apartment. He cooked ham and eggs to supplement his predawn coffee. Neither the food nor the unfiltered Pall Malls he chain-smoked after eating helped ease his growing guilt feelings, and he puttered around listlessly.

I really fucked up, Russ berated himself. *I should never have let Dan Madigan talk me into using my relationship with Suzy to get him off the hook. It's made me a pratboy on one hand, a God-damned pimp on the other.*

He continued dawdling until almost ten o'clock – by then Suzy's taping session with Dan Madigan was certain to be over. He finally decided against telephoning her. Whatever had transpired during the interview, the chances were that Suzanne's mood would be worse and not one receptive to apologies. I'll make it up to Suzy somehow, he assured himself, once again realizing how much she meant to him.

Lighting yet another Pall Mall, Russ went into his living room, morosely dumping his six-foot-one frame into an armchair and turned on the radio, tuning in WAVA-FM, an all-news station.

'... National Guard units continue to stand by in Detroit,' a newscaster's voice grated. 'Local authorities have once again emphasized that there are no racial over-tones to the rioting that has wracked the Motor City for several days ...'

Down and dirty reverse psychology, Russ thought. The riots in Detroit and other industrial cities were violent demonstrations by jobless people of all races who were in desperate straits because there were no more funds available to pay them unemployment compensation. Strident denials of 'racial overtones' only made an uneasy, gullible public think that race hatreds were, after all, the actual cause of the riots.

'. . . More grim news from the Republic of Basanda, where rebels yesterday massacred five hundred innocent men, women and children . . .'

Neat offset, Hatch applauded in bitter silence. Makes black Americans believe we're agonizing over the fate of black Africans.

'. . . But embattled Basandan Loyalists are to receive aid from an unexpected quarter. The Israeli Government has announced it will send them quantities of arms and ammunition . . .'

Which explains why the Pentagon only last week agreed to give Israel an extra billion dollars worth of weapons, Russ thought. A double-shuffling arm twist in the old Henry Kissinger tradition. We'll give you a pile of brand new military hardware if you'll ship some of your older stuff to Basanda. The gambit scored points for the hawks. With Israel helping Basanda, American liberals and a large segment of the U.S. Jewish population would start rooting for the Basandan Loyalists in a sort of sympathy-by-association reaction. Hatch recognized it as just another step in the Long March to American intervention.

'Shit!' he said aloud, angrily turning off the radio, his depression deepening. He was helpless to influence developing trends. I made a hell of a mistake going into politics, he thought. I've been a U.S. Senator – big fucking deal! – for over two years and haven't accomplished a single God-damned thing. I should have stayed in Portland, filing law-suits and writing briefs. At least I'd have the satisfaction of winning a case every now and then.

Russell Hatch had been nudged into politics by a mixed

bag of events. His wife's sudden death from peritonitis following an ectopic pregnancy left him rudderless, lost, and the demands of his law practice failed to fill the void. When friends urged him to take active part in the 'Renew America' campaign launched by Presidential hopeful Charles Talbot, Russ reluctantly agreed. To his astonishment, he was next urged to run for the Senate. He did, barely nosing out his opponents in the primary. But, benefiting from the Talbot landslide, he received a large majority in the final election.

Russ had familiarized himself with Talbot's record. He had been first a Congressman and then a Senator from Pennsylvania, but no more than a professional politician, a plodding Party drayhorse. During the three years prior to his election as President, however, Charles Talbot served as Senate Majority Leader and in that post displayed previously unsuspected talents and abilities. He was spectacularly successful in unifying discordant Party factions, reconciling differences between bitter rivals, acting as moderator and arbitrator between both parties when important issues were at stake.

Like almost fifty million other Americans who voted for Talbot, Russ was convinced these were the very qualities a shaken and divided nation needed in its Chief Executive. Unfortunately, while Talbot was a master persuader and conciliator, he had virtually no experience in making decisions and implementing them. Instead of wielding authority after taking office Talbot delegated – and relegated – it. Consequently, Cabinet Departments, bureaus, and agencies went their own ways, often operating at cross-purposes.

Maybe Suzy was right, thought Russ, gloomily recalling their early-morning bedroom-bathroom dialogue. She had described Talbot as 'a dum-dum glad-hander manipulated by whoever shakes his hand last'.

Maybe, Russ told himself. But Talbot's all we have for this year and next. When a country elects a President, it marries him for four years. And while the country doesn't have to love, honor, and cherish its chosen mate, it sure as hell has to put up with him until divorce papers can be filed at the next Presidential election.

Forcing his spirits up a few notches, Russ decided it was time to leave for his office – if for no other reason than to answer the day's crop of inane letters from his constituents.

Jordan B. Rickhoven III's personal Boeing 727/100 landed at Washington National Airport on its ETA dot: 10.45 A.M. There would have been hell to pay otherwise. Billionaire Rickhoven, head of the Rickhoven Family Dynasty and its global industrial and financial empire, was a stickler for punctuality – and a man with enormous pull and power. That was why National Airport flight controllers had ordered incoming commercial airliners into holding patterns and given Rickhoven's Boeing priority landing clearance.

Jordan Rickhoven himself never hurried. There was no need. He tugged the strings; others leaped, sprinted, or genuflected. Totally self-assured, even his manner of dress advertised to any who did not already know that Jordan B. Rickhoven III did not give a good Goddamn for customs, conventions – or rules and regulations. He wore his expensive, flawlessly tailored clothes with a careless, insolent nonchalance that matched his outward manner and personality.

Six feet, four inches tall, angular of face and build, Rickhoven made his casual way through the airlines terminal, his superbly cut shadow-striped shirt unbuttoned at the collar, heavy silk tie loosened, pale cashmere overcoat tossed over a shoulder. He was flanked by aides who walked a deferential half-step behind. Their collars were securely fastened, neckties snug, somber overcoats neatly buttoned – and they carried large black attache cases.

A Cadillac limousine was waiting. Rickhoven dismissed his aides with an easy nod; they had received their instructions aboard the Boeing. When the Cadillac started moving, Rickhoven touched a switch. A sheet of thick, tinted glass sealed off the chauffeur's compartment. He next lifted the leather-sheathed lid of an armrest in which a radio-telephone was recessed and reached for the handset.

Daniel Aloysius Madigan had succeeded Charles Talbot as Senate Majority Leader. Madigan took full advantage of the prerogatives the post and his fourth-term senatorial seniority conferred. His office suite in the Everett Dirksen Building was huge – twelve rooms, including a two-room hideaway apartment. The rooms in which his assistants and secretaries worked were furnished in Megacorp Modern style. His own were opulent.

Madigan's private office contained a fortune in art and antique furniture commandeered from Federal art galleries and museums. Although lacking clearcut legal sanction, these institutions lend national art treasures to top-ranking members of Government and legislators with influence over budget appropriations.

Priceless paintings from the National Gallery of Art hung on the walls of Dan Madigan's private office – among them a Tintoretto and a Vandyke. Visitors could sit on Louis XV sofas or matched Queen Anne armchairs. Madigan's desk, a magnificent Charles Cressent rosewood table, had originally belonged to Thomas Jefferson. The fourth-term Senator from Illinois had pried these items away from the Smithsonian Institution by dropping a hint that he might instigate a special Senate probe into the Smithsonian's annual expenditures.

Daniel Madigan had clawed his path from a Chicago slum and up the treacherous Machine-made cliffs of Illinois politics by catering slavishly to those above yet never hesitating to perform favors for those below. En route he acquired a deep love of luxury and a smattering of culture. His costly clothes somehow fell short of the quiet Social Register elegance he sought to emulate. His thinning hair was a shade too meticulously combed, his shoes a shade too brightly shined. Madigan's constituents were blind to these minor flaws. They – North Shore tycoons or Downstate dirt-farmers – could rely on him to remember their names, assist them when they had problems, and ram through beneficial legislation.

Much pleased by the outcome of his morning encounter with Suzanne Loring, Madigan sat at his magnificent desk. His features – blurred slightly by self-indulgence and frequent excess – were alert and expectant. His manicured hands toyed with an onyx paperweight. His eyes were steady, though, fixed on a desktop telephone. He was waiting for it to ring.

Most Secretaries of State have felt their work surroundings should be consistent with the prestige of their position and the nation's wealth and power. Not so MacDonald Pearce, who believed that frills distracted and reduced efficiency.

Upon his appointment, Pearce ordered the Secretary's offices on the seventh floor of the State Department Building redecorated – or, more accurately – undecorated. They were stripped of their plush carpets, costly panelings and theatrical, twelve-pronged chandeliers. Rooms used by his immediate staff were made austere. His own private sanctum was spartan. Only the mandatory paintings of George Washington and Abraham Lincoln, autographed color photo-portraits of President Charles Talbot and Vice President Alvin Dunlap and a world map adorned the walls. The ascetic decor, Pearce believed, served notice on foreign diplomats that the United States had at last returned to a no-nonsense foreign policy.

The Secretary's desk was strictly functional, and it was devoid of esthetic appeal. Much the same could be said of the Secretary. Portly, sixty years old, MacDonald Pearce had a severe, humorless face and habitually wore drab, dark suits. A professor of political science, he had come to State from Harvard University. Although adopting requisite liberal protective coloration on domestic matters while there, Pearce was ultrareactionary in his approach to foreign affairs. He had responded to the summons from Washington as though to a Higher Calling, a zealous missionary sworn to erase any and all doubts about America's supremacy in the world. MacDonald Pearce peered through old-fashioned rimless bifocals at the unopened blue-plastic bound report that lay on his desk. Like Daniel Madigan, he was waiting.

Madigan's telephone was the first to ring.

'I've arrived Dan,' the Senate Majority Leader heard Jordan Rickhoven's voice say. 'We'll lunch at the club. At noon.'

'I'll be there, JB – hungry and thirsty.' Daniel Madigan, connoisseur of borrowed national art treasures, knew the fine art of mixing respect and bonhomie in correct proportions when speaking to a superior.

State Secretary MacDonald Pearce thrust aside the report he had not been reading and lifted his telephone receiver. The call was the one he expected.

'Good morning, Jordan. Did you have a good flight?'

'Smooth as silk, Mac. The club for lunch – at noon.'

'Of course, Jordan.'

The Lieutenant General was in full, fruit-saladed uniform. The Walter Reed Hospital Chief Pathologist, a Medical Corps Brigadier General, wore a white smock without insignia. They faced each other over the Chief Pathologist's desk.

'. . . legally a person is considered intoxicated when the alcohol content of his blood reaches ten one-hundredths of a per cent,' the medical officer was saying. 'Our tests show over three times that – but of course, that fact will be omitted from our reports.'

'You'll have to do a lot more than that,' the Lieutenant General declared. 'A hell of a lot more.'

'What – in a hit-and-run accident case? Why, for God's sake?'

'Keith had a girl friend – she's Black – and lives on the same block where he was killed. He must have been going to see her.'

'My God!' The Army could not afford to have *that* made public. 'How do we handle it?'

33

The Lieutenant General had come directly from a conference of Army brass hastily convened to discuss the 'Weidener affair'. He recited the scenario that had been concocted. 'Weidener died of a heart attack in his quarters at Fort McNair. Around five-thirty, he went downstairs to make a cup of coffee. Mrs Weidener heard him groan and fall. She found him lying on the kitchen floor and phoned Walter Reed for an ambulance. He was brought here – dead on arrival.'

'Will Mrs Wiedener back the story?' the Chief Pathologist asked.

'Betty Weidener's an Army brat. Her father graduated from the Point. She knows how these things are done.'

'Then we're clear.' The Chief Pathologist had no concerns over the Walter Reed staff. They, too, knew how 'these things are done'.

'I'll have someone notify the press and the President that General Weidener is dead,' the Lieutenant General said.

'What version does the President hear?'

'The *only* version – heart attack. Otherwise, he might order a gung-ho search for the hit-and-run car and the dirt about Weidener would be dredged up and spread open by the press. Our President isn't . . .'

'Isn't too bright.' The Chief Pathologist grimaced. 'That's hardly classified information.'

'Hardly. Be sure the reports and death certificate are done right.'

'Yes, sir. They will be – down to the last deleted detail.'

The Dorian on F Street is among Washington's most elegant private clubs and safer safe-houses. Top Secrets may be discussed, deals of staggering magnitude transacted, bribes taken and received – all with complete confidence in the Dorian's soundproofed third-floor private dining rooms. A member booking one may have his own technicians inspect it to insure that no listening devices have been planted. Jordan B. Rickhoven's aides completed this task before noon, when the billionaire and his two guests met in Dining Room One for lunch.

Rickhoven drank an extra-dry Gibson. Daniel Madigan had a double scotch and water. MacDonald Pearce sipped sherry. Purple-jacketed waiters brought food and wine on carts and vanished.

'We'll serve ourselves,' Rickhoven said. 'No interruptions.'

They were seated around the table and had begun on their food when Rickhoven asked Pearce: 'You saw Talbot?'

'Yesterday, Jordan. He hasn't yet reached a decision.' The Secretary of State cleared his throat. 'I stressed the national interest . . .'

Holy Jesus and all twelve apostles, Dan Madigan groaned inwardly. *Pearce gave Talbot lecture number 238 and now we'll have to sit through a playback.* He drained his wine glass, wishing he could have another double scotch, but Jordan Rickhoven had ordered the wine.

'. . . I pointed out that Basanda now supplies twenty per cent of our imported crude oil and much of our nonferrous base metals . . .'

With Rickhoven companies producing the oil and owning half the mines, Madigan remarked silently, pouring himself more wine.

'. . . He countered that our industrial production had fallen so low that we had excess stockpiles of oil and metals . . .'

'Goddamn it!' Madigan broke in angrily. 'Production won't go up until we move troops into Basanda and give industry a hypo with defense contracts! I've told Talbot that a hundred times . . .'

'Obviously, he didn't listen, Daniel.' MacDonald Pearce was piqued at having his monologue derailed. 'It appears that peace-at-any-price advocates have his ear.'

Jordan Rickhoven shifted attention to Madigan. 'How do you read the latest Congressional mood, Dan?'

'At the moment, the doves have an edge,' Madigan replied. 'It can be whittled away, though – given a few convenient incidents and some straight talk in the back room. But it won't happen overnight.'

'Handy incidents are your department,' Rickhoven said

to Pearce. 'While I'll contribute my share, the main load is yours, Mac.'

Pearce's cheek muscles pulsed. 'Needless to say, I will do whatever . . .'

A door-buzzer sounded. Rickhoven frowned, went to the door, opened it and was confronted by a thirtyish State Department type.

'My apologies, sir. I have an urgent message for Secretary Pearce.' Rickhoven stood aside. Pearce went out into the corridor, returned and closed the door behind him. He remained standing.

'Shocking news,' he announced. 'General Weidener died of a heart attack this morning.'

'Sorry to hear that,' Jordan Rickhoven murmured. 'He was a fine soldier, a brilliant commander.'

'Greatest since MacArthur,' Dan Madigan said, face impassive. *Praise the Lord and pass the coronaries*, he added silently.

'A tragic loss,' MacDonald Pearce intoned.

Bullshit, Madigan thought. *The Numero Uno peace-at-any-pricer has marched off to join the Great Majority. Hurray for our side.*

Pearce said that Weidener's death created problems requiring his return to the State Department. He shook hands, departed.

'Staying over tonight, JB?' Madigan asked after Pearce left.

'Probably – why?'

'I'm paying Lady Norworth a visit tonight. Care to join me?'

Rickhoven waited a moment before replying, then a slow, strange smile formed on his face. 'Yes, I'd like that. Very much.'

Talbot was informed of Weidener's death at 11:30 A.M. Stunned, he did not question why, if Weidener suffered a fatal heart attack at 5:30, there had been a six-hour delay before he was notified. But the implications of Weidener's death gradually worked their way through his brain. The barrier Weidener had provided against an American military adventure in Africa was gone. A new Chairman of the Joint Chiefs would have to be appointed, and all the qualified generals were avowed hawks.

Talbot had told his daugher he wished to confer with two people before making any decision on Basanda. He could no longer put off calling them. He used the direct outside line which the Secret Service checked hourly for taps and reached Supreme Court Chief Justice Avery Braithwaite before the venerable jurist left his office for lunch.

'I'm honored, Mr President,' Braithwaite said.

'Drop the Mr President crap, Avery. I hear it so often I forget my own name.'

'Objection sustained, Chuck. How may I be of service?'

'Any chance of your coming here this evening at five?'

'Certainly.' To Avery Braithwaite, an invitation from the President of the United States was a command.

A maid's voice answered Talbot's second telephone call.

'Lady Marjorie Norworth, please,' Talbot said. 'Tell her it's an old friend who hasn't talked with her since two years ago this January.'

Moments later, he heard the warm husky tones and modulated accents. 'Is this who I think it is?'

'I've never known you to guess wrong, Marjorie.'

She recognized the voice, carefully avoided using his name. 'Your grammar and syntax have improved. They used to be worse than Eisenhower's. When he was nominated for his second term, I told everyone that Washington would be better off if he took a first-term course in English instead.' Lady Norworth laughed throatily. 'My remark made all the columns, but it was attributed to Perle Mesta. I was furious.'

Talbot grinned. Some people never changed, and Lady Marjorie Norworth headed the list. 'Marjorie, I'd like to see you tonight.'

'Isn't that a bit risky?'

'A little, I suppose, but I have to talk with you. I'd like to drop by at midnight – less chance of being seen then – and use the back entrance.'

'Of course. You'll be more than welcome.'

Talbot was grateful. The meeting was certain to be helpful. No one had sounder worldly opinions or could offer more down-to-earth practical advice than Marjorie Norworth.

3

Washington, D.C.: Tuesday, February 16. Afternoon.

MacDonald Pearce had long deplored the rivalries between
State Department, Defense Department, Central Intelligence Agency, and special Presidential emissaries in the
conduct of foreign affairs. As Secretary of State he convinced
key men in Defense and the CIA that a new era had dawned.
Under his aegis, their aims would be identical, their activities closely – if often covertly – coordinated. The United
States would be restored to its rightful preeminence in the
world.

His success was marred only by General Keith Weidener,
Chairman of the Joint Chiefs of Staff. The bemedaled hero
of Korea and Vietnam, having known war at first hand as
few men did, was an ardent advocate of peace and an
intractable opponent of policies or plans that might lead to
armed conflict.

With Weidener gone, it was conceivable that the scales
could be tipped.

Hurrying back to State from the Dorian Club, Pearce
called a crash-conference with Defense Secretary John
Kurtz and CIA Director G. Howard Denby.

'Part of our dilemma has been solved for us,' Pearce told
them. They needed no further elaboration. 'We can take
new initiatives,' he declared, mindful of the urgings he had
received from Jordan Rickhoven.

The pipe-puffing Kurtz allowed that he had been thinking
along those very lines, while Denby, bland-faced and
notoriously taciturn, made no comment.

'Basanda's Prime Minister has made himself a liability,'
Pearce continued. 'He has cast away all discretion and
prudence.'

'Odu Mwandi is the strong man Basanda needs,' Kurtz objected.

'A strong man, yes – but Mwandi has outlived his usefulness. He should be replaced with someone with more – ah – finesse.'

'Changing figureheads doesn't eliminate dry-rot in the hull,' John Kurtz said. A yachting enthusiast, the Defense Secretary often used nautical similes.

Pearce, who knew little about boats, tried to match him. 'A bright new figurehead might persuade the unconvinced that it's worthwhile for us to scrape off the barnacles and repair the hull.'

'It's worth a gamble,' Kurtz nodded. Ends justified means.

Denby's colorless eyes showed no expression. 'Mwandi can be taken out,' he said. 'Give us a week – ten days.'

'No sooner?' Pearce asked.

'We have to navigate carefully – or end up on the reefs,' Kurtz said.

Daniel Madigan returned to his Everett Dirksen Building office, poured himself a large scotch, gave the sad-faced Madonna in his borrowed Tintoretto a wink, went to the Jefferson desk and settled down to work. He signed correspondence prepared by his secretaries, took some telephone calls, refused others until a pert, bosomy girl entered, clicked the doorlatch locking-button. 'It's four o'clock, Senator.' Her moist, voluptuous smile failed to vitalize her vapid expression.

'Hi, Debbie,' Madigan said. The girl started across the room, unbuttoning her blouse. Too bad she's so dumb, he thought. Oh, hell, it didn't matter. Her $19,760-a-year secretarial salary was paid by the taxpayers, and he had others who could take dictation, type, file.

She stood beside his chair, blouse open, braless. 'I'll be watching you on the Suzanne Loring show tonight,' she gabbled. 'I'm dying to see you on TV.' She knelt on the carpet, hands moving to his thighs.

The remark activated a memory-valve in Madigan's

brain. Momentarily ignoring the girl deftly opening his fly, he reached for his telephone. 'Get me Senator Hatch,' he said, then cupped his hand over the mouthpiece. 'Easy, huh, Debbie. I have to talk to somebody.'

The girl had begun fondling his genitals. 'So do both – it's an extra kick.'

Why not, Madigan thought. 'Edge over a little, honey.' He turned his swivel chair to avoid the Madonna's gaze.

Hatch rated only cramped quarters barely adequate for himself and his small staff in the old, stage-set, Correct Classic-style Richard Brevard Russell Senate Office Building. He was studying a proposed Timberlands Bill to determine whether it was of benefit to the Oregon lumber industry.

His phone buzzed. 'Senator Madigan,' his secretary announced.

Russ cursed silently. 'Put him through.'

'Hello, Senator.' Madigan's voice was amiable. 'I should've phoned you earlier, but got tied up. I wanted to say thanks . . .'

'For what?' Russ couldn't resist making Madigan specify the reason he was beholden. Small consolation, but Russ was in dire need of whatever balm he could find for his lacerated conscience.

Madigan clapped his free hand over the transmitter. 'Not so fast, Debbie.' The hand moved from the transmitter to the girl's large breasts.

'Uh – you've got a great future in the Senate business, my boy,' he said into the phone. 'I'm grateful to you for' – right hand went from breasts to mouthpiece again, covering it – 'Slow down, huh?' The hand resumed his breast-kneading. He spoke to Hatch once more. 'I was saying I'm grateful to you for interceding with your lovely lady.'

Hatch's curiosity got the best of him. 'How did it go?'

'Great,' he heard Madigan reply.

'No claw marks?' *I wish Suzy had mauled you as she intended.*

'Not even a scratch.'

'I'm glad.' *Like hell I am.*

'Russ.' The switch to a first name basis was significant, Hatch realized, waiting for more, but there was another silence.

Debbie's lips and tongue were bringing Dan Madigan to the edge. He could not hold off much longer. He had to end the conversation quickly.

'I never forget favors, Russ . . .' Debbie's head bobbed violently between his thighs. 'Look, Russ – unff – I'm in a real bind today. Give me a ring tomorrow.' Madigan spoke rapidly. 'We'll make a date, get together. Don't forget, Russ.' Slamming down the receiver, he seized the girl's head with both hands and, muscles straining, thrust deeper into her throat.

I hate to admit it, but I am glad after all, Russ mused, at once rueful and elated. *Seems I've found the UP escalator at last – thanks to Suzy, and maybe she's in a forgiving mood.* He dialed the Continental Broadcasting Network and was told, 'Ms Loring has left for the day' by the CBN operator. He tried Suzanne's apartment. Three rings and she answered.

' 'Afternoon, Ms Loring,' he began.

'What is it, Russ?' Her voice was even more chilly than it had been that morning.

'Suzy, can I do the apology bit over dinner tonight?'

'Sorry, I'm busy.' Not chilly. Gelid.

'Tomorrow night?'

'I can't talk now.' She sounded evasive.

Click.

Russ glowered at the dead instrument. No wool-dyed male chauvinist, he was still conditioned to believe that women followed predictable patterns of emotional response. Suzy's pissed off at me for using her – fair enough, he thought. But she's more pissed off at herself for letting me do it, and blames me for that, too. So she's hitting back by going out with some other guy. He might even have been in bed with her when I called. That would explain the tone and evasions. Russ replaced the receiver slowly, guilt turning into jealousy.

*

Jordan B. Rickhoven III's limousine took him from the Dorian Club to the pretentious IM Pei-designed structure housing the Basandan Embassy on Massachussets Avenue, where he was expected.

Basanda was one of the many former British colonies whose ruling and educated classes eschewed native dress and clung to English manners and customs. His Excellency, Percival Kwida, Basandan Ambassador to the United States, was Cambridge educated and Savile Row tailored. Kwida's black moon face beamed a toothy smile, radiating English country-manor hospitality as he greeted Jordan Rickhoven.

'Tea – or perhaps a spot of whiskey, Mr Rickhoven?'

'Neither, Your Excellency.' Rickhoven owned Percival Kwida, just as he owned Basanda's government and most of its natural resources through his network of multinational companies. It amused him to observe the formalities, but no further than the 'Your Excellency'. He sat down before being invited, crossed his long legs. 'I want you to send Prime Minister Mwandi a message by diplomatic pouch.'

'Certainly.' Ambassador Percival Kwida snapped alert.

'Inform him you have unimpeachable information there will be no more American aid for Basanda and there are even plans to recall U.S. military advisers already assigned there.'

Kwida's mouth was agape, his features mirroring horrified alarm.

'Mr Rickhoven! This is disastrous. The Prime Minister will withdraw troops from outlying areas to protect the main province. Many mines will be lost. The Basandan Army may well stage a *coup d'état*!'

'Yes.' Jordan Rickhoven's smile was acute-angled, predatory. 'Let's be frank, Kwida. The Prime Minister has become a huge liability. A new government would be a huge asset.'

Kwida's face showed growing comprehension. A few American mines lost, a few Americans killed or taken hostage by the rebels – and U.S. public opinion would demand retaliation. A cosmetic change in the Basandan Government could well prove of enormous advantage.

Rickhoven read the crucial question in Percival Kwida's eyes, answered it. 'You were educated in England. You've served as Ambassador here for several years. If someone of your background and stature were to succeed Mwandi, our legislators, press and public would hail the event as a re-birth of democracy in your country.'

Kwida's last shred of hesitation vanished. 'The message will be sent today, by air-courier, Mr Rickhoven.' Kwida's eyes glazed over as he mentally contemplated a vision. The Prime Ministerial Palace in Kinsolo, the Basandan capital, was the finest in Africa. The huge park in front of it was called Odu Mwandi Square. He saw himself occupying the former and renaming the latter in his own honor.

Lexa Talbot slept late, did not see her father until after three – and only for minutes. A delegation from the New England Council of Small Businessmen had just been ushered out of the Oval Office. The Governors of Colorado, Arizona, and New Mexico waited to be ushered in.

'The Small Businessmen wanted tax cuts.' President Talbot sighed. 'The Governors will ask for more Federal money. So it goes.' He shrugged, smiled. 'What's on your schedule?'

'I'm dedicating a new hospital wing in Baltimore at six,' Lexa replied. 'There's a Hospital Board banquet later.' *And a far-out party elsewhere afterwards – if I can manage to lose the Secret Service goons.* 'Don't fret, *mon cher père*, I'll survive.' She started out. 'Promise me you won't get up before dawn again tomorrow morning.'

'I promise, Puss,' Talbot said. *I won't have to*, he added to himself. *It's about when I'll be getting in.*

President Talbot received Supreme Court Chief Justice Avery Braithwaite in the second floor Presidential Family Quarters study. They sat in deep chairs. Talbot poured straight rye, which they both favored.

'Mud, Judge.' He raised his glass.

'To old times, Chuck.' Braithwaite was sixty-five and

looked it. His face might have been rough-carved from granite, but it was intelligent and knowing. 'Shall we talk about them as a warm-up?'

Talbot emptied his glass. 'Avery, I was a good legislator . . .'

'You were.'

'But I'm a lousy President.'

'We've had worse.' Piercing black eyes fixed on Talbot. 'You're simply out of your accustomed league, Chuck. In the House and Senate, you campaigned, said the right words, won elections. The Senate Majority leadership was an extension of the same principle. Instead of cultivating Pennsylvania voters, you cultivated your colleagues. Now you're at the top – but you're still campaigning when you should be snapping out orders and raising holy hell if they're not obeyed. However, I assume you want to talk about specifics, not generalities.'

'I do.' Talbot swallowed more rye along with his pride. For the next half-hour he delivered a bleak recital of the nation's more critical problems. Although fully aware of them, Chief Justice Braithwaite wanted to hear how they appeared from Talbot's Presidential perspective.

'. . . and I'm asking for your advice on the big picture scale – the Constitutional aspects, statutory provisions, and legal precedents,' President Talbot concluded. 'What can – and should – I do?'

Braithwaite rubbed his craggy jaw. 'Chuck, every judge sometimes renders snap verdicts – Lord knows, I have. But when possible, he has to restrain himself . . .'

'Disqualifying yourself, Avery?'

'You know me better than that, Chuck. I must have time to think, to weigh and evaluate.' *To agonize*, Braithwaite added to himself. *To agonize – the only means whereby a just verdict may be reached when great issues are involved.* He rose from his chair. 'You'll hear from me.'

Talbot's spirits rose. Avery Braithwaite had accepted part of the load and could be relied upon to carry it.

Talbot returned to the Oval Office, his workday far from

over. Pentagon brasshats were to arrive at seven, bringing the proposed plans for General Keith Weidener's pomp-and-circumstance funeral that would call for a Presidential eulogy, no less. At eight, Talbot, his Domestic Affairs Adviser and his Press Secretary would watch the Suzanne Loring show and assess how much damage or good her interview with Dan Madigan had done the Administration. After the show they would dine together and discuss public relations strategies. The working-dinner would probably last until eleven.

That left an hour until midnight. Talbot was already impatient, looking forward to his meeting with Lady Norworth. Braithwaite would eventually produce broad-scale, long-range ideas and advice, but what Talbot felt he needed most were practical stratagems that would produce instant results. Marjorie could supply these. God knows, she's had the experience, done it for others, Talbot reflected. She learned early – and she's been doing it most of her life.

Charles Talbot seated himself behind the Presidential desk feeling reassured, confident – and more hopeful than he had felt for weeks.

4

The World of Lady Marjorie Norworth.
Warm Springs, Georgia: Saturday, March 8, 1941. Night.

The Great Man lay naked. As always, his expression had a smug quality, stemming from the awareness that he was an illustrious personage with immense power. Taking a heavy gold cigarette case from the bedside table, he opened and offered it.

The young woman lying next to him also enjoyed a degree of fame. Countless publications had described her in their trite journalese as 'the ravishing, raven-haired debutante (bride, widow, millionheiress, top-drawer Washington hostess)'. She glanced at the cigarette case, shook her lovely head languorously, spoke:

'I can still taste you. Smoking now would be like eating persimmons after beluga.' And require effort, she added silently. I'm exhausted. The Great Man had astounding vigor and stamina.

'People can accustom themselves to anything.' The Great Man laughed, inserting a Camel into a black cigarette-holder. 'I imagine one could eventually come to like even the combination of caviar and persimmons.' He clamped the holder between his teeth. It was his trademark. He would not have been wholly in character without it – even in bed.

'Or even addicted – as you are to those things.' Stretching catlike, she indicated the cigarette.

'Winston smokes great, fat cigars.'

'How well I know. I once told him they were phallic symbols, and he blew smoke in my face.'

'A charge you cannot level at me, my dear.'

47

'Ah, but I can. You did, just over a year ago at Cissie Patterson's ball.'

'I can't remember the ball, much less the incident. How can you?'

'One, I have a phenomenal memory' – she did – 'two, I keep a daily diary' – she had for years, in meticulous and clinical detail – 'and three, because everyone thought you did it deliberately. Eleanor was there. The McLean bitch claimed you did it expressly for Eleanor's benefit. The story was passed around for weeks. Now do you remember?'

The Great Man tipped ash into a cut-crystal bowl on the nightstand. 'Am I to assume your social standing plummeted as a result?'

'Don't play the fool. It doesn't suit you.' The young woman's startling violet eyes narrowed and her tone was tinged with acid. Washington's inner-circle lapped at every shred of gossip. Wealthy women fought with back-stabbing savagery to achieve social prominence in the capital. The smoke-in-face story, magnified and embroidered with each retelling, had caused her serious damage. Finally, she counterattacked. She maneuvered the Great Man into inviting her to join the select group aboard his special train during a 1940 campaign swing through Ohio and Kentucky. Then the gossip became envious, and the lost ground was regained.

'You delight in intrigue, Marge.' A smoke-ring floated upward.

The patronizing remark rankled. 'How charming – coming from you, the Grand Master of machination . . .'

'I take that as a compliment.' Although said with sarcasm, there was an underlying note of pride. The Great Man justifiably believed he could have outpointed Niccolo Machiavelli with ease. 'Our power drives are innate, yours and mine,' he said, suddenly turning philosophical. 'They merely operate at different planes . . .'

Do they, really Marjorie thought. *Kings, dictators, presidents have power, but they, in turn, can be influenced – even manipulated – by others. Who then possesses the actual, the final, power?*

'. . . My ambitions are political, yours social. I've beaten

48

my opponents. You, unfortunately, haven't yet bested yours. Mesdames Patterson and McLean remain unconquered.' He was the amused Olympian observing petty strife between lesser, mortal creatures.

The Great Man's brain had a near-limitless capacity for throwing off brilliant, icon-smashing ideas, especially when activated by his deep-seated sense of the sardonic. 'How many rooms are there in your house, my dear?' he asked abruptly.

Black-fringed eyelids blinked in puzzled surprise. 'Forty-three.'

'You're wealthier than Patterson and McLean and far more beautiful,' he said. The smile that had done much to help make him the Great Man took on a conspiratorial quality. 'Vanquish them both at one stroke.'

'Short of poisoning their food, I can't imagine . . .'

'An appalling suggestion – and unimaginative, which is worse.' His nasal drawl was whimsical, his look vulpine. 'Transform part of your house – say ten rooms – into a replica of the White House.'

Marjorie sat bolt upright, stared at him.

'Be lavish, spare no expense,' he went on blandly. 'Improve on the originals . . .'

'You can't be serious. It's too utterly gauche.'

'No city on earth equals Washington in gaucherie.' The Great Man laughed. 'And it's populated by sheep. *I* shall attend your first party – held in the magnificently recreated State Dining Room – and view the splendid duplicates of Lincoln's Bedroom, the Red Room, and the rest.' He paused. 'I'll see to it that my most devoted courtiers also attend. Hull, Frankfurter – we mustn't ignore the Jewish vote – Ickes . . .'

'They'll sneer – and their wives! I shudder to think!'

'*Au contraire*. When I declare that the copies surpass the originals and rave over the effect you have created, their cries of rapture will shake the walls – and all Washington.'

Marjorie nodded slowly. Yes. With his stamp of approval, it could be a *coup de main* for her, a *coup de grâce* for Cissie Patterson and Evelyn McLean.

'Another point, Marge. Patriotism is the rage at the moment. Even American Firsters will applaud you for spending a fortune to reproduce the rooms in which the nation's history has been made.' Inner laughter convulsed him. *The Emperor's New Clothes*, he thought. *There were – thank God! – hilarious sides to the exercise of power.*

Sharp doubt cut into Marjorie's growing elation. 'But Eleanor . . .'

'. . . will be outraged.' Inner laughter boomed into the open. 'She'll contrive a junketing crusade as an excuse to vanish from Washington.'

Marjorie Norworth contemplated the certainty of future triumph, pulse-rate soaring. She pulled away the sheet hiding the Great Man's thighs and legs, began the fondling and whispered the words that aroused him. His response was quick. Her voice husky, her movements frenzied, she mounted him.

Lady Marjorie Norworth – more correctly Marjorie, Lady Norworth – was born Marjorie Trumbull. In Minneapolis, Minnesota. An only child and sole heiress to the huge Trumbull lumber fortune, she was gorgeous and highly precocious. At twelve, she filched the key to a library safe where her father kept his small but comprehensive collection of erotica. The books were profusely illustrated with explicit drawings and color plates. By leafing through the volumes she obtained a sexual education surpassing that possessed by most medical men of the era, and her theoretical knowledge clamored for practical application. Marjorie forced the gift of her virginity on a hapless manservant by using a timeworn expedient.

'If you don't, I'll tell my father you did,' she threatened.

The servant took what was offered with fear-inspired ineptitude. The next morning he decamped, neither giving notice nor collecting wages due.

'The man must be mad,' Henry Trumbull observed in his daughter's presence.

'He *was* awfully dumb,' Marjorie nodded sagely. But she

had learned a memorable lesson. Sex was a power unto itself.

Educated in Switzerland and France (where her imaginative mind contrived myriad stratagems for eluding supervision and gaining more practical experience) Marjorie made a dazzling debut in Minneapolis. It was followed by another in London, where she was presented at Court.

By then a widower, her father misread signs of Marjorie's expanding interest in power as simply a desire for position and prestige. A year later – and at a cost of two million dollars – Henry Trumbull arranged for his daughter to marry an English nobleman.

Adrian Norworth, fifteenth Baron of his line, boasted an impeccable genealogy (there were even a few drops of royal Stuart blood in his veins), a magnificent country estate in Surrey (impossibly mortgaged) and a degree from Magdalen College, Oxford. His other assets included an aristocratic chin (properly receding), staggering debts (they consumed over half of Marjorie's dowry before the wedding), and an exclusively homosexual orientation. The freshly minted Lady Norworth was delighted with her title and by no means dissatisfied with her unattractive husband or his sexual proclivities. She could indulge her own variety-loving libido with no conscience pangs.

Lord Norworth's murder in 1931 caused a scandal still periodically rehashed in Britain's lurid Sunday newspapers. He was battered to death in South London by a trio of rough-trade youths who were soon apprehended, tried and sent to the gallows for their crime.

Marjorie returned to America. Six months afterward, her father died of prostate cancer. He had wisely invested his wealth in Government bonds before the 1929 Crash. The Trumbull fortune was intact, and Marjorie was sole beneficiary of her father's will.

While in England, Marjorie fell short of fully realizing her social aspirations. The uppermost levels of English Society viewed her as just another American Dollar

Princess whose father had been grossly overcharged for the shoddy goods he – and she – received. Naturally, once back home in Minneapolis, she reigned supreme and was avidly sought after as the city's most desirable widow. Yet the narrow provincialism of Minneapolis palled. New York City lured her, but she knew that moving there would require a laborious climb up the ladder, for New York Society was rigidly stratified and not overly hospitable to newcomers from the wilds of the Midwest. Marjorie pondered long and hard over where else she might best – and most rapidly – achieve her ambitions.

Under the Coolidge and Hoover Administrations, Washington, D.C. was a dreary backwater. Anal-retentive Calvin Coolidge fretted over his constipation and the reluctance of European nations to pay their war debts. His successor Herbert Hoover – porcine and eternally choking in his starched, detachable shirt collars – bumbled through the first half of his term. During the second, he issued statements denying there was a Depression and ordered troops with fixed bayonets to drive ragged, hungry Bonus Marchers from their pathetic Anacostia Flats camp.

Franklin Delano Roosevelt's 1933 Inauguration wrought total transformation overnight. Pennsylvania Avenue supplanted Wall Street (jeeringly called Poverty Row) as the nation's true power center. The stodgy bumblers were out. A new breed of dynamic braintrusters took their place. Many, like Roosevelt himself, were Ivy League university graduates, wealthy, and had long entries after their names in the New York Social Register. Washington became the place where it was all happening.

While in Europe and England, Marjorie had observed how much influence clever wealthy women could exert on affairs of state in their salons and drawing rooms. Recognizing that the New Deal was creating a New Elite in Washington, she reasoned that her natural beauty, inherited fortune, and repatriated title were qualifications for entrée into the charmed circle. Devising her strategies with the thoroughness of a field marshal planning a major offensive, Marjorie invaded Washington, taking a seven-room suite at the Mayflower.

After proper introductions led to invitations, Marjorie leased a townhouse near Dumbarton Oaks, contributed generously to the Democratic Party and the right charities, gave small but elegant dinner parties and was accepted.

Her next step was the purchase of a four-acre plot on Foxhall Road. A château-style mansion was constructed on the site. When it was completed and sumptuously decorated she gave much larger dinner parties and lavish balls. Before long, Lady Marjorie Norworth was acclaimed one of Washington's leading socialites and hostesses. But to be 'one off' was not what Marjorie wanted.

An affair with the distinguished, much sought-after British Ambassador (whom she handily usurped from his long-time mistress) enhanced her status. Another with tycoon Jordan B. Rickhoven Jr (who was frequently in Washington protecting his wealth by cultivating New Dealers) added more luster.

Liaisons of varying duration and intensity with other influential men followed. Marjorie dispensed her sexual favors as she did her magnanimous hospitality – selectively and with cool calculation. Men found her irresistibly charming, sympathetic, an excellent listener, magnificent in bed – and unfailingly discreet. Nearly every male who met Lady Marjorie Norworth was enhanced by her. Large numbers were infatuated. A notable exception was General Douglas MacArthur. Marjorie made an allout effort to seduce him, but he was impervious. Many years later, he would have reason for deeply regretting his refusal.

Each affair consolidated Marjorie's position further, and she took pains to remain friends with her lovers after ardors cooled into platonic relationships. Of course, Washington's Very Important Wives hated her passionately – all the more so because they dared not show their hatreds. To do so would be an admission of envy – and, what was more, Marjorie knew too much about them and their husbands. As for Marjorie, she cared little what most women thought.

In Washington, influence and power were held and wielded by men.

However, her many triumphs – social, political, sexual – were not sufficient to gain Marjorie the preeminence she desired. Evelyn Walsh McLean and Eleanor 'Cissie' Patterson remained firmly entrenched at the social peak, yet nonetheless watched her every move with uneasy trepidation, for Marjorie did possess potentially decisive advantages. She was younger, lovelier, richer, a widow – and she disdained moral codes and strictures.

Marjorie Norworth bided her time, waited for her Main Chance, seizing it after Franklin Roosevelt's 1937 Inauguration. She gave what *Life* was to label 'The Party of the Century' – a great ball ostensibly for the benefit of FDR's favorite polio foundation charity, augmenting the proceeds with a personal donation of $100,000.

Franklin and Eleanor Roosevelt were the guests of honor. Marjorie had met FDR on numerous previous occasions, and they were already friendly. At the ball, she evinced keen interest in the polio foundation as a pretext for an hour's private conversation with him. She overwhelmed him with charm, fed his ego with flattery, regaled him with choice bits of the racy Washington gossip he loved to hear – and made an indelible impression on him. Within weeks, she was one of his confidantes.

Marjorie had expected a miracle. It failed to materialize. Although her friendship with the President eliminated all lesser contenders once and for all, it only placed her on a par with Evelyn McLean and Cissie Patterson. They shared the peak and fought a three-cornered no-quarter battle for clearcut supremacy.

Marjorie consoled herself with the knowledge that she had gained a considerable degree of power. Favor-seekers of all types fawned over her, for she had direct access to FDR and to many others at the highest levels of Government. She could be – and often was – instrumental in having men appointed to office, promoted – or demoted. She was *au courant* with capital intrigues and conspiracies and frequently able to influence their course and outcome. She knew of major decisions well in advance of most – and her advice was sometimes asked before they were made. But she had still not reached her goal.

Marjorie's mind was concentrated on the Great Man's idea for duplicating White House rooms in her Foxhall Road mansion. She had already adopted the idea as her own and was mentally making plans. But she remembered a promise she had made a few days before in Washington.

'There's something I meant to ask you.'

A grunt signified that the Great Man was listening.

'Do you know Bradford Cooley?'

A contemptuous snort. 'Alabama's stripling contribution to the Congressional Dixie stew on which I'm constantly gagging? Yes, I know him – and of him.'

Young, exceptionally handsome Bradford Cooley had won a first-term Congressional seat from Alabama in 1940. Not yet twenty-seven and the scion of a rich land-owning family, he was – as the Great Man saw fit to remind Marjorie – 'an Isolationist, a budding Bilbo who votes the straight Dixie Dinosaur line.'

'Outward appearances often mislead,' she countered.

'Is that so?' The Great Man considered his judgments of people to be infallible. Irked, he reached for cigarette and holder.

'Brad Cooley is unusually bright. He went to Columbia . . .'

'In itself, neither recommendation nor apology.' The resonant voice was sarcastic. 'But do go on, my dear.'

'He'll be up for reelection next year and expects very heavy opposition in the primaries.'

The cigarette holder tilted up at a sharp angle. 'I suppose you are lobbying for me to support him.'

'An uncannily accurate deduction.' She tickled his ribs, cajoling.

There was a silence.

'What quid does Cooley offer for my quo?'

'He'll vote with the Administration.'

'I said before that he's a diehard Isolationist.'

'Brad agrees to switch his stand. I told him he must.'

Another silence. Such an abrupt *volte-face* had great political value and could be exploited further. The Great Man chuckled. 'This is a night to remember, my dear. I begin by laying inspiration at your feet – then I find myself incapable of refusing you anything.' His lips curled back, displaying strong teeth. The cigarette holder angled even higher between them. 'With your patronage – and my endorsement – Representative Cooley's future is assured.'

5

Washington, D.C.: Tuesday, February 16. Evening.

Foxhall Road begins at the western edge of the Georgetown University campus and traverses terrain that slopes down gently from lushly wooded Glover-Archbold Park. Famed, percipient columnist Russell Baker describes Foxhall Road as 'Lined with enormous houses on enormous lots ... it appears to have the highest concentration of wealth in Washington. What its people do, Heaven only knows. A lot of the women practice "hostessing". . .'

Grandest of the Foxhall Road houses is Lady Marjorie Norworth's château. Atop a hillock dominating the surrounding area, it is set like a gargantuan arched and pillared jewel in the midst of lawns and formal gardens. The entire four-acre plot is enclosed by a high stone wall. Visitors are permitted entrance only by invitation or by summons. Sapient Washingtonians have long called Lady Norworth's mansion the House on the Hill.

Alabama Representative Bradford 'Big Brad' Cooley was one of the fortunate elite who enjoyed a standing invitation to the House on the Hill. Barely more than five-feet-seven tall, he was tagged 'Big Brad' because of his girth – and because of his stature as a ranking member of Congress and the importance of his position as Chairman of the prepotent House Appropriations Committee. But these were not the reasons why he had carte blanche entrée. Cooley was Marjorie Norworth's oldest and dearest friend.

A squat mound of fat wrapped in a shapeless suit, Cooley occupied almost the entire breadth of an exquisite Sheraton sofa in Marjorie's replica of the White House Green Room. Almost bald, his head was fringed with off-white hair. A black string tie dangled below his numerous chins, and his hands clutched a cut-crystal tumbler filled with straight bourbon.

But Cooley's eyes were alert and worldly-wise. At the moment, they were amused as he gazed at the green watered silk that covered the walls of the room. 'Ah swear, ah nevah git tahd o' thet green movray,' he drawled in a grotesquely exaggerated cottonfields-and-Old Crow accent.

Lady Marjorie, seated opposite him, grimaced impatiently. 'Stop that nonsense, Brad – it's a bit tiresome after all these years.' Her tone was maternally reprimanding, even though they were almost the same age. Marjorie, however, appeared much younger. In her late sixties, she looked a vital fifty at most, her appearance a tribute to science and art – medical, surgical and cosmetic – and to her own iron self-discipline. Her black hair, artfully streaked with silver, waved softly away from her face, emphasizing violet eyes and a majestic profile.

'Old habits – like old soldiers – never die,' Cooley said with a grin, his speech now free of Alabama backwoods inflections.

Marjorie stared at her hands. They were smooth, unflawed by the mottling of age, in their way as perfect as the huge emeralds adorning her long, graceful fingers and encrusting the magnificent bracelet on one slender wrist. (She preferred wearing emeralds when receiving guests in the Green Room. The greens of the gems matched the silk moiré on the walls. She felt a momentary pang of nostalgia. *You were once such a handsome young man, Brad*, she thought. *A beautiful young man – and that was the trouble, I suppose.*

Then Cooley's remark about 'old soldiers' registered. Marjorie frowned, stood up, her body remarkably lithe beneath her flowing Halston gown, and walked to the convex mirror over the marble fireplace. Gazing into it, she studied the distorted reflections. Bradford Cooley was calmly swallowing bourbon. She turned, faced him.

'Keith Weidener was an old soldier,' she said. 'He died today.'

'Ironical.' Cooley's expression was bland. 'He survived two wars but couldn't survive Washington.'

'Brad. Keith died before dawn. The White House and press heard nothing about it until nearly noon.'

'The efficiency of your grapevine never fails to astound me.'

Whatever happened – or was about to happen – in Washington, Marjorie was usually one of the first to know. Men in high places who owed her debts of gratitude – and they were many – and others eager to curry her favor passed her information and gossip the moment they themselves learned anything of interest or importance. Her intelligence network, albeit personal, unofficial, and informal, was formidable. Precious little transpired in the capital about which Marjorie Norworth did not hear, and she stored all in her capacious memory banks. Such knowledge was a form of power in itself.

Marjorie again showed impatience, ignored Cooley's comment. 'At eight-thirty this morning, Keith's mistress was visited by a man who gave no name, showed no identification. He handed her a package containing thirty thousand dollars in cash and told her to leave Washington within seventy-two hours – or, he said, she would be very sorry. The girl called a friend – who, in turn, called me.'

Congressman Cooley shrugged. 'Weidener was the Great American Hero Figure, Chairman of the Joint Chiefs and – ostensibly, at least – a happy, faithful husband. But he had a mistress – a black girl, I believe.' Big Brad Cooley had his own, efficient spy net in Washington. 'Were she to talk – or be tracked down by the news media – a scandal would result. The Weidener image would disintegrate – and so, by extension – would that of the Army and military establishment.'

He paused, poured himself more bourbon from a decanter.

'The armed services have gigantic slush funds hidden in their budgets. Thirty thousand dollars is a cheap price to pay for riddance of a distressingly dangerous young lady. I'd say it's as simple as that.'

Marjorie Norworth's classic features tightened. 'You're clever and devious, Brad – as I've been aware since 1941.'

A gentle jab to remind Cooley he would not be where he was, had it not been for her. 'Intuition tells me there's more. I scent something.'

Cooley sighed. 'Perhaps there is, but *my* intuition tells me you should let sleeping dogs and dead generals lie.' He might have said more, but Holcomb – Lady Norworth's majordomo and most trusted retainer since the House on the Hill was completed – entered. A giant black with a prizefighter's musculature and snowy hair, he announced that Senator Daniel Madigan and Mr Jordan Rickhoven had arrived. The three men knew each other well. Madigan and Rickhoven were Marjorie's long-time friends and frequent guests.

'I still maintain your Green Room makes the Pennsylvania Avenue version seem a tatty imitation,' Jordan Rickhoven said, smiling.

'Your father, Jordan Jr, told Eleanor much the same in 'forty-three,' Marjorie laughed. 'I understand she sulked for days.'

They all chatted while Holcomb served drinks, then moved chairs and sofas so they would face the beige-green-and-coral-striped draperies drawn across the windows. Holcomb worked the controls that lowered a shiny metallic screen from its ceiling recess. He left, returned wheeling a table on which there was what appeared to be a compact motion picture projector, and positioned it carefully on the nineteenth-century Turkish carpet. Marjorie and her guests seated themselves. Holcomb turned on the machine and withdrew.

Larger-than-life color images of two beefy women playing tug-of-war with a sheet of paper toweling appeared on the metallic screen. '. . . stronger than the strongest housewife – so let Tufftowels do the tough work for you,' a male voice-over urged. The scene wiped to a quick-flash of the Continental Broadcasting Network logo. An unseen brass band played eight bars of 'The Stars and Stripes Forever' deliberately off key and another male voice announced: 'And now, from the nation's capital, Suzanne Loring and "Washington Inside Out".'

'Break a leg, Dan,' Marjorie said as though telling Madigan he was going on stage instead of watching an interview he had taped that morning.

'Hi, there.' The camera was on Suzanne Loring in a St Laurent tunic, close-cut brown hair emphasizing her unique glamorous-gamin quality, her arched right eyebrow knowing and skeptical.

Cool sex, a touch of the tomboy topped off with worldly sophistication, Marjorie thought admiringly. A terriffic package. Perfect.

'. . . my guest tonight is Senate Majority Leader Daniel Madigan.'

The camera shifted to Madigan, tense in a white molded chair. Suzanne's voice: 'Senator, you've been in the Senate for more than fourteen years . . .'

'A long sentence – and no time off for good behavior,' Madigan interrupted, laughing at his own wisecrack.

Suzanne and Madigan exchanged standard-fare preliminaries. Then she grew serious. 'Senator, the unemployment rate keeps going up and up. What are you and your colleagues doing to reverse the trend?'

'All we can – and we'll do more.' Madigan's TV face grew solemn, sincere. 'You must remember that President Talbot inherited an ongoing recession from previous Administrations . . .'

She's letting him deliver a speech, Marjorie Norworth thought with increasing astonishment as the show progressed. Suzanne Loring's questions and comments glossed rather than probed, gave Madigan openings to make more partisan speeches. Brad Cooley had like reactions. The fight was fixed, he mused, wondering what – or who – was behind it.

When the show ended, a smirking Dan Madigan turned off the projector, switched on table lamps. *Like a free commercial for the Party and me*, he chortled inwardly and winked at Jordan Rickhoven, who returned an amused nod.

Marjorie knew the three men wanted to have a private chat. 'I'll see that everything will be ready for you later, Dan, Jordan,' she said, excusing herself. Brad Cooley would be leaving when the conversation ended. She kissed his cheek. 'Come again, soon, Brad.'

The atmosphere in the Green Room underwent drastic change, became like that which prevails at hard-dealing board meetings.

'We had lunch with Pearce today,' Madigan told Cooley.

'I heard.'

'You're laconic, Brad,' Rickhoven observed amiably.

'Merely cautious. Your fangs are showing, JB, and I have a feeling this isn't just another chummy House on the Hill get-together.'

Senate Majority Leader and billionaire exchanged significant glances. Big Brad Cooley was not in a tractable mood. Madigan spoke up bluntly. 'Brad, your Appropriations Committee's delaying the emergency aid bill for Basanda. When can we expect you to report it out?'

'Never. I'm bottling the bill.'

Dan Madigan flushed. Jordan B. Rickhoven III was silken. 'What would induce the sommelier to pull the cork?' he asked.

'Those days are gone, JB. I can afford to let my conscience be my guide, and Uncle Sam can't afford to throw another billion dollars down that African rathole.' Cooley looked part Alfred Hitchcock, part Sidney Greenstreet as he spoke. 'We've pissed away too much in third-rate Third World countries. Ninety percent of aid funds go into the pockets of the tinpot dictators who run them. Five percent is fed back to Washington in bribes – to get more aid. With luck, five percent is spent for legitimate purposes.'

'Not true in this instance,' Madigan protested.

'Dan, stop spoutin' horseshit. Y'all might stain the purty carpet.' Dropping the overdone Alabama backwoods dialect, Cooley added: 'South Korea, Vietnam, Basanda, Ruritania – they're all alike.'

Rickhoven cleared his throat. 'I abhor mentioning past favors.'

'*Past* is the operative word, JB, and I abhor reminding

you that any you ever did me were repaid – many times over.'

'We can squeeze.' Madigan's tone had a sawtoothed edge.

Cooley grinned. 'You'll have to squeeze damned hard. This load of flab I carry makes a fine cushion.'

'We might squeeze from other directions,' Madigan said.

Cooley recognized the nature of the threat but retained his composure. He had passed the age and stage where it frightened him. 'I'll double my sentries,' he said airily. Heaving his large bulk from the sofa, he shook hands congenially and departed.

'Think he'll come around?' Rickhoven asked after Cooley left.

'We'll make him come around, somehow,' Dan Madigan replied.

Marjorie Norworth returned to the Green Room. 'Holcomb will take you upstairs first, Dan,' she said.

Madigan followed the butler up the familiar broad staircase and along corridors to an equally familiar door, where Holcomb left him. Madigan opened the door, entered, closed the door behind him. The room made no pretense of imitating any in the White House, but then, only ten of the total of forty-three were replicas. It was a bedchamber fit for a prince – spacious, sumptuously furnished and decorated. The walls boasted a Fragonard, two Watteaus and works by lesser-known artists. The huge ornate bed had belonged to Marie Antoinette. Candles in gilt museum-quality French Renaissance wall sconces provided illumination. In sum, the room epitomized the luxury Daniel Madigan craved.

So did the young women who were waiting for him. There were two – one a blonde, the other a brunette – sleek, long-legged and naked. They had never met Madigan before, but they had been briefed. Thoroughly. They greeted him with deferential courtesy, not using his name – for that was against his rules – and awaited their instructions.

A silk damask covered chaise was on a raised platform near the Marie Antoinette bed. Madigan reclined on it.

'Undress me,' he murmured.

The girls removed his clothing slowly, using their hands and mouths with skill on his body as they bared it. He wallowed in sensation. Class, he thought as a tongue flicked at his scrotum. Class and finesse. Not like the every weekday afternoon head I get from that dumb broad. He was completely nude. The blonde sucked gently at the flesh of his inner thighs. The brunette caressed his upper body.

'Lemme see you play games,' he said hoarsely. The girls went to the bed. 'Your head this way,' he gestured to the blonde. 'And you . . .'

The brunette had anticipated his instructions. Madigan's penis was erect, straining. He loved having it stay like that while he watched the young women's long legs twine around each other's necks and listened to the moist lapping sounds and the moans of pleasure. At last their moans rose to muffled cries, and they strained against each other. When their bodies separated, he leapt from the chaise and wedged himself between them on the bed. His mouth searched – and found. The wetness of one girl's saliva on another's thighs and pubic hairs raised his excitement to an unbearable pitch. His hips began thrusting wildly. A hand encircled his penis and guided it into a tight, throbbing sheath.

Madigan hardly knew which was the blonde, which the brunette – and didn't care. He lost himself in sensation – the most luxurious of sensations, he thought, an instant before his orgasm exploded.

Holcomb took Jordan Rickhoven to another wing of the mansion, departing hurriedly, as the libretto demanded.

Rickhoven stood in the corridor. His self-assurance had vanished. He shuddered with the fear that titillated. The angular face of the despot who headed the Rickhoven Dynasty turned ashen. His hands trembled and he bit deep into his lip. At last, he tapped on the door.

'Please.' His voice was a whimper. A door-bolt was drawn. He wanted to flee. It was too late. The door was flung open. A blowsy woman wearing heavy makeup, black leather corselet and trousers, and spiked-heel boots flicked the whip she held in her right hand.

'Inside, you piece of shit!' she ordered. Rickhoven cringed, crept past her. She shut the door, drove the bolt home.

'Strip!'

Fingers fumbling, he tried to obey, but was too slow. The woman drove a boot heel down on his instep. The pain was excruciating, exquisite. 'Speed it up, you bastard!' she rasped.

Rickhoven nodded silently, submissively – lost in the ecstatic throes of fearful apprehension. Tearing off his clothing, he edged away from the heap of garments he flung to the floor. The woman snarled another command. He went to his hands and knees, groveling, his flesh tingling in expectant, erotic horripilation. The woman's right arm flashed up, then down, whip cracking as it cut into Rickhoven's back. He mewled gratefully. Each successive blow brought Jordan B. Rickhoven III closer to the ecstatic release brought by pain and total degradation.

Marjorie, going to her own bedroom suite, spoke to Holcomb.

'When Senator Madigan and Mr Rickhoven come down, make my excuses – I had a ghastly headache.'

The butler inclined his head affirmatively.

'And at midnight, wait for my special guest at the service entrance and bring him up in my private elevator.'

She saw no reason to caution Holcomb that he must avoid giving any sign that he recognized Charles Pendleton Talbot. It was far from the first time that Holcomb would usher in a U.S. President secretly during the middle of the night, take him directly to her rooms.

6

Washington, D.C.: Tuesday, February 16. Midnight.

Back home in Portland, Oregon, Russell Hatch was noted for being mature, eminently sensible and, unless gravely provoked, even-tempered and good-humored. The Russell Hatch who irately paced the floors in his Cleveland Park apartment was showing none of these qualities. He lit one Pall Mall after another, intermittently muttered disconnected splenetic phrases and acted as though a smoldering fuse would – more probably sooner than later – set off a megaton explosion inside him. His face was livid, the freckles splashed across it standing out like disease spots – which was not entirely surprising, for Russ was suffering from a severe case of pulverized masculine pride.

He had watched Suzanne Loring's show some hours earlier, and it enraged him. *Suzanne turned the interview with Dan Madigan into an absurd, ugly charade to spite me, rub my nose in my own shit*, Russ told himself, *and she did it in front of twenty million people.* For some reason, the very fact that the audience could not possibly guess Suzanne's aims and motives made him angrier yet and further intensified his feelings of humiliation.

It was imperative that he talk to Suzanne – even though he wasn't quite sure what he would say to her. He lost count of the telephone calls he made to her Potomac Plaza number. Each time he dialed, there was no answer. At midnight, he gave a final try, with the same result. He slammed down the receiver, frustration and primal sexual jealousy compounding resentful anger. *She's twisting the knife*, he thought. *She's out with someone else, probably balling him – the classic vengeful female's reprisal pattern, Goddamn her!*

66

Russ suddenly discovered himself thinking along lines that basic integrity and fairness never before allowed his mind to follow. He recalled his marriage, began making comparisons between his dead wife, Virginia – or rather, his somewhat faded yet equally idealized memories of Virginia – and Suzanne Loring. Virginia was loving, forgiving, conciliatory, he reflected. She would never . . .

He stopped, reason prevailing. *Given the same circumstances, Virginia would have acted the same way Suzy has,* Russ admitted to himself. *Virginia had her bitchy moments too, but because she's gone and we were happy together, I block them out of my mind. I've also been happy with Suzy – sure, on a far different, no-formal-strings basis – but it seems I ignored a mass of circumstantial evidence that should have warned me. Suzy's bad-news marriage and divorce, her career and her obsession about being free, self-sufficient, and independent are elements that can produce an infuriating species of super-bitch – and so they have.*

'Oh, fuck it!' Washington swarmed with women. They weren't all Suzanne Lorings – not by a long shot, Russ conceded glumly – but by God plenty of them were attractive, congenial – and available. Stalking to his liquor cabinet, he downed a four-finger shot of Remy and started toward his bedroom. He hoped the cognac would induce sleep.

Suzanne Loring invariably watched her weekly television show at home – and with critical objectivity. She seldom sat through the 44 minutes and 30 seconds of program (14 minutes and 30 seconds of commercials brought it up to an hour) without thinking of the tattered phrase, 'You've come a long way, Baby.' She was proud of what she had accomplished in life, prouder still that she had done it on her own.

This Tuesday was an exception. Glowering at the screen, Suzy was disgusted at how far she had fallen in her own esteem – and that of anyone possessing an ounce of perception who might have been watching her performance with Dan Madigan. Not that she worried about network officials or sponsors. Her reputation and popularity were solidly established. They could not be dented by one clinker. It was that she hated herself for having over-reacted, thrown a sort of childish temper tantrum, gone to an absolute extreme of punch-pulling.

Why had she done it?

Asking herself the question, Suzy did not need search for the answer. *Because I felt Russ was exploiting our relationship, and I was hurt, furious, and vindictive. I wanted him to feel small, cheap, guilt-ridden.*

Suzanne took another step in painful, shaming self-analysis of her emotional responses and thought-processes.

Again, why – and more particularly, why did she strike out against Russ? Of all the men she had known, Russell Hatch was the one who neither patronized nor sought to dominate her. He was supportive and protective when necessary, but made no capital out of being either. They seldom if ever quarreled or bickered unless they staged hilarious mock-battles over which restaurant they would go to for dinner or whether a new piece of furniture she bought should go against this wall or that.

Each of them respected the other as a person – or had, until that morning. They weren't adversaries. They were equals who meshed. These were the reasons their relationship had lasted, gained depth and dimension, and was so mutually gratifying. These – and the sex, of course, Suzanne reminded herself. Russ was not only magnificent in bed, he could sense her needs and moods, be infinitely tender or marvelously passionate. His lovemaking was imaginative, uninhibited – and more.

'Going to bed with a lot of men after my divorce taught me how great my ex-husband had been in bed,' she admitted to Russ one night about three months after they met. 'But you're – Christ, I don't know how to put it into words, Russ. I really don't.'

'Two-way street,' he said simply, sincerely, firing up a Pall Mall and brushing the back of his hand against her cheek. 'We bring things out in each other – with apologies to Dr Comfort, the joys of sex among them.'

Remembering the conversation and the night of delicious

lovemaking that followed it – in Russ's apartment that time – Suzanne felt her glands activate, start to pump juices. They inevitably did when she thought of Russ in a sexual context – and often when she merely thought of him in any other.

She willed a turnoff of glandular response, forced herself back to a purely cerebral level. The moment of truth, she thought miserably, for the first time squarely facing the realization that she was in love with Russ and needed him. Having at last admitted this to herself, Suzanne at once gained a degree of understanding and was plunged into deep depression.

She now recognized that her staging of the Madigan fiasco was caused by violent resentment against being in love with Russ to the extent that she would even consider giving in to him. Her vindictiveness had not been directed at Russ – but at herself, for being weak, dependent and acceding to him. Instead of taking delight in having found what she knew to be the true explanation, Suzanne was dejected – and not a little unnerved and frightened. Being in love implied a surrender of independence and individuality – not far beyond which lay subjection, submissiveness, loss of freedom: emotional, mental, even personal. Suzanne saw herself threatened by the possibility of an Anthony Loring replay, and her stomach knotted.

Suzanne often worked odd – and slept odder – hours. Her telephones were equipped with switches which, when flicked, prevented them from ringing audibly. Instead, lights set below the dials flashed when someone was calling. She had set the silencing switch when she came home. From eighty thirty on, the lights flashed so frequently that Suzanne told herself the apartment looked like an amusement gallery filled with pinball machines. She guessed that some – probably many – of the calls were being made by Russ and others from people she knew who wanted to ask what-the-fuck caused her to make Daniel A. Madigan come on – like a glorified Mister Clean. She could not bring herself to speak with Russ – her brain was in too much of a turmoil – and had no desire to talk to anyone else. She ignored the blinking lights.

Two Seconals, and Suzanne went to bed, falling asleep by nine-forty-five. The sedative wore off after a couple of hours. She went to her bathroom medicine cabinet and took another capsule. Returning to bed, she saw the bedside telephone light flashing again, turned on her side, and closed her eyes. She was thinking of Russell Hatch as she once more fell asleep.

Lexa Talbot had dedicated the new hospital wing in Baltimore with a speech written by the man she asked her father to place on the White House payroll. Short, suitably crafted for the occasion, it contained all the requisite ingredients, eulogizing medical science, the hospital staff, and especially the private donors whose contributions paid for constructing and equipping the structure. She concluded with a variation on the political soft-sell theme that characterized every public address she made.

'Just before I left the White House to come here this evening, Daddy asked me to give you his personal message. I jotted it down.' Lexa picked up a scrap of paper – it was blank, but only she knew that – and pretended to read from it. '"Both as President and as a private individual, I would like to express heartfelt praise to each and every person who helped make your hospital project a reality. I hope for – and will myself work toward – the day when all American communities may have medical facilities as fine and modern as those you are helping to provide for your city."' A two-beat pause, followed, and Lexa's features formed into an expression appropriately reverent. '"I join my daughter in saying God bless you all."'

Swelling with self-esteem, those present had applauded loud and long. 'That's some young lady,' a florid-faced donor told his reed-thin wife, who nodded vigorously. 'Gorgeous – she could be a movie star,' she said, then amended her remark. 'No, a girl like that is too nice and refined . . .'

Lexa, sensing she had made another smash hit, was

effervescent at the formal banquet that followed. Remembering the names of everyone who counted, she made them laugh heartily with amusing (and apocryphal) anecdotes about life in the White House, dispensed compliments and flatteries, injected sobering references to the many problems President Talbot faced and how he worked day and night to solve them.

The banquet ended before eleven. One of the Secret Service men detailed to guard Lexa approached her timorously. 'Miss Talbot – uh, the guys on duty last night were chewed out for losing you. Please, Miss Talbot, you won't shake us off tonight, will you?'

Lexa's smoky-gray eyes were wide with innocence. 'I promise.'

She held her silver-gray Jaguar J72 at a patriotic, fuel-saving fifty miles an hour on the Baltimore–Washington Parkway. The Secret Service agents in the security backup car relaxed, tooled along a hundred yards behind the Jag.

Once into Washington, Lexa made for Rhode Island Avenue, the short-and-easy course leading toward the White House. Knowing routes and traffic-light rhythms, her timing was perfect. At the New Jersey Avenue intersection Lexa accelerated at the same instant that the traffic light turned red and made it across – barely, for traffic streams spurted into movement on New Jersey Avenue. The security car was cut off. Its driver slammed on the brakes, cursed.

Lexa tight-cornered to the right at the next intersection, zigzagged at high speed through side streets to Scott Circle, which she circumnavigated and drove into the Holiday Inn underground garage. Guiding the flashy car down inclined ramps to the lower garage-level, she parked, got out and took an elevator back to the ground-level garage entrance. There, she gave the night attendant his usual five-dollar tip. He had hailed a taxi when he saw her drive in, it was part of their agreement. Lexa got in the waiting cab and again congratulated herself. Her Jaguar was unique in Washington, immediately recognizable. But who – even the smartest Secret Service man – would ever dream that she parked it in the garage of a Holiday Inn located only seven short blocks north of the White House?

The taxi took Lexa to a narrow, two-story brick house on the outer – and sleazier – fringes of Georgetown. She went up three steps to the front door and stood directly in front of the fish-eye scanner, rang the bell. Several seconds passed before the door was opened by a man in his mid-fifties. He would have been attractive except that he was unshaven, wore a shabby bathrobe, and his eyes were glassy.

'Been rash with the hash, Jim?' Lexa asked, stepping inside.

'Pos-i-tive-ly gluttonous.' The man closed the door, swayed, steadied himself. 'Hey, talked to your Old Man about me?'

'Uh-huh,' Lexa nodded. 'With him and the clown who handles the paperwork. You're in. Now let's fuck.'

Security regulations provided that a minimum of six Secret Service agents accompany the President whenever he left the White House. Charles Talbot selected men whose personal loyalty to him was beyond question. They used private, unmarked automobiles. Two agents led in one, another two rode with Talbot in the second, and yet another duo followed in the third car.

The small convoy did not use the main – Foxhall Road – entrance to the House on the Hill. It drove onto the grounds by the side gate, drew up in front of the service entrance, where Holcomb waited and quickly whisked Talbot inside.

Employing extravagance and ostentation as means to further her ends, Marjorie Norworth herself favored quiet elegance. This was clear from the impeccably subdued taste with which her personal suite – reception parlor, bedroom, dressing room, and bathrooms – was decorated. The small elevator in the rear of the mansion went directly to her private apartment. She kissed Talbot fondly when he stepped out of the elevator.

'Welcome back, Charlie.'

He returned her kiss, stepped back, studied her, smiled. 'When I talked to you this afternoon, I told myself you never change, Marjorie. You don't. You look just the same.'

'Sit down, Charlie – and stop campaigning for my vote.' Marjorie knew her appearance hadn't altered in two years – and not very much in ten, for that matter. She waited for Talbot to settle into a generously cushioned armchair. 'Care for a drink?'

'Please. Big rye, little water. May help me unwind.'

Marjorie had exchanged her emeralds for rubies. She enjoyed basking in their red glow late at night. Besides, she believed they went better with the decor of her suite, sharply counterpointing its muted colors. Jewel facets flashed crimson, reflecting light, as she reached to touch a switch. A section of bleached mahogany wall-paneling slid aside to reveal a well-stocked bar. '*You've* changed, though,' she said, pouring his drink. 'You never needed liquor to unwind before. You always drank to have fun.'

'I don't have much fun these days,' Talbot said, taking the glass she handed him. Marjorie had poured herself fresh orange juice. She never drank anything stronger. Total abstinence had been part of her youth-and-figure-preserving regimen ever since she was forty.

'Thanks for the booze.' Talbot raised his glass. 'Thanks even more for letting me come by.'

Marjorie tipped back her head, laughed. 'FDR used to put on his sternest look and tell me, "Never deny the exalted in their hours of need." He made it sound like a Biblical proverb, and I took it to heart.' She sat down on a chair matching that occupied by Talbot, her movements graceful, her off-white full-length gown swirling. 'What can I supply now that you're exalted and in dire straits, Charlie?'

He took a large swallow of his drink before replying. 'A sense of perspective – or maybe call it a barometer reading. You know everybody worth knowing in this town, hear what they say. I'd like to get an idea of – well, the consensus about me and my Administration.'

Marjorie had guessed that was it. 'There are some of

73

those ghastly mentholated cigarettes you like on the table next to you,' she said. 'I suggest you light one. Along with the drink, it might act as a partial anesthetic.'

'That bad, huh?' He took a Salem from the box on the table, lit it nervously.

Marjorie Norworth sighed. 'I'm afraid you're not exactly first in the hearts of your countrymen, Charlie. The consensus – God, how I despise that idiotic word – the consensus is that you aren't leading. You're following, trying to keep in step with a hundred and one different drummers.' Her violet eyes softened, looked at him sympathetically. 'Perhaps I shouldn't have been quite that blunt, but you did ask . . .'

'Christ, no apologies, please.' Talbot's hands shook slightly. 'I'm isolated on Pennsylvania Avenue, surrounded by people who tell me what *they* think I should hear. I never get a straight answer.'

'I've listened to the identical complaint from more than one of your illustrious predecessors.'

Talbot inhaled cigarette smoke. 'They asked you for advice . . .'

'Often.'

'And you gave it.'

'Naturally.'

'Will you do it for me?'

'Of course.' Marjorie inclined her head, waited.

Talbot began speaking, telling Marjorie much the same things he told Braithwaite, but placing more emphasis on problems demanding immediate solutions. He talked steadily for over an hour, pausing only whenever Marjorie saw that his glass was empty and insisted on refilling it.

'That's how things stand,' he finished. 'Whatever I've left out isn't important, and I haven't added any filigrees. So –' he broke off, frowning. 'Goddamn, Marjorie! You're smiling like a schoolteacher who just heard a little kid complain . . .'

'Precisely how it sounded.' She smoothed the folds of her gown, her rubies flickering as her hands moved. 'Remember that I was initiated into the mysteries of governance by the all-time master.' She chuckled. 'In his lighter moods, he would say that the only difference between a ward-heeling politician and a statesman was that the statesman had a bigger bag of tricks and a better sense of timing.'

'A good line, but . . .'

'He had an even better one. "People can't tell the difference between movement and action – a lot of the former makes them believe they're seeing a great deal of the latter."'

'Marjorie . . .'

'Shush! I listened without uttering a word for an hour or more – a record for me, I should imagine. It's my turn. What you – and the country – need, and fast, is some high drama and razzle-dazzle. To start off, there being no breast like a clean breast, make one and beat it publicly. Go on television and confess that you – more than anyone else – are aware the country is on the verge of nothing less than calamity, catastrophe, and chaos . . .'

'*What?*' Talbot was aghast.

'Charlie,' Marjorie's tone was calm, soothing, yet faintly tinctured with sardonic humor. 'Confessions made by the high and mighty gain sympathy and support. Imagine the grassroots reaction when the President shows himself honest and courageous enough to admit that the Utopia he envisioned failed to materialize because he has been hampered and hindered . . .'

'I'll be damned. You may be right.' It was beginning to sink in.

'I am right, and wait until you've heard the rest of my scenario. You declare that you've sought to take positive steps, but have been blocked by divisive elements within your own Administration – and, of course, even more so by the opposition party. You practically have tears in your eyes when you implore the opposition to put partisan politics aside and guarantee to put your own bailiwick in order.'

'How?'

'By a wholesale reorganization of your Administration – quote, to clear out problem-makers and bring in problem-solvers, unquote.'

Talbot was thoughtful. 'The idea's great – but I doubt if our people in Congress and the party bosses will buy it.'

'They will, provided you take the most reliable stalwarts into your confidence, make clear it's mainly movement, not action – diversionary sound and fury to gain time. You'll only dump the expendables – and discredit them completely so no one will pay attention to their howls of protest, much less believe their claims and charges.'

'Firing people in key positions is risky.'

'You *are* an infant!' Marjorie Norworth shook her head in exasperation. 'I remember Lyndon Johnson holding forth in the Red Room – mine, that is – and telling Hubert, "Everyone in the Goddamned Government is expendable except me!" That's the attitude to take.' She stood up, went to a desk, returned with a pad of her embossed memo paper and gave it to Talbot. 'Jot down a few notes.' She returned to her chair and spoke for three-quarters of an hour.

'There,' she concluded cheerfully. 'Follow the scenario and doubters will become believers long enough for you to maneuver and find some really constructive formulas. Oh, yes – one other point. You'll need a front-runner. Someone young, with a squeaky-clean record and carloads of charisma. The public has to like and trust him, believe every word he says when he hard-sells the rejuvenated Talbot Administration.'

'Have you anyone in mind?'

'No. Dan Madigan should be able to find a White Knight, though. A younger, cleaner version of Ted Kennedy.'

Talbot nodded, frankly awed. No wonder Marjorie Norworth was acknowledged to have been the power behind so many thrones. 'I should have talked to you sooner,' he said – and meant it. 'Between you and Avery . . .'

'Avery Braithwaite?'

'Uh-huh. I saw him this afternoon.'

Aha – well, that means I'll be hearing from the distinguished Chief Justice soon, Marjorie thought, concealing her amusement. She gazed at Talbot from under hooded lids, a sense of triumph warming her. After more than three decades, she was still official Washington's confidante of last resort, influencing – even guiding – the men who held and wielded power. Now – as never before, not even with The Great Man – she would be exercising much, perhaps even complete, control. She gloated – for President Charles Talbot was reading over the notes he'd written on the memo pad, studying them exactly like a schoolboy bent on memorizing his lessons.

7

Washington, D.C.: Wednesday, February 17. Day.

As its first daily chore, official Washington scans the Washington *Post* and New York *Times*. This morning, the *Post* headlined:

NATIONAL GUARD KILLS SIX
IN RENEWED DETROIT RIOTS

The *Times*:

MICHIGAN GOVERNOR MAY REQUEST
U.S. TROOPS TO END VIOLENCE

But official Washington pays little attention to headlines and hard news, concentrating instead on syndicated columns, editorials, and financial pages. Along the Potomac, it is an Article of Faith that these are the true and reliable indicators of the National Pulse.

President Charles Pendleton Talbot did his required morning reading in the Oval Office. Most columnists and editorial and financial writers focused on the worsening economic picture, deploring or damning and calling for swift, decisive action by the Federal Government. Talbot was almost smug as he read. The clamor was much the same as it had been for months, but now he discerned how well it fitted the strategy Marjorie Norworth had proposed. Razzle-dazzle movement would not only silence the critics. It would flatter them into believing that the pressures they brought to bear had been felt and had produced results.

Talbot put the newspapers aside, summoned his chief White House aide, Kenneth Ramsey. Beefy, bettle-browed, Ramsey had the appearance and air of a nightclub bouncer, an impression he cultivated. This – and his easy relationship with Talbot – enabled him to intimidate other members of the Presidential entourage.

'Cancel my morning appointments,' Talbot instructed Ramsey. 'Use any excuse.'

Ramsey nodded and withdrew, much gladdened by having observed that the President was apparently in better spirits than he had been for some time. Talbot added insurance to his orders. He depressed a desk-side control console, activating electrically operated locks on the Oval Office doors and turning on red lights mounted outside them. The latter warned all and sundry that the President was not to be disturbed under any circumstances short of imminent nuclear attack.

Satisfied he was immune from interruptions, Talbot took a leather-bound folder from a desk drawer. It contained the names of all Executive Branch personnel – from Cabinet members down – whom he could fire or force to resign. Laying the folder before him, he picked up a Parker ballpoint. A check mark beside a name would mean the individual stayed; an 'X' that he was to be jettisoned and small circle that he was a borderline case.

The task was time-consuming. Each individual decision had to be made carefully, cautiously, with many political factors evaluated and weighed. Talbot changed his mind in several instances, blacking out one mark, making another, then changing it back again. At last, he was satisfied. He closed the folder, returned it to the desk drawer and placed a telephone call to the Senate Majority Leader. While it was too early for him to take Madigan into his confidence fully, the next move had to be made.

'Dan, we have to find a torchbearer,' he told Madigan after they exchanged greetings. 'I'm looking for a party paragon – youngish, clean as a whistle – who'll not only toe the line but walk it to hell and back if we ask him.'

'From the Senate?' Madigan wondered what Talbot had up his sleeve.

'If at all possible – and I want him fast.'

Lexa Talbot paid no attention to warning lights or protests from security guards and secretaries. Leaning across the executive secretary's desk, she punched down an intercom key. ' 'Morning, Daddy. Am I ostracized, too?'

A chuckle came over the intercom. 'You're the exception, Puss.'

A muted click indicated the doors were unlocked. Lexa gave everyone in the anteroom a dazzling smile and went into the Oval Office. Her father remained seated behind his desk. She leaned over to kiss him. Her long blonde hair brushed against his face. Talbot noticed she was wearing a tartan-plaid skirt, white sweater, and black velvet blazer. Sexy-chic, yet Junior League correct, he thought and remembered that she was scheduled to spend her afternoon at the U.S. Soldiers' Home. The costume was ideal for the occasion.

'I'm in a rush,' she said. 'My monthly stint of paying homage to our brave boys. I'll have a sore face tonight from holding a dumb smile while I listen to all those corny war stories again.'

'The hospital thing go okay?' Talbot asked.

'Another triumph for the Talbots. I worked in all the usual plugs for you, Mr President.'

He gave her a closer look. 'Hey, you look radiant.' She did.

'I had a good night's sleep,' she lied. He psyched that it was a lie but said nothing. 'You seem perky yourself, Daddy. Did you sleep in late?'

'My night was good, too,' he evaded.

'Glad to hear it – see you later.' She kissed him again and hurried out.

The scent of Lexa's perfume lingered. Like hell she had a good night's sleep, Talbot mused with permissive complaisance. Lexa had the full-bloom glow of a woman whose sleep – if any – had consisted of brief dozings between orgasms that replenished even as they exhausted.

I'm a Goddamned fool, Talbot berated himself. I went to see Marjorie last night and didn't take care of my own itch. It would have been a cinch. She would have set it up for me. I'd have stayed a little longer – that's all. Visions of indulging in pleasure – pure, raw sexual pleasure – kaleidoscoped in his mind, resisted his efforts to erase them, created urgent, painful tensions. Lexa had kissed his cheek moments before. Remembering it now evoked fantasies of women's lips, open and moist, covering his mouth . . . He emitted a groan of frustration.

'Mr President,' a concerned voice came over the intercom. 'Are you all right?'

Talbot jolted, groped for the talk-key, pressed it down.

'Uh – what? Yes, I'm all right.' He paused. 'Why?'

'We heard a moan over the intercom. It sounded like you'd hurt yourself.'

Jesus, Talbot thought, struggling to recover his composure, think of an excuse. 'Uh – yes, I did. I banged my shin and cussed. Sorry.' He neutralized the talk-key, swiveled his chair to the right and again cursed the day that he had been installed in this office.

Jordan B. Rickhoven III was jaunty, even jovial as he boarded his Boeing 727/100, favoring aides and crew members with pleasantries. He went amidships to the roomy compartment that served as his inflight headquarters and communications center. Settling into a white-leather-upholstered lounge chair, he fastened the seat belt. The pilot brought the flight plan and Kennedy Airport ETA.

Rickhoven nodded approval. His conference with the presidents of the Rickhoven National Bank, Jersey Continental Oil, Rickhoven Consolidated Mines and Metals and other giant corporations he controlled was scheduled for midafternoon. He would arrive in New York City in ample time.

The billionaire had not bothered telephoning good-byes to anyone in Washington. There was no reason why he should.

They would be notified when he wished to see them again.

Rickhoven asked a stewardess for coffee. She hurried to the galley, encountering the copilot, who was making a final pretakeoff cabin check. 'JB must have brought off a big deal,' the stewardess remarked. 'He's acting like a cat that swallowed a whole aviary.'

'He's always bringing off big deals,' the copilot shrugged and lowered his voice. 'More likely he feels so good because he laid some cute chick – like you.' He leered, goosed the stewardess, and headed for the flightdeck.

The decline of the FBI began in 1972, when J. Edgar Hoover died. Revelations of corruption and power-abuse followed, further weakening the once sacrosanct bureau. Legislators, long intimidated by the confidential files Hoover held over their heads, passed laws that whittled away the bureau's responsibilities and authority. Whatever was taken away from the FBI was given to the CIA.

Emmett Hopper was the present Director of the greatly enfeebled FBI. Outwardly an IBM-punchcard bureaucrat who operated – and lived – strictly according to the rule book, Emmett Hopper was obsessed with restoring the FBI's power and status. The shortest route to the goal lay in discrediting the CIA and its chief, G. Howard Denby.

Hopper had been in Denver, addressing a National Police Chief's convention and returned to his J. Edgar Hoover Building office shortly after noon on Wednesday. His Deputy, Bodley Wallace, greeted him exultantly, flourishing a large manila envelope.

'Too bad it isn't your birthday,' Wallace chortled. 'You couldn't ask for a finer present.'

Hopper pulled a sheaf of 16 by 20 glossy photographs from the envelope, spread them out on his desk. 'My God – they're fantastic!' he exclaimed, eyes wide and gleaming.

'Denby's crew is getting careless,' Wallace said. 'They took him to the Shoreham. Our agents picked up every word, knew in advance where they'd take him from there. We sent a car and two men ahead to park and wait near the corner. These are only a few sample blown-up stills from motion picture footage taken with a long lens and fast film . . .'

'Fantastic!' Hopper repeated. 'The license number on the Lincoln stands out like a neon light and Weidener is easily recognizable.'

'What next, Chief?'

'Put everything in a vault. Denby and Company think they're riding high and Pearce can protect them. At the auspicious moment we'll produce the material – then watch the havoc.'

Between weekly shows, Suzanne Loring went more or less daily to the CBN studios, studying background information gathered by researchers and doing the preliminary planning for her next telecast.

Awakening late and with a slight Seconal hangover – quickly cured by black coffee – Suzanne arrived at the studios just before noon, lunched at her desk with her secretary and the research department head and pored over newsclips and summaries until three-thirty. Deciding to call it a day, she fine-tuned in on the subject that had been intruding on her thoughts since she woke up.

Russell Hatch.

Okay, she capitulated mentally, *I am in love with him. And what people insist in calling feminine intuition tells me he's in love with me – only like me, he's been afraid to admit it, dodging it, doing his Goddamndest to stay cool and uncommitted while we've been spending the last two years getting more and more – and more – involved with each other. Hell, we're both grownups. We should be able to handle it. But we've both been acting like a pair of brain-damaged adolescents since yesterday morning. Or I have, at least. Russ was conned – victimized – by Dan Madigan. He's sorry, regrets it. He tried to apologize yesterday afternoon, and I wouldn't listen, wouldn't even give him a chance to talk. I know he tried again – I'm certain it was Russ who kept my phone flashing last night – and I've been a cunt. A dumb, ego-tripping cunt.*

She reached for her telephone, punched numbers.

Hatch's secretary knew Suzanne and of her relationship with her employer.

'Oh, you missed him by minutes, Miss Loring,' the secretary burbled. 'He's on his way to see Senator Madigan. He rushed out – it must be important. Would you like to leave a message?'

'No. Thanks.' Suzanne replaced the instrument in its cradle, her mind and feelings once again in total disarray.

My ex used to tell me everyone, without exception, in Washington was a hypocrite, a liar, and a double-crossing, opportunistic son of a bitch, Suzanne reflected. *I didn't believe him at first. But he and a parade of other males made me a believer – with a vengeance. After that, along came Senator Russell Hatch, and I thought that at any rate, I'd found one – maybe the only – exception. Now I'm back to the Shitty Square One of yesterday morning. Russ must have made some kind of deal with Madigan.*

Russ had practically come right out and said as much. What was his line? Oh, yes. 'A nod from Madigan is all I need.' Well, I knuckled under, and Russ must have gotten his nod – it looks as though he's running over to give the nodder's ass another lick right this minute.

Another voice inside Suzanne spoke up in rebuttal. *Don't do a repeat of the dumb cunt act. In the first place, Russ Hatch is innocent until he's proved – or proves himself – guilty. In the second, even if he's guilty, he can be used. Then – for Christ's sake – you only just threw in the towel and admitted you were in love with the jerk. You can repair the damage, shape him up – steer him in any direction you want.*

'Seems I've still got a long way to go – Baby,' Suzanne murmured audibly. She had no clue as to how she really felt when she went into her office bathroom to freshen up before calling for the limo to take her home.

Having finecombed the Senate roster, Daniel Madigan narrowed the field of eligibles to eight and had their personal dossiers brought to his office. He went over these for hours, culled out three probables – one of them being Russell Hatch. He stared at the Hatch file and broke into laughter – at himself.

'I must've balled myself silly last night,' he muttered aloud. 'I'm not thinking.' Russell Hatch was it, a natural.

What citizen could possibly doubt anything the spotless junior Senator from Oregon with the Tom Sawyer image might say?

Hatch had telephoned earlier, but Madigan – deep in his dossiers – pretended to be out. He now called Hatch, apologized profusely and asked, 'Can you shoot over here right away, Russ? It's top priority – and I can't discuss it over the phone.'

When Russ arrived, Madigan gave him the strong grip and the jovial-sincere look. That ceremony concluded, the Senate Majority Leader poured them both drinks and launched into exploratory talk, testing for signs of ambition, obtained positive results – for Russ freely admitted he was ambitious to make his mark in Washington.

Madigan was convinced. Hatch could be safely dished up as the White Knight – provided he was made to believe in the virtues of his mission. However, it would be Charles Talbot's job to convince him of that.

'President Talbot and I've been talking about you, Russ,' Madigan said, replenishing empty glasses and beaming his thousand-kilowatt sincere look. 'We remembered how terrific you were in Oregon during the big campaign,' Madigan was improvising, 'and the excellent impression you've made on me and others in the Senate. I also told him about the favor you did for me with your lady friend . . .'

He stopped as Russ's expression underwent abrupt change and guessed what must have occurred between Hatch and Suzanne Loring as a result of the 'favor'. The luck of the Irish, he thought. They're pissed off at each other – or maybe it's only that she's pissed off at him. No matter. Any rift between Russ and Suzanne Loring would make the task of political seduction all the simpler.

'Almost six,' Madigan said, glancing at his Patek Philippe wrist watch. 'Let's knock off and continue this gabfest later tonight – at Lady Norworth's.'

Russ did a double take. He had of course heard of the House on the Hill, but being low in the Washington pecking-order, had never been invited there before – and an invitation was, in itself, at least a one-rung boost.

'Sounds great to me, Dan.'

'Good. I'll pick you up around nine.'

At six o'clock Avery Braithwaite telephoned Marjorie Norworth.

'My dear Marjorie, would it be possible for me to have the Lincoln Bedroom tonight and . . .'

'You don't have to go into details, Avery. I'll see it's made ready for you.'

Marjorie had expected to hear from Braithwaite ever since Charles Talbot mentioned him. She did not expect the call she received shortly afterwards from Daniel Madigan. He requested an invitation for himself and for Senator Russell Hatch.

Marjorie knew that Hatch was a novice solon, a political nonentity. If Madigan wished to introduce him into her charmed circle it meant Hatch was being groomed – or gulled – by the Senate Majority Leader. She would certainly learn which before the night was over.

Marjorie's credo paraphrased the adage about knowledge conferring power. Knowledge of the men who wielded political power conferred a higher form of power, above which there was only God. But Marjorie Trumbull Norworth did not believe in God.

8

Washington, D.C.: Wednesday, February 17. Night.

Russell Hatch had visited the White House on those ritual occasions when even junior Senators were included on the guest-list. Thus, he instantly recognized the meticulously reproduced Diplomatic Reception Room into which he and Dan Madigan were ushered. Never underestimate the powers of a woman, he mused. Not when she has fierce ambition, iron will, and two or three hundred million dollars.

It must have cost a fortune to duplicate the American scenic-landscape wallpaper alone. The original, dating from 1834 and made in Alsace, was priceless, an acknowledged artistic masterpiece. The huge Aubusson-style carpet, its pattern formed by seals of various states of the Union, was superior in quality and hand-workmanship to that woven for the White House.

Hatch cut short his survey of the decor, whistled inwardly. None of the countless photographs of Marjorie Norworth that he had seen did her justice. The woman who came to greet them was what, he thought – 65? She must be, for she was already an internationally known beauty in the 1930s. But it was impossible to believe. Her carriage was erect, almost regal. Her face was still beautiful, that of a woman of forty – and a well-preserved forty at that.

'Dan, you scoundrel.' She embraced Madigan, the enormous diamonds on her hands and wrists flaring. Marjorie always wore diamonds on evenings when she had more than a handful of guests. Diamonds bedazzled and intimidated. Even the most cloddish bureaucrat recognized their immense value. All Washington (for that matter, most of the world) knew she owned such famous gems as the Wanderfill and Quahinat diamonds. Some years before when Richard Burton and Elizabeth Taylor were still married and in the midst of their diamond-buying mania, Burton offered her two million for the Quahinat. Piqued that anyone thought she would ever consider selling any of her jewels, Marjorie sent him a curt, icy note of refusal which, gossips claimed, had sent Elizabeth Taylor into a two-week depression. Marjorie was wearing the Quahinat tonight – as a bangle hanging from a bracelet on her right wrist.

Dan Madigan started to introduce Russell Hatch. Marjorie stopped him with a laugh and extended her hand to Russ. The Quahinat practically blinded him.

'Hello, Senator Russell Hatch,' she said warmly. 'You're from Oregon, thirty-nine years old and serving your first term. You see, Dan forgets that I memorize names, faces and facts. I even know you're an attorney – or were – in Portland. A lovely city. I opened the Rose Festival there once, many years ago . . .'

Interesting, Hatch thought. The Grand Dame – Grand Duchess – of Washington enjoys giving the impression of being a compulsive chatterbox, but one who knows everything about everyone. He listened until she finished, said the right words in response, and looking into her stunning violet eyes wondered how many men had drowned themselves in their compelling depths.

Marjorie read his thoughts as she studied his open, freckled face, admired his tall, wide-shouldered frame, and made her initial evaluation. He's attractive, she told herself, and far more intelligent and perceptive than someone like Dan Madigan would imagine. Senator Russell Hatch could go far – with a little coaching and a guiding push every now and then.

'Come, meet the others,' Marjorie said, taking Russ's arm.

Several men were talking and drinking in Marjorie's replica of the White House Blue Room. Russ knew two already – both senior Senators from their respective states.

Paunchy, balding Aaron Kugelman from New York and gaunt, sallow-complexioned Early Frobase from Mississippi – an important Washington figure, for he was President Pro Tempore of the Senate. Hatch liked Kugelman, an effusive but intelligent and conscientious man who often larded his conversation with Yiddish words and phrases. But Russ despised Frobase, who was a virulent racist and had amassed considerable wealth from graft and outright bribes. He found it surprising to see Kugelman and Frobase sitting together, apparently the best of friends and in total harmony.

Among the others to whom he was introduced, Hatch knew only three – and by sight and reputation only. The Secretary of Agriculture and two veteran Representatives from the Midwest. They sat apart, clearly deep in serious discussion. Russ surmised they were probably cooking up some new farm-subsidy rape of the Treasury and taxpayer. The Agriculture Secretary greeted Dan Madigan as an old companion-in-arms and wryly asked if Madigan were aware the National Gallery had recently acquired a new Rembrandt.

'It'd look good over your desk, Dan,' he said, laughing.

'The Gallery should buy another,' Kugelman said. 'A big *macher* like Dan should have them hanging in pairs.'

'You mean he doesn't?' Frobase teased. 'Way I hear it, you always get two of everything, Dan.'

'Sure, when I can steal 'em,' Madigan retorted.

A crisply white-jacketed waiter moved about, bringing trays of drinks and canapes. One of the Midwestern Congressmen eyed Russ. 'Are you on the Agriculture Committee?'

'No, afraid not.'

'Oh.' The congressman turned to the Secretary of Agriculture. 'We have to get more support on the Senate side.'

'Don't worry, Hank,' Dan Madigan said over his shoulder. 'You'll have it. The fix is in. Your home-state farmers'll grow fatter on the pork we dish out from the old barrel.'

Surreal, Russ thought. Here there aren't any political Parties, or separations of powers, interests, secrets. He could not help but feel excitement – mingled with something akin to shock. The entire vast and intricate apparatus of government boiled down to this. Political leaders gathered at the House on the Hill, ignored ideologies, joked about the illegal and illicit, prearranged what would later be made to appear as the result of democratic processes – and fuck the voters.

Russ remembered a fragment of an Ogden Nash couplet. *Raping is a crime – unless you rape the voters, a million at a time.* He drained the glass of Remy he held.

Shit, maybe this is – and always has been – the democratic process. Marjorie Norworth sat near him, sipping orange juice. She turned to him, spoke in a low tone.

'You can't possibly be that naïve,' she said. Russ blinked, stared at her. 'I'm psychic,' Marjorie smiled. 'You're hardly the first wide-eyed tyro I've seen.' She flicked a glance at the waiter, who immediately brought Hatch a fresh Remy. 'You're an attorney,' she went on. 'I find it difficult to believe that you conducted your practice in a fairy-tale world.'

'I'm sorry. I don't understand . . .'

'There were never deals made between opposing counsel – or with prosecutors and judges?'

Russ was about to say the comparison was unfair, that what happened in his law-practice in Portland was one thing, the Federal Government quite another, when Marjorie's words triggered sudden insight. Of course the comparison was fair. The two differed only in their comparative scale and scope.

'I've been overlooking the obvious,' he said – and was amazed that he, at thirty-nine and after two years in Washington, had been doing precisely that. Pensive, he withdrew into himself, but only for a moment.

'. . . and, gents, you better keep your eye on Russ here,' he heard Dan Madigan saying. 'He's going places, I guarantee you . . .'

Russ almost spilled his cognac. It was practically a formal

announcement that he was slated for important assignments. Considering the men who had heard it, word would be all over Washington tomorrow.

Marjorie saw the pieces fall into place. She had told Talbot he needed a front-running Sir Lancelot. Madigan had found him. Another of her complex manipulations was taking form. *Too bad I find myself liking Hatch,* she reflected – then suddenly erased the regret. *While the machinery can't be reversed, I* can *keep Russell Hatch from getting hurt, take him in hand, make something of him.* She glowed inwardly. *The more intrigues the merrier.*

Frobase had now consumed enough liquor to embark on his favorite tirade.

'Take Detroit. What's the problem there? Nigras. Same here in Washington, same everywhere . . .'

'For God's sake, Early, find some new lyrics.' Madigan yawned.

Kugelman came to Frobase's defense. 'Maybe Early does go off the deep end, but the *schwarzers* make trouble.'

So much for Kugelman, the Great Liberal, Russ thought, his liking for him evaporating.

Marjorie recognized the familiar Frobase symptom and, pressing a call-button, diverted the conversation. 'Did I ever tell you the story about Ike and General Vaughan . . .'

Holcomb appeared in the doorway.

'Has Miss Quigley arrived?' Marjorie asked him. Holcomb said she had. 'Show her in, please, Holcomb.'

The majordomo ushed in a statuesque platinum-blond girl of nineteen. 'Early, Miss Quigley would like to see you,' Marjorie said.

Frobase got to his feet. 'Thanks for a marvelous evening, Lady Norworth.' He nodded to the men. 'Be seeing you all.' He made his way to the girl, took her hand. Holcomb stood aside. Frobase and Miss Quigley disappeared.

'It was Ike's first term,' Marjorie picked up the thread of her promised story. 'Harry Vaughan rang me up . . .'

Early Frobase and the Junoesque Miss Quigley went upstairs, turned a corner along the main corridor, stopped.

Frobase gave her a fifty-dollar bill. 'You'll go out the back way, right?'

'Sure. Thanks, Senator.' She walked away, hips swinging.

He opened the nearest door, entered a bedroom. A corpulent black woman with great pendulous breasts stood nude, waiting. Frobase seized her, embraced her feverishly.

'Tits! I want to come on your tits!' His voice was ragged.

'Come anywhere you want, honey – after you get your clothes off and we're on the bed.' She raised an arm high, guided his face to her armpit. 'You want this first though, don't you.'

Frobase went wild, hungrily inhaling the heavy, sweaty odor.

The Secretary of Agriculture chuckled. 'Early sure goes for 'em young and lily white. He'd probably have cardiac arrest if he so much as stood near a woman with a deep suntan.'

Marjorie's eyes were hooded. She laughed inwardly at the elaborate pretense, so often repeated. The strident racist invariably used a young blonde as camouflage, terrified that other men might discover his pathetic secret. Unless he could ejaculate on the sagging breasts of a middle-aged – and unwashed – black woman, Frobase was totally impotent.

Another hour of talk and drink, and the guests began to take their leave. Madigan signaled Hatch to stay a little longer. Russ was amused at the way the other guests' manner had changed toward him since Madigan had remarked that he was going places. Each wrung his hand and swore that if Hatch ever wanted a favor – 'just call me, Senator'.

Russ and Madigan stayed only a little longer. Dan had requested nothing from Marjorie Norworth but an invitation to visit. When bringing a guest to the House on the Hill for the first time it was understood that only after Lady Norworth had scrutinized the newcomer and indicated approval could future requests be made. Madigan waited for her verdict on Hatch. She gave it when he and Russ made ready to depart.

'You're always welcome here, Russ,' she said, flicking a

significant glance at Madigan. 'Please do come again – and soon. Telephone me whenever you'd like to drop by.'

Dan Madigan hid his surprise. Seldom did a single visit give anyone carte blanche entrée. Maybe Russ turns the old on, he speculated. The idea struck him as being howlingly funny – Lady Marjorie Norworth trying to seduce Tom Sawyer. Which, of course, was what Marjorie intended doing – but not at all in the way Dan Madigan imagined.

Like Talbot the night before, Avery Braithwaite arrived at midnight. Unlike Talbot, he drove his own car, entered the grounds through the Foxhall Road gates and drew up before the main entrance to the mansion.

Marjorie took Braithwaite to the now-deserted Blue Room. He looked haggard, his granitelike features pale and drawn. She knew better than to offer him anything alcoholic on a night when he'd asked to use the Lincoln Bedroom. 'Would you care for coffee, tea . . . ?'

'Thank you, no,' Braithwaite said. He had not eaten or drunk – not even water – since his talk with Talbot. Fasting was a form of selfpurification enabling the mind and body to utilize every bit of inner energy and force in withstanding infinitely more severe rigors.

'Care to talk a little?' Marjorie inquired.

'Not tonight, my dear.'

'Shall I have Holcom take you upstairs?'

'Please.'

A tattered, soiled garment, hardly more than a loincloth, was laid out on the large and ornately carved mahogany bed in the Lincoln Bedroom. Other furniture had been moved against the walls, leaving a cleared space in which an almost ceiling-high wooden cross was erected and securely fastened. One stepladder stood in front of the cross, another off to its side.

Holcom helped Braithwaite remove his clothing and hung each item neatly in the bulky, dark-wood cupboard. Braithwaite took the torn garment off the bed, donned it.

'Exactly five minutes, Holcomb.'

'Yes, sir.' The butler left the room.

Braithwaite, barefoot, wearing only the sorry cloth draped around his loins, knelt beside the bed and prayed – prayed as he believed Abraham Lincoln must have before signing the Emancipation Proclamation in the White House original of the room. Fervently striving to establish communion, he pleaded for strength to bear the coming ordeal, begged for the guidance and enlightenment that could be granted only through the agony he was about to experience.

'. . . Amen.' He stood up, face shining with inner light.

Holcom entered with a man and a woman. The man was dressed in the uniform of a Roman legionary – helmet, rough tunic under a metal breastplate, flat openwork sandals. A shortsword was slung on his belt. He carried a spear. The woman wore a loose, white hooded cloak. Her face was garishly painted to resemble a Mask of Tragedy.

'Ready, sir?' Holcom asked.

'Yes.' It was a whisper. Braithwaite climbed the stepladder in front of the cross. On the top step he turned, spread his arms wide, held them against the horizontal beam. Holcomb produced leather thongs, mounted the other stepladder, lashed Braithwaite's left wrist tightly to the beam with a thong. He climbed down, moved the stepladder, repeated the process with Braithwaite's right wrist. Climbing down again, Holcomb used a third, much heavier thong, to secure the Chief Justice's ankles to the vertical beam. He removed the stepladder and Braithwaite gasped as the support went from under his feet and his body sagged, almost wrenching his arms from their sockets.

'Thank you, Holcomb.' Dismissed, the butler withdrew from the room. The woman and man knew their roles. She knelt at the foot of the cross, head bowed. The Roman soldier struck an insolent pose beside her and cursed. Braithwaite, his physical pain intensifying, stared down at them and felt a greater, deeper pain. He slowly raised his head, looked up at the ceiling that was now to him the open sky.

'Father, help those who beseech Thee.'

The Roman legionary mouthed obscenities. The woman sobbed.

'We are Thy children, lost without Thy mercy . . .'

Braithwaite cried out in anguish as the legionary jabbed the wooden spear shaft into his ribs.

'I beg Thee to show me what is righteous and Thy will . . .'

Another, harder jab of the spear shaft, and the soldier spat up at him and snarled: 'Son of a whore!'

'Father . . .'

'You have no father!' the legionary taunted. Braithwaite looked down. The soldier seized the woman, flung her to the floor. She wept, struggled. The legionary pulled her cloak up around her waist and, laughing savagely, mounted her, began thrusting. Every fiber in Avery Braithwaite's body shrieked with pain, but it was as nothing to the inner agony caused by what he was forced to witness. He bit blood from his lips, strained against his bonds.

'God, Thou art all-knowing . . .'

'Watch us!' the legionary ordered, his body pounding against that of the woman.

'Help me,' she begged, turning her head so Braithwaite could see the Tragedy Mask of her face contort even more.

'We are all imploring Thy help, Father.' Braithwaite raised his head again – and waited for the first tremors to start.

The legionary brayed as he reached orgasm. Braithwaite gazed down, wept. My agony is complete, he thought. In a moment, his own body would shudder in physical release – and the release would be accompanied by enlightenment.

Minutes passed. Woman and legionary remained in frozen tableau. At last, Braithwaite realized that he had failed. There were occasions when release and revelation eluded him. My agony was not sufficiently great, he thought and, in a hoarse whisper, said, 'Take me down.'

The man and woman leaped up. The legionary's short-sword was real, sharp enough to cut the thongs, and they helped Braithwaite down from the cross and to the bed. He slumped down on it.

'The money is on the desk,' he said.

They said nothing. They were not to speak a word other than their rehearsed lines. Braithwaite closed his eyes. He heard the man and woman move about the room, then leave it, closing the door behind them. He lay on the bed for an hour while pain ebbed and some of his strength returned. At last, every move torment, he got up, took off the tatters and dressed himself.

Clothed, he sat at the copy of the desk Abraham Lincoln used while temporarily residing at the Old Soldiers' Home during the most critical period of the Civil War. Hands trembling, he scrawled a note. He folded the paper, made his way out of the room and to Marjorie Norworth's suite. Slipping the note under her door, he went downstairs. Holcomb, still awake, brought his overcoat, draped it over his shoulders.

'May I assist you, sir?' Holcomb asked, opening the main doors.

'Thank you, no, Holcomb. Goodnight.'

Marjorie had not gone to sleep. She heard Braithwaite's shuffle outside her door and guessed he was leaving her a note – he sometimes did. She found it on the rug.

'My Dear Marjorie: I am most grateful to you. May I possibly have the Lincoln Bedroom again tomorrow night?'

Marjorie had her own means of knowing that his visit was a failure. Going to her bedroom, she touched a concealed switch. A large mirror, apparently built into the wall, rolled aside on hidden tracks, exposing a safe that would have done credit to a bank's branch office. She worked the combination, opened the armored steel door and removed the current volume of the diaries she had been keeping for decades. She smiled as she glanced at the dozens of volumes ranged along two shelves in the safe – and at the many scores of small, square and labeled cardboard boxes stacked on other shelves. Living history, she thought.

She took her diary to the dressing table, entered the day's events in her clear, flowing script, and pasted Braithwaite's note to the bottom of the page.

Reading the note again, Marjorie was seized by a fit of girlish giggling. What would the American public do if it ever learned what the Chief Justice of the Supreme Court meant when he said he 'agonized' over important questions? The giggled faded. Countless other Great and Famous men – past and present – had even more bizarre quirks. The details – and the proof – reposed in her safe.

9

The World of Lady Marjorie Norworth.
November, 1941–December, 1947

Prodigious expenditure of money translated the Great
Man's suggestion that Marjorie Norworth reproduce ten
White Rooms in her home into reality with astounding
speed. Hiring outstanding architects, art historians, de-
signers, and decorators, Marjorie spared no costs and
promised them munificent bonuses if the work was completed in six months. They met the deadline and, on
Tuesday night, November 18, 1941, she gave a landmark
'House Warming' party.

Franklin and Eleanor Roosevelt attended, as did some
five hundred members of Washington's political and social
elite and numerous representatives of the press, FDR was
effusive in his praise of Marjorie's imagination, taste, and
patriotic spirit. As the Great Man had predicted, the sheep
dutifully brayed even louder and more grandiloquent
accolades.

Only Cissie Patterson and Evelyn McLean were silent,
sullen with rage. Overnight, Marjorie Trumbull Norworth –
in their eyes a concupiscent parvenu – had become the undisputed Queen of Washington Society, relegating them
both to second place. Worse, they could not hope to re-
taliate. Scarcely three weeks later, the Japanese attacked
Pearl Harbor and America went to war. Press and public
would tolerate no resumption of High Society status-struggle
while men fought and died. Marjorie's position at the peak
was secure for the duration.

Her home became the hub of Washington social life.
Invitations to attend her dinners, parties, balls were

accepted as Imperial Commands. Reveling in the knowledge that she could socially make or break by inviting or omitting, Marjorie was highly selective in choosing names for her guest lists.

But the Great Man did nothing throughout his life that could not somehow be later used in his own self-interest. Having been decisively instrumental in raising Marjorie to the rank of Washington's Number One hostess, he demanded payment for services rendered – and she deferred to his wishes and whims. Often, when desiring to cast a subordinate into limbo, he asked Marjorie to give a dinner-party to which he and the marked individual's colleagues were invited – but the condemned man was not. It was the Great Man's cruelly devious way of informing one and all that the conspicuously absent vassal was Out. Conversely, he would have Marjorie invite him, a number of men who held high positions – plus a comparative unknown. The next morning all Washington understood the message. Yesterday's nonentity was today's new favorite.

The Great Man frequently used Marjorie's Foxhall Road mansion to hold secret and momentous conferences with party bosses and men of great wealth and influence. The decision to scuttle Vice President Henry Agard Wallace was made long before the 1944 elections – in Lady Norworth's Red Room. Somewhat later, Great Man and kingmakers hammered out what they contemptuously called 'The Missouri Compromise', agreeing that Harry S. Truman should be the Vice Presidential candidate. That meeting took place in Marjorie's Blue Room – and the Great Man's open scorn of Truman was transmitted to Lady Norworth – and the effects were to cost her dearly.

Being at the epicenter of momentous decisions and events further enhanced Marjorie Norworth's status and influence, and she reigned unchallenged – until April, 1945.

The Great Man's physical and mental health deteriorated. His body wasted away. His mind, never at safe distance from megalomania, roiled with delusions of omniscience and omnipotence. With the European war nearing its end, he visualized a world that he and Josef Stalin would share equally between themselves. His plans and decisions lost touch with political reality. He issued orders that would have brought catastrophic results – but appalled subordinates ignored them, something they could do with impunity, for his memory-span was now short.

Ever since the beginning of the war, the Great Man had been guarded day and night by platoons of military police and security men. He was accompanied everywhere by a horde of aides, including advisers, experts, personal physicians, valets, and others – a swollen entourage he disparagingly called 'My Plague of locusts'. Yet, when he died in April 1945, a docile press and a public stunned by his passing did not question why – on that one day – he was in the rambling house at Warm Springs without guards, aides, staff, or servants. Indeed, the official version stated he was alone save for 'his longtime friend, the fabulously wealthy and famed Washington hostess, Lady Marjorie Norworth'.

It was true that Marjorie had been alone with the Great Man. She was puzzled by the absence of his usual retinue, but said nothing. He seemed unaware that the men – in and out of uniform – who always swarmed through and around any building in which he happened to be were nowhere in evidence. But then, he was concerned solely with the purpose for which he had summoned Marjorie to Warm Springs from Washington.

The Great Man's entire body was now thin and shriveled. His face was cadaverous, his eyes sunk deep into their sockets. Only the dream of soon becoming ruler over half the globe kept him alive.

When the OSS men burst into the room Marjorie was pulled away, sent sprawling to the floor. A hand holding a silenced .45-caliber Colt automatic flexed twice against its trigger, pumped two bullets into the Great Man's head.

Marjorie screamed, kept on screaming until a hypodermic needle was thrust into her arm and fast-acting sedatives closed off her conscious mind. She was not aware that men took her limp hands and fingers and pressed them against the trigger, butt, barrel, and magazine of the Colt, which they then dropped into a plastic bag.

Marjorie regained consciousness hours later in another bedroom. Men she knew well – men who were high in the councils of state stood by her bedside. Memory returning, she could only stammer: 'They – they murdered him . . .'

A white-haired Cabinet officer for whom she had held a gala reception only a week before took her hand and spoke gently. It had to be done, he declared. There was no alternative, for the Great Man's mental condition and irrational actions were a grave threat to the national interest. The decision to assassinate him was made unanimously by officials at the top level of government. Marjorie found herself not only understanding but agreeing – even approving. Yes, she admitted—to herself, his mind had gone Killing him – quickly and painlessly – before the world learned the truth was an act of mercy. She wept. The men allowed her to weep, knowing that any attempt to comfort or console would be futile.

One of her friends – a ramrod-straight military man in ill-fitting civilian clothes – now disclosed the precautions that had been taken to insure her silence. He showed her the plastic bag containing the Colt.

'Your fingerprints are on it, Marjorie. I regret this, but we have to be absolutely certain.'

She nodded wanly. They dared not risk her talking. She dared not talk as long as they had the weapon with her fingerprints on it.

Marjorie was given an affidavit. It stated that she and the Great Man had been talking in the solarium of the house. He suddenly cried out and fell from the chair in which he was sitting. She rushed to help him, realized he was beyond help, and tried to telephone for a doctor. The telephone was out of order, but moments later an official car drove up. She ran out of the house, told the occupants of the car what had happened – and fainted. Marjorie signed the document.

Once released, the version was universally accepted as

historical fact. The Great Man suffered a massive brain hemorrhage which turned his face and head a hideous, purple-black. It was for this reason that his casket was sealed and he was buried without being viewed by any of the millions who mourned him.

When President Franklin Delano Roosevelt died, Marjorie Norworth lost a dear friend. She was also – and immediately – dispossessed of her social preeminence. But this was her own fault. Like so many others, she thought that FDR – being only sixty-three – would certainly live to serve out his fourth term. And, also like many others, she looked down on Vice President Harry S. Truman as a ludicrous cipher, a country bumpkin and former haberdasher whose social graces were limited to playing poker (well) and the piano (badly). His wife, Bess, was a formidable Midwestern *hausfrau* type who cared nothing for *haute couture* or the *haute monde*. Marjorie Norworth had avoided any attempts to cultivate the Trumans' friendship.

The new President and the end of the war brought drastic changes in Washington power-patterns, life-styles – and the world of Lady Marjorie Norworth. She no longer had a patron in the White House, nor even access to the man who occupied it. Peace relaxed restrictions, and the scramble for social supremacy resumed. Women who had long envied (and thus hated) Marjorie leaped at the chance to depose her. New contenders, Perle Mesta and Gwendolyn Cafritz among them, entered the fray. They had money to spend and the new power-players of the Truman Administration at their beck and call.

Lady Norworth's invitations were no longer Imperial Commands. Many Washington women who had formerly fawned over her now deliberately ignored them. Only holdovers from the FDR regime remained loyal, remembering hospitality shown, favors done, and Marjorie's intercessions on their behalf. However, when invited with their wives to the Norworth mansion, they came alone with increasing frequency, giving lame excuses why Ellen or Jocelyn or Bar-

bara could not attend. Marjorie soon found herself presiding over dinner tables at which there were only male guests and being asked only to those garish charity affairs or Diplomatic Row parties where practically anyone was welcome.

Bradford Cooley was foremost among the men who remained her steadfast friends and champions. Cooley had never forgotten that it was through Marjorie's importunings of the Great Man that he won a second Congressional term in 1942. Thereafter, his Alabama constituents reelected him as a matter of course, and Marjorie continued to be a staunch and active ally. By 1947 he was an influential member of the powerful House Appropriations Committee. But he was no longer an almost breathtakingly handsome young man: he had grown overly plump in six years, his face resembled that of a dissipated cherub, and he was already balding.

Years before, Marjorie had desperately desired to have an affair with Cooley. Trusting her implicitly, he confessed the secret why it was impossible. He was a fixed homosexual – and had been since the age of fourteen. 'I practically raped the local druggist,' he confided. The confession somehow greatly strengthened their friendship.

One evening in mid-December, 1947, Bradford Cooley dined alone with Marjorie. She made a brave outward show, trading morsels of capital gossip, laughing at his cutting remarks about Truman Administration bigwigs. He readily saw through the façade.

'You do feel badly battered and bruised,' he said.

There was nothing to hide from Cooley, Marjorie thought and, toying with a dessert fork, nodded wanly. 'I wouldn't have minded abdicating gracefully – God knows I had a long and happy reign – but to be suddenly deposed' – she forced a wry smile – 'to be defenestrated . . .'

She sipped champagne (it was before total abstention became of her regimen) and watched Cooley pour himself more bourbon from the Waterford decanter that was always placed beside his plate when he came to dinner. Glass filled, he raised it in a mock toast.

'To your myopia – may it be cured, and quickly.' He drank.

'Is that some kind of arcane Alabama wit?'

'It's a diagnosis. You're shortsighted, unable to see that what appears to be defeat may be turned to advantage. You fail to discern that, despite your "defenestration" – an utterly sublime word – you retain myriad potent weapons in your armory.'

'Namely?'

'Ah'm a-comin' to thet, ma'am.' His counterfeit Alabama dialect both amused and irritated her. Having achieved the desired effects, he dropped it. 'Where to begin the inventory? With money, I suppose. Interest on that mountain of Trumbull wealth you inherited resists your most extravagant efforts to dent the capital sum. Next, beauty. Yours is undiminished.' Cooley drank more bourbon. 'Wish I could say the same for mine, but we aren't here to shed tears over my sins and sorrows. Then, you have a sizable hard-core nucleus of devoted friends . . .'

'All men. The women have ostracized me.'

'More myopia. You equate the social whirl with influence . . .'

'Of course.'

'Yes – when there is an autocratic FDR in the White House and you are his confidante and enjoy his special favor. No – when a Harry Truman sits in the Presidential chair. He has cronies – all male. His sole female confidantes are Bess and Margaret.'

'But Gwen Cafritz, Perle Mesta, Cissie . . .'

'Give parties and balls, and they can influence the second-stringers. Not much, though, for they dilute their influence by concentrating on their own internecine catfights.'

Cooley emptied his glass and reached for the decanter.

'I'll return to my thesis. The weapons in your arsenal. You have this house with its renowned replicas of rooms in the White House. You have had infinite experience as Washington's leading hostess. There's your encyclopedic knowledge of all that has been said, done, schemed, plotted, and suppressed in Washington for a decade . . .'

'Unfortunately, you overlook . . .'

'*You* overlook, Marjorie. I repeat, myopia. Men in Government don't really enjoy the Cafritz-Mesta-*et al* extravaganzas. They go because they're dragged by their wives or feel they *must* make an appearance. God, how often I hear them complain!'

Marjorie gave a start. 'Did they complain about my . . .?'

'Never. FDR ruled, this was the hub, and you had a touch and flair the others lack. More important, while you gossiped, you kept confidences. The others talk, indiscreetly and incessantly.'

Marjorie sensed he told the truth, relaxed.

'Be honest,' Cooley went on. 'You couldn't have cared less about having women attend your affairs. The men were the means to your ends. Now you can have the ends – through the same means – but *sans* the extraneous and, I should imagine, tiresome female window dressings.'

She waited, intuition telling her he had an idea, a scheme. His talent for intrigue and machination rivaled that of the Great Man.

'Use the nucleus of men in high places – men who have remained your friends – as a new base,' Cooley murmured. 'Make this a place where those who govern – or whatever it is we do – may come. Be at ease, drink, and talk without their nagging wives. Capitalize on the concept.'

'You may be on the track of something, Brad.'

'There's more. Deep in the heart of every politician and appointed official in Washington there is a flicker of hope that eats like a cancer. Perhaps, by some miracle, he will some day be the Man in the White House.'

'Yes, I know that.'

'The hope – or cancer – is the most potent of all aphrodisiacs. Imagine what feats of sexual prowess a man could perform, the orgasms he would achieve, in Lincoln's Bedroom, the Queen's Bedroom – or the bedchamber of the President himself.'

'I don't have to imagine. I've experienced the effect even here in the replica rooms with various men. The meekest became bulls.'

'Your eyesight is improving,' Cooley leered.

It struck her then. 'My God, Brad! Are you suggesting I turn this house into a bordello?'

'Not quite. Into a haven where men who are the *crème* of the Establishment may gather and, on occasion, gratify their fantasies.'

'You have gone stark, raving mad.'

'I have never been saner. I propose you give parties and dinners for men high in Government and occasionally – not often and only as a special favor for select individuals – provide sexual partners for them. It would be understood that you take no money. Financial arrangements would be between them and their partners – except in cases where you wished to do some individual a particular favor and footed the bill yourself.'

'They'd still be using the bedrooms here.'

'In their minds, they'd be in the real White House rooms – in their ultimate fantasy-world.'

'I'd be operating a house of assignation. Under the law ...'

'Law?' Cooley chortled. 'The men you would invite are laws unto themselves. And you would simply be conducting the most exclusive *salon* in Washington.'

Salon, Marjorie reflected. Yes, DuBarry and Pompadour, *Mesdames* de Montespan and de Maintenon had their *salons* and arranged liaisons and assignations between important men and attractive young women. But this was the twentieth century.

'There are too many dangers,' she objected. 'The press might expose – and the women might talk.'

'No reason to fear either. The press may attack individuals or small groups – but, as you know, never dares reveal anything that might antagonize the Establishment as a whole. As for the women, their silence is assured by the importance and power of the men who would disport with them. They would fear the consequences, the retributions if they said a word.'

Marjorie was silent, thoughtful – then shook her head.

'Impossible, Brad. Most of the men are married and have their wives here in Washington. Inevitably, those wives would hear and create a scandal.'

'Wrong. Washington wives are notoriously selfish bitches and climbers terrified that their husbands might be compromised and lose prestige or position. Granted, they've recently danced with glee over your apparent downfall. But do what I advise, and while they'll be filled with hatred, they'll once more envy you – and, at the same time, treat you like a queen restored to her throne. They'll have no choice, because if they don't, it would be an open admission that *their* husbands are coming here for purposes they're not even supposed to know about.'

'A convoluted sentence, but it makes sense.' Marjorie smiled at him fondly. 'Your insight into female psychology often astounds me.'

'Insights endowed by my own sexual proclivities, I fear.' Cooley drained his glass. 'It was a magnificent dinner, Marjorie.' He tapped his lips with his napkin. 'One last thought. Assuming that you follow my Grand Plan, remember that simulating the White House is the key to it. Presidents and their wives will redecorate rooms, discard old furnishings, bring in new. You must make identical alterations – down to the last ashtray and antimacassar. The men using the rooms will be familiar with the interior of the White House. The illusion you create must be exact, flawless.'

'Brad, more than a few of our most *distingué* political figures require extremely elaborate paraphernalia and stagings for their pleasures.'

'True.' Cooley chuckled and pushed back his chair. 'You simply buy and store the items and materials needed for special effects. Any investment that insures the sexual gratification of Very Important Aberrants is certain to pay huge dividends – in the form of their undying, guilt-inspired gratitude and sense of obligation. You might put that down in your notebook as Cooley's Law.'

He stood up, went to Marjorie's chair and held it for her. Marjorie was smiling enigmatically. Her mind went back to the March night in 1941 when the Great Man had suggested she reproduce White House rooms in her home. She followed his advice – and it worked. She could almost hear his sardonic laughter, for he would have been the first to endorse Bradford Cooley's Grand Plan – and assure her that it, too, would work.

10

Washington, D.C.: Thursday, February 18.

During the Nixon Administration the White House switch-board had seventeen trunk lines. Twenty operators worked in shifts handling between six and ten thousand calls daily. Trunk lines, operators and daily traffic-load had since more than doubled, and the system worked with commendable efficiency – until this morning.

By 9:00 A.M. there was almost total breakdown. Incoming calls poured in at a rate estimated to be over five thousand an hour. Most were long-distance, sparked by overnight developments that preempted newspaper front pages and caused television and radio stations to interrupt their regular programs for frequent news-bulletin updates.

MICHIGAN GOVERNOR MAKES FORMAL REQUEST FOR REGU-LAR ARMY TROOPS TO MAINTAIN ORDER IN DETROIT ... TWELVE MORE KILLED, HUNDREDS INJURED IN RENEWED MOTOR CITY VIOLENCE ... Evidently reacting to events in Detroit, mobs rampaged through the streets of Pittsburgh, Cleveland, St Louis and Los Angeles – cities with extremely high unemployment rates – and defied police efforts to disperse them ... LABOR LEADERS WARN OF POSSIBLE FULL-SCALE CIVIL UPRISINGS ... Last night, the heads of national labor unions united in urging their members to start a massive 'Telephone-the-President' campaign. A major union spokesman declared, 'ten or twenty million calls to the Chief Executive might finally awaken him to the urgency of the situation ...'

President Charles Talbot smiled as the three men filed into the Oval Office. The smile was neither forced nor grim,

Defense Secretary John Kurtz noted with surprise. Senate Majority Leader Dan Madigan thought Talbot was merely keeping up a brave front. Chief Presidential Adviser Kenneth Ramsey grinned back confidently. He knew why Talbot had summoned Kurtz and Madigan to the White House posthaste.

'Make yourselves comfortable,' Talbot told the trio. 'We're in for a longish session.'

Kurtz filled his pipe. Madigan lit a Cortez y Vilar panatela.

'John.' Kurtz stopped his finger-pokings into the pipe bowl, looked up at the President, listened. 'I want an airborne brigade flown to Detroit. The troops are to camp outside the city limits, take no action unless I give orders.' Talbot's smile broadened. 'Then, an infantry battalion on the same basis to each of these cities: Cleveland, St Louis and Los Angeles.'

'No formal requests have been made by authorities in any of those places,' Kurtz objected.

'I don't give a shit. We can order troops anywhere – on training exercises, good enough?'

'You left out Pittsburgh,' Kurtz said sarcastically.

'Only because you interrupted me, *Mister* Secretary,' Talbot said, topping the sarcasm. 'The battalion of Green Berets we keep at Fort Meyer goes to Pittsburgh. All troops to be en route by five today.'

'The Green Berets are your Washington security reserve force!' Madigan protested.

'Uh-huh. They sure are. But they're going to Pittsburgh.'

The son of a bitch, Kurtz thought. He's playing to the gallery as usual, sending his elite guards to a city in his home state. 'Well, Mr President,' Kurtz shrugged. 'I suppose the show of force will help cool down the rioters.'

'You'd make a lousy politician, John,' Talbot said. He glanced at Ramsey. 'Read out the statement we're going to leak, Ken.'

Ramsey read from a typed sheet: 'A highly placed Administration source says the troops being dispatched would be held in readiness to prevent further overreaction by local law enforcement authorities and National Guard units which are under the command of State Governors.'

The pipe dropped from Kurtz's mouth. He caught it. His look of consternation was equalled by that of Madigan.

'Did I hear right?' Madigan croaked.

'You did,' Talbot assured him. 'Uncle Sam is protecting the weak and helpless. Can you think of any better gimmick to stop the rioting for a while and quiet the labor unions?'

Madigan chewed that over, broke into a grin. 'No, by God, I can't. It's beautiful.'

Talbot looked smug, having all but forgotten that the idea and even the wording of the statement to be leaked had been given him by Marjorie Norworth. 'Use my phone, John. Get on to the generals.'

Kurtz obediently called the Pentagon. After fifteen minutes – during which he listened as much as he talked – he hung up and said, 'They'll pull the levers, but they're not happy about it.'

'Tough,' Talbot growled. He opened a leather-bound folder lying on his desk blotter. 'John, both you and Dan brace yourselves.' He paused, spoke again. 'Gentlemen, this Administration is about to be rejuvenated. It's going to have one hell of a shake-up.'

Kurtz and Madigan stared at each other, stunned.

'You and Mac Pearce stay, John,' Talbot said. 'Can't change Defense and State Secretaries without telling the world our foreign policy is fucked up, too. However, we can convince the public' – he remembered Marjorie's phrase – 'that we're going to clear out the problem-makers and bring in problem-solvers.'

A hardened pol, Madigan tuned in on Talbot's wavelength and grinned, the panatela between his teeth levering to a jaunty angle as the President went down his list. The nation's farmers were no less dissatisfied than Labor, Talbot said, so the Agriculture Secretary would have to go. The same for the Secretary of Treasury – a change in that office invariably perked up Wall Street.

Madigan voiced an objection. 'You put him in on Jordan Rickhoven's recommendation . . .'

'Explain things to Rickhoven. He'll no doubt come up with a substitute.' Talbot's eyes returned to the open folder. 'Justice and Interior stay – we can't overdo this. Commerce is okay, but a new Secretary of Labor is a must. Somebody the unions will think is the greatest thing since Frances Perkins.'

'A thought there,' Ken Ramsey spoke up. 'A woman Secretary of Labor. Kill two birds with one appointment.'

Kurtz was thawing. 'Some very liberal lady,' he said.

Talbot nodded and continued. 'A lot of lower-echelon shuffling in HEW should do the trick there. No change in Transportation, but a big noisy one in Housing and Urban Welfare. A new Secretary who zooms in, announces plans for sweeping programs.' He closed the folder. 'Those will be the openers.'

Kurtz puffed his pipe. 'Maybe I am a lousy politician – but what are we really going to gain, Mr President?'

'Breathing space, John. Now beat it over to the Pentagon and make sure the brasshats are doing what they've been told.'

Ramsey and Madigan remained.

'You have the toughest job, Dan,' Talbot declared. 'I want a ten billion dollar emergency appropriation to replenish unemployment compensation funds – and I want it fast. Use every trick in the book, including the IRS bit. Tell any holdbacks I'll give the new Treasury Secretary orders not to question their returns – no matter what they report or don't report.'

'That should buy a majority,' Madigan nodded. 'But appropriations bills have to originate in the House, and . . .'

'Talk to Brad Cooley.'

'Hell, he's bottled the Basanda aid bill . . .'

'Perfect tradeoff. Cooley's big beef is that we've been laying out too much for defense and foreign aid, not enough for use at home. We drop the Basanda bill, tell Cooley he convinced us it was all wrong and give him the pitch about helping the unemployed . . .'

'Slogans make Brad puke – right in your face.'

'He can't repudiate his statements about the need for domestic aid funds. He'll push the ten billion through his committee.'

Madigan frowned. 'Where does that leave us with Basanda?'

'There are Executive Branch discretionary funds.' Talbot looked at Ramsey. 'Did you find out how much is lying around?'

'One-point-two billion piled up here and there,' Ramsey replied. 'I'd say we could divert half a billion with nobody being the wiser.'

'That a satisfactory gap-stopper, Dan?' Talbot asked.

'Yep.' Madigan beamed. Half a billion now, more later. Rickhoven couldn't complain. 'How do we kick off the big rejuvenation?'

'I'll make a nationwide speech.' Talbot stroked his jaw. 'I might even drop a hint tomorrow when I deliver General Weidener's eulogy.' He stared up at the ceiling, ad-libbing. 'How can one pay adequate tribute to the memory of this bravest of men? By promising him and all who have served and are serving the nation – in uniform or out – that we shall soon embark on a new course that will bring prosperity at home, peace abroad – et cetera. How does that sound?'

'Okay, but it'll take a lot of polishing,' Ramsey said.

'What the hell do we have speechwriters hanging around for?'

'So they can jack off on Government time,' Madigan wisecracked. Talbot shot him a sudden, inexplicably fierce, glare. *Maybe he wants me to leave*, Madigan thought. 'Is that all, Charlie?'

'Yes – uh, no. Made any progress on our White Knight project?'

'I've got him, trussed up and ready for the oven. Russell Hatch. The guy they say looks like Tom Sawyer.'

Talbot remembered Hatch. By God, he sounds right, he thought. 'Bring him over today – Ken, clear me for an hour between three and four. Make it then, Dan.'

Talbot lunched with his daughter Lexa in the Family

113

Quarters. His mind was on the nationwide address he planned to make, and he worried over it. The White House speechwriting staff was, in his opinion, a sorry unimaginative crew. The speech would require force, sparkle. He eyed Lexa. Maybe, he thought – just maybe.

'Puss, that young man you mentioned to me, the writer . . .'

'He's not exactly young – almost your age. Name's James Zander.'

Almost as old as I am, Talbot mused. I must have been wrong when I figured Lexa had slept with him. 'Is he really good?' he asked.

'Yes, I think he's probably very good.'

'Can you tell him to see me this evening at five-thirty?'

'I'll bring him over myself, Daddy.'

'Thanks, Baby. Another favor. It's very possible we'll be seeing quite a bit of a Senator Russell Hatch around this lunatic asylum. Give him the full charm and hospitality treatment, will you?'

'Never fear,' Lexa grinned. 'I'll bewitch and beguile.'

Talbot talked. Madigan and Hatch listened. Russ was tense but bursting with enthusiasm, for his original confidence in Talbot was not being vindicated.

The President frankly reviewed the problems facing the country and his Administration, then swung into an outline of what he had already done (ordering troops to five cities) and what he intended doing in the immediate future. Talbot is taking hold, Russ told himself elatedly, at last exercising the authority a President should. Nonetheless, he was troubled by doubt. Why was Talbot telling him, a first-term Senator with only two years of seniority, about plans and proposals that Senators of far greater seniority had not yet been told?

The question was answered when Talbot wound up his remarks.

'We need new blood. I must have young men with open minds and sincere motives behind me. Dan' – Talbot nodded toward Madigan – 'vouches for you a hundred percent.'

Back to Russ with a man-to-man grin. 'Knowing Dan, he probably checked out everything about you – including your toilet habits.'

A chuckle and Talbot resumed.

'We'll have plenty – more than plenty – for you to do after I reorganize the Administration. At the same time, Dan and I want you to take on additional responsibilities in the Senate. You'll be given a seat on the Labor and Public Welfare Committee. But that's not all. My new program will require a special watchdog committee. Dan and I want you on it – and I hope you'll consider yourself my personal watchdog, keeping the other members on their toes.'

Russ had to restrain himself from shouting with joy when he and Madigan left the Oval Office. He asked if he could make a telephone call – right away. Madigan took him into Ken Ramsey's office.

Russ telephoned the CBN studios and asked for Suzanne Loring. She was in.

'Suzy!' He was ebullient. 'Are you free tonight? I've got loads of news – good news – to tell you.'

'I'm glad, Russ – but not tonight. I'm dead tired.' *And I need another day to get my muddled brain, shook up nerves and whipsawed emotions back to some stage approaching whatever passes for normal. If I saw you tonight, I'd probably break down and cry and say a lot of damned fool things.* She forced her tone to be light and playfully affectionate. 'I have a seven o'clock date, Senator – with a boiling hot bath, a set of cool, clean sheets and a guy named Morpheus.'

'Not even a drink?'

'Uh-huh. Not this evening – but do Senators with good news give out rain checks?'

'Only when absolutely necessary.' Although disappointed, he made himself match her tone. At least there were signs the storm had blown over – and that was more good news. 'How about tomorrow night?'

'Yes, Russ.' *I should be all together by then,* Suzy thought. *God only knows what I'm liable to do if I'm not.*

'Pick you up at the studio?'

'Call first, I may go home very early – or not come in at all. If I don't, or I'm gone, phone me at home and I'll have the camomile tea ready by the time you get there.'

'Right, honey.'

Odd, Russ thought. *Here I am in the White House and I've been in the Oval Office with the President – and when I came out of it, my first and only impulse was to talk to Suzy.* When explanations as to why began forming in his mind, he shied away from them skittishly, even fearfully.

James Zander wore a casual air, an old tweed jacket and not very well-pressed contrasting slacks. President Talbot could not make up his mind whether he liked Zander or not and wondered how on earth she met him and why she recommended him so highly. But, as the two men talked, Talbot began to realize that James Zander was bright and had a good – and realistic – grasp of politics.

'Maybe I should fill you in on my curriculum vitae, Mr President,' Zander volunteered after a quarter of an hour of general conversation. 'I'm fifty-one. I wrote three novels before I was forty – all flops. My employment record is what personnel managers call "spotty" as they turn up their noses. I've worked – never for long – as a p.r. man and a reporter. I've ghosted speeches – even did a stint in the Republican Party press office during the last months of the Nixon Administration. Frankly, I'm not too good at taking orders from most people, and I have lazy spells.' Lexa had coached him to be frank and forthright. *Okay*, he thought. *I have been, to a point. Let's see what happens next.*

He's honest about himself, Talbot mused – something he considered a mark in any man's favor. Most professional politicians do – because it is a quality they cannot themselves possess if they expect to receive votes. *But I'm not playing Diogenes. I'm looking for crack speechwriter*, Talbot reminded himself.

'Mind taking a test, Mr Zander?' he asked.

'Not at all, Mr President.'

Talbot said he would be delivering the eulogy at General

Keith Weidener's funeral and cautiously sketched out what he wanted injected into the speech. 'I don't want to talk more than fifteen minutes,' he said in conclusion. 'How long will it take you to write it?'

'Half an hour, forty-five minutes. If I can borrow a secretary's typewriter . . .'

Talbot had Ken Ramsey take him to an outer office. Zander was only minutes over his self-imposed deadline, but then, he had to wait while the President took a call from Defense Secretary Kurtz – who reported that all the troop lifts were under way.

'The media are going out of their minds,' Kurtz said.

'Good,' Talbot said. 'They've been driving us out of ours for two years.'

The conversation over, he had Ken Ramsey admit Zander. The writer gave him some typed sheets. They were drafts, but Talbot had not expected finished copy. He started to read skeptically, but after a few paragraphs, all reservations vanished.

'Congratulations, Mr Zander,' he said. 'My daughter was right. You're good – very good.'

At 8:00 P.M., Kenneth Ramsey reported that the 'leak' about the 'real reason' behind the troop movements had been planned – and the White House press corps had lapped it up. President Talbot then had a simple dinner alone – and went to bed. He slept well.

Chief Justice Avery Braithwaite returned to the House on the Hill and the Lincoln Bedroom at midnight – again without avail. Marjorie Norworth found another shakily written note slipped under her door.

'Marjorie, my dear: Please permit me to use the Lincoln Bedroom once more tomorrow night. I shall be most humbly grateful to you.'

She put the note aside, returned to doing what she had been doing all evening and night – listening to continuous news broadcasts. What she heard gave her pleasure and satisfaction that bordered on the sexual. The scenario she had prepared for Talbot was being followed to the letter. At last, she made her nightly diary entry and went to bed. She slept a contented child.

II

Washington, D.C.: Friday, February 19.

'ADMINISTRATION MOVES ELECTRIFY NATION ... Union leaders
interviewed last night lauded President Talbot's action,
citing unimpeachable sources that have said the Army units
would protect demonstrators if this proved necessary ...
DETROIT HAS QUIET NIGHT AS GOVERNOR WITHDRAWS NATIONAL
GUARD FROM CITY ... Rumors that President Talbot will
soon seek massive appropriations to help the nation's un-
employed spread through Washington yesterday ... CAPITAL
INSIDERS CLAIM MAJOR CABINET RESHUFFLE POSSIBLE ...'

Most editorial writers and columnists gave Talbot
cautious tentative praise hedged with predictable ifs and
buts. A few openly hailed his courage and decisiveness. A
few others were openly skeptical, urging the nation to adopt
a 'wait-and-see' attitude. However, the overall pattern was
decidedly favorable.

'Hey, what time is it?' Lexa Talbot demanded, sitting up
in bed and trying to focus her eyes.

'Who cares?' Jim Zander laughed. He grasped her hand,
guided it to his hardening penis. 'Play with this a little –
then we'll ball.'

'I care,' she said, glancing over his shoulder at the alarm
clock. It was a few minutes past nine. 'I have to be at that
damned funeral.' She freed her hand. 'Sorry, Jimbo –
politics come before sex, even in the dictionary.'

General Keith Weidener was accorded a full-dress cere-
monial funeral. Services were held in the Gothic-style
Washington Cathedral and attended by generals, admirals,

political figures, and foreign dignitaries. President Talbot and his daughter sat with Weidener's widow and family.

The traditional cortege to Arlington National Cemetery followed. President Talbot delivered the graveside eulogy before a large crowd of mourners, gawking tourists, reporters, and television cameramen. Speaking into a battery of microphones, he delivered a moving tribute to Weidener's heroism in two wars and his outstanding service as Chairman of the Joint Chiefs of Staff, then shifted gears.

'General Weidener will lie here at Arlington with many thousands of others who lived – and died – for their country. It is a fitting place for me to take a solemn oath. We shall end strife and dissension, poverty, and hunger in our country and among our people. The orders I shall soon issue and legislation I shall soon urge Congress to pass without delay will be tributes to Keith Weidener and all our heroic dead, dedicated to the nation in their names, in their memory.'

As expected, the news media interpreted the words as confirmation of the rumors that had made the Washington rounds since the previous evening. There were big things in store.

Moon-faced Basandan Ambassador Percival Kwida developed a diplomatic asthma attack to avoid the funeral. The message he had sent to Prime Minister Odu Mwandi at Jordan Rickhoven's instigation was producing a tidal wave of responses from Kinsolo, the Basandan capital. Not the most stable of men, Prime Minister Odu Mwandi was reacting in hysterical – and increasingly irrational – panic and rage.

One radio message from Kinsolo ordered Ambassador Kwida to obtain an immediate audience with President Talbot. The next, arriving minutes later, countermanded the first. Fifteen minutes afterward, a third recalled Kwida to Kinsolo. Another half an hour, and the recall order was cancelled and Ambassador Kwida was instructed to issue a threat to Jordan B. Rickhoven III:

'... AID REDUCED AND MILITARY ADVISERS WITHDRAWN

WE WILL DESTROY MINING AND OIL FIELD INSTALLATIONS . . .'

Then Kwida's friend, the Basandan Foreign Minister, radioed:

'OUR GLORIOUS IMMORTAL PRIME MINISTER MAY BRING ALL TROOPS BACK FROM REMOTE AREAS TO PROTECT CENTRAL PROVINCES.'

At noon – again from the Foreign Minister:

'UNITS IN NORTH HAVE BEEN ORDERED TO ABANDON THEIR POSITIONS.'

At 12:47 P.M. – from Prime Minister Odu Mwandi:

'ALL MEMBERS OF YOUR FAMILY HAVE BEEN PLACED IN PROTECTIVE CUSTODY THEIR SAFETY DEPENDS ON RESULTS YOU OBTAIN IN WASHINGTON.'

This horrified Percival Kwida. Under the Odu Mwandi regime, tens of thousands of people had been placed in 'protective custody'. Precious few survived. Kwida telephoned U.S. Secretary of State MacDonald Pearce and, pleading 'utmost urgency', obtained an audience with Pearce, told him of the messages from Kinsolo.

'The troop withdrawals have begun?' Pearce asked, his facial muscles twitching. Kwida said yes, they had. Pearce took off his rimless bifocals, fiddled with them for a moment.

'I will have word for you later, Your Excellency,' he said.

Kwida departed. Pearce ordered an aide to track down Jordan Rickhoven and reach him by telephone. He, himself, placed a call to CIA Director G. Howard Denby and told him, 'I must see you immediately.'

Jordan Rickhoven was located in Paris. Pearce gave him an Aesopian briefing on the latest developments reported by Percival Kwida. Rickhoven expressed a suitable degree of concern – for the record, in case anyone between Washington and Paris was eavesdropping on the line. Inwardly, he smirked. Before long, the United States would have no option but to intervene in Basanda.

'Keep me informed, Mac,' he said. 'I have complete faith and confidence in you.' *And more in myself and my calculations.*

Someone once said that if G. Howard Denby pissed at all, he

pissed ice water. The remark got back to Denby, who considered it an accolade. The CIA chief had no nerves, allowed no feelings to intrude when performing his official duties. This is what had enabled him to make his agency what it was.

Denby waited until MacDonald Pearce talked himself out, made only a laconic comment! 'There's a hell of a problem ahead, Mac.'

Pearce cleared his throat. 'Mwandi must be eliminated – and quickly. We can't wait a week or ten days now.'

'The specialist teams went out Wednesday,' Denby said with a small shrug. 'We might bring it off sooner, but it'll be risky – and damned expensive. Odu Mwandi has a battalion-strength palace guard. The guard commander, junior officers and non-coms will have to be bribed with so much cash that they won't think twice.'

'How much do you estimate?'

'Two million for the commander – he'll have to leave Basanda for good, or someone will wipe him in revenge. Two hundred thousand apiece for the junior officers, fifty thousand for each non-com. With incidentals, close to fifteen million, I'd say.'

'You have secret funds . . .'

'Sorry. I'm not using Agency money for your crash-operations. I want the funds transferred from State.'

'Very well,' Pearce capitulated. 'When will Mwandi go?'

'Forty-eight hours after Agency couriers fly the cash into Basanda. With luck, a little sooner.'

Madigan went to the Weidener funeral services at Washington Cathedral but not to Arlington Cemetery. A visit to Cooley's offices in the monstrously ugly Rayburn Building took priority.

The debonair Senate Majority Leader and the corpulent House Appropriations Committee Chairman in his baggy suit shook hands and Madigan began their conversation with an apology.

'JB and I pushed you hard the other night at Marjorie's. Please write it off to too much booze and tension, Brad.'

Booze and tension my flabby ass, Cooley thought.

'We're both sorry,' Madigan added.

Cooley played along. 'Forgiven and forgotten,' he said – but his expression urged that Madigan get to the point of his visit.

'President Talbot asked me to tell you he wants the Basanda aid bill killed, Brad.'

'That makes him an accessory after the fact. I've already choked it to death.' Cooley was wise to the ways of Presidents. 'You're here to soft-soap me, Dan. Good. I like plenty of lather – but I'm an old farmboy and recognize the smell of horseshit. Talbot withdraws the bill – and plugs the gap with his secret discretionary funds.' The last was a shot in the murk, but Cooley realized, seeing Madigan's lips twitch, a bull's-eye. 'I can't stop him, but if the truth ever comes out, he'll have to take full responsibility. What else?'

Madigan filled him in on Talbot's plans, wound up with the information that the President would request ten billion dollars for emergency domestic use.

'He's having the bill drafted at top speed. Can we expect support and quick action from you and your committee, Brad?'

'Naturally,' Cooley nodded. It would be political suicide to create obstacles or delay any such measure. 'With one proviso, Dan.' His shrewd eyes twinkled. 'Charlie Talbot waves a magic wand and shifts fifty million or so of those discretionary funds we're tossing around to Alabama – and right away. The people down there are in bad shape.'

'A deal.' Madigan grinned, appreciating Cooley's practical politics. Always think of the home state constituents first, get all you can for them. 'I might put the same kind of squeeze on Charlie for Illinois.'

Returning to the White House from Arlington, Talbot closeted himself in the Oval Office with Kenneth Ramsey.

'How did I come across?' Talbot asked.

'Couldn't have been better. Wasn't a dry eye in the house.'

'Ken, get Zander cracking on the big production – and

pull the levers. I want an hour of network prime time Sunday.'

'You're cutting it damned close. This is Friday, and . . .'

'Have to cut it close. I want to spring the Cabinet reorganization before the people I'm tossing out have a chance to get together and start making waves.'

'The media will call it another Sunday Night Slaughter.'

'Maybe I'll come right out and call it that myself.'

'Want a Cabinet meeting scheduled?' Ramsey asked.

'Monday, when the sacrificial lambs are reeling and bleeding.'

'What about the lists of possible substitutes?' They had only forty-eight hours to select the possibles, have superfast security and personal background checks run on them – and make contact with the individuals to determine whether they would accept appointments.

'Madigan's handling it. We have too many other things to do.'

Talbot fell silent, rose from his chair and went to the windows, staring through them at the gardens outside. He had become conscious of the huge gambles he was taking and was suddenly assailed by doubts and anxieties.

'How's the wind blowing?' he asked, almost as if afraid to hear the answer.

The poor, insecure bastard is going to need plenty of bolstering, Ramsey thought. Luckily, he had mainly favorable reports to offer.

'Switchboard's worse off than yesterday, only the calls are congratulatory rather than critical. Telegrams are running three-to-one in your favor. The Governor of Michigan isn't too happy, but who cares? The press is yowling for statements, but the correspondents aren't showing their old chip-on-shoulder hostility . . .'

'No statements before Sunday,' Talbot said, beginning to recover.

'I figured that. Let's see, what else? Cabinet and Bureau heads are basket cases because of the rumors . . .'

'Great. It'll do 'em good to sweat.'

'Your ten billion bill is being drafted over in the Executive Office Building. I swore everybody over there to secrecy.'

Talbot's mood was up again. 'You don't just swear them Ken,' he laughed. 'I know your methods. I can probably quote you verbatim. "Listen you cocksuckers, any leaks and you'll be fired so fucking fast your balls will crack open when you break the sound barrier.'

'Pretty close, Chief.' Ramsey grinned.

'You deserve a medal, Ken. Now get Jim Zander over here. I'll brief him on what I want for Sunday.'

Mindful that Russell Hatch's star was in rapid ascendant, Marjorie Norworth decided to hold one of her impromptu, spur-of-the-moment receptions in his honor. Every guest she telephoned and invited to attend accepted with alacrity. It was ever thus whenever official Washington heard conflicting rumors and sensed upheavals in the offing. The House on the Hill was where they were likely to gain accurate inside information.

Marjorie called Russ last. 'Be here at eight,' she told him pleasantly. 'My guest-list is impressive – and it *is* in your honor.'

Hatch, knowing he could not refuse, accepted gratefully and graciously. Afterwards, he remembered his date with Suzanne. He called her, first at the studio – she hadn't come in that day – then at her apartment, and reached her there.

'Honey, much as I hate to do it – and I mean that – I'll have to stand you up tonight.'

Suzanne had been building herself up to what – in effect – was to be a joyous reunion. The letdown was numbing.

'Don't tell me you're working late at the office,' she said, managing to keep her hollow disappointment out of her voice.

'Nope – but I will be working. Glad-handing the big wheels.' He told her about Lady Norworth's invitation. 'I'm sorry . . .'

'Don't be. We both have careers' – *and neither of us can give*

125

them up, or would even if we could because we're too ambitious and into them too deep – 'and we can't afford to miss boats. Call me tomorrow.' She barely avoided adding a heartfelt 'Please, darling'.

'I will – and give you an A-to-Z rundown on everything that's been going on.'

Russ was astonished by the turnout. The main floor of Lady Norworth's house teemed with legislators, Cabinet officers, bureau chiefs and agency heads and the next-in-line deputies. He was amused – and despite himself, flattered – by the attention he received from the other guests. Men who had never before deigned to recognize him were eager to shake his hand, trade jokes, suggest luncheons and dinners. It's insane, he mused. From rags to riches in three short days – via a political variation on the Horatio Alger theme. *I didn't marry the boss's daughter, but I did subborn Suzy – and Eureka! – they're standing in line to lick my boots.*

Russ could not deny that it was an exhilarating, ego-bloating experience. For the first time since coming to Washington, he was getting a firsthand taste – a bare sip, but a taste nonetheless – of what power was all about, what it meant and implied. He felt a pang of regret that Suzanne was not with him to share the experience. In fact, he had a vague, undefined wish that he could share it all with her – the present and the apparently bright and shiny future. He pushed the thoughts aside sheepishly. As Suzanne had said a few hours earlier, they both had careers. She was already an established success in hers. By comparison, what seemed to him a Great Leap was political arena small beer.

Russ spent nearly two hours circulating, talking, listening, absorbing the scene and patterns, learning more about how Government actually worked than he had in his two years as a back-row Senator. Then he encountered Aaron Kugelman, whom he had met at Marjorie's two nights before.

'Dan Madigan tells me you and I are going to be on the new watchdog committee,' Kugelman said. 'We should get better acquainted.'

'We *are* acquainted,' Russ retorted sourly. 'You're the fighting liberal who can't stand *schwarzers*.'

Kugelman's face flushed scarlet. 'That was empty talk for Early Frobase's benefit. He'd just agreed to switch his vote on a bill I'm sponsoring. I had to throw him a bone.'

Who and what the fuck can you believe in this town? Russ thought. It's all Max Ernst, Hieronymous Bosch and Alice in Wonderland. He moved on into the Red Room. Marjorie Norworth, ablaze with diamonds, silk-chiffoned by Dior, intercepted him. She took his hand, led him upstairs.

'I'm merely heeding FDR's dictum,' she said. 'Be quick to pay homage to the successful.' She laughed. They had stopped before a paneled door. 'My oblation is an *intime* dinner for you. Unfortunately, I'm too old for you – otherwise we would be having it together.' She opened the door, nodded him inside. 'Enjoy yourselves.' She closed the door.

Russ found himself in the sitting room of a splendid suite. Light was provided by a silver Lamerie candelabra in the center of a table richly set for two. A sterling silver champagne bucket contained a magnum of vintage Roederer Cristal. A girl – petite, with exquisite features that had an exotic, almost Eurasian touch – held out her hand.

'I'm Christine – and I know you're Russ.' Her voice was soft, seductive, her hand tiny and warm.

'I didn't know I had a blind date tonight,' he said, then added a sincere compliment: 'I couldn't have hoped for a lovelier one, though.' Another surprising fringe benefit of success, he thought – only this one I sure as hell couldn't share with Suzy.

Christine wore a simple red sheath accentuating the curves and planes of her body, amplifying their sensuality. 'The pleasure is mutual,' she murmured – 'or should I say I'm sure it will be.'

Holcomb served them dinner. It would have put the Tour d'Argent to shame. Christine's conversation was lively, witty, her every movement a subtle promise that aroused him, sent blood pumping to his loins. She tantalized him, eating slowly, sipping champagne, lingering over coffee until, at last, his desire was at its peak and they went into the adjoining bedroom. She drew Russ to her, sensual lips moist, kissed him, her tongue thrusting deep, fluttering inside his mouth, then stepped away.

'Let me undress you,' she said, slipping off the red sheath. She wore nothing beneath it. Her breasts were high, firm, the nipples coral-pink and distended. 'Sit on the edge of the bed, Russ.'

She offered her delicious body to be stroked and caressed while she removed his clothing. Her lips and tongue flicked over his body.

'You're huge – beautiful,' she marveled, cupping his massively swollen organ between her hands, brushing her lips against its tip.

He seized her, not roughly but with the urgency of his physical hunger, and they fell on the bed. He could feel her hot moisture against his thigh. She was soaked, her entire body pleading.

Sensing that he desired vaginal intercourse first, she opened her thighs, held his penis, and with a slow, sensuous movement of her hips, swallowed it up inside her. Later, after his first orgasm exploded simultaneously with her own, Christine quickly discovered that Russ delighted in variety, had no inhibitions. Some hours later, they told each other that they had been magnificent together. They both meant it.

Experience told Lady Marjorie Norworth that it would be a long night. Her guests would continue to drink, talk, speculate, pry, and probe at each other for information – or hints that might provide some degree of additional enlightenment – and drink yet more.

The pattern was very familiar to Marjorie. It was always the same whenever Washington had premonitions of impending political convulsions. It had been thus during the Cuban Missile Crisis, in the days immediately prior to Lyndon Johnson's announcement that he would not run for President in 1968, during the week-long death watch before Richard Nixon finally resigned from office.

At such times, the House on the Hill was a sanctuary for

men who feared eventual consequences and loss of power (or held hopes of gaining more) – and Lady Marjorie Norworth was Oracle, Mother Figure, and Regnant Queen.

Shortly after midnight Supreme Court Chief Justice Avery Braithwaite entered by the back service entrance to avoid any possibility of being seen by Marjorie's guests. Holcomb took him to the Lincoln Bedroom via the back stairs and noted that Braithwaite's face was a sickly putty color, his eyes bloodshot and sunken.

The drama was reenacted yet again, exactly as before save for an added embellishment. Before mounting a stepladder to be lashed to the cross, Braithwaite – his voice barely audible – asked the Roman legionary to make a pretense of beating the hooded woman mercilessly with his fists.

Clad in the tattered loincloth, Braithwaite was secured to the cross and he welcomed the pain tearing at his shoulder sockets when the support was taken from under his feet.

The ritual began.

'Father, help those who beseech Thee . . .'

The legionary cursed, struck the woman with his clenched fist. She sobbed. The soldier drove his spear shaft into Braithwaite's ribs.

'I beg Thee to show me what is righteous . . .'

The spear shaft jabbed again, with greater force. The soldier spat up at the crucified figure and snarled, 'Son of a whore!' He set about battering the woman. He flung her down on her back, pulled the cloak up around her waist, went on beating her. Mouthing obscenities, he mounted the woman.

Avery Braithwaite's mouth opened. 'Father, I thank Thee!' His cry was ecstatic. Tremors shook his body, building up in force until his straining muscles quivered violently. 'Aaah – Father!' Wrists and ankles fought against the leather thongs binding them. His body twisted contorted. 'Aaaah . . .!'

Physical eruption, elemental and molten, brought the bright glare that starkly illuminated the answer he sought.

Thank you, Father, for the grace of Thy enlightenment, Braithwaite said silently – and fainted.

'He finally made it,' the woman said, getting to her feet. 'Call Holcomb. We'll need help getting him down.'

The Roman legionary looked up at the crucified figure. Yes, he had lost consciousness and his inner thighs glistened wet with fresh semen. The soldier removed his theatrical-property helmet, edged around the cross and pressed a call-button to summon Holcomb.

12

The World of Lady Marjorie Norworth.
December, 1947–

Perle Mesta was to give a mammoth New Year's Eve Party.
Capital society columnists predicted it would be 'the biggest,
most brilliant bash since before the war'. The guest list ran
the gamut from the Trumans down to second-term Congressmen and Undersecretaries of Cabinet departments.
Lady Marjorie Norworth's name was pointedly omitted
from the list.

Inspired by Bradford Cooley, Marjorie made the first
move in the the complex chess game of her renascence. Most
men attending (or forced to attend) Perle Mesta's party
were certain to drink far, far too much. They were even
more certain to have monumental hangovers the next
morning. The married ones would have to contend with
their wives' naggings, scoldings, and bitchy monologues
about the party, what other people said and what other
women wore.

During the last week of December, Marjorie told her
loyal men friends that she was holding a For Men Only
open house on New Year's Day. A January First First-Aid
Party, she called it. Men requiring safe haven and healing
potions – be they black coffee, Alka-Seltzer, ice-cold
stingers, or straight twenty-five-year-old bourbon – were
welcome to seek refuge and cure in her mansion.

'The staff will be prepared to handle any and all
casualties,' she laughed. 'And *do* spread the word.'

She hired a dozen extra maids, the prettiest available, and
ordered nurses' uniforms for them. Holcomb, her regular
barman and two others employed for the occasion were

given doctors' white smocks – and stethoscopes to hang around their necks. (Hadn't The Great Man said no city in the world equaled Washington in gaucherie?)

Marjorie anticipated that perhaps a hundred and fifty males in various stages of hangover distress would show up during the day. By one P.M., there were almost seventy – including two Cabinet officers, the Speaker of the House, and President Truman's military aide. By 3:00 P.M. the number had more than doubled. Before the open-house ended (at two o'clock the following morning) some three hundred males had gotten drunk all over again. Their appreciation of Marjorie Norworth's theme-party was unanimous and unbounded. Thereafter, her January First First-Aid Party became an annual event.

Marjorie had planned the New Year's Day affair with shrewd foresight and consummate skill. During the evening, she singled out a very senior Democratic Senator, a Cabinet officer and a leading Republican Congressman. Each was notorious for harboring Presidential aspirations. With Holcomb's connivance, she managed to get all three only slightly less than paralytically drunk. She insisted they go upstairs (aided by servants) and sleep it off before leaving.

The Republican Senator was given the Lincoln Bedroom. The Cabinet officer was put to bed in the Queen's Bedroom. The very senior Democratic Senator was half-carried to the bedroom duplicating that used by the President himself in the White House.

After varying periods of sodden sleep, each man awoke to find himself in bed and not alone. A 'nurse' – naked and eager – was curled next to him. Each man blearily asked similar questions: 'God, where am I?' 'How did you get here?' Each received parallel replies: 'I'll turn on a light so you can see where you are?' 'Don't you remember, you asked me. I sneaked upstairs. Nobody saw me.'

The reassuring answers relieved anxieties, eased hangover pangs and fed masculine egos. The naked bodies activated glands. The illusion of being in White House bedrooms had megaton-force aphrodisiacal effects. Later (in the case of the very senior Democratic Senator, not until noon) each girl chanted the same refrain.

'You were fantastic! Don't worry, I'll slip down the back stairs.' Offered money, each young woman refused ('Oh, no! I wanted to!'). This provided more food on which the men's macho could feed and batten. As each went down stairs, he found Holcomb waiting with black coffee and the message that Lady Norworth had long since retired. She was very fatigued after the party.

Later in the day, Marjorie received masses of flowers, messenger-delivered notes apologizing 'for having passed out' and thanking her for having been so kind, considerate, hospitable. Understandably, no mentions were made of the young women who had so unexpectedly turned up in the various bedrooms and beds. But, being men, none of the three politicos could long resist the temptation to boast about their experiences in front of male friends and colleagues.

'She was about nineteen and gorgeous.' (Said with an appropriately modest and mystified look.) 'Can't understand what she wanted with an old fart like me, but she was like a wildcat.' (Voice lowered, almost reverent.) 'And Christ! Doing it in the same bed Lincoln slept in – fantastic!'

'There I was, screwing my head off in the room where Royalty stays!'

'Haven't a clue how Harry does it with Bess, but I sure found out what *I'd* do if I ever got to use that Presidential bed . . .'

Biding her time, building discreetly on her 'new base', within a year Marjorie Norworth regained all the ground she had lost and took even more. She was restored to a loftier throne, high above and far removed from the mundane battlefield on which the Mestas, Cafritzes, and McLeans continued their catfights for ordinary, everyday, social supremacy. By 1950, even though she was still ignored by the Trumans themselves, Lady Norworth's *salon* was once again the undisputed Power Exchange where commodities of political influence were traded, brokered, bought and sold, and where the value of politicians' personal stocks (and futures) were established. At last – in 1951 – even Harry Truman had to unbend somewhat.

The Korean War was going badly and Truman was in a bind. General of the Army Douglas MacArthur publicly criticized his policies and orders and grew increasingly insubordinate. Pressed to dismiss his Far Eastern commander, Truman vacillated. MacArthur had powerful supporters in the legislative branch and enormous popular appeal. 'Firing Mac' was bound to cause widespread and damaging repercussions.

Truman could not bring himself to visit the House on the Hill personally. On a rainy day in April, he toyed with his much-publicized THE BUCK STOPS HERE desktop sign and conferred with his gregarious (and controversial) military aide Major General Harry Vaughan.

'They tell me nobody has an ear closer to the political ground than Lady Norworth,' Truman said and, when Vaughan admitted this was probably true, continued, 'I'd like you to have a talk with her and find out how feelings are running on this MacArthur business.'

Vaughan did as the President instructed. Marjorie put on her most serious face. 'The President may be damned if he kicks Douglas out, but most of the people who come here privately feel that he'd be a weakling and damned fool if he doesn't. Douglas should have been put out to pasture long ago.'

General Vaughan reported back to President Truman. Whether this was the final touch that tipped the scales is a moot question – but in all probability it was. Two days later, on April 10, 1951, Truman removed MacArthur from his command.

Marjorie purred with satisfaction. She had evened two scores. When he first came to Washington, Douglas MacArthur had icily rebuffed her attempts to have an affair with him – now she had helped to end his military career. Harry S. Truman had consistently snubbed her since FDR died. His dismissal of MacArthur would unquestionably be a major factor in finishing his political career. Revenge was sweet; the power to obtain revenge against the high and mighty even sweeter.

Marjorie Norworth had no partisan loyalties. Political parties – Republican, Democratic or Vegetarian – were all the same. She regularly contributed large sums of money to the party in power and, during electoral campaigns, to the party she believed would win (her guesses were unfailingly correct). Yet she wisely maintained equally close and cordial relationships with members of the opposition, and not merely because today's OUTS could be tomorrow's INS. The earliest lesson she had learned from the Great Man was that when their selfish interests coincided, opponents disregarded party lines and became staunch allies. Marjorie appreciated the advantage of having a string to all the marionettes, regardless of the side of the stage on which they stood.

Adlai Stevenson was an exception to her self-imposed rule. She wrote him off without a second thought in 1952. He was an idealist and an intellectual – a lethal mix for any Presidential candidate. In any event he never came to the House on the Hill, and the men who did laughed about his egghead political naïveté. Although realizing that Dwight Eisenhower's election was a foregone conclusion and that he had limitless campaign funds at his disposal, Marjorie gave $200,000 to his campaign committee.

She was invited to Eisenhower's official Inaugural Ball and had fifteen minutes of private conversation with the new President wroth every penny of the $200,000 it had cost her. She had again achieved entrée to the White House and access to its occupant. The raging envy this inspired in Washington's socially prominent women was a delicious premium return on her investment.

Marjorie knew of the Kay Summersby episode in Eisenhower's life (Marshall had told her about it in 1944) and had full knowledge of his many and difficult personal problems. During his two terms in office, he frequently

consulted Marjorie Norworth and poured out his troubles –
official and personal.

Marjorie recognized the serious flaw in Dwight Eisenhower.
A career soldier conditioned to remain detached while staff
officers pondered and finally made recommendations, he
carried the habit with him to the White House. He relegated
virtually all responsibility to a staff headed by his Chief
Administrative Assistant, former New Hampshire Governor
Sherman Adams – who, many claimed, was the *de facto*
President while Eisenhower devoted himself mainly to
playing golf.

Marjorie resented Adams because he made himself the
sole dispenser of White House favors and soon had an
exclusive monopoly on influence over Eisenhower. One
evening, a group of Republican Party kingmakers and
Senators angrily discussed Adams in Marjorie's facsimile
of the White House Red Room.

'Sherman Adams has Ike under his thumb,' Jordan B.
Rickhoven Jr complained bitterly. 'And we can't do a
thing about it.'

Marjorie remembered Ike making a passing – and good-
natured – remark about how Sherman Adams enjoyed
receiving gifts. 'He gets oriental rugs – someone even gave
him a vicuna coat that must've cost so much I couldn't
afford it myself, if I wanted one,' Ike said.

Marjorie asked the men in the Red Room a question.
'Who on the White House staff wants Adams's job most?'

A Senator supplied a name. The others nodded
agreement.

'Bring him around – soon,' Marjorie smiled.

The man came with Jordan Rickhoven Jr a few nights
later. Marjorie overwhelmed him with charm, invited him.
to return a few days later. When he did, she greeted him as
an old friend, drew him aside and, confiding the chink in
Sherman Adams's armor, offered advice. A week later, the
aspirant for the position held by Sherman Adams had
obtained detailed proof and leaked it to the press. In the
overblown influence-peddling scandal that followed, Adams

was forced to resign. Eisenhower never suspected Marjorie Norworth's role. Deprived of the steady flow of advice poured out by Adams and not entirely at ease with the man who was his successor, Ike resumed the habit of frequently asking Marjorie for counsel. Her status and influence in Washington soared higher than before.

During his years as Congressman, then Senator, from Massachusetts, John F. Kennedy was a frequent guest at the House on the Hill. Lady Norworth saw he possessed many traits and qualities like those of the Great Man – charm, ferocious ambition, a pragmatic approach to all things, and more than a touch of ruthlessness and megalomania. But he lacked the Great Man's intelligence, breadth of vision, tact, and deft touch. She contributed to his campaign only because she knew he would win. The deal assuring Kennedy a paper-thin, political-machine-made edge was consummated at her dinner table. However, she was singularly unimpressed by his Camelot-on-the-Potomac.

'Charisma and glamor simply aren't enough,' she remarked to Brad Cooley a few months after Kennedy was inaugurated.

He was even more negative. 'I know Jack – what's more, I can see through him. While I have no delusions about democracy with freedom and justice for all, I'm uneasy about him.'

The expression 'Kennedy Kith and Kin,' shortened to KKK in a snide play on initials, was already in vogue among Washington insiders disenchanted with the new President. Some carried the play even further, referring to 'the six K's' – the Kennedy Kith-and-Kin Ku Klux Klan. A deferential press bowdlerized both versions into the watered-down, mildly bantering 'Irish Mafia' that gained wide public currency and had little or no pejorative connotation. Cooley preferred the original.

'Jack and his KKK are dangerous,' he said. 'Their behind-the-scenes operations are outrages against the few pitiful shreds of political morality still extant.'

*

Marjorie's supersensitive antennae picked up the first faint signals in March 1963. Politicians of both major parties who gathered in the House On The Hill were growing restive, worried, traded rumors about ominous developments purportedly being hatched by the Executive Branch. By June, they talked of 'plans on the six-K drawing boards' that could well dislocate the nation's economic, social, and political patterns, but agreed they were helpless to interfere.

'Kennedy has the media and masses hypnotized. They'd lynch anyone who suggested he isn't the greatest President since Washington.'

Two months later, intuition fine-honed by vague hints and random, veiled remarks warned her that a rewrite of the 1945 Warm Springs libretto was in the offing. She had no desire to become involved, not to any extent or degree. The man heading the anti-Kennedy faction within the Democratic Party had once been her lover, and they trusted each other implicitly. She asked him a single, one-word question.

'When?'

'Before the end of the year,' he replied, realizing that she had been told – or had deduced – the secret.

'I'm going to Europe,' Marjorie said and ran her fingertips over her cheeks. 'I have lines and wrinkles – and Switzerland has the world'st finest plastic surgeons. It's time I rid my face of the former.'

She closed up the House on the Hill in September, went to Switzerland, had her face lifted and stayed on in Europe.

The event took place on November 23, 1963. In Dallas, Texas. Marjorie Norworth was in Paris when she heard the first bulletins. A week later, she returned to Washington, reopened her mansion.

By then, Marjorie Trumbull Norworth was so firmly established that changes in Presidential Administrations – even when brought about by assassinations – did not require her to alter any facet of her life. Indeed, she felt the new Johnson Administration had been designed for her personal benefit, for never before had it been so easy for her to influence and manipulate.

Marjorie barely had to lift a finger, and Bradford Cooley was made Chairman of the House Appropriations Committee. She introduced Lyndon Johnson to Jordan B. Rickhoven III (JB Jr had died in 1961), an introduction from which both profited handsomely – and for which they were boundless in their gratitude.

Lyndon Johnson was aware Marjorie had distrusted and disliked John F. Kennedy – whom Johnson hated. This fact alone made LBJ trust her, cater to her wishes (and she in turn, saw that his boorish whims were fully satisfied at the House on the Hill). When an Undersecretary of State made disparaging remarks about Lady Norworth during lunch at the Dorian Club, LBJ demanded his immediate resignation. A man Marjorie liked was given an important ambassadorship because she spoke to Johnson on his behalf. The gun used at Warm Springs in 1945 and bearing her fingerprints, the photographs of the prints lifted from it (and pertinent documents held in reserve to incriminate Marjorie if it became necessary) were all turned over to her.

She enjoyed countless other Presidential favors. Lady Bird gave a party in her honor at the White House – and another at the LBJ Ranch in Texas. (Marjorie was hilariously amused by the latter – for she discovered that, no matter what the Great Man claimed, there *were* places immeasurably more gauche than Washington, after all.) In 1967, a young woman who had entertained a number of political figures in the upstairs bedrooms of the House on the Hill – but apparently unaware of the power of the Establishment – tried to blackmail Marjorie. She demanded $50,000, or she would reveal all she knew to the *National Interrogator*, a raucous weekly publication with five million circulation that thrived on printing lurid exposés.

Marjorie informed Johnson – who sent an order to J. Edgar Hoover. Within hours, the girl was picked up, shown her FBI dossier, told there was enough in it to justify her arrest on a dozen different charges – and warned to keep her mouth shut. Or else. Added emphasis was provided by District Police – who promptly arrested her on shoplifting and prostitution charges and held her for forty-eight hours in the women's drunk-tank. When finally released, she begged Marjorie to 'take off the pressure' and swore she would remain forever silent. Marjorie was forgiving and told Holcomb to give the girl a hundred dollars. It had been the first blackmail attempt, and it was the last. The secrets of the House on the Hill remained inviolate.

Lyndon Johnson's errant, arrogant blunders over Vietnam did not alienate Marjorie Norworth. At an emotional level she abhorred the Vietnamese war. Cerebrally, she accepted it as a historical inevitability. Antiwar demonstrations, protest-marches, riots – whether over the war or over racial issues – all left her unmoved. They, too, were historical inevitabilities and did not encroach upon her private world.

When, in March 1968, LBJ announced he would not seek renomination, Marjorie Norworth made an uncannily accurate prediction.

'Lyndon won't live more than three or four years after he leaves office.'

Johnson relinquished the Presidency in January 1969. He did in January 1973. Marjorie had known him well enough to understand that he lived only for power. Once deprived of it, his life force drained away. She felt no sense of sorrow when Johnson made his announcement, nor when he vacated the Presidential office – nor even when he died. She knew that power remained power – and that those who wielded it subtly, invisibly, behind the thrones survived those who had the outward trappings but only rose and fell, emerged and disappeared.

Marjorie felt a distinct antipathy toward Richard Nixon, yet supported him generously with large campaign contributions. Instinct told her he would squeak through to be the victor. Beyond this, she considered him the lesser of two evils, for she judged Hubert Humphrey a clumsy, prating buffoon surrounded by woolly-headed incompetents.

Having been so bountiful with her campaign donations,

Marjorie was invited to Nixon's official Inaugural Ball and a month later, to tea with the Nixons themselves. He was pleasant. Patricia Nixon chatted and smiled – rather stiffly and mechanically, Marjorie observed to herself.

'You'll be placed on the A-list, Lady Norworth,' Nixon said when Marjorie took her leave. 'Whenever you telephone you'll be put straight through to one of my principal aides instead of being bucked up the line from one secretary to the next.'

Eisenhower and Johnson had given her their private, direct-line numbers, Marjorie mused. She suspected that Nixon would institute rigid bureaucratic procedures in the White House – and intended to use aides as protective shields, hermetically sealing him off from the outside world.

A year later, one of the 'principal aides' paid an announced visit to Marjorie. He was polite, but there was an underlying note of demand – almost of coercion – in his tone and manner.

'Since you were so generous during the Presidential Campaign, we have you down for fifty thousand dollars to be used in the off-year elections.'

Marjorie was furious. No one approached her for political contributions. Those she had made – and they were many and huge – were made of her own volition. She told Holcomb to eject the aide and telephoned the White House. It was one of those increasingly rare occasions when Nixon was in the Oval Office and not off on a vacation or a junket, and by some fluke, her call was switched over to him. Relating what had occurred, she received stammered, obviously hastily improvised apologies and excuses. There must have been a mistake, a slipup. 'I – that is, I knew nothing about it, Lady Norworth. I'll talk to Bob – or Maurice – and make sure it doesn't happen again.'

Clearly, Richard Nixon was not kept posted – or did not keep himself posted – about what his aides were doing in his name.

During the very beginning of Nixon's second term, a CIA assistant director who owed Marjorie many favors asked her to take a short walk with him in her gardens. She protested it was bitter cold outside.

'Wrap yourself in sables,' he said. 'It's an important walk.'

Once away from the house he asked, 'You've been redecorating again, haven't you?'

'Keeping up with the Nixons' White House refurbishings.'

'Marjorie. Some of the workmen were plumbers.'

'You're joking!' She already knew what the word 'plumbers' meant under the Nixon regime and was aghast. If the conversations that took place inside her house were bugged and recorded . . .

'No, I'm not. You should hire technicians to go over the house. Every room has been bugged – but please, for God's sake, don't let anyone know I told you.'

Marjorie acted the same day. The electronic eavesdropping devices were located and removed. But the incident gave Marjorie an idea. In the weeks that followed, she had other – much more elaborate and sophisticated – electronic gear installed. For her own amusement and, she thought, quite possibly for her own protection and benefit.

Marjorie was neither surprised nor ruffled by Watergate and its aftermaths. Nothing was revealed that she did not already know – and she knew much more that was glossed over or entirely suppressed. She literally laughed through the two years and six months of the bumbling Ford Administration (as did most of the men who gathered at the House on the Hill).

She was stunned by the Democratic Party's choice of Carter as its Presidential candidate, but contributed handsomely to his campaign chest (through devious channels) – again because she felt he would be the winner. It was the same with his successor – during whose hopelessly corrupt and inefficient Administration the nation went into the worst economic downslide in its history and every problem that had plagued previous Administrations was compounded many times over.

Marjorie had known Charles Pendleton Talbot since his

second term in Congress. She liked him, but recognized him for the professional politician that he was: not overly bright, no more honest than most of his peers in the House – and later, in the Senate. However, Talbot demonstrated an ability to mediate and conciliate while serving as Senate Majority Leader. When he announced his candidacy for President, she foresaw his victory – and, she admitted to herself, even Charlie Talbot would be an improvement over the incumbent who would be his opponent in the election.

There are always means by which laws may be circumvented. Marjorie shrugged at restrictions on political contributions and made the largest campaign donation of her life – half a million dollars – passing the money through a series of purifying sieves into Talbot's campaign coffers.

After his spectacular landslide victory – he carried every state except Hawaii – Talbot floundered, unable to get his bearings. The conciliator, it became evident, had no ability to take command. He thought he could rely on the men he appointed to carry out their tasks and recoiled from criticizing or admonishing them – for he considered them all his friends and loyal political allies. Hadn't they all promised – sworn – to support and implement the broad (and glowing) promises he made during the campaign? For their part, the underlings waited to be given crisp, well-defined and forceful orders from their President. After realizing that they waited in vain, each embarked on his own, private empire-building projects. Conditions at home and abroad grew steadily worse, and President Charles Talbot could not understand why propitiating words, gentle coaxing and back-slapping cajolery did not improve them.

The State of the Union did not disturb Marjorie Norworth unduly, for her own world – of wealth, status, influence, power, and the manipulation of the powerful – remained intact. What counted was that Charles Talbot, the President of the United States, had come to her not merely for advice, but for step-by-step guidance.

Marjorie was exultant. She had reached the ultimate pinnacle – from where she would exercise direct control over the President, and thus shape the decisions and events that determined the fate of the United States – and much of the world.

13

Washington, D.C.: Saturday, February 20.

Suzanne Loring awoke at nine, considerably earlier than
she usually did on Saturdays. Russ should be telephoning
her at any time to relate a quick-skim account of his
evening at the House on the Hill and make a date for
later in the day, when he would doubtless fill her in on the
details. And, Suzanne told herself, we'll spend the night
making love. She yearned to be kissed and held and loved
by him, yet hoped that she would be able to retain a
reasonable degree of control over her down-deep emotions,
avoid being oversentimental. She loathed weepy, dramatic
females and the scenes they made, and knew Russ felt much
the same.

When he hadn't telephoned by 9:45 A.M., Suzanne
assumed he must be sleeping off a king-sized drunk. It was
common knowledge that the politicos who gathered at
Marjorie Norworth's often turned her parties and receptions into colossal boozing-bouts. But then, Suzanne reflected, why should Lady Norworth's be different from almost any other place in Washington where parties were
given? The District of Columbia and its bedroom suburbs
in Maryland and Virginia had by far the highest per-capita
liquor consumption rate of any area on the face of the earth.
Poor Russ, she thought lovingly, pouring her fourth mug
of coffee, he'll have a hell of a hangover. She sipped coffee,
smiled happily to herself. I'll apply all the conventional
cures – and some not so conventional, but (at least in
Russ's case) even more effective.

At ten, he still had not called, but Suzanne heard the
downstairs doorman's signal chime and picked up the house

phone. Eagerly. Perhaps it was Russ, who had come directly from his flat without phoning first.

Anyone visiting residents of Potomac apartments was required to undergo screening by doormen and be announced.

'A Mr Noah Sturdevant wishes to see you, Miss Loring,' she heard the doorman's voice.

Suzanne was incredulous. Noah Sturdevant was the tyrannical board chairman of the Continental Broadcasting Network. He seldom left New York, especially not on weekends, and never – but never – paid personal visits to the homes of people employed by CBN, no matter what their capacity.

'I don't believe it,' she said. 'It must be an impostor.' Then she chuckled. It could also be Russell Hatch gagging it up.

'The gentleman insists he *is* Mr Sturdevant, Miss Loring. Would you care to switch on your closed-circuit scanner?'

Suzanne's eyebrows climbed. She turned the knob of the closed-circuit television receiver mounted on the wall beside the door. Noah Sturdevant's prognathous features came into focus on the screen. Suzanne sighed, both baffled by the reasons behind Sturdevant's unprecedented visit and resigned to accept whatever they may be. Also, she was not a little glum over the prospect of having to sit through one of the CBN chairman's harangues. No matter what Sturdevant had to say to anyone, it was invariably a harangue. Anyway, thank God I'm dressed and the maid has cleaned up, Suzanne thought.

'Please show Mr Sturdevant to the elevator,' she said into the house phone. And I'll brace myself for the mysterious session with CBN's Little Hitler.

She greeted him at the elevator. He bustled past her, into the apartment, removed his overcoat and handed it to Suzanne's maid without a word. He gave the large living room a split-second scan, unerringly selected the most comfortable chair, took it, and leaned forward before Suzanne had time to sit down.

'Miss Loring.' Noah Sturdevant disdained using first

names. 'My trip to Washington is a secret.' He spoke as though he had taken elocution lessons by watching old March of Time shorts. 'Our conversation must be in complete – absolute – confidence. Please make certain your maid cannot eavesdrop.'

The maid had already vanished into the kitchen, closing the two intervening doors behind her.

Suzanne made polite hospitality noises. 'Would you like a drink or . . . ?'

'Much too early for a drink. And nothing else. I'm flying back to New York in an hour.' Without asking permission, Sturdevant thrust a large cigar into his thin-lipped mouth, performing fellatio until satisfied he had it lit. Suzy remained silent. Conversation with Noah Sturdevant was one-way. Everyone else listened until he asked direct questions.

'Your show last Tuesday was lousy . . .'

The Madigan interview will haunt me for the rest of my life, Suzanne reflected gloomily.

'. . . but *I* saw through it. I was the only person who did.' The massive cigar-bearing lower jaw worked, expressing prideful self-congratulation. 'You picked up advance information that Talbot was going to do something spectacular . . .'

Suzy put on her most enigmatic face.

'. . . there, I knew it. By greasing Madigan, you ingratiated yourself with the decision-makers. Clever move. I want you to carry on, ferret out all the details of whatever is behind Talbot's actions.'

'Mr Sturdevant, I have an interview show . . .'

'I am familiar with its format.' A reprimand. 'You continue as you have been – but also play detective.'

You're nuts, Suzy thought, but you're also the Big Boss. However, I suppose I should try and set you straight. 'Talbot's going on all the networks tomorrow night with a special message. He'll probably lay out the whole story. Even if he doesn't, every political analyst and investigative reporter will be digging . . .'

'You have many advantages over them, Miss Loring.

When you've gotten to the bottom of things, I'll put your findings to the nation. You can count on a hundred thousand dollar bonus – tax-free.' Cigar ash fell to the carpet. Sturdevant stood up, ready to leave. 'Remember, this is our project – yours and mine. Make progress reports to me directly.'

Suzanne stood up, too. The project did have its appeal – if there were anything further to be unearthed, that is, she thought. And, if so, the special would have immense value for CBN.

'Not one hundred thousand, Mr Sturdevant. Two,' she said.

He glared at her. 'One hundred and fifty – top. Otherwise, I may feel constrained to suggest that the board review your contract. No one is irreplaceable, Miss Loring.'

Ja, mein Führer, Suzy said to herself. *And up yours.* Aloud, she told Sturdevant it was a deal, she'd do her best. The maid brought his overcoat, and he departed. Before Suzanne had a chance to give much thought to their brief talk, the telephone rang. It was Russ. Her pulse rate rose several points; she thrust all else from her mind but managed to keep her tone and manner lighthearted.

'Good morning, Senator – are you badly hungover?'

'Well, I did have a big night, honey.'

'I figured you would.' Oh, Russ, please get to the important point – when will I see you? 'Who else was there?'

'About half the Government, far as I could tell.'

'I'm dying to hear the details – and your other news.'

'What about this evening?'

Why not right away? Oh, hell, don't sound too eager. 'Actually, I'm not doing a thing all day – or evening. So . . .'

'I'd suggest lunch . . .'

Why don't you?

'. . . but I brought home a pile of reports and other junk. I'd like to go over the stuff this afternoon. How about six or seven – and where shall we go for dinner?'

'Six will be fine' – *if it can't be any sooner* – 'and we're not going anywhere. I'm having a dinner party tonight, and I'm doing the cooking myself just to prove that my kitchen does get used – and you're the only guest, only you'll still have to make coffee in the morning. *Late* in the morning, not like last time – which we should both forget.'

Russ laughed at the nonstop flow of words and asked: 'Shall I bring anything?'

'A few kinds words, you bastard.'

Bradford Cooley had inherited millions from his family. He could easily afford the home he built (in 1948) in Washington's Forest Hills district. Located only blocks from the house Lyndon Johnson occupied before becoming President, Cooley's residence shattered all Forest Hills architectural conventions. It was modeled after a First Century A.D. Roman villa, set on a generous plot of ground and completely enclosed an inner peristyle garden. The outer walls had only tiny barred windows set high, close to the tiled roof, making it impossible for anyone to see inside. This was frustrating to neighbors and passersby who might have wished a glimpse at the interior and some indication of Cooley's home life-style. Over the years, only a few very close friends had received invitations to the villa, and they remained silent about whatever they saw inside the walls.

Actually, the interior was luxurious, faithfully reproducing the home of a wealthy first century Roman. The inner peristyle was quadrangular, surrounded by porticoes and large windows that looked out on a garden and a reflecting pool. To the south of the courtyard was a spacious atrium, corresponding to a living room and lounging area. Corridors led off to a tablinum – another sitting room – to bedrooms, and to sunken baths that would have gladdened the heart of a Caesar. Furnishings were in total harmony with the architecture. Only the kitchen and such modern appurtenances as television and radio sets and telephones were anachronisms. Bradford Cooley lived alone, save for a single manservant, who enjoyed long weekends off – from Friday evening until Monday morning.

Big Brad Cooley eased his gross body off the huge Roman couch in the main bedroom. Barefooted, he went noiselessly into the adjoining bathroom, stepped carefully down the mosaic tiled steps into the sunken bath. The water, maintained at a constant – and hot – temperature, was perfumed. He soaked himself, rubbed at his skin with a natural sponge, climbed out and used an enormous sheet to dry his body. Several fresh togas hung on a rack. He selected one, put it on and fixed a jeweled brooch to its left shoulder. Slipping his feet into sandals, he went down a marble-walled corridor and began preparing brunch. For two.

Cooley charcoal-broiled filet steaks, poached plovers' eggs in a rich sauce delicately flavoured with herbs, and mixed *bellinis* – vintage champagne and fresh pear juice. Arranging all on a tray atop a wheeled serving cart, he added silver and linen napkins, wheeled the cart to his bed chamber.

A figure lay on the couch, still sleeping, lips parted. Cooley held the folds of his toga, bent over and kissed the partially opened lips, tongue probing gently between them. 'Good morning,' he said.

FBI Director Emmett Hopper opened his eyes, teeth nipping at Cooley's tongue, and sat up. Cooley took the *bellinis* from the tray, handed one glass to Hopper.

'Nectar fit for the gods.' Cooley smiled, raising his glass. 'I had my first of these in Florence, after the war.'

'Alone?' Emmett Hopper asked archly.

'Don't be absurd. A young Italian – handsome as Apollo – introduced me to *bellinis*. He made my Italian summer an eternal delight.'

Cooley and Hopper were old – if somewhat sporadic – lovers, and they chatted easily while eating brunch. Then Hopper made his own pilgrimage to the sunken bath and also donned a toga. The two men wheeled the serving cart to the kitchen together. Cooley scraped plates into the sink, where modern garbage disposal units made quick work of scraps. Then Hopper stacked dishes and silver into the equally ultra-anachronistic electric dishwasher.

Cooley made more *bellinis*, which they took into the atrium and semi-reclined on couches there.

'You said you wanted to talk seriously last night,' Cooley

declared. 'We never got around to it, though. Shall we now?'

'Why not? I'm looking for allies, Brad.'

'Intending to run for some office?'

'No. I'm content where I am – or would be if the Bureau could be revitalized.'

Cooley stared into his glass. 'A difficult job, that. Denby and the CIA are riding high.' He sighed. 'They have full backing from Talbot, Pearce, and Kurtz – to say nothing of Jordan Rickhoven et al. Best I could do is plump for some modest appropriation increases.'

Hopper eyed him sharply. 'Brad, the CIA murdered Weidener.'

Cooley showed no surprise. 'I suspected the heart-attack story.'

'Three of Denby's agents lured him to a Shoreham suite on a pretext, got him drunk. My agents keep tabs on the CIA. They followed, used listening devices and learned where Weidener was to be taken – to his mistress's apartment building. An FBI car was sent out to wait near the scene. The agents obtained photographs.' Hopper described what the agents saw and recorded on film. 'Pearce and Denby wanted Weidener dead because he opposed their African adventure.'

'Now the Administration is dropping the Basanda aid bill,' Cooley mused aloud. 'Talbot is to fill the gap with his discretionary funds. The cabal has an intricate game-plan worked out.'

'With potentially lethal long-term consequences,' Hopper said. 'I'm holding the photographs and other evidence until the moment when they'll have the maximum impact – but they won't be enough. That's why I need . . .'

'Allies,' Cooley nodded. 'Powerful allies.' A pause. 'I think we can obtain them.' An idea was forming in his brain.

President Talbot and his Chief Adviser were in the Oval Office. Kenneth Ramsey saw that Talbot was once more beset by doubts and anxieties and sought to reassure him.

'You're all set on air time for tomorrow, Chief. Every candidate for the new Cabinet has been queried – and said yes. By Monday, you'll have the whole country solidly behind you.'

'There can always be slipups.'

'Chief, for God's sake, think positive, will you?'

'What about my speech?' Talbot opened a drawer, took out a bottle of Valiums, swallowed a ten-milligram tablet. 'When will I be able to read it over?'

'Later today. Zander's over in the Executive Office Building putting together his final draft.' Ramsey grinned. 'Lexa's with him – suggesting touches that'll grab the women.'

Talbot had a sudden thought. 'Has anyone gotten around to running a security check on Zander?'

'Lexa told them at the EOB to put him on the payroll and skip all the security investigation nonsense.'

'Oh,' Talbot said, but Ramsey's reply made him feel uneasy.

An hour later Avery Braithwaite telephoned and asked if he might come over without delay. Talbot was shocked when he saw him looking as if he had just risen from a sickbed.

'I'm merely a little tired,' Braithwaite explained, sitting in a chair beside the Presidential desk. 'I haven't slept much lately, but I believe my efforts have produced answers to your broad-scale problems.'

Talbot leaned forward. 'Avery, I'm damned grateful...!'

'Wait.' Braithwaite raised a sinewy hand. 'Listen to the conclusions I've reached. First, you must buy time with expedients – which you are doing. However, there can be no lasting solutions unless you are prepared to take draconian action.'

'You make it sound like a doom watch.'

'No. Disaster may be avoided provided that – at the propitious moment' – *which will be revealed to me* – 'you assert the strong special powers vested in you as President.'

'Huh?' Talbot's eye bugged. 'You aren't saying I should declare a national emergency or . . .'

'It is an option. If the African crisis escalates, you will have a firm basis . . .'

'My God, Avery – are you for military intervention?'

'I am for whatever best serves the interests – and the destiny – of our country, Chuck.'

'Congress won't stand for it!' Talbot protested.

'Legislators are not immune to fear.'

Talbot assumed that Braithwaite referred to fear of internal chaos. Nervously, he began to raise a question: 'The Constitution . . .'

'Mr President!' Braithwaite's eyes glowed. 'I can guarantee you a six-to-three majority in the Supreme Court, no matter what you may do. Working together, you and I will restore the United States to sanity, make our nation great again.' *That* has already been revealed me. 'Have faith that history is not an accident, but is guided . . .'

Yeah, I guess it is, Talbot mused, not catching the odd inflections of Braithwaite's tone. That's what we're all in Washington for – to guide what they call history.

'. . . we'll talk again next week, Chuck. By then, I will have a full study of legal precedents completed for you.'

Russell Hatch brought roses – red, long-stemmed and several dozen in number. Having longed to see Suzanne again, but still feeling guilt over the Madigan interview – and now additional (and, he tried to convince himself unreasonable) guilt over his marathon sexual bout with Christine at the House on the Hill, he seemed almost abashed as he held out the enormous florist's box.

Suzy sensed the reticence of his manner, took it as just another manifestation of the boyish quality in his nature and tingled with the warmth she had long described to herself as affection, but had finally realized was love. Deep love.

'Hello, freckle-face,' she said, accepting the box and putting it on a table so that she could kiss him – at first in fondly welcoming greeting and then, as their mouths locked and inner emotional-current switches closed, passionately.

Suzanne was wearing a white-and-beige dress with a scooped neckline – and nothing beneath it, Russ realized as she pressed her body against his. She pulled herself free, laughed happily.

'Mix the drinks, Senator. I'll try to round up enough vases to accommodate this rose garden.' She took a step, paused, glanced over her shoulder. 'Mix a lot of drinks. I changed my mind after talking to you. I thought a midnight supper would be more fun than dinner.

Russ made a pitcher of super-dry martinis. She sat close to him on a couch and, unable to contain himself longer, he began relating all that had happened with Madigan and President Talbot – what he had heard and seen, what Talbot was doing and planning, and the promises made to him by the President and the Senate Majority Leader.

The first pitcher of martinis was empty and a second had been half depleted before he finished his recountings.

'. . . so it looks like we have a fascinating future on the banks of the Potomac, honey.' Russ grinned, lopsidedly – a little drunk, but more from the pleasure of telling Suzy than from liquor.

Maybe it's the gin working in me, Suzanne thought, but her blood raced at his use of the first-person plural 'we' when referring to the future.

'Oh, God, Russ!'

She leaned closer to him, tipped up her face. He bent his head to meet her open lips. Her dresstop slipped from her right shoulder. Russ pulled her to him, his kiss starved, his hands frenziedly renewing their knowledge of her body even as they searched for the fastenings of her dress.

'Suzy . . .'

'Don't talk, Russ – please.' *If you do, I'm liable to say things I might be sorry for afterward – things I won't say, I can't bring myself to say until I'm sure. Sure of you – of us. Sure that the 'we' wasn't an unintentional slip.*

Guiding his hands to the concealed fasteners, Suzy moved her shoulders, twisting her torso. The top of her dress fell away. Her nipples were eager for his touch, rose tauter as he cupped and kissed them.

He held her and they rolled from the couch to the thickly carpeted floor. God, but I want him, Suzanne thought. I'm soaked, and he's merely touching me and I have to bite my lips to keep myself from coming. But nothing could stop her gathering orgasm. His lips were on her breast, and her moan rose to a cry of joy as her muscles corded.

Russ moved away, tore himself free of his clothes and flung himself on her. Guilt, masculine ego seeking to redeem his desire for Suzanne, produced a degree of arousal that almost frightened him.

14

Washington, D.C.: Sunday, February 21.

President Talbot would address the nation from the Diplomatic Reception Room in the White House. It was there – before the advent of television – that Roosevelt had delivered his famous Fireside Chats. (The choice was one of FDR's inside jokes. The Diplomatic Reception Room's fireplace was the only one in the White House that did not work. This inspired an atrocious – but telling – pun. 'The wise politician always speaks from a cold hearth,' Roosevelt had told Harry Hopkins.)

Talbot was to speak seated at a desk brought up from the White House storerooms and hastily polished. A briefing kit prepared for the news media alleged it had been used by both Presidents Theodore Roosevelt and Woodrow Wilson. The desk was flanked by American and Presidential flags – and two people were to be seated at the desk, flanking Talbot himself. On his right, Vice President Alvin Dunlap. On his left, Lexa Talbot.

The announcement that Alvin Dunlap would be present brought snickers from the White House press corps. Dunlap was an old school Vice President – a perpetually invisible man. Since his election, Vice President Dunlap had made no domestic or overseas junkets and almost no public appearances or statements. On the other hand correspondents unanimously agreed that Lexa Talbot would dress up the proceedings, add class and sex appeal.

Television and radio network crews arrived with their complex gear early in the morning. After being subjected to Secret Service checks and inspections, they set up for the evening broadcast. Ken Ramsey saw to it that they were supplied with copious food and reasonable rations of liquor throughout the day.

The broadcast was scheduled for 8.00 P.M., Eastern Time. At 10.00 A.M., Talbot pored over the final draft of his speech. At first, he considered it an excellent piece of work. On his second and third readings, he grew jittery, began to have reservations about certain passages. He made some changes. By noon, he had completely butchered the script and summoned Kenneth Ramsey and James Zander to the Oval Office. The speech would have to be rewritten, Talbot announced to Zander's horror. Ramsey was unmoved, excused himself, and returned minutes later with the U.S. Navy medical branch Rear Admiral serving as the President's physician.

'Mr President, you need some sleep,' the Rear Admiral said, noting that Talbot was by then extremely nervous and agitated.

Talbot followed him out of the Oval Office meekly. Jim Zander stared at Ramsey, waved the altered script. Entire paragraphs had been crossed out, barely legible sentences were scrawled in page margins. 'Now what?' Zander asked.

'Nothing,' Ramsey grinned. He took the pages, fed them into the shredder. 'The doc'll give him a shot so he'll sleep till five or so, then another that'll wake him up, relax his nerves and act as an antidepressant. At seven-thirty, we'll give him another copy of the original – and he'll give an Academy Award performance.'

Zander lit a cigarette. The smoke was acrid.

'That pot?' Ramsey asked mildly.

'Uh-huh.'

'Then for Christ's sake stand close to an exhaust vent, huh?' The request was good-natured. Any man able to churn out speeches of the quality that Zander wrote was too valuable to fire – or even reprimand – simply because he smoked a little grass.

The President's physician knew his uppers, downers, tranquilizers, antidepressants, energy boosters – and his illustrious patient. When Talbot entered the Diplomatic Reception Room with his daughter and Vice President Dunlap, he was in top form.

It was ten minutes before air time. Talbot spoke a few impromptu words to the TV crews and correspondents.

'Normally, I'd greet you all with the customary ice-breaking jokes. But I can't try to be funny tonight – you'll understand why. I'd like to apologize to you, though, because you'll have to stand while we' – he indicated Dunlap and Lexa – 'will be seated.'

He held Lexa's chair, waited politely until Dunlap took his place and then seated himself at the desk, laying the script of his speech in front of him.

'No advance printed copies,' an AP man observed to a colleague.

'Well, we'll soon find out if it's another snow job or if he really has something to say.'

A last flurry of activity, sudden silence, and Talbot was on, full face into the camera lenses, his expression serious, sincere.

'My fellow Americans. Most Presidents in our history have been accused of making mistakes. Few – if any – have ever publicly admitted making them.' A one-beat pause. 'I am here tonight because I feel that precedent must be broken – and to state openly and honestly that my Administration has been guilty of many grave mistakes and errors.'

There were audible murmurs of astonishment from television crew members and White House correspondents.

'I take full blame and responsibility for permitting slip-shod planning, inadequate coordination and other deficiencies that have created crisis after crisis. If you are un-employed, it is my fault for allowing the Government to pursue wrong economic policies. If one of your loved ones was killed or injured in the riots that have swept many of our cities, this too is my fault.'

'He's committing political suicide,' a cameraman whispered.

'Don't be too sure – yet,' his assistant said.

Talbot continued.

'This is a democracy. I am an elected President, not a dictator. Nonetheless, a President has certain powers – powers that I should have exercised to prevent violence and bloodshed . . .'

Daniel Madigan, MacDonald Pearce and John Kurtz watched the telecast in a private room at the Dorian Club.

'By now, he's got the public's mouths hanging open so wide they'll swallow whatever he feeds them,' Madigan observed gleefully.

'Maybe.' John Kurtz would not commit himself further yet.

'And maybe not,' MacDonald Pearce said dryly. 'It depends on what he has to say after he takes off the hair-shirt.'

'. . . the troop movements I ordered Friday were belated, but I pray they will halt killing and destruction and bring local law enforcement agencies as well as rioters to their senses . . .'

Suzanne Loring cocked a skeptical eyebrow. According to Russell Hatch, Talbot had promised to castigate local authorities for having overreacted and caused the slaughter of rioters. She turned to Russ, who was sitting up beside her in bed, watching the telecast.

'He's backing off,' she said. 'I knew he would.'

'Wait.' Russ squeezed her hand, kissed her temple. On the television viewing-screen, Talbot could be seen turning a page.

'I have reason to believe that the demonstrators were frequently provoked into rioting,' the President's voice went on. 'I shall order Federal agencies to conduct full investigations . . .'

'See?' Russ gloated, rumpling Suzanne's short brown hair.

I wish I could see, Suzy thought. *See into Charlie Talbot's head and get the inside story of the whole con job, because my intuition tells me it is a con job, pure-but-not-simple.* Her ambition

159

apparatus was activated. *God, to have it all wrapped in a neat package, and deliver it exclusive on a network special.*

Talbot turned another page of his script. Here comes the big pitch, he warned himself, remolding his expression into a look of courageous determination.

'Mistakes can be corrected. The steps taken must be swift and drastic.' Pause. 'Tomorrow, there will be several men in my Cabinet who will shout to the world that I am ruthless, for I shall then hold a special Cabinet meeting and demand immediate resignations of those who failed to live up to the promises I made to you. The problem makers will go. They will be replaced by problem solvers . . .'

Ramsey stood in the back of the room. *Beautiful switcheroo,* he thought, *it sounds even better than it read. The Chief pounds his breast – mea culpa – and the public can't believe it. Here's an honest man. A paragon. Only, he's suddenly shifted the blame – and the public will go along, take the honest man's word without a question.*

'This will only be the beginning,' Talbot continued. 'Next week, I shall ask the Congress to enact an emergency bill to provide ten billion dollars for the replenishment of unemployment compensation funds and provide aid for farmers and small businessmen. If more money is required, I shall not hesitate to ask for additional appropriations . . .'

'But *I* shall hesitate to push further appropriations until I see what you've done with the first ten billion,' Bradford Cooley said to the President's television image.

Cooley and Emmett Hopper had changed into street clothes. The togas were hung in a locked closet, to be used again on some other weekend. They sat in the tablinum, watching the Talbot telecast.

'You won't find it easy to block him – not after this piece of theater,' Hopper said, giving Cooley a sour look.

'Emmett, we've talked at length about the – um, resources we have and are likely to obtain. Correct?'

'Yes.'

'We'll block him – if it becomes necessary, never fear.'

*

'. . . Some may oppose increased Federal spending. To them, I say charity begins at home.' Talbot set his jaw. 'We have long poured out billions in aid to foreign countries – without receiving so much as thank-you in return. We can no longer subsidize others while our own people are in need. We must slash our giveaway programs. I have already had an Administration-sponsored bill giving the African country of Basanda a billion dollars withdrawn. We shall take care of our own.'

Talbot doubled back, taking viewers and listeners into his confidence.

'I've talked about programs and policies. Now, I'd like you to hear the specifics about the changes I am making in the Cabinet.' He read off the names of the Cabinet officers whose resignations he would demand Monday. His look and tone made 200 million Americans feel he was sharing a top State secret with each of them personally, that they were his friends bound together in a common cause against incompetents and villains. It was magnificent theater, and Talbot knew it.

'Finally, let me explain why Vice President Dunlap and my daughter Lexa are with me here tonight. Vice President Dunlap will be my personal ombudsman in Washington, keeping a close eye on the progress of our new programs, and the new officials who are to implement them. I have a job for my daughter, too. I will form an Office of Direct Public Access to the White House.'

Talbot turned, smiled at Lexa, turned back to the cameras.

'The office will receive your suggestions – and your complaints – study them and recommend what action should be taken. Lexa will head the agency – without pay – and will be *your* direct link to the Executive Branch of your Government.'

He stood up, extended one hand to Lexa, the other to Dunlap. They rose to their feet. 'Good night, my fellow citizens,' Talbot said into microphones and cameras. 'May God bless you all.'

The reaction of the media representatives in the Diplomatic Reception Room was without precedent. They broke into applause and cheers.

Ken Ramsey had ordered a full switchboard staff to be on duty. It proved a wise precaution. Incoming-call traffic topped all previous records, tying up local and long-distance circuits. Half an hour after the speech ended, an initial count showed the calls were running 100-to-one in enthusiastic favor of President Talbot.

'We should all have a drink to celebrate,' Lexa urged.

Talbot demurred. He wanted to be alone in the Oval Office for a while. 'And then I'm going out,' he told her.

Once inside the Oval Office, he telephoned Marjorie Norworth.

'You were fabulous, Charlie,' she congratulated him. 'You made yourself George Washington, Abraham Lincoln, and FDR all rolled into one.' *By following my scenario to the letter – and rest assured I shall be preparing many more for you.*

'Is it all right if I come over tonight, Marjorie?'

'For more advice?'

'I'll be needing it later, but not tonight. I . . .'

'Aha! You feel just like Franklin did after his Fireside Chats.' Sexually aroused, turned on FULL. 'Any particular room?'

'Any – long as there aren't any White House trimmings.'

'I'll take care of everything.' Marjorie did not need to ask more. She instinctively knew Charles Talbot's specifications – a girl with long blonde hair and not more than twenty-five years old.

Ramsey had a drink with Lexa and Jim Zander, said good night and went home to his wife and children.

'Come upstairs to the family quarters.' Zander recognized the look Lexa was giving him.

'Think that's smart?' he said. 'This place is neck-deep with security men, servants . . .'

'So what? I'm Lexa Talbot. I can have anyone visit with me.'

They went to the Family Quarters. Lexa led him to her

sitting room. He lit a cigarette, inhaled deeply, passed the cigarette to her.

'Never dreamed I'd get to ball in the White House,' Zander chuckled, glancing around him. 'Sure your old man is out?'

'Positive.' Lexa passed the cigarette back to him. 'I'm positive I can guess what's on your mind – the bulge is showing.' Her eyes grew hot. 'Let's use his bed!'

Balling the President's daughter in the Presidential bed – was wild, the wildest turn-on of all time, Jim Zander reflected, inhaling. He gazed at Lexa. I'll be damned, she wants it even more than I do, he realized and burst into lewd laughter, allowing her to lead him to Talbot's bedroom.

15

Kinsolo, Basanda: Monday, February 22

In 1854 a British Colonial Office cartographer drew an uneven, curving line on a map of West Africa. The line marked off a 450,000-square-mile area inhabited by some fifteen million natives belonging to no less than twenty major (and mutually hostile) tribes. The boundaries of the new British colony of Basanda were thereby established.

British rule was benign. Colonial administrators and soldiers halted the thriving slave trade, maintained peace among the tribes, built roads, schools, and hospitals. (In the process, they also contracted malaria, dengue fever, and various other high-mortality-rate diseases.) Kinsolo, a hideously squalid seacoast town was rebuilt and transformed into Basanda's reasonably clean, English-pattern capital city.

By 1900 Britain had succeeded in training a body of native civil servants and establishing some semblance of local democracy. Most Basandans cheerfully accepted British rule and protection. Many eagerly learned English; the educated classes in Kinsolo and provincial capitals emulated British dress, manners, and customs – even unto forming crack cricket and rugby teams.

White settlers raised tobacco, cotton, grain, peanuts, produced palm oil, and harvested timber. Lacking in vision and understanding, they ignored the possibility that Basanda might possess more valuable natural resources. (A few prospectors did come to the colony, but they sought gold and diamonds. Finding none, they departed.) Basanda and Basandans profited from the British presence. However, the almost entirely agricultural economy failed to make the colony self-sustaining. The British Treasury regularly made up the huge annual deficits.

The British Empire began disintegrating after World War Two. Colonies and possessions clamored for independence – all but Basanda, which had no desire to cut free of the British umbilical cord. But by 1967, Britain's faltering economy could no longer afford to subsidize the African colony. Independence was literally forced on Basanda. By then, its population was nearly thirty million and, in the vacuum created by sudden independence, ancient tribal hatreds were rekindled.

Two million Basandans died in tribal warfare and massacres. The country was leaderless, in chaos. A faction made up of several large tribes formed around Odu Mwandi, a former sergeant in the King's Own Basandan Rifles, a regiment that fought on the Allied side during World War Two. Eccentric, erratic, and self-styling himself as General Field Marshal, Odu Mwandi ended the internecine warfare by using brutal and savage methods. Entire villages were wiped out; tribes were decimated. Starvation and disease followed, taking more lives.

New armies descended on Basanda – armies of American geologists, mineralogists, and other specialists. Within months, they were discovering immense deposits of base-metal ores – and oil. The United States Government sent cash, food, weapons, and other supplies to back Odu Mwandi and insure that he became the Prime Minister of Basanda. Upon taking office, Mwandi's first official act was to grant giveaway mining and oil concessions to American-owned companies – most of which were owned or controlled by the Rickhoven dynasty. Mwandi next ordered the construction of a Prime Ministerial Palace in Kinsolo, decreeing that it should surpass every other structure on the African Continent in size and grandeur. He insisted it be an ultra-modern rendering of Buckingham Palace – but four times larger.

The result was a monstrous parody of Buckingham Palace constructed of black marble and stainless steel. Outside its walls, Odu Mwandi Park was an expanse of green lawn and shady trees rivaling any park in London – save that its use was forbidden to the general public. Mwandi installed himself in the palace with a army of concubines and an even larger army of personal bodyguards and ruled Basanda with terror, hangman's noose, and machine gun. His spies, torturers, and executioners were everywhere, and mass slaughters were commonplace.

American companies operating in Basanda ignored all this. Mwandi held native-wage rates down to preposterously low levels. Mines and oilfields yielded prodigious profits. What more could corporate officers and stockholders desire? As for the United States Government, it was delighted to have a 'staunch ally' on the African continent.

The Basandan revolt was sparked by what, according to standards prevailing there, was a trivial incident. Odu Mwandi wanted a summer palace compound in the cool uplands and sent troops to evacuate and raze a village he had chosen as its site. A hundred and twenty villagers – members of the proud Sawila tribe, resisted; they were gunned down and their bodies burned.

Sawila tribal belief holds that cremation after death consigns the soul to eternal wandering. News of the mass slaughter and cremation spread to other Sawila villages. A Sawila force ambushed the soldiers and massacred them. Odu Mwandi ordered all Sawilas exterminated, a formidable task, for there were more than 300,000 in the tribe.

Battalions of Mwandi's American-equipped troops launched the campaign. The Sawilas dispersed into jungle and bush and began a guerilla war. They were soon joined by other tribes. The fighting escalated further. Under a 'Friendship Treaty', America was required to supply Basanda with financial aid, arms, and 'limited numbers of military advisers' when formally called upon to do so. Prime Minister Mwandi invoked this treaty provision. The U.S. complied, but the fighting continued and the rebels steadily gained strength.

Sandhurst-trained Colonel Leabua Rwati commanded

Prime Minister Odu Mwandi's personal bodyguard. Having heard of the report Mwandi received from the Basandan Ambassador in Washington and aware of the orders being issued to Loyalist units in outlying regions, Colonel Rwati had been infected by the rapidly spreading panic.

He had sworn undying loyalty to Odu Mwandi and lived up to his oath. The rewards had been great. Rwati owned enormous tracts of land (which Mwandi had confiscated and parceled out to his favorites), and he had almost a million dollars in a Swiss bank. But he scented disaster, and his survival instincts were strong. Consequently, he was affable and receptive when he met with the three American civilians in the operations room of the U.S. Basanda Military Advisory Group airstrip a mile east of Kinsolo. Among the aircraft parked along the strip were a four-engined jet transport and a large Bell helicopter, Rwati noted, and felt comforted.

'The money is all here, Colonel,' an American said, patting suitcases laid out on a table. 'Once it's done, you and others who must leave can be aboard that transport – with your cash – and headed for Switzerland or wherever you all agree to go.'

Rwati hesitated. 'There could be sudden changes of mind in Washington,' he said. There had been many in the past.

'No chance.' The tallest American shook his head. 'The decision is final. Mwandi passes into history – fast, if you cooperate, not quite so fast if you don't, but then you'll follow the leader. Down the drain.'

Oath or no oath, Leabua Rwati wanted to live long and enjoy the million already in Switzerland, the two million more he would receive.

'You will guarantee my safety?' he asked.

The trio of Americans in civilian clothes nodded.

Rwati squared his shoulders. 'Very well.'

The four men left the operations room, went outside to a waiting BMAG staff car and drove to the Prime Ministerial Palace in Kinsolo. Guards halted them at the gates, recognized Colonel Rwati, saluted and allowed the car to pass.

Sentries presented arms as Rwati and his companions

alighted from the car and entered the Palace. Rwati led the way along marble corridors to the wing where Odu Mwandi had his audience chambers and what he called his 'Command Post'. They stopped before ivory-inlaid doors. Rwati spoke in M'ba, the tribal dialect used by officials when not speaking English, and a Prime Ministerial aide ushered them into Odu Mwandi's presence.

Mwandi wore his gaudy General Field Marshal's uniform and was surrounded by officers of lesser rank. A giant with bulging eyes and a messianic beard, the Prime Minister barked an order dismissing his entourage, returned Rwati's salute, and glared at the Americans.

'These gentlemen have flown from Washington and have presented their credentials to me, Your Excellency,' Colonel Rwati said.

'Whose signature is on their credentials?' Mwandi demanded.

'That of the Secretary of State, MacDonald Pearce.'

Mwandi waved an imperious hand. 'What further perfidies have they come to reveal?' Odu Mwandi spoke like that. 'Have they come to cause more harm for the glorious nation I created?'

An American, of medium height and powerful build, spoke. 'Your Excellency, there have been serious misunderstandings. We have been sent to clarify matters and set your mind to rest about American intentions.'

'Money, guns – where are they? That is what I want to hear!'

'They will be forthcoming, Your Excellency. However, we must make an immediate survey of conditions and report by radio today.'

'*I* will tell you what to report.'

Taking turns, the Americans explained that they had specific orders. They were to request the Prime Minister to accompany them on a helicopter reconnaissance within a radius of one hundred miles from Kinsolo. If there were no signs of headlong retreat by Loyalist forces, Washington would rush aid. Naturally, they needed Odu Mwandi's personal interpretations of whatever they observed.

'I will accompany Your Excellency and protect your person,' Rwati said, patting the holstered automatic on his belt.

Mwandi deliberated. There would be no evidences of military withdrawals in the Kinsolo area. The Americans would see nothing to alarm them. But if he refused to make the reconnaissance flight, they were certain to become suspicious, send damaging reports to Washington.

'We go,' he announced.

A sizable convoy left the palace grounds. An armored car led. Two jeeps with stanchion-mounted M-60 machine guns followed. Odu Mwandi's bulletproof and gold-plated Rolls Royce was next. Then the staff car. Behind it, another armored vehicle.

Prime Minister General Field Marshal Odu Mwandi donned a parachute provided for him and boarded the Bell helicopter. Rwati followed. The three Americans climbed into the craft, the tallest of them sliding into the pilot's seat. Moments later, the engine caught and the rotor blades started whirling. The copter lifted off, rose to 2,000 feet altitude, leveled and cruised directly east.

'Everything looks normal to me,' the pilot said after several minutes. 'Road traffic is average, two-way.'

'Perhaps you should fly over your American operated oil fields,' Odu Mwandi said, laughing loudly. 'They will not be American-operated long unless you send aid. I shall first expropriate them. If rebels advance into the main province, I shall have them blown up, completely destroyed.' His laugh rose to a shrill cackle.

The motherfucker is a certifiable lunatic, the American pilot thought. He went to 2,500 feet, banked left, flew straight for perhaps ten miles, banked right, reduced power.

'What's down there?' he asked his colleague in the copilot's seat. They were over rocky ground. 'There – near that little hill?'

The other man used binoculars, studied the terrain below.

'Can't see anything clearly through this damned plexiglass,' he said.

'Slide open the door, you damned fool!'

Americans shouting at each other angrily was a source of amusement to Odu Mwandi. Chuckling, he undid his seat belt and leaned forward to obtain a better view.

'Okay,' the pilot said. 'Get it over with.'

Colonel Rwati unsnapped his seat belt. The man in the copilot's seat tossed the binoculars aside. They seized Odu Mwandi, pulled at his heavy body – while the third, the powerfully built American pushed. Prime Minister Mwandi was flung out of the open door. He screamed as he fell, clawed at his parachute ripcord. The chute failed to open. A few drops of solder in the right places insured that it could not.

The pilot swung the chopper sharply to the right and gave the engines full throttle.

BMAG had direct radio contact with Washington via communications satellite, and its transmitter-receiver was equipped with scrambler devices. The tall American who had piloted the helicopter encountered no problems reaching G. Howard Denby's deputy in charge of special operations.

'A-plus,' the agent in Basanda reported. 'Scratch Mwandi.'

'What about his bodyguard?'

'Rwati and most of his officers collected theirs and took off for Zurich an hour ago. A few officers opted to stay, and they're passing the cash out to their noncoms and men. We've got no sweat at all here – except we have to know who's taking over.'

'State has that wrapped up. The Number One there' – Pearce – 'talked to our Number One' – Denby – 'and Percival Kwida's en route. Have a giant-sized BMAG honor guard ready when he lands. He'll make a speech at the strip – announce that Basanda has been liberated from tyranny – the usual crap – and promise free elections as soon as the rebels are defeated.'

'Any further orders for our team?'

'Yes. Stay where you are and make sure the new Prime Minister doesn't fall out of any choppers.' There was an odd, scratchy-gurgling noise. Scrambler devices have one notable failing. They distort laughter.

16

*Washington, D.C. and Wilmington, Delaware: Monday,
February 22.*

The Secretary of the Treasury sent a coldly formal letter of
resignation by messenger. Otherwise, every seat at the
Cabinet Room table was occupied. The men being axed
were grim-faced, resentful. Those who would remain were
tense – except for MacDonald Pearce and John Kurtz,
whose expressions verged on the smug.

'Mr President.' Duane Tillinghast, the rubicund,
counterfeit-liberal Labor Secretary, was determined to
have his say. 'I want to express my indignation at the
manner in which you publicly humiliated me and other
members of this Cabinet. Never in history . . .'

'Oh, balls!' Charles Talbot snorted – and grinned. He
was in excellent spirits. Press and public were acclaiming
him. The visit to Marjorie's had done wonders. He didn't
give a damn *what* Tillinghast thought. 'You're a horse's
ass, Duane. I brought you into the Cabinet because you
swore you could tame the unions and keep Labor happy.
You did nothing. So don't give us any static this morning.'

'I protest . . .'

'Write a letter to *Pravda*, for all I care.' Talbot lit a
Salem, jetted smoke through his nostrils. 'Only remember I
have a file of the Your-Eyes-Only memos you wrote
recommending – and I quote – "harsh measures to subdue
militant labor leaders." We can have those Xeroxed and
pass copies out to the news media in five minutes flat.'

Duane Tillinghast subsided into purple-faced silence. A
glance at the others seated around the table told Talbot he
had gotten his message across. The Talbot Administration

would make mincemeat of any outgoing Cabinet Officer who kicked up a fuss.

Feeling a surging sense of power, Talbot said: 'Polite letters of resignation received before noon will receive polite letters expressing my thanks for services rendered et cetera.' He puffed lazily on his Salem. 'There being no further business to discuss, I declare this meeting to be adjourned.'

Pearce and Kurtz met with the President in the Oval Office after the meeting. Ramsey joined them.

'You said it was important,' Talbot addressed Pearce. 'You didn't say why.'

'Prime Minister Odu Mwandi is dead,' Pearce announced.

Talbot's gray eyes widened. 'You mean the rebels . . .'

'No. It was an accident. He was making an aerial reconnaissance by helicopter and fell out of the craft.'

Ramsey shot the Secretary of State a penetrating look. 'Who did the chopper belong to – Basanda or BMAG?'

'Ah – BMAG,' John Kurtz replied.

'Interesting,' Ramsey murmured. 'I flew choppers in Nam during two six-month tours. I saw people shot out of copters, saw some jump, and a few pushed. Never saw one fall out accidentally.'

'That is the report we received.' MacDonald Pearce was prim.

'What counts is that he's dead,' Talbot said, his spirits slumping. 'The whole damned Basandan Government may fall apart.' He bit his lower lip. 'Defense ought to draw up plans for evacuating our people – civilian and military – and as for that half-billion . . .'

'The situation is under control,' Pearce declared with assurance. He adjusted his bifocals. 'Mwandi was not – ah – the greatest of assets. His death will not be mourned by those who were so critical of his – ah – sometimes high-handed methods.'

Mwandi was a fucking butcher, Ramsey commented to himself.

'His successor has already been designated by unanimous agreement of the Basandan General Staff,' Kurtz said, fondling his pipe.

'Who is he?' Talbot asked.

'You've met him often at diplomatic receptions,' Pearce replied. 'Percival Kwida, the Basandan Ambassador – or he was, until John arranged to have him flown to Kinsolo by Air Force jet when we received word that he was the General Staff's choice.'

'Kwida, eh?' The President was trying to get things in focus.

'An admirable choice,' Pearce clucked. 'He went to school in England – to Cambridge – and his long experience in Washington has made him most familiar with our American ways.' He saw that Talbot was gratefully swallowing the sugared pills.

'Kwida will rally the Loyalists,' Kurtz said. 'I see no reason for us to make evacuation plans. In regard to the discretionary funds, I recommend they be made available to Kwida immediately.'

'I concur, and fully,' Pearce nodded.

Talbot's spirits soared again. Pearce and Kurtz were right. Hell, Percival Kwida was practically an Anglo-American. He would boost Loyalist morale, make their cause more palatable to Americans and to the governments of Western democracies.

'Okay,' he said. 'You've sold me.'

It was hastily improvised, but Talbot wanted a quick check on how Hatch handled himself in public and how the public reacted to him. He had a brief talk with Lexa, telephoned Dan Madigan, told him to bring Hatch over at eleven-thirty.

Upon his arrival, Madigan exuberantly waved a copy of the Washington *Post*. 'The lead editorial starts off: "In a precedent-shattering address that has apparently galvanized the nation . . ."'

'I haven't had time for reading today,' Talbot broke in.

'Take it from me, no sour notes anywhere,' Madigan said. 'What's the feedback from up on the Hill?'

'All positive – and then some. The ten-billion appropriation should sail through both Houses. I'll bet any odds you'll have rubber-stamp okays on the people you appoint to the Cabinet.' Dan Madigan rubbed his hands.

Talbot looked at Russell Hatch, who had been following the conversation with interest not unmixed with amusement but could not understand why Madigan had brought him along.

'What's your opinion, Russ?' the President asked.

'I think everything you've done so far is great, Mr President,' Russ answered readily enough, then became thoughtful. 'But the-momentum will have to be maintained with tangible results.' That made his stand fairly clear. He would do whatever Talbot and Madigan asked – provided the brave words were really translated into action.

'Agreed,' Talbot nodded. 'There're mountains to be climbed.'

The Oval Office doors opened and Lexa Talbot entered. Madigan and Hatch leaped to their feet.

'Hello, Daddy, Dan and' – Lexa came forward, hand outstretched – 'unless I'm mistaken, Senator Russell Hatch.' Her handclasp was firm, her smile dazzling.

'Call him Russ,' Talbot smiled. 'I do – and he's likely to be a frequent visitor.'

'You Russ – me Lexa,' she laughed, released Hatch's hand, and went to the Presidential desk. She *is* a raving beauty, Russ thought, watching her lean across the desk and kiss Talbot's cheek.

'Please sit down – Dan, Russ,' Lexa said, turning to face them. 'I only stopped by for a minute to ask Daddy a question.' She looked at Talbot again. 'Have you corraled anyone for tonight?'

Talbot feigned total bafflement. 'What's tonight?'

Lexa sighed in exasperation. 'Don't tell me you've forgotten! I have that Men-and-Women Voters' League meeting in Wilmington . . .'

'God, l did forget.'

'. . . you were going to find someone to go with me and give the audience a male-viewpoint talk.'

Lexa shook her head. 'That's my Pop,' she said with an

elaborate shrug. 'Guess I'll be on my own – no, hey, wait.' Her great gray eyes flicked to Russ, locked on him. 'Russ, how long has it been since a female flung herself at you? No, don't answer that.' She laughed. 'As the President's daughter, I do have some prerogatives – lassoing Senators among them. You're stuck with the job of sharing the Wilmington High School auditorium platform with me!'

Russ had a date with Suzanne. However, he could hardy refuse Lexa, not in front of her father, who was expressing approval.

'I'll have to whip together some sort of speech,' Hatch said.

'Why? I'm going to talk ex-tempo. You can, too. We'll rough out something while I drive you to Wilmington this evening.'

So I even get to ride in the famous silver-gray Jag, Russ thought.

'We won't have to talk much,' Lexa went on. 'We'll probably spend most our time fielding questions about Daddy's speech and plans.'

' I'll wear a double-padded mitt,' Russ said.

Lexa parodied a curtsy. 'Thanks for rescuing a damsel in distress.' She grew serious. 'Where do you live, Russ?' He told her. 'My Secret Service goons and I'll pick you up at five-thirty – and, oh, black tie. They like their politicians to look formal in Wilmington – even when they're tall, redheaded and handsome like you, Senator.'

She blew her father and Madigan a kiss, hurried out.

'You scored a ten-strike with my daughter,' Talbot grinned.

She scored more than that with me, Russ thought – then reminded himself that Lexa *was* the President's daughter, which made her Off Limits and Out of Bounds to all junior senators and other rabble.

Russ phoned Suzanne Loring at the CBN studios.

'Honey, I have to stand you up tonight. I'm giving a talk in Wilmington, of all dumb places.'

Suzy's right eyebrow shot to its apogee. That didn't

sound right. Senator's speaking engagements were scheduled far in advance.

'Take me along. I'd love to hear you orate.'

'Uh – I can't. I'm going with Lexa Talbot.' He explained what had happened in the Oval Office.

I will be damned, Suzanne mentalized. *The Talbots (plural) and Dan Madigan are giving Russell Hatch the full Royal treatment – and, smart as he is, Russ is falling for it. No doubt he's already started to fall for Miss Twinkle Tits Talbot, too. They all do. But the blond bitch certainly isn't going to be in any future that we – Russ and I – have, in this town or anywhere else. I'll make sure of that.*

'Knock 'em dead, Senator, and call me in the morning,' Suzanne said. 'I'll be dying to know if she's on the Pill or you have to use a condom.'

Afternoon television and radio broadcasts and newspapers carried bulletins about the death of the Basandan Prime Minister and reported he would be succeeded by Percival Kwida – a diplomat known for his democratic attitudes. By some weird distortion of nonlogic the development was made to appear as another brilliant triumph achieved by the rediscovered genius of American politics, President Charles Pendleton Talbot.

Jordan B. Rickhoven III spoke to MacDonald Pearce from New York.

'Fine job, Mac.' Rickhoven's words were cautious. 'I thought of you when I had lunch – at my desk. Had a sandwich with four thick slices of Swiss cheese in it.'

Pearce understood. Four thick slices – $100,000 each – would be deposited to the Swiss bank accounts of MacDonald Pearce, John Kurtz, G. Howard Denby, and Daniel Madigan. For extraordinary services rendered.

Lexa Talbot's rainbow-swirl gown was all the sexier for its apparently demure design, and she drove the powerful Jaguar as though she were a part of the machine.

'I'll talk about Daddy and how he worried himself sick

before making his big decision,' she told Russ, her gloved hands at nine-o'clock–three-o'clock on the steering wheel. 'You give them a sort of background briefing and plug his plans. Okay?'

'Sounds all right to me, Lexa.' Hatch glanced over his shoulder. The security backup car was holding steady behind them. 'I hear they sometimes make you feel uncomfortable,' he remarked.

'Mmm, they do, and then I shake them. Remind me to show you how it's done one of these days.' A pause. 'Or nights.'

The Wilmington High School Auditorium was jammed and platoons of police and security men lined the walls and stood in back. Lexa and Russ went through the traditional formalities backstage. Effusive local dignitaries (all oozing wealth, for this was E.I. Du Pont Company country) fawned over Lexa while their shrill wives gabbled. When Lexa introduced Russ, the men shook his hand and the women eyed him with varying degrees of lustful appraisal.

At last, they were led onto the stage. The audience applauded loudly.

Lexa and Russ were given the seats of honor at a long table. The preliminary speeches by officers of the Voters' League, local officials, and their wives were hackneyed, pointless, and interminable. At last, Lexa was given the floor. The applause was thunderous.

'Hello, everyone.' Lexa's smile outshone the spotlights. 'I love being in Delaware because of statistics. Delaware is the forty-ninth State in terms of area, forty-sixth in population – and first for having wonderful people with warm, open hearts.'

That brought down the house. She does have a touch, Russ mused. The house grew quiet. Lexa launched into her extemporaneous speech. She fed the audience what they believed were intimate glimpses into the life and workloads of President Talbot, larded in appealing – and sometimes seemingly revealing – anecdotes that extolled his countless virtues. She spoke for the twenty minutes alloted her, then asked for questions. They were predictable, asked mainly by women.

'Miss Talbot, do you manage household affairs in the White House?'

'I try. Thank heavens there are competent people to help, or I'd make a horrible mess of things.'

Laughter.

'Do you cook for President Talbot?'

'Sometimes – when Daddy's tired and wants a quiet supper. We have a small kitchen in the Family Quarters.'

'What do you make for him?'

'Oh – I'll fry chicken or put together an omelette.'

Solemn murmurs of praise for the loving, dutiful daughter.

Fifteen minutes and the question-period was over. It was Russell Hatch's turn. He stood up, received appreciably less applause than Lexa.

'Good evening, ladies and gentlemen. As your distinguished Voters' League president said when he introduced me, I'm from Oregon. Our state motto out there is "The Union". Yours here in Delaware is "Liberty and Independence". We're smack on the same wavelength.'

A round of polite applause. Then a heckler jumped to his feet. 'Screw your mottoes!' he bellowed. 'Talbot ran for President on a motto – "Renew America" – and the country's ready for the junkyard.'

Guards moved to seize the heckler. Russ, recognizing an opportunity, spoke loudly into his microphone. 'Leave the gentleman alone, please.' The guards halted, edged back to their posts.

'I ran on that motto, too,' Hatch said, reverting to normal tones. 'For two years, President Talbot has been making every effort to renew America. I can attest to that.' *Can I? No, but Talbot's moved off his ass and I've given my word to help him.* 'President Talbot himself admitted he hadn't done too well on Sunday night, and he announced fresh efforts . . .'

Applause started. Russ held up his hand. It stopped.

'. . . President Talbot took all the blame in his own shoulders – but the mistakes were really made by other men. That includes many of us in the Legislative branch.

179

We delayed on his programs. Now, perhaps, led by the President, we'll all get cracking and carry out his pledge to renew America. To do this, we need your support – not gibes and hecklings.'

Good, solid outbursts of handclapping and some cheers.

Russ used the remainder of his twenty-minute time-ration to paraphrase much of what Talbot said on Sunday night and received loud – although by no means deafening applause. He asked for questions. The queries from the floor were largely concerned with Talbot's announced proposals for new legislation to help labor, farmers, and small business. Hatch made generalized replies, but made them sound as though they were direct, specific. The audience was satisfied. The tall, frank-faced young Senator with his unruly mop of red hair could not be possibly telling anything less than the whole truth. Russ was rewarded with an ovation.

The customary post-orgastic reception followed. It was held in the suburban home of an extremely wealthy officer of the Wilmington Voters' League.

'Hear you're a lawyer,' the host said, drawing Russ aside.

'Yes, I had my practice in Portland.'

'Your own firm?'

'A partnership. I sold my share when I was elected.'

'Sure.' A wink and a jovial smile. 'My companies do considerable business out in Oregon. They're always on the lookout for reliable law firms, and they pay high retainer fees.'

The hoariest of influence-buying ploys, Russ thought. A legislator's former law firm collects fat fees and kicks part of them back to him. Some people have said I look naïve. I sure as hell must, or this asshole would have at least been more subtle.

'Sorry,' Hatch said. 'I'm not a peddler.' He walked away.

The sweaty industrialist stared after him. Well, cover me in shit, he mused. An honest Senator.

Lexa and Russ eventually managed to extricate themselves.

Russ offered to do the driving back to Washington. Lexa refused.

'I like to drive,' she said.

Russ studied her finely etched profile. She does, he reflected. It gives her a sense of having control. 'The universal Washington obsession,' he said, grinning. 'Everybody wants to be in the driver's seat.'

'Pretty much the same everywhere else, no?'

'Allowing for a matter of degree, I suppose you're right.'

Lexa slid him a sidewise look. 'Don't tell me you haven't any higher ambitions.' Her eyes went back to watching the road. 'Political ambitions, I mean.'

'None beyond racking up a decent record during my term in the big debating society.'

Lexa laughed. 'What, no secret hopes running for President?'

'Nope. I doubt if I'll even run for reelection to the Senate.'

She took her right hand from the steering wheel and patted his shoulder. 'You're kidding yourself, Russ.' The scent of her perfume tantalized Hatch. 'The bug will bite – just wait.' She took her hand away. 'My guess is it already has, but you don't realize it. *I* do, though. I watched you on that dopey stage, drinking up the applause, getting almost as big a kick out of it as I did – and always do.'

Did I? Russ wondered, mulled for a moment or two, and reluctantly admitted to himself that he had enjoyed the experience.

'You were the one who brought down the house, Lexa,' he said.

'Long practice – plus the Lexa Talbot mystique built by Christ knows how many of Daddy's p.r. men.' She grinned broadly. 'We made a great act together, though. Talbot and Hatch, the dynamic duo with their adult patter and clever chatter.'

'You make it sound like straight show business.'

'Show biz, politics – same difference. Haven't you noticed?'

'I have.' And how. 'Like the old Romans said. Give 'em bread and the circus.' Politics and Government were

Barnum and Bailey. Jugglers, clowns, brass bands, tight-rope walkers. Suzy called me a Talbot Administration tightrope walker last week. Maybe I am at that.

'Next time, we'll use your car and you can drive – be in the driver's seat,' Lexa said suddenly.

'Next time?'

'Why break up the act? We might even put it on the road.' There was a husky undertone in Lexa's voice. It carried hints of promise that made Russell Hatch's blood pump faster. No, he decided, best not to read – or misread – anything into it.

'We need a good agent,' he said, holding the conversation at a bantering level.

'We have the best, partner.'

'Namely?'

'President Charles P. Talbot – who else?'

17

Washington, D.C.: Tuesday, February 23.

A daily log of the President's movements and activities is kept by his Appointments Secretary. While literally a minute-by-minute record, it lists only the barest facts. Whatever transpires between the President and the people with whom he meets or speaks is recorded elsewhere – or nowhere save as parenthetical recollections in the minds of the individuals involved. On February 23, President Charles Talbot had a full day – as the log showed:

0810: The President had breakfast.

(Lexa joined her father, pronounced the Wilmington foray a success and urged that she and Russell Hatch make other public appearances.)

0833: The President went to the Oval Office.

(Talbot read news-media summaries. They were highly favorable.)

0855–0931: The President met with Senator Daniel Madigan and Representative Bradford Cooley.

(Talbot told Cooley he would make $50 million in discretionary funds available to Alabama under Section XXI of the Miller Act. Cooley promised prompt action of the $10 billion domestic aid bill.)

0932–0956: The President met with his Chief Adviser, Kenneth Ramsey.

(They discussed routine matters.)

0958–1019: The President met with Secretary of State MacDonald Pearce and Defense Secretary John Kurtz.

(Pearce and Kurtz gave encouraging reports on the situation in Basanda. The new Prime Minister had rescinded the late Odu Mwandi's orders withdrawing Loyalist troops from outlying areas.)

1024–1132: The President held a meeting in the Roosevelt Room.

(Party kingmakers, including Jordan B. Rickhoven III, converged on Washington for an inside briefing on Talbot's intentions. They left content that while he was putting on a great show, he still toed the line and, in the end, they would gain much.)

1140–1202: The President met with Senate President Pro Tempore Early Frobase.

(Talbot bartered a promise to soft-pedal civil rights issues in return for Frobase's guarantee of a 'solid South' for six months.)

1205–1220: The President greeted nominees for vacant Cabinet posts.

1225–1335: The President lunched with the Cabinet nominees.

1341–1402: The President met with Representative Earle Clay of New Jersey.

(Clay was Black and the de facto spokesman for black legislators in both Houses. Talbot bartered a promise to press for more civil rights legislation in return for Clay's guarantee that his black colleagues would support the Administration's new policies and programs.)

1409–1415: The President met with Defense Secretary John Kurtz.

(They agreed General Merle Littlefield should succeed General Weidener as Chairman of the Joint Chiefs of Staff.)

1420–1455: The President met with Senator Aaron Kugelman of New York.

(His eye ever on the Jewish vote, Talbot promised yet more aid to Israel and said the United States would buy more oil from Basanda, saying, 'That'll squeeze the Arabs a little.' Kugelman in return pledged he would beat the drums for the Administration among his constituents and the numerous Jewish organizations to which he belonged.)

1501–1509: The President met with Legislative Counsel Lester DeMont.

(DeMont stated the $10 billion emergency appropriations bill would be ready for submission to Congress within a day or two.)

There were twelve additional log entries for the day, the last being:

2105: The President departed from the Mansion to attend a private social function.

After his inauguration, a newly elected American President traditionally enjoys a 'Hundred-Day Honeymoon' with the news media and even political opponents. He is allowed the grace period in which to effect the transition of power, adjust and acclimate, and formulate policies. After it is over, he and his Administration are fair game.

Charles Talbot had been no exception to the unwritten rule. But, a little more than three months after he took office, the 'Honeymoon' ended. Media criticism and public dissatisfaction began and mounted. Opponents in and out of Washington sniped at his Administration. Anti-Talbot sentiment grew steadily, reaching a virulent peak after he completed the second year of his term.

But when Talbot ordered troops to trouble-plagued cities, made his moving speech at General Weidener's graveside, and then followed it with his February 21 speech, he worked a miracle. The tide of criticism was not only stemmed, but reversed. On Tuesday morning, a quick-skim Gallup poll showed that Charles Talbot's nationwide popularity rating had soared an incredible twenty-one points.

Lady Marjorie Norworth had had one of her spur-of-the-instant inspirations. At 8:30 A.M., she telephoned Daniel Madigan at his home.

'I have a fantastic idea, Dan! Charlie is on top again – it's as though he's just been reelected by another landslide. I want to give a very special party for him *tonight* – a huge party with a Second Honeymoon theme. He should be able to come, don't you think?'

Madigan's instincts told him such an event would be of immense benefit to Talbot and his political party.

'Brad Cooley and I are meeting with him in fifteen minutes,' Madigan said. 'I'll ask him and call you back pronto.'

Madigan broached the subject to Talbot during the 0855–0931 meeting (noted in the daily log) that he and Cooley had with the President in the Oval Office. Brad Cooley agreed with Madigan that Marjorie's party idea was excellent. They both urged Talbot to attend.

'Hell, yes!' Talbot said. He was riding a crest and could afford to show himself – and be one of the guys again. 'Tell Marjorie I'll be there – no, I'll do it myself.' He reached for his private-line telephone and called the House on the Hill.

Marjorie Norworth and her domestic staff spent a hectic morning and afternoon. Caterers, decorators, florists and others had to be called and told, 'Price is no object, but everything *must* be done – and to perfection – by this evening.'

Marjorie and her social secretary went down the long list of men to be invited, telephoned them. All were acutely aware that Charles Talbot had become very much The Man In Charge. They grasped the implications of the 'Second Honeymoon' party theme and realized it was an event they could not afford to miss. Their political futures could well depend on their being present to pay Talbot homage.

Marjorie's own female servants and the caterer's waitresses wore white bridal costumes. Male servants – hers and those furnished by the catering firm – were dressed like best men at formal weddings. A piano player engaged for the occasion managed the improbable task of hastily arranging a tune that blended melodies of 'Here Comes the Bride' and 'Hail to the Chief'. Buffet tables set up in the replica of the State Dining Room of the White House were laden with foods sufficient for an army of gourmets – or gourmands.

There was more fresh caviar (at $132 per pound) than ever seen at Russian or Iranian embassy receptions, more (and finer) vintage champagne than any French Ambassador ever provided for his guests. Knowing the special tastes of her guests in all things, Marjorie made a final check with Holcomb and her chef.

Charles Talbot doted on lobster thermidor. Aaron Kugelman preferred smoked Nova Scotia salmon to caviar. Fresh pear juice for Brad Cooley in case this would be a night when he preferred *bellinis* to straight bourbon. And so down the list of American political figures to the foreign Ambassadors. Blazing-hot curry for Sir Leslie Holloway, the ramrod straight and brilliantly dry-witted British Ambassador. (He and his Scottish-born, delightfully charming wife, Margaret, were among Marjorie Norworth's favorite people. She had known them for years and regretted that her parties were invariably stag affairs. She would have loved seeing Lady Margaret Holloway.) The Yugoslav Ambassador drank only absinthe, although technically illegal because of its powdered wormwood content, it was readily available in Washington – if one knew a source, and Marjorie naturally did. At last satisfied there had been no omissions or oversights, Marjorie went to her suite, where she bathed and dressed for the evening.

She was ecstatic. And why shouldn't I be, she asked herself, humming a few bars of a Cole Porter tune. Charles Talbot may be the official guest of honor, but this party is really for me. Charlie would still be drowning in manure if I hadn't instructed him, chapter and verse – down to the last line, word and syllable.

As was his habit whenever Marjorie Norworth gave an elaborate party, Bradford Cooley arrived half an hour early. Overplump fingers curled around a glass of bourbon – it wasn't a *bellini* night – he waddled at Marjorie's side as she took him on a tour of the ground-floor rooms in which the party was to be held.

'Corn,' Cooley snickered when they completed the circuit and sat down in the facsimile of the Green Room. 'But your guests will glut themselves on it, and the assembled notables will prostrate themselves before Talbot.'

He took a swallow of whiskey, grimaced and said, 'Sad to say, I doubt if his second political honeymoon will last very long.'

'That depends on Charlie,' Marjorie said. *Or, to be more accurate, on me*, she added to herself.

'Only within very narrow limits. Others are doing the fishing. He's merely cutting bait for them, although he doesn't realize it.'

'And you're *dangling* bait in front of me. What have you been hearing, Brad?'

'Remember our talking about Weidener some days ago?'

'Yes.'

'Emmett Hopper . . .'

Marjorie interrupted him with a chuckle. 'Never has any Washington love-affair lasted longer.'

'It has lasted, hasn't it?' Cooley smiled, then turned serious. 'But I didn't mention Emmett to start a discussion of my sex life. Emmett has conclusive evidence that Weidener was killed by Howard Denby's CIA thugs.'

Marjorie showed no emotion. Many deaths said to be 'due to natural causes' were anything but.

Cooley went on, telling her what he and Hopper knew – and what they suspected. 'Pearce, Rickhoven, Kurtz, Madigan, Denby,' he ticked off the names. 'They're all the ingredients necessary for the unmaking of a President.'

A deep frown distorted the classic planes of Marjorie's face. She believed Cooley. Inwardly, she was boiling with rage. Working in concert, the men he named could manipulate Charles Talbot however they wished. This would destroy her own Grand Plan for making herself the power behind Talbot and his Administration.

'The evidence Emmett has simply isn't enough. It only implicates the CIA agents directly involved, and Denby – as everyone knows – considers them expendable.' Cooley sighed. 'Unfortunately, Emmett and his downgraded FBI have no J. Edgar Hoover-type dossiers with which to exert influence and pressure . . .'

'With which to blackmail,' Marjorie corrected.

'Mere semantics,' Cooley shrugged. 'My point is that you

have the materials for overkill on a scale that staggers even my utterly depraved imagination. I refer, of course, to the stores of information you've told me you have, but which I have never seen.'

'Nor will you – or anyone else.' Marjorie forced a smile. 'I'm afraid you and Emmett, the co-conspirators . . .'

'Co-*counter*conspirators would be closer to the truth.'

'Mere semantics, as you just said. In any case, what do *you* hope to gain, Brad?'

'Personally, little if anything. I've passed the age and stage where I'm driven by ambition. But two more years of a Charles Talbot controlled by a Madame de Maintenon is infinitely preferable to what we'll have if he's controlled by Rickhoven, Pearce *et al*.'

Marjorie was silent, solemn, then brightened. 'We'll talk about it again,' she said. 'Tonight, I'm going to concentrate on my party and on being a nonpareil hostess.'

Nearly three hundred formally attired guests milled about, gathering in knots, trading information and gossip, discussing Charles Talbot's astounding 'comeback', or simply drinking and listening. When the arrival of the Presidential limousine was announced, all conversation ceased. Men gravitated – some pushed and shoved – toward the entrance foyer. Holcomb held the doors open. Lady Marjorie Norworth was poised to welcome Talbot. The pianist pounded out his mélange of 'Here Comes the Bride' and 'Hail to the Chief'.

Talbot strode inside, bringing with him an aura of the conquering hero and half a dozen Secret Service men. He and Marjorie hugged and kissed each other. Normal rules of protocol did not apply at the House on the Hill. The men who thrust themselves forward most forcibly, not those of highest rank, were the first to shake the President's hand. Following Lady Norworth's instructions, each guest saluted Talbot with the same words:

'Happy Second Honeymoon, Mr President.'

Talbot noted that Marjorie had accomplished several improbables and impossibles. There were politicians of both major parties present – and several members of each who hated each other personally and made a practice of avoiding social affairs at which they might encounter one another. The turnout of foreign ambassadors was remarkable, for the party was patently an American political affair. Talbot preened himself, taking what he saw as proof that his triumph was universally accepted.

Russell Hatch was among the last to greet Talbot.

'Good seeing you, Russ,' Talbot grinned. 'Lexa tells me you did a fine piece of work at that Wilmington clambake. Thanks.'

Hatch moved on to let the next well-wisher approach the President.

MacDonald Pearce took a demure sip of champagne.

'Lady Norworth does have a flair for entertaining,' he said. The remark was banal, even inane, but it served as an opener.

'If she wasn't so rich already, she could make a fortune organizing bar mitzvahs,' Aaron Kugelman said. *Okay, Pearce, the next line is yours*, he thought. *I'm curious to hear what it'll be.*

The Secretary of State screwed his face into what he considered a jolly expression. 'That conjures up an amusing picture, Senator. Imagine everyone here going to a Lady Norworth bar mitzvah.'

'Wearing *yarmulkas* – a scream.' *Get to it, schmuck!*

'Yes, a scream. Absolutely.' Pearce wet his lips with champagne again. 'Oh, incidentally – has President Talbot spoken to you about his intentions to increase aid to Israel?'

'He did. This afternoon.'

'You might pass a hint along to the Israeli Ambassador – without quoting the President or me directly, of course.'

Kugelman was anything but a fool. 'So what's the t\ztkeh for *tschatchkeh*?'

'I'm sorry, but . . .'

'The tit for the tat, Mr Secretary.'

'Ah, you've read or heard the statements made by the new Basandan Prime Minister, I assume.'

'Sure. He's promising free elections – in the future. Which might be the Hereafter, for all we know.'

'Come, come, Senator. We have the whip hand. We'll hold him to his word, and you can do much to help. You have a large – ah, liberal – following among people of all religious persuasions. If you would make a statement or two indicating approval of the new Prime Minister, it would make the State Department's task that much easier.'

'Toss in a sweetener, and we have a deal. Your Department leaks just enough confirmation on more aid to Israel so that people don't think I'm talking through *my yarmulka*. Then I'll shout at the top of my lungs that Percival Kwida is a latter-day George Washington. Agreed?'

MacDonald Pearce nodded. 'Agreed, Senator.'

The Agriculture Department Secretary-designate found himself cornered by Early Frobase.

'One question,' Frobase drawled. 'What about cotton and tobacco subsidies?'

'I'll recommend to the President that they be raised as much as possible,' came the reply.

'All I wanted to hear,' Frobase chuckled. 'You won't have any problems with the Senate. We're going to get along fine and dandy.'

Frobase sought out Dan Madigan, led him to a deserted corner of the Blue Room.

'Some of our folks down South haven't been too happy about getting mixed up any deeper in Basanda,' he began – unnecessarily, for Madigan knew all too well that Frobase and several of his Dixie colleagues had taken a dovish stand. 'We're not raring to pull chestnuts out of the fire for a bunch of African nigras.' He leered. 'That doesn't mean we can't reassess our stand, though.'

'What'll it cost, Early?'

'I just talked with the bird who's taking over the Agriculture Department. He mentioned he'll try to up cotton and tobacco subsidies. You willing to bring the Northern boys in the Senate in line?'

'Yep.'

'Dan, I figure the South can get color blind – forget that Basandans are nigras, if you get my drift.'

'I do, Early. Consider the logs rolled.'

There was a scream and a crash of breaking china and glassware. A Texas Congressman had thrust his hand up the skirt of a bridal-gowned waitress carrying a heavily loaded tray. Another Congressman – from Utah – promptly punched the Texan, who thereupon kicked the Utah Representative in the genitals. Secret Service agents and security guards hired by Lady Norworth grabbed both men and led them off.

John Kurtz was spooning caviar into his mouth. He felt a hand touch his shoulder, turned.

'Oh, hello, Eccleston.' Mark Eccleston was a three-star general and Chief of the Army's Ordnance Department, but like the other guests, he wore a civilian dinner jacket.

Eccleston made certain there was no one within hearing distance. 'I'm leap-frogging the chain of command, Mr Secretary.' His eyes mocked the gravity of his voice. 'I considered it in the best interests of the service to report to you directly. Someone fouled up.' Both men knew this was no report, but confirmation that a prearranged gambit had been played.

'Oh?' Kurtz maintained the pretense nonetheless. 'What happened?'

'Ten unarmed air-rescue copters were supposed to be shipped to BMAG. There was a snafu. Ten gunships went out instead – aboard C-5-A transports that took off at six this evening.'

'It would be a waste of money to recall them,' Kurtz said. 'I suppose the BMAG commander can have the guns removed – if that's what he decides to do. What about your paperwork and records?'

'Damn it, sir, that's another goof. All the documents seem to have gotten lost in the shuffle. I can't estimate how long it'll take to find them.'

'Do your best, Eccleston.' Kurtz winked. 'No one could expect you to do more.'

The President and a dozen of his former Senate colleagues were trading stories from the days when Talbot was the Majority Leader in the Upper House. A Secret Service man interrupted them.

'Chief Justice Braithwaite would like to have a word with you, Mr President.'

'Be right back,' Talbot said over his shoulder, followed the agent to the foyer. Braithwaite was ready to leave.

'I wanted to say good night and God bless you, Chuck,' he said. 'You'll enjoy far, far more than a second hundred-day honeymoon. But as yet, only you and I know that.' He clasped Talbot's hand in both of his, and there was an almost fanatical glow in his eyes.

Damn, but Avery seemed odd, Talbot mused as he returned to his Senate friends. Oh, hell, he probably just had a drink too many.

The party was growing more boisterous. Marjorie Norworth singled out Emmett Hopper, led him to a tiny, secluded sitting room. She told him that Brad Cooley had spoken to her.

'I thought I could put what he said out of my mind – at least for tonight – but I can't,' she declared. 'I'd like a short, straightforward cross-reading from you, Emmett.'

'Certainly. There are people who want to involve us in what at very best, will be a limited war – and at worst lead to allout nuclear conflict. Even if the war is limited they envision declarations of national emergency by a President who mutely takes orders from them. Then, two years from now, a rigged election – or no election of any sort . . .'

'Impossible!'

Hopper only gave a tired shrug.

'You and Brad want me to involve myself . . .'

'Neither of us will try to influence you further, Marjorie. Any decision will be your own.'

*

The Chairman of the Securities and Exchange Commission was very drunk.

'You motherfucker!' he bellowed at the Undersecretary of Commerce and swung an empty champagne bottle at his head. The Undersecretary, also drunk, staggered back. The bottle missed, but he fell on the floor of the Green Room and began to vomit.

It was 2:15 A.M. Time, Lady Marjorie thought, to bring the party to an end and ease the thinned-out crowd on its way home.

Many of those who took her hints and obediently left were surprised that Charles Talbot, the guest of honor, was not in the foyer to accept their good-night obeisances. However, some noticed that his Secret Service bodyguards remained, trying in vain to appear inconspicuous. The departing guests had to content themselves with thanking Lady Norworth profusely for what, they all agreed, was an ingeniously conceived and magnificently executed party.

Dan Madigan alone asked the direct question, whispering it into Marjorie's ear as he kissed her cheek. 'Where's The Man?'

'None of your business, Dan,' she whispered in reply.

Madigan leered knowingly. Obviously, Marjorie Norworth, the *ne plus ultra* of Washington hostesses, had carried the 'Second Honeymoon' party theme through to its ultimate conclusion. The President of the United States was upstairs – getting laid.

18

Washington, D.C.: Wednesday, February 24

Kenneth Ramsey sat near the Presidential desk, reading out summaries of news media reports and comments.

'Amost all kudos and kowtows,' he commented. 'You couldn't ask for more or better, Chief.' He thought Talbot would be cheered, happy. But the President was withdrawn, remote, and there were deep circles under his eyes. Probably has a hangover, Ramsey guessed. It must have been one hell of a party. 'Would you like to have the doc give you a shot or pill?' he asked solicitously.

'No!' Talbot snapped. 'Just get out of here and see that I'm left alone this morning.'

That's no hangover talking, Ramsey thought, leaving the Oval Office. He's in lousy mental shape – but why, now that he's sitting on top of the world again? What could possibly be eating away at him?

Russ studied the Van Dyck portrait in Dan Madigan's private office. 'It's great,' he observed. 'From Van Dyck's Genoese period.'

'Christ, are you an art expert?' Madigan asked.

'Hardly. Once took a few courses in art history, though.'

A point to remember, the Senate Majority Leader thought. The artsy-craftsy set would flip over a Senator who knew about art and artists. 'The President wants you briefed ASAP, Russ,' he said. 'I'm squeezing in half an hour this morning to start you off.' He leaned forward, resting elbows on desk. 'Sit down. I'll make it quick. Everybody says you were terrific in Wilmington. The Administration's going to be using you to present its case to the public – speeches, TV and radio appearances . . .'

'Dan, except for Suzanne Loring, I haven't any media contacts.'

'You don't need 'em. The strings will be pulled by p.r. people on the White House payroll. They get in touch with network executives who support the party or want something from the Administration. As for clubs, organizations, colleges – shit! They're always asking for speakers. Some even pay two, three thousand bucks plus expenses.'

'The lecture-circuit gravy-train,' Russ interposed dryly. Senior members of both Houses augmented their salaries with fees for 'speaking engagements'. He grinned. 'Freshman senators don't ride it.'

'Holy Mary and nine archangels! You're Talbot's Fair-Haired Boy. You'll be swamped with invitations.'

Russ frowned. 'And I'll be expected to give speeches canned for me by the Party, I suppose.'

'Nope. Write 'em yourself, or talk extempo, like you did . . .'

'Hold on. First I'm told I'll be getting two committee appointments. Now, it's speeches . . .'

'Right. Where's the problem?'

'How will I find time to do committee work and also read up and do research on subjects I know nothing about?'

'Son, committee work is a cinch, ask any old-timer. And whenever you make a speech, the press-relations monkeys do the research for you.'

Hatch lit a Pall Mall. 'Like I said, canned material. Suppose I don't like the *research* that's packaged and given me?'

'Goddamnit, be realistic. If you don't agree with basic Administration policies, you're on the wrong team. If you differ on minor points, go ahead and express your own opinions – that's healthy.'

'You mean a little meaningless dissent will make the main thrust all the more convincing.'

This bastard may not be so easy to keep tame, Madigan reflected, but so what? It's as easy to knock a front man down as it is to build him up. 'Sure,' he nodded. 'Give a little, gain a lot. It's sound psychology, even sounder politics.' He would have said more, but a female voice came over his intercom.

'The VFW delegation has arrived, Senator Madigan.'

'I'll be right out,' Madigan told the intercom, and turned to Russ. 'Veterans lobbying for more benefits – what else is new? – and I've got to salute. Drop by at four. We'll pick up where we left off.'

Suzanne Loring reached Russ by phone after he returned to his office.

'Care to take me to lunch, Senator?'

'Stupid question. I'll book a table at the Sans Souci for one o'clock.'

'The Sans Souci?'

'I'm making a survey of upper-class eating habits. Incidentally, I have more news with which to fascinate and regale you.'

'I'll promise to listen, guru.'

The girl slept until ten-thirty, showered, dressed, and, following instructions given her the night before, went to Marjorie Norworth's suite. Marjorie, wearing a white quilted satin robe, was just starting on the breakfast Holcomb brought to her sitting room. Her breakfast menu never varied: orange juice, yogurt, whole-grain toast (one slice, unbuttered) and black coffee.

'Hungry, Claire?' she asked the girl, who was unusually attractive and had long, straight blond hair. 'I'll ring Holcomb if you are.'

'No, thanks, Lady Norworth.'

'Not even coffee? There's an extra cup and saucer.'

'Yes, I'd like some coffee,' Claire smiled. 'Would you like to hear the details?' Marjorie nodded, grinning, and poured coffee. 'Well, it went just as you said it would,' Claire said.

'I wasn't *quite* that positive, my dear.'

'You told me certain things would probably happen. They did.'

'Please go on. I can't stand suspense.'

'Okay. I was wearing the satin wedding dress and the gray contact lenses. He came into the room. He couldn't see me clearly, only the tiny lamp was on, but he wasn't at all surprised . . .'

'He knew there would be someone.'

'First thing he noticed was the wedding gown. "Marjorie sure can wrap a honeymoon present right," he said. Anyway, the dress had all those little covered buttons down the back. He started undoing them, but stopped every now and then to stroke and kiss my hair . . .'

'Ah-hah!' Marjorie Norworth's eyes narrowed.

'When he undid about half the buttons. I switched on the lamp that's like a spotlight. It shined on my face. My God, what an effect! He stared at me and began to tremble – and I mean tremble.'

'You spoke to him?'

'Like you told me to. I asked him if there was anything wrong. He sort of groaned and said, "You have gray eyes, too."'

'All honor to whoever invented tinted contact lenses.'

'He was wearing all his clothes but he had this fantastic erection.' Claire drank coffee, giggled. 'I was afraid it might punch right through his trousers. He finally got himself to talk again and asked me what my name was. I gave him the answer you said I should. "It's Alexandra, but my friends call me Sandra for short."'

The girl drained her coffee cup, continued. 'He really freaked out then. "Has – has anyone ever called you Lexa?" he asked me, stammering and stuttering. I told him no, but he could. That did it. He ripped the wedding dress off me, kept on repeating "Lexa, Lexa" – and I found out what it's like to be with a sex maniac. He kept on for hours – came *five* times, can you imagine?'

'I can,' Marjorie chuckled. She went to her desk, took money from a drawer and gave it to the girl.

'Lady Norworth!' Claire exclaimed. 'This is a thousand – double what . . .'

'You've more than earned it, my dear.' Marjorie Norworth now felt certain of something she had long suspected, and the knowledge would strengthen her hold on Charles Talbot. I'll test, flex my muscles, she thought when the girl departed. Picking up her telephone, she punched out the direct-line Oval Office number.

The President remained alone after ordering Ramsey out of the Oval Office. He sat staring into space, unable to clear his mind of the thoughts and images boiling through it. When his private telephone gave off its muted hum, he reached for it gratefully. Any diversion would be welcome – as long as he did not need to see another person.

'Yes?'

'Good morning, Charlie.'

Talbot paled. Marjorie Norworth's voice served as a deep-stabbing reminder. Her call might mean something even worse. 'I – I was going to call you later and thank you for the party,' he stammered.

'You're more than welcome. You deserved it, Charlie. It reminded me of the old days and FDR . . .'

Talbot's tensions eased off a half-turn. She was chattering.

'. . . but I have a reason for phoning you . . .'

The tension screw tightened.

'. . . I read the papers and had a brainstorm. The soldiers you sent to Detroit and other cities – order them back to their bases . . .'

'Uh – what's that, Marjorie?'

'Here's your keynote. The people are showing confidence in their elected representatives. Therefore, the Government is showing its confidence in the people. Trim it with tinsel about State's Rights and the fundamental common sense of the American public, and you'll hear more and louder hurrahs . . .

Talbot unspooled. Marjorie was calling to give him good advice – and for no other reason, thank God.

'. . . don't delay or allow anyone to talk you out of it . . .'

'I won't, Marjorie – and thanks again. For everything.'

Replacing the receiver, Talbot called for Ken Ramsey.

'Sorry I was so cranky this morning, Ken.'

Ramsey smiled. Talbot was looking much better.

'Get Kurtz. I want the troops we sent to trouble-spots recalled immediately.' Talbot was emphatic. 'I mean *immediately*.'

Ramsey blinked. 'Isn't that being dangerously premature, Chief?'

'Nope. Here's the press statement. The fundamental common sense of the American public has prevailed. The people have demonstrated confidence in the Administration – no, make it in their elected representatives. It behooves Government to demonstrate its confidence in the people. The Federal Arm must not usurp State's Rights except in grave emergencies – blah-blah. You fix it up.'

Not bad at all, Ramsey found himself concurring. There were times when Charles Talbot had ideas that were pure genius.

The Sans Souci on 17th Street is outrageously expensive. It is more showcase than restaurant, catering to those at the uppermost influence-and-power levels who wish to flaunt their wealth and connections. The cuisine is French and, while good, not superior. The decor strives to be altogether luxurious – with dark wood paneling, rich leathers, elaborate crystal chandeliers and masses of fresh-cut flowers. The walls are adorned with reproductions of French Impressionist paintings. These are too-perfect copies, like so much else in Washington, pretentious counterfeits.

Suzanne Loring and Russell Hatch were led to a banquette. She ordered a bloody mary, he a bullshot. The drinks arrived in a moment.

'You missed my show last night,' Suzanne said, reaching for her glass. 'I dismantled Joey Skeffington, God's gift to God.'

Russ laughed. The Reverend Joey Skeffington – silver-haired, golden-voiced and all-dross phony – made Big Business out of Old-Time Religion and had served as ex-officio Religious Adviser to four Presidents. All Washington despised him, but feared his power among Bible Belt voters.

'The Second Honeymoon blowout at Lady Marjorie's was quite a show, too,' Russ said. 'I gawked like a tourist.'

'You should have swaggered, old buddy. I drink to your meteoric rise.'

Hatch sampled his bullshot. 'It's left me baffled about the whys and wherefores, honey.'

You're being set up as a fall guy, Suzanne told him mentally. Aloud, she said: 'Everybody has to win occasionally. Now tell me the latest.'

'For one thing, they want me to do a lot of speechifying, some of it with Lexa . . .'

'Lexa Talbot?'

Russ failed to notice the sharp cocking of Suzanne's eyebrow or the acid in her tone. 'None other than. Y'know, she's got terriffic presence. The audience in Wilmington went wild over her.'

Not only the audience, Suzanne mused sourly, claws out as she saw Russ's expression when he spoke of Lexa. 'I think I'll invite her to appear on my show, bill it as the Battle of the Bitches.'

'Oh, shit, honey. She's not like that . . .'

'But *I* am?'

Russ flushed, completely disoriented. He drained his glass, signaled for another round. 'Jesus Christ! I said nothing of the sort. I meant . . .'

'Never mind,' Suzanne relented. 'Regale me – like you promised – with tales of last night's revels.'

Russ breathed a sigh of relief. 'Except for the frills, it was straight Washington. Talbot was smothered with congratulations. Some characters got together and made their deals. Others swapped information, lies, dirty jokes or all three. Late at night, when everybody was practically drowned in booze, a few punches were thrown.'

'Were Pearce and Kurtz there?'

'Of course.'

'How did they act – glum, pissed off?'

'Hell, no. Calm, collected, happy. And why not?'

'Because they're hardlining hawks. Talbot junked the Basanda aid bill they've been pushing. How could that make 'em happy?'

'Talbot cleaned out the Cabinet, but he let them stay. My guess it was a trade-off. They agreed to back down on the bill in exchange for job security.'

'Possible.' But I don't believe it. 'By the way, did you hear that Talbot ordered the Army out of Detroit and other points east, west, north, and south? It came over the Telex as I was leaving the studio.'

Hatch was startled. 'News to me. Did the bulletin say why?'

'Our Fearless Leader is quoted as saying that Government has to show confidence in the public or some such crap.'

Russ called for a menu.

'Another flash,' Suzy went on. 'The Loyalists claim advances in Basanda. That's a strange and sudden switch, no?'

Russ stared his menu, shrugged. 'Maybe the new Prime Minister rallied his troops – or the Israeli arms arrived.'

Suzanne's deep brown eyes were fixed on her own menu. 'Mmm, the bouillabaisse tempts.' She glanced up. 'Coincidences are proliferating, Russ. Mwandi falls out of a copter. He barely hits the ground before Kwida flies out of Washington to take his place. In the meantime, back on Pennsylvania Avenue, Talbot withdraws the aid bill – leaving our African allies in the lurch. But they claim victories all of a sudden.'

'Huh? Oh, sorry – I was debating between duck and the *crabe en chemise*.' He frowned. 'When you put it that way m'love, I must admit there may be a fishy smell – and not from the bouillabaisse or crab.'

'Why not track the spoor, Senator?'

'I may. Could be somebody's double-shuffling behind Talbot's back. I'll do a little Sherlock Holmesing.'

Just as I am, Suzanne thought, then asked: 'What are you doing for dinner tonight?'

'Honey, that's not only the non sequitur of the century, it's a sign of gluttony. We haven't even ordered *lunch* yet.'

'But I'm going to cook again. After.'

'In that case, I'll walk over hot coals to be there.'

I'm making progress with him, Suzanne mused, giving Hatch a loving glance. I've stirred doubts in his mind, and being the kind of man he is, Russ won't rest until he's resolved them. He may even help me get my big scoop. She wanted it very much.

Defense Secretary John Kurtz occasionally lunched in one of the Pentagon's atrocious, concessionaire-operated snack-bar cafeterias. He gagged on the blotting-paper sandwiches and watery, chicory-flavored coffee. But he believed his presence among very junior officers, enlisted men and low pay-grade civilian employees boosted their morale.

Today, he spooned down what purported to be tomato soup, ate a ham sandwich and drank a Coca-Cola instead of coffee. Then, putting his trademark pipe into his mouth, he made a great show of taking cardboard plate, plastic bowl, and spoon and paper cup to the proper disposal receptacles. 'Hey, look – it's the Big Wheel himself,' he overheard a pink-cheeked corporal tell his companions. It was a gratifying reward for the atrocities he had committed against his palate and digestive tract, John Kurtz thought, and trudged through the maze of corridors to his office.

Two decoded EYES ONLY radio messages were waiting for him. Both had been sent by the BMAG commander in Kinsolo. The first read:

> PRIME MINISTER KWIDA HAS GIVEN HIMSELF TITLE OF NATIONAL SAVIOR AND IS PURGING BASANDAN ARMY. FORTY-THREE EXECUTIONS HAVE TAKEN PLACE IN KINSOLO ALONE DURING LAST FEW HOURS.

The second:

> CONTRARY TO KWIDA REGIME REPORTS OF LOYALIST VICTORIES, REBEL FORCES ARE ADVANCING ON BROAD FRONT. IN THE NORTH

THEY HAVE OVERRUN THE RICKHOVEN INTER-
NATIONAL METALS CORPORATION COPPER MINE
AT GIDUNA. ALL COMMUNICATIONS WITH GIDUNA
ARE OUT. WE HAVE NO INFORMATION FATE OF
AMERICAN CITIZENS EMPLOYED AT MINE BUT
BMAG HELICOPTERS WILL CONDUCT RECON-
NAISSANCE MISSIONS IF THESE ARE AUTHORIZED.

Kurtz had enormous difficulty keeping tomato soup, ham
sandwich and Coca-Cola down while he instructed an aide
to place five top-priority telephone calls. To Jordan B.
Rickhoven III, CIA Director G. Howard Denby, Secretary
of State MacDonald Pearce, Senate Majority Leader
Daniel Madigan – and President Charles Talbot.

'In that order, sir?' the aide asked politely.

'Goddamnit, yes – and move!' Kurtz barked. He poured
himself a glass of water from the thermos carafe on his desk,
drank it at one gulp, and hoped it might calm his churning
stomach.

19

Washington, D.C.: Thursday, February 25. Very Early Morning.

It had taken a very long time to locate Jordan B. Rickhoven
III. He was finally reached in London, and while he agreed
to leave for Washington without delay, his plane could not
possibly arrive before 1.00 A.M. Since no council on the
Basanda situation could be held without his presence, the
conference was scheduled for two o'clock in the morning.

Inside the White House, the atmosphere was tense,
volatile. Most of the regular staffers – aides, assistants,
secretaries – had been ordered to remain on duty through
the night. As yet, they had been given no work. Many
napped fitfully on couches or with heads resting on their
desks. Some even stretched out on the carpeted floors of
their offices. In the West Wing press lobby, a horde of media
correspondents clamored for statements, information, some
word from the President. They clamored in vain.

Charles Talbot, nerves held together by the hypodermic
injections his physician administered, was locked in the
Oval Office with Kenneth Ramsey. They said little to each
other as they listened to radio newscasts and waited.

'. . . and still no comment from White House or Defense
Department . . .'

Ramsey fiddled with a Chinese ceramic vase on the fireplace mantel. *There won't be any comment until Jordan Rickhoven has his say*, the President's Chief Adviser thought
bitterly.

'. . . the fate of over one hundred American supervisory
personnel and their dependants at Giduna remains
unknown . . .'

'What's your guess, Ken?' Talbot groaned. 'Are they alive?'

'I'm not guessing, Chief. I'm praying.'

'. . . some quarters speculate that Washington had advance warning of the developments. This theory is bolstered by yesterday's withdrawal of U.S. Army contingents from the five American cities to which they were sent only last week. All crack units, they may now be needed to form a strike force . . .'

Ramsey crossed the room, switched off the radio. His tough-guy features softened in sympathy for Talbot, who seemed to have shrivelled.

'That wasn't why the troops were recalled,' Talbot protested hoarsely. 'I was aiming . . .'

'To soothe and conciliate,' Ramsey nodded, finishing the sentence. 'It would have worked beautifully – except for the timing.'

The intercom announced that the men scheduled to attend the 2:00 A.M. conference had arrived. Ramsey went to the doors, admitted them. Pearce entered first, then Kurtz. Rickhoven and Denby were next. Madigan brought up the rear. Each shook hands with the President, then all five seated themselves. Ramsey stood, leaning against the fireplace.

'Who's been the closest to this thing?' Talbot asked.

'Imagine I have,' Kurtz replied. Opening an attaché case, he took out a sheaf of documents.

'Update me – fast,' the President said.

Kurtz looked at the papers in his hands. 'At eleven last night, I received a message from the BMAG commander stating that Prime Minister Kwida had carried out another two hundred executions in Kinsolo. The next message – some minutes later – said three of our CIA agents have been placed under arrest . . .'

'The ones aboard the chopper Mwandi fell out of?' Ramsey broke in.

'Can't tell,' Denby lied. 'No names were listed.'

'What's the difference?' Talbot snapped. 'They're our people.'

'As are those at Giduna,' Rickhoven interjected piously.

Kurtz lit his pipe. Madigan took a cigar from his pocket. Talbot directed his attention to MacDonald Pearce.

'What action have you taken, Mac?'

'Our Ambassador will lodge formal protests . . .'

'Striped pants routine,' Talbot growled. 'What about you, John?'

'BMAG personnel are on red alert,' Kurtz replied.

Talbot scowled. Dan Madigan's cigar glowed brightly as he spoke to the Defense Secretary. 'John, you told me there was a request from BMAG for authority to send copters to Giduna . . .'

'We don't dare,' the President interrupted. 'All BMAG aircraft are unarmed. The rebels can blast them out of the air.'

'Mr President.' John Kurtz spoke around his pipestem. 'The Ordnance Department yesterday made a serious blunder for which we can now thank God. By some mistake, ten helicopter gunships were airlifted to Kinsolo. They've arrived.'

Cocksuckers, Ramsey fumed silently. This is a fucking conjob, rehearsed down to the last throwaway line.

'I had prepared an order for their immediate return,' Kurtz added. 'It was to go out this afternoon. I've held it . . .'

'Lucky you did,' Madigan nodded sagely.

Talbot was silent. He felt trapped, back at Square One. He wished desperately that he could talk to Marjorie Norworth, ask her advice. It was impossible. The five men watching him intently had brought a complex of problems requiring instant decision.

'Can gunships protect rescue copters?' he asked finally.

'They should be adequate,' the Defense Secretary declared.

'What about Kwida?'

Pearce's bifocals flashed reflected light. 'He can be brought to hell. None of the discretionary funds have been made available to him yet. Our Ambassador will give Kwida an ultimatum. No aid will be forthcoming until he releases Denby's agents and halts the purges and executions.'

'My personal representative in Kinsolo will follow up,' Jordan Rickhoven said smoothly. 'Basanda derives much of its revenue from interests I control. We'll threaten to close all our mines and oilfields unless Kwida behaves himself.'

Like going to the dentist, Charles Talbot thought (he suffered intense dental anxiety). Fear, even terror, before. Then one momentary peak and the tooth is yanked. He gripped the arms of his chair – exactly as he did in dentists' offices.

'I'll authorize an air-evacuation mission, and send the gunships in to provide protective cover.' There, the tooth was out. Talbot relaxed his grip on the chair arms.

Ken Ramsey groaned audibly. No one took notice. The Chief fell for it, he thought. We're escalating – for the Greater Glory of the Rickhoven Empire. There was worse to come. He could see Talbot squaring his shoulders, winding up to make another pronouncement.

'As I recall, we're allowed to have limited combat forces to protect our advisory personnel,' Talbot said.

'Yes,' Pearce confirmed. 'We've sent none, though.'

'Situation never called for any before.' Talbot was regaining confidence, exercising his macho. 'Airlift two companies of the Green Beret battalion we pulled out of Pittsburgh, John. Make it clear they're not to fire a shot except to protect American lives.' He turned to Madigan. 'Dan, you'll explain what we're doing and why to the Senate and huddle with our leaders in the House. They can talk to me direct if that doesn't satisfy them.'

'Check,' Madigan nodded, asked, 'What about the press?'

'Ken, find Jim Zander,' Talbot said to his Chief Adviser. 'Get him at his home or wherever he may be. I want him here ASAP. We'll prepare statements for the new media. I think we have everything wrapped up for the moment – agreed?'

Everyone save Ramsey nodded and, led by MacDonald Pearce, stood up, shook hands with Talbot, told him he had made the right decisions – and filed out of the Oval Office.

*

Half an hour later, Ramsey reported that Zander was not to be found. 'He doesn't answer his phone, and I sent a man to his house in Georgetown. Nobody there.'

'Hell!' Talbot frowned. 'He's the only speechwriter who can craft the kind of statement we should issue.' The frown vanished, to be replaced by a lopsided grin. 'Get Emmett Hopper out of bed.'

'Hopper? What for?'

'He's sore because his FBI doesn't get any attention from me or the Administration. Tell him he'll make points with me if his agents can find Zander and bring him here by – what time is it now, three-fifteen? – by five o'clock. He'll bust his ass. Especially when you add that his people can kick down every door in the District if necessary. I'll cover them.'

'Chief . . .'

'Don't argue. Go yell in Hopper's ear.'

Despite its loss of status and reduced manpower, the FBI remained highly efficient. This was a result of Emmett Hopper's untiring efforts to hone the Bureau into a formidable instrument against the inevitable day when the CIA would lose favor.

Roused from his sleep, Hopper snapped alert when he heard Ramsey's voice on the telephone. When Ramsey had passed on the President's instructions, Hopper hung up and then used his scrambler-equipped phone to call the Night Agent-in-Charge at FBI headquarters in the J. Edgar Hoover Building. He relayed the information Ramsey had given him about James Zander.

'Send out every agent on night duty, call others – about thirty more, I'd say – and have them start scouring, too,' Hopper ordered. 'We have a clear field. Talbot seems to think it's important, and he'll back us, regardless. I'll be over there myself in twenty minutes.'

Informed they had 'a clear field', the score of agents on night duty went into action with a vengeance. Fists battered on the doors of Zander's neighbors. Blue-on-white FBI identification cards were flashed, agents pushed their way into entrance halls and living rooms, bombarded residents with questions, threats, more questions.

But it was the two FBI men who went to Zander's own house, picked the front door lock and went inside who struck paydirt. The interior of the house was shabby, unkempt. There were mats, but no furniture in the living room, and hash pipes were scattered around on the floor. Upstairs, the beds had rumpled, semen-stained sheets and there were jars and plastic bags of drugs in the bureau drawers.

'Jesus, we'll put this bastard away for life,' one agent said.

'I doubt it,' his partner retorted. 'We're supposed to take this bum Zander to the White House, not the slammer. We better tread carefully, friend – or we may find ourselves up to our ears in shit.'

He went downstairs, found a cheap memo-and-date book next to the telephone in the hallway. He flipped it open. An address on A Street Northeast was scrawled on the Wednesday, February 24, page. He copied it down, called to the other agent. They returned to their car, radioed headquarters and, after making their initial report, heard Director Emmett Hopper's voice come over the receiver.

'Leave everything as you found it,' Hopper said. 'Check out that address.'

'The whole neighborhood's swarming with our cars, sir. Shall we tell the agents . . .?'

'We'll worry about them. You worry about A Street.'

Part of A Street NE is lined with century-old houses that have been renovated and made into pleasant homes. Another part is a grimy slum. The address taken from the date book was that of a slum house, sagging, and scrofulous. The doorbell was disconnected or out of order. The door was equipped with three locks. The agents picked two, forced the third. They found a light switch, flicked it on, and saw a living room that was a seedier, dirtier version of Zander's – and a dozen or more naked figures lay in juxtaposed tangles on the mats. A few stirred, opened their eyes, promptly closed them again. A girl squirmed away from another girl, moved closer to a man. He did not move.

'Orgy – and they're all stoned.'

'Thanks for telling me – I never would have guessed – but we're looking for Zander. Lucky we have a good description – so let's start wading through the flesh.'

They found James Zander quickly, shook him. He failed to respond. 'Wiped out. I'll check in, you stay here.' The agent who spoke picked his way among the bodies, suddenly stopped dead. 'Holy Christ! Come over here.' He pointed to a blond girl who lay with her head nested in a man's crotch. 'Am I nuts, or is that . . .'

'It is, pal. That's Lexa Talbot.'

Emmett Hopper listened, gave orders.

'Photograph them all – particularly the girl – but don't move her. She stays. Carry Zander to your car and bring him here. We'll hypo him into something approaching consciousness. Work fast!'

Hopper chortled inwardly. First the Weidener file, now this. The Bureau was gradually making a comeback.

The suit that had been provided for Jim Zander was a size too small, and his mouth tasted foul. But the drugs from the FBI's pharmacy had done their work. Zander was functioning and aware. All the same, he was glad that two FBI men held his arms as they walked down the corridor toward the Oval Office, for his legs were still rubbery.

'The FBI has Zander outside,' Ramsey told the President.

Talbot glanced at his desk-clock. 0451. Nine minutes under the deadline. 'Phone Hopper my congratulations and have Zander brought in.'

The agents steadied Zander as they entered the Oval Office.

'Mr Zander was a bit drunk, Mr President,' an agent said, following Emmett Hopper's instructions. 'He was home, just didn't hear the phone or doorbell. A cold shower and black coffee did wonders.'

'I'm sorry, Mr President.' Zander's voice was only slightly fuzzy.

'Everybody's entitled to get loaded once in a while,' Talbot said. He nodded to the FBI men. 'Thanks to you and the Bureau for your work.' The agents said polite good nights and withdrew.

'Feel up to composing some of your poetry?' Talbot asked Zander.

'A speech?'

'No, some statements to the press.'

'I think so,' Zander replied. *I hope so. I'm scared shitless. If I don't deliver, I've had it. If this guy ever learns about Lexa, I've had it double – and the same unless I do what Hopper wants. God, those photographs, the statements he had me sign.* 'Yes, I think so, Mr President.'

'Good. Ken Ramsey and I will brief you. Then you can settle down behind a typewriter and put together words that sing.'

20

Kinsolo, Basanda: Thursday, February 25. Afternoon.

The Commanding General of the U.S. Army's Basanda Military Advisory Group had only two stars and avidly aspired to a third. When the radio message from Washington arrived, he exulted. I'll be a Lieutenant General by next month, he assured himself. A Lieutenant General with a Distinguished Service Medal. Added stars and DSMs came quickly, automatically whenever there was any shooting. He issued crisp, terse commands. Every BMAG air-rescue helicopter and the newly arrived gunships were to take off without delay, fly to Giduna.

'The mission is to rescue Americans held by rebel forces. Gunships will fire only in defense or to cover evacuation operations.'

Once over Giduna, the choppers were caught in a storm of fire from rebel antiaircraft machine guns hidden in the dense foliage. Three unarmed rescue copters were shot down. All burned; their crews were presumably dead. The gunships were of no avail.

'We shot up real estate, period,' the gunship crewmen reported at their de-briefing. Several of their craft had been holed by rebel machine gun bullets. One gunner had been killed, two seriously wounded.

The mission had been a disaster.

A slovenly servant escorted the American Ambassador to the audience chamber where National Savior Percival Kwida presided in place of the late Odu Mwandi. The insult was calculated, crude, unmistakable. The U.S. Ambassador feigned indifference and delivered the ultimatum radioed by Secretary of State MacDonald Pearce.

Percival Kwida snickered contemptuously.

'Inform your Government that I am holding an auction,' he said. 'The rebels are backed by the Soviet Union. This disturbs the Chinese, who yesterday made me a formal offer of considerable aid in money and war materiel. I shall await the American counterbid with great interest, but not for long. Shall we say seventy-two hours? We shall. The audience is ended, Your Excellency.'

Frederick Dollinger fared no better. Dollinger was executive vice-president of Rickhoven International Properties (Africa) Inc., the holding company that owned Rickhoven operating companies in Basanda. Under the Mwandi regime, Frederick Dollinger was a force to be reckoned with and Odu Mwandi had treated him with deferential respect.

'Your Excellency . . .' Frederick Dollinger began.

'Silence!' Percival Kwida rasped. 'I fear you have not read my decrees. All persons not holding diplomatic rank are to address me by my title, National Savior, and use the third person when speaking to me.'

Dollinger swallowed, wet his lips and swallowed again – this time his pride. 'With the National Savior's permission, I have been instructed to deliver a message to him from Mr John Rickhoven.'

'You may proceed.'

'Mr Rickhoven is deeply concerned over recent events. He wishes' – *I'll have to make this flowery*, Dollinger thought – 'With utmost respect to the National Savior, he wishes that I convey his fears that it may become necessary to suspend mining and oil production. Unfortunately, as the National Savior doubtless appreciates, such action would also necessitate the suspension of royalty payments.'

Percival Kwida laughed derisively.

'Rickhoven is a bloody fool! My signature on a single document can instantly nationalize all mines and oilfields. Then he will save his pathetic royalty payments – and lose his mountains of profit!'

Frederick Dollinger abruptly awakened to the realization that he – and the Rickhoven Empire – were being shoved to the wall and made a last effort.

'With the utmost esteem, may I remind the National Savior that Mr Rickhoven has been extremely generous in the past?'

'You are unbelievably stupid, Dollinger.' Kwida's moon face was a total sneer. 'What do I care for a few hundred thousand dollars deposited in Swiss banks when I own – I *own*, do you hear me? – one of the richest countries on the African continent? Tell that to Rickhoven. It might shock him into being less of a fool and make him more respectful and cooperative.'

The BMAG Commanding General – like most military men – mistrusted the press, resented its pryings into matters that concerned the armed forces. He also feared adverse publicity that might injure his reputation. Besides, he reasoned, the Defense Department had issued the orders for the Giduna air-rescue operation – and it should therefore carry the can in announcing any news of the debacle. He permitted no communique on the operation to be released. It was a grave error of judgment.

Percival Kwida gleefully seized on the BMAG commander's failure to give out the facts and held a press conference. Kwida knew the underlying chauvinistic streak in Americans. If their country was humiliated, they demanded revenge and retaliation. He calculated that news of the Giduna fiasco would – if properly managed – arouse U.S. public opinion against the rebels. This could well force the American Government's hand to give him unlimited, unconditional financial and military aid. With luck, it might even bring about full-scale U.S. intervention – on his terms, with the American forces being placed under his overall command. Once they had destroyed the rebels, he would order them out of Basanda – and then nationalize American holdings.

After leaving Kwida's press conference, journalists filed harrowing dispatches.

'. . . only a single American helicopter returned to its base . . .'

'. . . scores of U.S. Army officers and men are said to have been killed or wounded . . .'

'. . . Prime Minister Kwida expressed astonishment that BMAG had employed gunships without prior consultation . . .'

'. . . Kwida flatly declared he and his General Staff would have vetoed the Giduna operation had they been informed of it beforehand as required by U.S.-Basanda treaty provisions . . .'

21

Washington, D.C.: Thursday, February 25. Midmorning to Night.

As the Percival Kwida-inspired bulletins were made public, it became increasingly apparent that the United States presence was now nothing more than a very bad joke, and U.S. policy on Basanda was in shambles.

The statements which James Zander prepared and which were distributed to the White House press corps at 7:30 A.M. proved worse than useless. Correspondents ignored the element of the time-difference between Washington and Kinsolo. The statements were construed as unbelievably clumsy attempts to cover up.

Talbot slumped in an Oval Office armchair. He stared at MacDonald Pearce and John Kurtz, who sat opposite. They had come to the White House with the latest BMAG messages.

'BMAG blundered, acted precipitately, with insufficient advance planning,' Kurtz said, trying to shed all responsibility.

Talbot exhaled breath like a man resigning himself to execution. 'What options do we have left?' he asked

'Only two,' Pearce replied. 'Total withdrawal – with the attendant destruction of American credibility and prestige . . .'

'I've ordered a Sixth Fleet carrier task force in the Med to proceed at full speed for Kinsolo,' Kurtz broke in. 'It's a precautionary measure in the event we have to evacuate. There are about three thousand American civilians – plus BMAG and diplomatic personnel – in Basanda.'

Talbot passed a hand over his face. 'What's the second option?'

'Punitive action against the rebels,' Pearce said.

'There has to be some other way. Kwida . . .'

'Mr President.' Pearce cleared his throat. 'Kwida has started negotiations with the Chinese. He's allowed us seventy-two hours . . .'

'Get rid of the bastard!'

'Impossible. We gave him our official blessing after Odu Mwandi's – ah – unfortunate accident. If we exert pressure to remove Kwida so soon, we'll be accused of openly turning Basanda into a puppet state. I'm afraid we must meet his demands – for the moment.'

'Give me another rundown on what that involves,' Talbot said wearily. His head felt like it would explode at any second.

Kurtz hid behind his pipe-filling ritual.

Pearce ticked off the points. 'We hand over the half-billion out of discretionary funds immediately. We take token retaliatory action against the rebels with what we have available over there – the gunships and the two Green Beret companies that will land today.'

'Yes on the money,' Talbot muttered. 'No on retaliation. Not for now. We'll review the decision again after the task force arrives and we have some muscle over there.'

'We should airlift some reinforcements to play safe,' John Kurtz said. 'Our people at the mines and oil fields are scattered over wide areas. If the rebels break through, we'll need more ground-based men and planes to bring them out and cover the evacuation.' He shifted his pipe. 'I recommend one airborne brigade, one squadron of tactical fighters.'

'Solely to protect American lives and property?' Talbot asked.

'For no other reason.'

'All right.'

Kurtz and Pearce exchanged significant glances.

Suzanne Loring mentally blew a good-bye kiss to her $150,000 tax-free bonus and telephoned CBN's New York headquarters. As usual, her call had to be filtered by secretaries before she was permitted to speak directly with Noah Sturdevant, the network's board chairman.

'Ah, yes, Miss Loring. What have you got?'

'My period.'

She heard Sturdevant splutter indignantly, then his acid tones saying, 'You are not under contract to us as a comedienne, Miss Loring.'

'I should be, considering the sit-com running down here – but it won't sell. No suspense. Everybody knows the payoff.'

'Miss Loring. Have you been drinking?'

'Only bitter dregs, Mr Sturdevant. There's no longer any story for me to run down. It's public property. Talbot was laying down a smokescreen – farting like a dove but pouring out hawkshit.'

He spluttered again.

'For Christ's sake!' Suzanne almost screamed. 'You wanted a special that exposed what Talbot was really doing. He gave it all away this morning. He got us into a shooting war!'

'There have been confused reports – nothing certain.'

'Balls! A carrier task force is sailing full speed ahead toward Basanda. Part of an airborne division and fighter planes are being flown over. It's an Instant Replay of Vietnam.'

'Where did you obtain this information?' Sturdevant demanded.

'Off the record –' *From Russ, who got it from Dan Madigan* '– There should be an official statement issued any minute.'

Noah Sturdevant had many conceits, an image of himself as a conceptualizer being among them. Suzanne Loring was right. However, he could still steal a march on the other networks.

'Miss Loring.' His voice was treacly. 'I don't want you to lose that bonus or a chance to enhance your reputation.'

'When both you and money talk, I'm riveted, Mr Sturdevant.'

'Leave for Basanda this afternoon.'

'*What?*'

'I'll have a camera crew flown over from New York.

You'll tape next week's interview with some common soldier, a rear-rank private, and give the public an on-the-scene insight . . .'

'No, thanks.' I'm not going near that mess, not for any amount of money. I can't go.'

'Why not?'

'I told you. I'm having my period.'

'The connection escapes me, Miss Loring.'

Suzy grimaced at the telephone mouthpiece. 'There aren't any Tampons available in Kinsolo. The native women use boiled rags – and they're running short of those. Good-bye for now, Mr Sturdevant.' *And up yours.* She could picture CBN's Little Hitler turning puce with rage. Wiping the picture, she smiled pensively. Russ had been downcast, depressed when he called and told her what he'd learned from Madigan. It was a good sign. Maybe now – at long last – he would see through the Talbot Administration façades and become his own man again – independent, open-minded – and, she told herself, the smile deepening, altogether wonderful.

Chief Justice Avery Braithwaite came to the White House unannounced, but the President said he was to be admitted to the Oval Office. He rose from his Presidential chair to greet his visitor.

'Glad you came by, Avery,' he said. 'Right about now, there's nothing I can use more than the sight of a friendly face – and the sound of a few kind words.'

He shook hands with the Chief Justice. That's funny, he thought. Avery's palm is sweaty, clammy. Never was before. He took a closer look at Braithwaite. The roughhewn face was flushed. Forehead arteries throbbed. Talbot resumed his seat, surreptitiously wiping his own palm on a trousers leg.

'Strikes me you're wrought up about something, Avery.'

Braithwaite took a chair near the Presidential desk, drew it even closer. 'Are the doors locked and recorders off?' he asked.

Talbot worked the door-locking mechanism, nodded.

'You have brought off a magnificent coup,' Braithwaite said.

'Coup?' Talbot echoed, completely baffled.

'Yes, coup.' Braithwaite's eyes burned. 'Your action on Basanda will be the solution – the salvation – of America!'

'Avery, shooting-scrapes in Africa, of all fucking places . . .'

'Every man has his destiny, Mr President. Yours is to unite our nation by reasserting the might of the United States. The law will stand at your side . . .'

'You mean legal precedents . . .'

'I am speaking of the Law that transcends those made by men – call it the law of historical continuity.'

Their conversation continued for ten minutes – but Talbot could not quite grasp the point and purpose of Braithwaite's ponderous – frequently portentous – remarks. Their meaning eluded him. He spoke with Kenneth Ramsey after the Chief Justice left.

'Braithwaite looks feverish – ill, maybe – or did you notice, Ken?'

'He did seem a little peculiar, Chief. Anything you want me to do – like check with his doctor or . . .'

'No.' Talbot shook his head. 'I guess at Avery's age, a man picks up bugs, has bad spells.' He hauled himself back to matters of closer concern. 'What's next on the agenda?'

'A million pieces of paper – and Senator Kugelman's been hanging around. He had an appointment, but Justice Braithwaite arrived . . .'

'Send Kugelman in and stick around while he's in here.'

Senator Aaron Kugelman was grim-faced.

'The Israeli Ambassador gave me an advance tip-off, Mr President. His Government is reneging on the guns-to-Basanda agreement.'

'They can't do that!' Talbot protested. 'By God, we'll cancel the billion in aid to Israel!'

'Ungood,' Ken Ramsey interposed. 'We'd be telling the whole world it was a phony, under-the-table trade from the start.'

Talbot squirmed. 'What's the Israeli excuse?'

'If they send arms now, after the big *tzimmis* over our raid on Giduna, the Reds and Third World bloc will land on them for being puppet-partners in imperialist aggression,' Kugelman replied unhappily. 'They can't afford the risks.'

When Kugelman had gone, Talbot gave Ken Ramsey a gloomy, dispirited look. 'We're sinking deeper and deeper,' he said.

'You'll find a lifeline, Chief.' Ramsey tried to make himself believe it.

MacDonald Pearce attended many social functions at the House on the Hill but went there alone only when inner and outer stresses and tensions reached unbearable levels. On such occasions, he drove an Avis-rented car, used the side gates and entered by the service entrance. Having telephoned Marjorie Norworth early in the day to request an invitation, he arrived at 10:00 P.M., was met by Holcomb, and led upstairs to the replica of the Presidential Bedroom.

Until his late twenties MacDonald Pearce dreamed (and daydreamed) of someday being the President of the United States. Eventually, he was forced to admit that any elective office was beyond his reach, precluded by his temperament and personality, which alienated potential voters. His political ambitions could be realized only by appointment to high office. As Secretary of State, he had reached an apex, but the old dream remained lodged in some remote recess of his brain. Using the Presidential Bedroom – albeit only a reproduced version – rekindled the dream and, by a process of psychological alchemy, revitalized Pearce, endowed him with remarkable vigor.

'H'lo!'

The girl in the transparent, virginally white nightgown seemed no more than thirteen. Pearce licked his thin lips, his eyes peering at her ravenously through the prissy bifocals he wore. The girl's breasts were not yet formed, mere tiny buds. 'Turn around, please,' he said. She obeyed. Her buttocks were small, flat, and her flesh smooth (he had a phobic dread of touching skin marred by pimples or blackheads). He began undressing methodically. 'Take off your nightgown.'

'Anything you say.'

Pearce presented an unappetizing figure when naked. His body was flabby, his penis short and abnormally thin, even when erect – as it was now. Putting his eyeglasses on the nightstand, Pearce climbed into the Presidential bed, lay on his back.

'Want to start?' the girl asked.

He grunted affirmation. She took an open jar from a bureau top, went to the bed. Pearce took the jar, scooped Vaseline from it with a forefinger, set it beside his glasses. 'I'm ready.'

Having been coached, the girl hiked herself up on the bed. Her knees straddled his thighs, but she faced away from him, toward the foot of the bed – toward his dopey-looking feet, she thought, bending over almost double. She reached for her buttocks with both hands and spread them wide.

Pearce took sensual delight in coating her anus with Vaseline, easing his forefinger deep inside to lubricate the narrow passage. His scrawny penis grew harder, throbbed. He withdrew his finger. 'Lower yourself.' He gripped his thin shaft, guided it. The girl squatted atop him, her constricted sheath swallowing his penis.

'Ride me!' he croaked. She began jouncing up and down. He reached for her minuscule breasts, rubbed vigorously at their nipples.

Pearce shut his eyes. He was a boy again. A boy of twelve in the throes of puppy love for a girl his own age, a grammar school classmate. He took her to a movie once, a Saturday matinee, and they sat in an otherwise empty seat row. He tried to touch her breasts – they, too, were unformed, tiny. She leaped from her seat, fled. He remained alone, terrified that she might 'tell on him', but sexually excited. He closed his eyes and masturbated. He pictured her sitting on his lap, facing the screen, submitting to his commands, riding him while he kneaded and crushed her breasts. One day, I'll be President, he swore to himself, flaying away at his penis, and I'll *make* her do it, because Presidents can make anybody do anything.

This remained his masturbatory fantasy until his undergraduate days at Harvard, then transliterated itself into a fixation . . .

'Ride me faster!' His fingers pinched the girl's nipples. She winced, accelerated her movements. 'Bounce harder!'

The girl was grateful when Pearce's slack muscles grew taut, and he twisted his head to one side, biting into a pillow. Then he thrust her away, rolled over on his stomach and wept like a child.

Marjorie Norworth sat with Bradford Cooley and Emmett Hopper in the parlor of her suite. She had examined the photographs and documents they brought to show her.

'So – Keith Weidener was killed and Lexa Talbot took part in an orgy,' she shrugged. 'Shades of J. Edgar and the "Official and Confidential" files he used to intimidate Washington.'

'Exactly – mere shades,' Cooley said. 'Much more is needed to prevent a whole catalog of calamities.'

'Don Quixote and Sancho Panza tilting at windmills!'

'Wrong, Marjorie,' Hopper said. 'We're motivated by the instinct for self-preservation and survival.'

'Candor is refreshing – but dull. I much prefer artful deceit. Any fool can be frank and truthful – see, I've coined an aphorism.'

But they were getting through to her. Marjorie could visualize fascinating new dimensions to the games of intrigue and manipulation she loved. The men pulling and pushing at Charles Talbot are clever, powerful, she mused. There would be boundless satisfaction in proving that I can outwit and outmaneuver them all.

'Allow me to sleep on my decision – Don Quixote and Sancho.' She kissed Brad Cooley, gave Emmett Hopper a fond pat on the cheek. When Holcomb escorted them downstairs, she double-locked her door.

Marjorie operated a hidden wall switch. A panel like that

masking her bar slid back and exposed a complex electronic console surmounted by a 21-inch television screen. She pressed a lever. The screen came to life in sharp focus and full color.

MacDonald Pearce's muddy eyes were swollen from weeping, but he lay on his back, forefinger digging into an open jar. The girl was shifting her position to straddle him properly.

'Spread yourself again.'

The girl gripped her buttocks, leaning her torso forward until her head almost touched his legs. The forefinger poked and probed.

Marjorie switched off the viewing set, careful not to press the levers that would stop the audio-video taping apparatus. I must remember to screen the Talbot Second Honeymoon tape, she reminded herself. It was something she hadn't yet done, and Claire's description of the night had been hilarious. Oh, I most certainly have the weapons, Lady Norworth thought. The question is do I want – or have any valid reason – to use them, and if I do, how can I employ them most effectively?

22

Washington, D.C.: Friday, February 26.

The Washington *Post* bannered:

> SOVIETS DENOUNCE AMERICAN MILITARY MOVES,
> THREATEN REPRISAL ACTION

The New York *Times* headline was comparatively restrained:

> TENSIONS MOUNT AS U.S. REINFORCEMENTS SPEED
> TO PROTECT AMERICANS IN BASANDA

Dan Madigan was orchestrating an outwardly spontaneous pro-Talbot display in the Senate. At 9:30 A.M., he conferred with Russell Hatch.

'We have to give the President full backing, Russ.'

Hatch's lips tightened. 'His African safari doesn't exactly inspire me to yell rah-rah.'

'Be objective. The original treaty was done with Dick Nixon's blessings. Jerry Ford praised it to the skies. The goody-goody Goober Boy from Georgia cheered it lustily' – a wry grin – 'or maybe he had lust in his heart for some chick in Kinsolo.' The grin vanished. 'Past Administrations piled up the manure, and then the whole stinking load was dumped in Talbot's lap.'

True enough, Russ conceded silently. Nonetheless . . .

'The rebels have Gidanu and over a hundred American prisoners – or corpses,' Madigan went on. 'There are thousands more of our people in Basanda. Where do we stand if they're captured – or slaughtered?'

Hatch stared at the floor, slowly exhaling cigarette smoke. *Oh, shit*, he thought. *Sometimes you have to fly now, pay later. There were lives at stake.* 'You want me to do – what?'

'Make a short speech on the floor this afternoon. Express confidence in the President and suggest – don't move, simply suggest – that the Senate might think about a resolution in the same vein.'

'That's a job for someone with more seniority.'

'President Talbot asked that you do it.' *Your Honest John looks and country-bumpkin appeal are what we need, buster.* 'Well, Russ?'

'I'll go along.' *Only because at this stage, I can't see any alternative to supporting Talbot.*

When she had awakened on Thursday morning in the A Street house, Lexa Talbot was furious to find Zander gone. Pulling her drug-fragmented self together, she dressed, left the house and hailed a taxi. Retrieving her Jaguar from the Holiday Inn garage, she drove to the White House. It was in turmoil. She met Zander as he hurried down a West Wing corridor, grabbed his arm.

'You son of a bitch!'

Zander tore his arm loose. 'We better stay away from each other for a while,' he said. 'Don't even phone me. I'll explain later.' He rushed off.

Lexa saw her father in the evening, worked in a casual reference to Zander. 'He acted odd this morning.'

'Poor guy had it rough,' Talbot said. 'We needed him in a hurry around three A.M. and sent the FBI to find him.'

Lexa's blood froze. 'The FBI? Oh – where was he?'

'At home, drunk. Hopper's agents delivered him, though.'

My God, Lexa thought. *The FBI men must have tracked Zander to the A Street pad. No wonder he looked scared and told me to keep away from him.* Fear knotted her stomach. *Did the agents see me? Not likely, or they would have taken me along, covered up for me as they obviously covered up for Jim. Or would they?*

Wracked by anxiety, Lexa did not sleep Thursday night.

On Friday morning she told her maid she had a cold and would remain in bed.

The President read the Friday morning news summaries, and his nervous system took savage punishment. Pro and con opinions were about evenly divided. The former elated him, the latter brought bleak dejection. The ambiguity left him depressed. His first appointments of the day provided no uplift.

MacDonald Pearce reported continuing stalemate in the diplomatic sector. Kurtz was next, declaring that the military situation in Basanda remained 'fluid'. The two Green Beret companies had dug in around BMAG's headquarters and airstrip. The first airborne brigade contingents had arrived and were awaiting further orders.

'The supply-lift is under way,' Kurtz added. It was a throwaway line. The escalation pills had to be fed gently, gradually.

'Huh? I didn't authorize any supply-lift . . .'

'You authorized men and planes.' Kurtz mimed bewilderment. 'We can't send them unless we also send equipment, supplies.'

Damn it, that never entered my mind, Talbot realized.

'All available Air Force freighters are on shuttle runs,' Kurtz continued. 'Plus twenty more chartered from civilian airlines.' They were airlifting material to sustain two full divisions – the strength he and Pearce contemplated for the next step in the buildup. Talbot would soon be finessed into giving his retroactive approval.

The President reviled himself for having overlooked the supply question – and thought of the cost-aspect. 'John, where the fuck is the money coming from? Defense appropriations . . .'

'Always have a little fat hidden in 'em,' Kurtz winked.

'What's this cost us so far?'

'Barely half a percent of the Defense budget,' Kurtz replied blithely. Talbot's arithmetic was poor. Even if he remembered that the budget topped $140 billion, he would not grasp this meant $700 million.

Kurtz left. Talbot sank deeper into gloom. The curved walls of the Oval Office gave him a feeling of claustrophobia. He longed for temporary escape. Ken Ramsey entered, carrying documents.

'Lexa down yet?' Talbot asked. She could cheer him up.

'No. Her maid says she has a cold.'

'Hold things off, Ken. I'll go see her.'

Lexa lay in bed, electric sheet drawn to waist level, golden hair loose on the pillow, breasts clearly visible through the sheer, silvery fabric of her Fernando Sanchez pajamas. Her face was inordinately pale. Talbot sat on the edge of the bed, felt her forehead.

'No fever, that's good.' He smiled.

'Fever? All I have is the curse. Hit me harder than usual.'

I should keep my stories straight, Lexa thought. She said, 'I told the maid I had a cold. My cycles are none of her business.' She sat up. The loose, deepcut pajama-top fell away from her perfect breasts.

Talbot's throat seemed to seal. He cleared it – with effort. 'Puss, you *will* catch cold unless you keep a cover over you.'

'Yes, doctor.' Lexa flipped the sheet aside – Talbot glimpsed the golden triangle beneath the silvery gauze of her pajama trousers – then she pulled the sheet up under her arms. 'There. I'm swaddled.'

Aware his heart was pounding, Talbot got to his feet. 'Take it easy today – rest, huh?' He bent down, gave her a hasty, perfunctory hug and kiss and hurried from the room.

Holcomb brought copies of the *Post* and *Times* to Lady Marjorie's suite with her breakfast each morning. Experience had taught her that newspapers should be read between their printed lines. The front pages were largely devoted to the Basanda crisis. Hard facts were sparse, padded out with rumors and speculations attributed to anonymous sources. Marjorie reflected that the sum total impression verified the fears expressed by Bradford Cooley and Emmett Hopper. Nevertheless, having 'slept on' their proposals, she decided not to take part in their schemes. I'll choreograph my own ballets, she mused and turned to the financial pages of the New York *Times*.

Marjorie viewed profligate Federal Government spending complacently. Waste and graft were not only the concomitants, but the very fuel of politics. Paradoxically, her attitude toward private enterprise was harshly puritanical. She could not abide dishonesty or even bad financial management in the private sector. Businessmen had an obligation and duty to preserve the free-enterprise system, maintain ethical standards, and treat investors' money as a sacred trust. Businessmen – and especially bankers and financiers – who transgressed were guilty of treason against their class and the free-enterprise system itself.

She merely intended to skim the *Times* financial section, but an article caught her eye.

'A Federal Reserve System official today revealed that three of the nation's ten largest commercial banks are on the System's "critical list" due to serious liquidity problems. He refused to name the banks, but said . . .'

Something clicked in Marjorie's brain. Putting aside the newspaper, she telephoned Samuel Goldwasser, senior partner of Goldwasser, Pritchard and Symes, her Washington attorneys. She mentioned the news item, asked, 'Find out where the Rickhoven National Bank stands, will you please, Sam?'

Goldwasser called back in minutes. 'Rickhoven National's at the top of the critical list . . .'

'Thank you, Sam.'

Formerly disjointed pieces fell into place with zero-tolerance for Marjorie. Jordan Rickhoven's bank, keystone of his financial and industrial empire, was in trouble. And banks with over $40 billion in deposits were at the head of the Federal Reserve's critical list only if the individuals who controlled them were either inept or incompetent – or dishonest and dishonorable.

Jordan Rickhoven III being neither inept nor incompetent, the remaining conclusion was inescapable. He had milked the bank, probably making huge loans to dummy corporations he and other members of the Rickhoven family owned through intricate, untraceable corporate chains. With the bank overextended, the entire global Rickhoven complex would be shaky.

That explains Jordan's terror of losing the Basanda mines and oilfields, Marjorie reasoned. The income they provide must be his main hope of preventing collapse. If he could manufacture a war, and a demand for metals and oil, his profits would soar. She sat in silent, solitary judgment and arrived at her verdict. Jordan Rickhoven was not merely guilty of treason against class and system. He was an arch-traitor, for he *was* a Rickhoven, his name a symbol – virtually a synonym – for the system he had betrayed.

'Woman's prerogative,' she murmured aloud, reversing her decision. Lifting her telephone handset, she called Bradford Cooley's office. He was in. She asked that he and Hopper come to the House on the Hill 'tonight, for a long and very private visit'.

Russell Hatch spoke on the Senate floor. Brevity added strength and conviction to his words.

'. . . If I believed for a single instant that President Talbot desired to escalate our participation in the Basandan conflict, I would condemn his actions and disown him and the party to which he and I belong. But any American President who failed to protect American lives would be condemned and disowned by this Senate, the citizens of our country – and by history . . .'

He concluded as Madigan had asked.

'Being a very junior member of this body, I do not feel qualified to offer proposals on momentous issues. I can only respectfully suggest that we demonstrate nonpartisan unity. Perhaps it might be fitting if a resolution were introduced expressing support of steps taken to protect our citizens . . .'

Hatch received considerable applause from his colleagues and an ovation from the public gallery. He did not suspect that Dan Madigan had pulled strings, filled the gallery with a trained-seal claque of men and women who held party patronage jobs in the capital.

At four in the afternoon, Jordan B. Rickhoven III strode insolently past aides and assistants and burst in on MacDonald Pearce.

'Jordan!' Pearce blinked consternation. He was not aware that the billionaire was in Washington. 'This is – ah – a surprise.'

Rickhoven threw himself into a chair. 'What are you doing about that bastard Kwida?' he demanded, glaring.

'Jordan, Percival Kwida was your handpicked choice . . .'

'So were you, Mac. I got you in, and I can get you thrown out. And I will, unless you flush Kwida down the drain by next Monday!'

'The schedule has been accelerated as much as . . .'

'Speed it up even more. How to do it is your business, but if you don't, I'll make you wish you had!' *Every day – every hour – counts. Reports that the Rickhoven National Bank was on the critical list were spreading. If Kwida nationalizes my holdings or the rebels win, everything will crumble. The Rickhoven Empire will be finished.* 'I've said my piece, Mac. I'll leave you to take care of the details.'

When the billionaire had gone, MacDonald Pearce wet his lips, overcame the tremors that caused his hands to quiver and reached for a telephone.

Suzanne Loring and Russell Hatch had cocktails at the Hay-Adams. Suzanne slowly worked her way through a Bacardi Manhattan and slow-roasted Hatch about the speech he made in the Senate earlier that afternoon.

'The idea didn't originate with you.'

'No,' Russ admitted. 'Madigan asked me, at Talbot's request.'

'So, bang! You knuckled under.'

'I was persuaded.'

'What did they promise you this time?'

'Nothing.' Russ gulped his double Johnnie Walker Black. He needed it. 'The arguments were logical and convincing.

Our people over there have to be given protection or, if worse comes to worst, brought out safely. Hell, we can't abandon them.'

'Suppose – just suppose – it's all a gussied-up excuse for escalation? Will you change your stand?'

'Honey, I said I would – and I will.'

'You may have to – and sooner than you imagine.'

'Crystal-ball gazing, Suzy?'

'Teletype watching.' As usual, she had made a last-minute check of wire-service bulletins before leaving the CBN studios. 'There are fairly solid rumors of an air supply operation that's way, way out of proportion. Defense has even chartered a fleet of civilian cargo planes and is running a shuttle.'

Hatch experienced a sudden queasy feeling in his stomach. The Air Force had more than ample cargo planes to airlift supplies for the numbers of soldiers that had been sent to Basanda. He signaled a hovering waiter for refills.

'If they're only rumors and there's no confirmation . . .'

'Assume the reports are verified, Russ. Then what?'

The waiter brought fresh drinks. Russ again downed his at a single gulp. He needed it more than the first.

'Then it'll mean we are escalating, and I've been euchred by Madigan and the President,' Hatch conceded with morose resentment. 'Talbot . . .'

'Don't be too quick about laying the blame on Talbot.'

'Christ, Suzy? Are you switching your sides?'

'Hardly. My opinion of Charlie T. remains the same as ever. He's even dumber than Grand Rapids Jerry was. Talbot not only can't chew gum and fart at the same time, he has to be told which end to put the gum in.'

'He's been acting a lot smarter lately,' Russ protested.

'The operative word is *acting*, freckle-face. Somebody – or a collection of somebodies – has been supplying him with prepackaged, smokescreen scenarios. He reads his lines like a good machine-made professional pol should. Damn it, Russ, you know as well as I do that Talbot isn't running the country. The only noises he makes on his own sound like he's still running for the Presidency.'

She saw his face grow thoughtful, then troubled.

'Your doubts gathering?' she asked.

'Afraid they've gathered. You make too goddamned much sense, m'love.'

'You deserve a payoff for those kind words, partner. You can take me to dinner. Then we'll spend the night at my place. That'll be *my* reward.'

Daniel Madigan was purposely omitted from the meeting. The demands and threats MacDonald Pearce had to relay would not carry the same force with Madigan as they would with Kurtz and Denby. Madigan was an elected legislator, with almost four years to go on his current Senate term; he could not be dumped summarily, not even by a Jordan Rickhoven.

Although Kurtz and Denby agreed with Pearce that Rickhoven's latest dictates were 'impossible', they were unanimous that it was even more impossible for them not to comply. But how? Various ideas were advanced, chewed over, discarded, and the afternoon wore on fruitlessly until Kurtz suggested that there were sufficient combat troops in Kinsolo to launch an attack on the Prime Ministerial Palace. The first reaction from Pearce was a blunt veto. Any such assault would be direct disobedience of Presidential orders that there was to be no shooting – save in self-defense or to protect American lives. Besides, Kwida headed what was ostensibly a friendly country, an ally.

Kurtz listened to Pearce's harangue on this score and had an inspiration. He turned to the CIA Director. 'Howard, what about your three men Kwida was holding at last report?'

'They're still prisoners in Kwida's palace.'

'That's it!' Kurtz exclaimed, grinning broadly. 'Full justification. We make it public that Kwida has imprisoned American citizens and refuses to release them . . .'

'Excellent!' Pearce's prissy face lit up. 'We have it on unimpeachable authority that they're being tortured – add that.'

I don't doubt they are, Denby mused placidly.

Kurtz, realizing he was on to the solution, extemporized the scenario. 'Airborne troops surround the palace to enforce our demands that the prisoners be freed. The Palace Guard will offer resistance – at minimum – and take some action that our commanders will interpret as menacing. Whereupon, they order their men to storm the palace and search for the prisoners – to save their lives. A squad – with a few of your men along, Howard – corners Kwida, whose bodyguards open fire.'

'If they don't, my men will make it appear they did.'

'Check. Our troops fire in self-defense. In the melee, a stray bullet hits Kwida.'

'Yes,' Pearce nodded. 'The President ordered American lives protected. The – ah – program you offer will prove that he was completely sincere and impartial. Our soldiers carry out their mission regardless of the side posing a threat to U.S. citizens.'

The Defense Secretary smirked. 'Afterward, ground and air units move on Gidanu in another fire-only-if-fired-upon rescue mission. They're bound to meet heavy resistance from the rebels, and we'll be forced to send over more reinforcements.'

'A question,' Denby interposed. 'Shouldn't the troops attacking the palace suffer some casualties?'

'It would make our case stronger,' Pearce nodded.

'My people will arrange it,' Denby said.

Avery Braithwaite telephoned Marjorie and requested a special invitation – and use of the Lincoln Bedroom – for the evening. He would like to come at 10:30, he said. At first Marjorie sought to discourage him. Braithwaite had not looked well on his last, quite recent, visit. However, he was insistent, almost pleading, and Marjorie agreed. She told Holcomb to ready the properties and costumes and call the performers.

Since she would be entertaining other guests in her suite, and did not wish to be interrupted, Marjorie added that Holcomb should take Braithwaite directly to the Lincoln Bedroom.

'Tell him I had a terrible headache and went to bed early,' she instructed.

'And give him your apologies for not being able to welcome him personally, Lady Norworth?'

'Naturally,' Marjorie smiled. 'Supreme Court Chief Justices must always be treated with utmost deference and politeness, Holcomb.' The smile became almost saturnine. She and Holcomb were the joint keepers of countless secrets. 'Chief Justices are august personages – deserving of our greatest respect, Holcomb.'

She laughed. The powerfully-built majordomo of the House on the Hill flashed a wide grin. 'Of course, Lady Norworth.'

Bradford Cooley and Emmett Hopper seated themselves in the parlor of Marjorie's private suite. Cooley savored mellow bourbon. Emmett Hopper quenched a genuine thirst with cold Coors beer. Their hostess, her splendid rubies glowing, held a glass of her usual freshly squeezed, lightly chilled orange juice.

They talked of the latest developments – international, national and local – in broad terms until Holcomb served dinner. Their conversation remained general, convivial during the meal. When they had eaten, two of Marjorie's footmen cleared the table. Brad Cooley settled himself in a wide armchair with more bourbon; Hopper sat in another, gently swirling fifty-year-old Otard. Marjorie occupied a couch facing them, leaning gracefully against one of its arms. She linked her fingers and smiled.

'Which of you has the gavel to call our meeting to order?'

Brad Cooley rapped a knuckle against the side of his glass. 'There. The floor should be yours to begin, Marjorie.'

'Then I'll make a carefully prepared statement. I insist we be direct and straightforward with each other. Agreed?'

The two men nodded.

'That being settled, exactly what is it you want from me?'

'Damoclean swords,' Cooley replied. 'Material that can be dangled over heads – and which would have a lethal effect if dropped.' He shrugged one obese shoulder ponderously. 'I thought we made that clear the other evening.'

'You did, Brad, but I prefer to be doubly certain – and to proceed one step at a time. You and Emmett intend using what I may – what I probably will – furnish against individuals, am I correct?'

'Yes.'

'You would go to, say, Senator Smith, then to Cabinet Secretary Jones and so on?'

'Yes.'

'I have a much better strategy in mind – but I'll come to that later.' Marjorie unlinked her hands, stroked the huge ruby on her right forefinger. 'Yes, I'll tell you later.' Her smile was enigmatic. 'Shall we move on to real names? Who are the most important? For example, do you agree with me that MacDonald Pearce is a key figure?'

'Denifitely,' Emmett Hopper declared.

'Rest assured. I have more than you'll need.'

'John Kurtz?' Hopper asked.

'Mmm, yes. Ample.'

'Dan Madigan?'

'Considering that he's a Papal Knight and his wife heads the Illinois Catholic Sodality, yes – to the point of overkill.'

'Charles Talbot?' Cooley asked.

'Oh, no!' Marjorie shook her head. 'You'll get nothing from me to use against Charlie. I have no objections to Emmett firing his opening gun with the Weidener photos, but Charles Talbot himself is my private property.' Her violet eyes were feline. 'Exclusively *my* property. I'll give you no swords, Damoclean or otherwise, to hang over his head.'

'Not even as a last resort, if all else fails?'

'All else won't fail,' she purred. 'You see, I hate nothing more than failure – my own worst of all. Ergo, I don't allow myself to fail.' She gazed at Hopper. 'You haven't mentioned Jordan Rickhoven, Emmett.'

Hopper shifted uneasily in his chair. 'Rickhoven has too much power, too many connections that extend far beyond Washington.'

'I see. Billionaires frighten you.'

'My concern is for the bureau. Rickhoven's influence is global. He can pressure foreign governments to cease co-operating with the FBI and weaken it even further. I wouldn't dare move against him unless there was something so overwhelming . . .'

'Wait a moment.' Marjorie stood up, went into her bedroom, returned minutes later with a plastic case containing a video tape. Half an hour afterwards, she was laughing heartily at the two gaping men, and asked: 'Still afraid to put Rickhoven on the list, Emmett?'

The FBI Director stopped gaping.

'No.' Hopper never dreamed that Marjorie Norworth possessed weapons of such magnitude. And she had confidently assured them that what they saw and heard was only a 'milder sample'.

Hopper's eyes glowed. 'Marjorie, with you helping us . . .'

'Emmett, the order of precedence has changed,' she corrected him sharply. 'What I have puts *me* in charge. You and Brad are the helpers.'

Cooley was about to speak, but there was an urgent knock on Marjorie's door. She opened it. Holcomb stood in the doorway. She read the question in his eyes.

'It's all right to tell me.' Whatever it was, Cooley and Hopper could hear.

'Justice Braithwaite – something happened.'

Marjorie's brain worked at top speed.

'Brad, Emmett – please leave. I'll talk to you again tomorrow.'

She hurried to the Lincoln Bedroom with Holcomb. The Roman legionary and the woman in the white robe stood against the far wall. They seemed to be frozen there, and they stared, terrified, at the loin-clothed figure of Avery Braithwaite rolling and thrashing on the floor. Slimy spittle ran from his mouth.

'He freaked out when we took him down,' the woman said.

'Hold him, get him dressed,' Marjorie ordered Holcomb and the other two. 'I'll only be gone a moment.'

She went quickly to her bedroom, took $2,000 in hundred-dollar bills from a desk drawer, held the money in her hand while she telephoned a topflight doctor she knew well. The physician earned enormous sums by answering – and handling – potentially embarrassing emergency cases for members of the Washington Establishment. He could be relied upon to remain silent, doctor his records as skilfully as he doctored his patients – or keep no records at all. He promised Marjorie he would come immediately.

Returning to the Lincoln Bedroom, she saw that Braithwaite continued to struggle, but was now wearing trousers and shirt. She had him and the rest of his clothes taken to an ordinary bedroom. Holcomb and the legionary lowered Braithwaite onto the bed. The majordomo held him down.

Marjorie gave the Roman soldier and the white-robed woman each a thousand dollars. 'Please change your clothes and go out quickly through the back,' she told them. They nodded and went off.

Lady Norworth knew there was no necessity to add warnings about remaining silent, and not merely because of the money. Most of those who served the sexual needs of guests at the House on the Hill were moonlighters, augmenting the income they received from sinecure government jobs Marjorie contrived to obtain for them. Were they to talk, Lady Norworth could – and would – have them fired instantly, civil service regulations or no. The two performers in the Braithwaite crucifixion charade were not exceptions to the rule. The robed woman was a $25,000-a-year GS-13 'systems analyst' in an obscure agency that had no systems to analyze. The Roman legionary earned $3,400 more annually – and was one notch up on grading scale – as an Interior Department auditing supervisor, a post that required him to make an hour-long appearance in his office twice a week. Neither would talk.

Marjorie locked the Lincoln Bedroom. Some minutes later, the doctor arrived. She took him to Braithwaite.

'Something's snapped up here,' the physician said, tapping the side of his own skull, after he examined Braithwaite and gave him a sedative injection. 'I can't be sure if it's only temporary or permanent – but I suspect it's the latter.' He gave Marjorie a shrewd look. 'How did it happen?' He meant how-did-it-happen-for-the-record.

'Justice Braithwaite and I were chatting in my parlor. Holcomb has just brought us coffee. He – Avery Braithwaite – suddenly clutched at his throat. He fell from his chair. Holcomb and I loosened his clothing and carried him in here. Then I telephoned you.'

The doctor's look became even shrewder. 'Wouldn't it be better if he was found in the street – oh, somewhere in the Dumbarton Oaks section. Holcomb could drive his car there.'

'Can it be managed?' Marjorie asked. Of course, the doctor would charge a high – a very high – five-figure fee, but it would be a bargain at any price.

'I think so. When – or *if* – Justice Braithwaite recovers, he'll have no memory of the circumstances under which he suffered the attack – probably none of the entire evening.'

He gazed past Marjorie at empty air and continued.

'My records will show I received an anonymous telephone call. Someone said there was a man slumped in his automobile. I responded because I live very near Dumbarton Oaks. I found the Chief Justice, sedated him, and called for a private ambulance to take him to the Bethesda Naval Hospital. The report will satisfy everyone.'

He looked at Holcomb.

'Shall we carry him downstairs?'

'I can do it myself, Doctor.'

Holcomb lifted the now-unconscious Braithwaite easily, slung him over his broad, muscular shoulders in a fireman's carry and walked out into the corridor.

23

Washington, D.C.: Saturday, February 27. Morning and Afternoon.

Charles Talbot awakened, cursed. Several appointments were scheduled for this Saturday and Sunday. Dry-swallowing an anti-depressant, he went into his bathroom.

The medication had not yet taken hold when he appeared in the Oval Office. Seeing that Kenneth Ramsey wore a worried expression, he grew edgy. 'Out with it, Ken!' Talbot snapped.

'Chief – Avery Braithwaite had a nervous breakdown last night. We've kept it quiet so far. He's in Bethesda Naval.'

'My God!' Talbot reached for a telephone. Ramsey stopped him.

'Don't. He's unable to talk to anyone and personal inquiries by you are bound to cause a flap at Bethesda. I'll stay in touch with the medics and keep you posted.'

'All right,' Talbot concurred wearily. 'Anything else?'

'Lady Norworth called shortly before you came down.'

'Early for Marjorie – must be important.' Talbot used his direct-line phone. Holcomb answered. After moments, Lady Norworth was on the line.

'Have you heard the dreadful news about Avery?' she asked.

'Yes.' Wait a minute, Talbot thought. Ken said it was being kept quiet. The knee-jerk response of doubt passed instantly. Marjorie always knew whatever happened in Washington before anyone else did.

'That isn't why I called, though,' she said. 'I spoke with Emmett Hopper last night. He has some information for you.'

'Let him send it through normal Justice Department channels.'

'*Quite* impossible. Please see him today – and alone.'

She's on my side, Talbot reflected, so it must be that what Hopper has is urgent. 'What's on the schedule for eleven?' he asked Ken Ramsey.

'The inter-service briefing you wanted on Basanda.'

'Cancel it. Emmett Hopper instead.' Ending his conversation with Marjorie, he addressed Ramsey again. 'Anyone waiting?'

'No, but a pile of papers need signing.'

Talbot brightened. He liked to sign official documents. Each signature he wrote was reassuring, a re-affirmation that he truly was the President of the United States.

Emmett Hopper placed an oversized attaché case on the Presidential desk, took the chair Talbot indicated. His anti-depressant having taken effect, Talbot was jovial. He complimented Hopper on the speed with which the FBI had located Zander, not noticing that this caused Hopper's lips to twitch with amusement. 'Well now,' Talbot said, tipping back his chair. 'What's the big problem that can't wait?'

'Mr President.' Hopper opened the attaché case. 'General Weidener . . .'

'It's a little late to rush. He died ten days ago.'

'He didn't "die", Mr President. He was murdered.'

'Ridiculous. The Army's autopsy reports . . .'

'Were fiction.' Hopper took several dozen photographs from the attaché case, began passing them to Talbot. 'Still enlargements of motion picture frames,' he said. 'First, Weidener walking along the sidewalk. Now, he halts. Next, he turns to his left. He starts across Upper Connecticut. Here, a Lincoln Continental moves away from the curb. Back to Weidener, part-way across the avenue. The car bears down on him. It hits him.' Hopper laid out a series of prints in sequence. 'These show the Lincoln deliberately driving over his body. I also have transcripts of taped conversations and my agents' depositions.'

Talbot, aghast, punched an intercom key. 'I'm locking

the doors and cutting off the intercom. No one is to disturb us.'

The secretary wanted to be certain. 'Not even Miss Talbot, sir?'

'Not even my daughter.'

Lexa Talbot whirled into the Oval Office anteroom at eleven thirty. 'Good morning, everyone.' She continued toward the Oval Office doors. A Secret Service agent blocked her path.

'Sorry, Miss Talbot. The President . . .'

'Don't be silly. Daddy never keeps *me* out.'

The secretary spoke. 'He said not even you, Miss Talbot.'

Lexa flashed her radiant smile, leaned across the secretary's desk to the intercom. 'I'll call in to him.'

'The President turned it off.'

'Nonsense.' Lexa pushed a key. 'Daddy, you have a rejected daughter out here.' No reply. The line was dead. The 'I-told-you-so' looks of secretary and Secret Service men infuriated her. 'Are you *sure* Daddy included me? If he didn't, you'll all be sorry!'

Kiss my ass, a Secret Service agent thought. There's a mile-wide bitch-kitty streak under all the sweetness and light.

'Who's with him?' she asked angrily.

'Mr Emmett Hopper.' There were no orders to keep that secret.

Lexa paled. The FBI Director had never been closeted with her father before. Fear made her leap to a conclusion. The only reason Hopper could be there – and herself excluded – was that he was telling her father about Jim Zander. And possibly about her. 'Has – has anyone seen Mr Zander?' she asked, her voice uneven.

'He was told he needn't come in today,' the secretary said. The reply seemed to confirm Lexa's fears. She left without another word. She had to see Zander. Immediately.

Losing a Secret Service back-up car at night is one thing, in broad daylight, quite another. Lexa drove her Jaguar to

Garfinckel's department store, double-parked in front of an F Street entrance, dashed into the store, hurried out through a 14th Street exit. She waved down a passing taxi, thrust a ten-dollar bill into the driver's hand, gave him Jim Zander's Georgetown address. 'I'm in a hurry.'

Zander slammed and double-locked his door behind them.

'Are you out of your skull?' he raged. 'I told you . . .'

'We have to talk. You alone?' Her tone was terrified, frantic.

He led her to the living room. It was tidy. The floormats were gone, replaced by cheap – but new – carpeting and furniture.

'Had to sanitize the place,' Zander said. 'Okay, talk!'

The frightened words came tumbling out. 'I heard the FBI was sent to look for you – Daddy told me – and I put things together. They must've found you over on A Street. Today, I wasn't allowed into the Oval Office. He – Daddy – was with Emmett Hopper. It must have something to do with you or us, and . . .'

'That motherfucker Hopper promised . . .'

'Why should Hopper promise you anything?'

She might as well hear it all, Zander thought. He poured two large shots of Seagram's. Lexa gulped hers. The liquor warmed the ice block that was her stomach. Zander drank, then spoke.

'Look. The FBI creeps took me from A Street to the Hoover Building like they found me, wiped out and stark-assed naked. They brought me around, gave me some clothes and hauled me in front of Hopper. They had photos of this place, the A Street scene, shots of you and me . . .'

'Oh, my God! No!'

'. . . and made me sign statements . . .'

'In trade for what?' There had to be a trade.

'They'd shut up if I agreed to tip the FBI off on what I saw and heard inside the White House . . .'

'You stupid prick!'

'Cool it.' Zander was thinking. Desperately. 'Listen. Your old man thinks the sun rises and sets in your asshole. No matter what Hopper tells or shows him, claim it's a frame-up, put on an act, threaten to commit suicide, use every trick. It's the only chance we have to save our necks.'

You're right – in part, Lexa thought. *I'll save mine. I'm not so sure about yours, though.*

By twelve thirty, Emmett Hopper had convinced Talbot there was an ongoing conspiracy against him. 'Luckily, you haven't passed the point of no return yet,' Hopper was saying. 'Make the men involved resign.'

'I can't,' Talbot mumbled. 'Not right after last week's Cabinet shakeup. I'd be firing the men I kept in, praised to the skies. The public wouldn't stand for it – while the press . . .'

'Mr President, there are means . . .'

'Chief!' Ken Ramsey was shouting through the doors. 'This can't wait! Open up!'

'I'll leave,' Hopper said. 'Whenever you wish to see me . . .'

Talbot nodded vaguely, unlocked the doors. Ramsey burst into the room. Emmett Hopper, attaché case in hand, slipped out. Ramsey thrust a decoded message-form at Talbot. 'The airborne outfit attacked Kwida's palace, shot him. He's dead.'

Talbot stared at the message in disbelief, finally managed to speak. 'Get Pearce, Madigan, Kurtz, and Denby over here.' *The point of no return,* he thought bleakly, and said, 'Please stick with me while they're here, Ken.'

Ramsey swallowed, nodded. 'Sure, Chief.'

It was a confrontation, not a conference, and Ramsey took Talbot's request literally, standing close beside the Presidential chair.

'Kurtz' – Talbot could not bring himself to use first names – 'who engineered this?' He held up the message-form, hand trembling.

'I take exception to the word "engineered", Mr President.' John Kurtz puffed his pipe serenely. 'You authorized combat troops to protect American citizens. Prime Minister

Kwida held three Americans prisoner.'

MacDonald Pearce picked up the ball. 'Our Ambassador made formal demands for their release. These were rejected.'

Back to Kurtz. 'In accordance with your directives, I ordered military action to rescue the men. The tragedy is that we were too late. They were executed before our troops reached their cells.'

As I anticipated they would be, Denby mused. They were the three CIA agents who had been in the Lincoln Continental and later aboard the helicopter with Odu Mwandi. All tracks were erased.

'Kwida was gunned down!' Talbot rasped.

'You slander our soldiers, Mr President,' Kurtz protested. 'Kwida's bodyguard started shooting. Our troops acted in self-defense. Unfortunately, the Prime Minister was caught in the cross fire.'

How fucking convenient, Ken Ramsey thought.

'Restrict our soldiers to their camps – without delay . . .'

'That's not feasible, Mr President.' The Defense Secretary shifted his pipestem. 'The airborne brigade is advancing on Gidanu.'

Talbot's facial muscles pulsed. 'By what authority?'

'Yours, sir.' Kurtz's smile was snide, mocking. 'The operation to protect Americans continues. The airborne unit will liberate U.S. citizens held by the rebels at Gidanu. Isn't that what you desired?'

'My God, I didn't approve offensive action!'

'You issued orders and statements guaranteeing the safety of Americans,' Pearce said unctuously. 'Legal experts at State and Defense consider the steps taken as being consistent with your orders.'

Kurtz came in on cue. 'I went even higher for an opinion – to Supreme Court Chief Justice Braithwaite. He kindly furnished me with a memorandum yesterday morning.' Kurtz unfolded a sheet of stationery, read from it. '"President Talbot agrees with me that our national honor requires forceful action in Basanda. We must shoulder the heavy burden of a crusade" – want me to go on?'

'Braithwaite's in a padded cell!' Ramsey blurted.

'All the more reason why his memorandum would be extremely embarrassing if released to the press,' Denby observed.

Talbot turned on him in fury. 'Denby – you had General Weidener murdered!'

'Charlie.' Dan Madigan spoke for the first time since entering the Oval Office. He felt sorry for Talbot. 'Watch what you're saying . . .'

'I protest!' Denby broke in. 'Even assuming that Weidener was killed, who could produce a shred of evidence it was at my instigation?'

Talbot understood. The CIA chief had covered himself. 'I want your resignations – now,' the President said in hoarse whisper.

'Mr President,' MacDonald Pearce said. 'Before you make more accusations or demands, I believe you should listen to this.' He took a sheet of paper from his inside jacket pocket.

Lexa Talbot returned to the White House in a taxi, hurried to the Oval Office anteroom. A new Secret Service team had come on shift. The secretary was not behind her desk. She played little-girl mischievous. 'Hi, Centurions. I bamboozled your buddies again – left my car in front of Garfinckel's as a joke. Have any idea what happened to it?'

'Security Chief had it towed back, Miss Talbot.'

She made her smile scintillating. 'I'd like to see my father. Okay if I go in?'

'No ma'am. We can't let anyone near the doors.'

Lexa pouted. 'Is he *still* tied up with Mr Hopper?'

'Sorry, Miss Talbot. We're not allowed to say.'

Can't be Hopper then, Lexa thought. 'Please do me a favor. When Daddy surfaces, tell him I'll be upstairs in his suite.'

'Be glad to, Miss Talbot.'

MacDonald Pearce adjusted his eyeglasses. 'Mr President, it pains me greatly to read you Article Four of the Twenty-

Fifth Amendment to the Constitution of the United States . . .'

You dirty bastards! Ken Ramsey bellowed inwardly. He put a hand on Talbot's shoulder, gripped it in a gesture that was supportive, protective. Pearce's voice droned on.

'. . . "Whenever the Vice President and a majority of either the principal officers of the executive departments or of such other body as Congress may by law provide, transmit to the President Pro Tempore of the Senate and the Speaker of the House of Representatives their written declaration that the President is unable to discharge the powers and duties of his office, the Vice President shall immediately assume the powers and duties of the office as Acting President."'

Talbot gasped. Ramsey tightened the hold on his shoulder.

'There are those who have expressed concern about your mental and emotional state, Mr President,' Pearce said with oily solicitude.

'Dan!' It was a cry for help. 'You can't make it stick!'

Madigan averted his eyes. 'Shit, Charlie, nobody wants . . .'

'Mr President.' Pearce cut Madigan short. 'Last week, you impulsively dismissed several Cabinet officers. Today, in an obvious fit of rage, you demand more resignations and hurl baseless charges against responsible officials. You deny – or forget – issuing certain orders and directives. These are hardly rational . . .'

'You can't make it stick,' Talbot repeated in a dull, hollow tone.

Madigan shook his head sadly. 'Probably not, but just starting it up will be enough to finish you, Charlie. An awful lot of people will pile on the lynch-Talbot bandwagon.'

'Alvin Dunlap won't,' Talbot said.

'Christ, man. Your invisible Vice President would give his balls to finish out your term and then run on his own.'

'Dan, the President Pro Tem of the Senate has to . . .'

'Early Frobase? You've forgotten what he's like, Charlie.

He'd perform a hysterectomy on his mother if he could sell her ovaries for an organ-transplant.'

Talbot fought down nausea. 'Get them out, Ken,' he whispered.

'Right, Chief.' Ramsey raised his voice. 'The meeting is ended.' He would have gladly battered all four men to death. 'Leave – fast!'

Pearce, Kurtz, and Denby were jaunty, confident they had won and Talbot was rendered impotent, helpless. Dan Madigan alone walked slowly, glanced at Talbot, wanting to speak – but he found no words.

'Cancel my appointments, Ken,' Talbot groaned when they had gone. 'I feel – I'd better go upstairs.'

Lexa Talbot moved around her father's sitting room, her anxiety and apprehension mounting. It was after four. She had been waiting for what seemed an eternity. She paused in front of a mirror, examined her reflection. Yes, the effect she wanted remained. Her face looked well-scrubbed, angelic – with a few cosmetic touches adding a seductive glow. Her hair, brushed to a sheen, hung free, as he liked to see it.

The door opened. She turned away from the mirror.

'Hello, Puss. They told me you were up here.'

Lexa stared. Her father looked terrible, and he was unsteady on his feet. She felt him sag as she hugged him.

'I'm tired. Beat.' His voice was faint, lifeless.

'Want to lie down, Daddy?' Lexa asked. He nodded. She helped him to his bedroom. He sat heavily on the bed. She knelt, removed his shoes and socks. He stroked her hair, wound a thick strand around a forefinger, gave a weak tug. She stood up, undid his necktie, aided him by removing his jacket.

'You must've had a horrible day,' Lexa fished.

'Worst in my life.' He fell back on the pillows, eyes shut.

'Because of Emmett Hopper?' she probed further.

'Guess it did start with him and those pictures.'

Lexa caught her breath. 'Pictures?' She braced for the worst.

'Uh-huh. He brought photos that show General Weidener was killed.' Talbot shuddered. 'By the CIA . . .'

Lexa experienced a sense of relief that she could not have described. 'It upsets you, Daddy. Don't talk. Try to sleep.' I'm safe – for the present – she thought. Not safe enough, though. I won't be until I get rid of Jim Zander and take out additional insurance. She believed she knew how to do both, and quickly.

Suzanne Loring wisely refrained from making comments when the first bulletins from Kinsolo came over her FM radio. But that had been two hours before and Russell Hatch continued to rant, make futile tries to reach Madigan, and rant more. He *has* to stop or he'll drive me bananas, Suzanne thought. She went to her living-room bar, mixed yet another Scotch highball, brought it to Hatch – who was a livid cursing machine slumped in the corner of a sofa.

'. . . the piss-complected son of a syphilitic whore . . .'

'You win, Russ.' She gave him the glass. 'I'm convinced.'

He took the drink. 'Convinced of what, honey?'

'That you know every obscene, blasphemous, and scatological word in the English language. Now wind down, or I'll wash your mouth out with ZAP, the miracle detergent that clogs your drains permanently.'

The grin flickered feebly, died. 'Madigan suckered me. Got any idea how it feels to be suckered – but like completely?'

His eyes strayed to the telephone on the table beside him.

'Go ahead,' Suzanne sighed. 'Try again.'

He called Madigan's residence. A maid said he had just come in. 'I'll tell him you're on the phone, Senator Hatch.'

Madigan scowled. He had been hoping to duck Hatch until Monday. He picked up an extension. 'My maid says you've been ringing up every ten minutes, Russ. What can I do for you, buddy?'

'Meet me somewhere. I want to have a talk . . .'

'Sorry as hell, Russ. Today and tomorrow are out.'

'Then I'll say my piece to the press without hearing your side.'

'Uh – wait. I'm due at Lady Norworth's at ten. Want to meet me there, I'll ask her if it's okay . . .'

'I'll phone her myself, Dan. You see, I can't quite trust you to deliver messages accurately any longer.'

The liberation of Senator Russell Hatch, Suzanne exulted lovingly and proudly, for she could take credit for bringing it about.

Lady Norworth next. Holcomb put Russ through to her.

'Don't you *ever* check in with your answering service?' Marjorie chided. 'I've been calling your apartment all afternoon. I'd like you to come over and join a small gathering at eight.'

'Eight? I just talked to Madigan. He said ten . . .'

'We have much to discuss before *he* arrives. Oh, yes. Please wear an ordinary business suit, not a dinner jacket.'

Hatch rang off. 'Lady N's cooking some kind of brew,' he said.

'I'd love to know what,' Suzanne said.

'You'll know, honey – soon as I find out myself.'

Russ was dressed in sports shirt and laze-around slacks. He left Suzanne's early, returning to his own apartment to change clothes.

24

Washington, D.C.: Saturday, February 27. Late Afternoon–Early Evening.

Lexa gave her father two Quaalude tablets. They would relax him, induce deep sleep, lasting for hours. She waited until he was snoring gently, left the bedroom, went to her own suite. She unexpectedly found herself slipping into an introspective mood, retrieving random data from her memory banks.

As a little girl, Lexa frequently played with modeling clay. She modeled human figurines – usually male – then twisted and squeezed them into deformed, misshapen lumps. Far-out Freudian precocity, she thought now, but what the hell, I'd rather be a Circe than a sculptor any day. Especially today. It's a real art, and I came by it honestly.

From childhood, Lexa's life had been a Total Immersion course in the techniques of people-manipulation, as might be expected in the case of any professional politician's only child. Maternal influence was non-existent, save as a negative, disorienting factor. Her mother was an unpleasant figure in Lexa's mind, a disgruntled, neurotic woman eternally commuting between solitary drinking bouts and expensive clinics that always promised cures but never delivered. Formative forces were supplied by her father and the men who came to their house and talked into the night about politics – about how to obtain this personal support, wean another away from the opposition, 'nail down' a ward, 'swing' the vote in a city, a county – or, finally – a state.

Shape, sell, buy, bludgeon, bamboozle . . .

Rough. Lexa snapped herself back to the here and now.

She changed clothes, selecting a simple black dress that was ideal for creating optical illusions. With a belt cinched tight at the waist, it was alluring, feminine, obliquely (but unmistakably) sexy. Without the belt it hung loose, seemed slack and rather dowdy. She rolled up the belt, thrust it into her capacious Vuiton shoulderbag, went to her dressing table. Renewing her makeup, she altered it subtly, muting flesh tones down to putty-hued pale, shading eyes and cheeks to appear somewhat sunken. Content with the results, she put on a fake-fur coat and went downstairs to Kenneth Ramsey's office.

Ramsey was visibly unnerved, distressed. Lexa asked no questions. Instead, she said her father was sleeping and she was going to visit some friends. 'Knock off, Ken – go home,' she suggested.

'I will, soon,' he said in a troubled voice. 'After I make a couple of phone calls.' And take a detour, he added silently, thinking of the tape cassette he had swept into a drawer when Lexa entered his office. 'Have a good time, Miss Talbot.'

'I will.' And how!

For once, Lexa Talbot made no effort to lose her security escort when she drove to James Zander's residence.

'You're not looking too good,' Zander said worriedly when they went into his living room. 'Your old man hassle you?'

'He's up the wall. He told me Hopper showed him your photograph. I couldn't find out why, he wasn't volunteering any information.'

'Only me, huh? Not you?'

'Seems not. Hopper must be holding them back – and I'm out of my mind. I'm afraid he plans to spring them on Daddy – or me – late.'

'Jesus Christ! What do you figure I can do?'

'You can't show at the White House, Jim. Daddy was raving about how much damage you can do him politically. He swore he'd "get you" – whatever he meant by that.' Lexa's voice broke. 'He gave me hell, too – blamed me for having recommended you to him.'

'Anything else?' Zander shakily poured himself a full tumbler of Seagram's, opened his gullet, tossed the whiskey down.

'Plenty. For a while, I even thought he knew all about us. He gave me a third-degree about our relationship. I stared at him like I hadn't a clue what he was talking about and said things like "Jim's always been a perfect gentleman" and "I only met him at parties and here in the White House".'

'He believed you?'

'Yes – finally.'

Thank God for that much, Zander thought. No telling what Talbot might do if he suspected I've been balling his daughter. 'How the hell am I going to climb out of this shitpot?' he groaned.

Lexa did something Zander – nor anyone else – had ever seen her do. She bit at her fingernails. 'Jim, I hate to say it, but maybe you should cut, disappear from Washington. I'm sure I can talk Daddy into keeping the bloodhounds off. I'll tell him he'd only cause the scandal he wants to avoid if he has you traced.'

Yes, she can probably do that, Zander mulled, and there's nothing to keep me hanging around here any longer. The house was rented on a month-to-month basis. Its contents were unimportant to him. I could pack my clothes and walk out in a minute, he told himself. But as usual, I'm broke. 'Shit, I can't afford to go very far,' he muttered dejectedly.

Lexa frowned. 'I can help you. I – I should. In a way, I'm partly responsible.' She opened her handbag, took out a checkbook and ballpoint. He watched silently while she wrote a check, tore it out gave it to him. 'Go to the bank first thing Monday morning. I'll phone the manager. You'll get the cash and be able to take off – to Monaco, Canada, wherever you want.'

Zander stared at the check. 'Five thou! A lot of bread. How come, Lexa?'

Eyes misting, she bit at her lower lip. 'Because we had

fun – no, why should I lie, that's not the reason. I'm protecting myself. If they get you – as Daddy said he would – it'll probably be on some phoney trumped-up Federal charges. The FBI – or the reporters – will dig and sooner or later, they'll find out about me.'

'Yeah, they would.' *She's scared – can't blame her for that* Zander thought, *and she's leveling, not handing me any horseshit. God, I never expected to see Lexa Talbot chewing her lip – and her finger nails – and ready to burst into tears at any second.* He reached for the Seagram's bottle. 'Can you use a little of this?'

'I could use it all. Only it's after six. I have to go back. I told Daddy I'd only be gone half an hour, and with the mood he's in . . .'

'Yeah, no use asking for more trouble,' Zander agreed. He fingered the check. 'Uh – thanks, Lexa. And we did have fun . . .'

Scratch one clay figurine, Lexa chortled. She drove two blocks, turned left and pulled over to the curb, killed the Jag's engine. She pulled down her sun-visor. An illuminated mirror was fixed to its back. Switching on the mirror-light, she once more renewed – and again altered – her makeup until she looked less wan and drawn, but rubbed at her eyes to redden them. Taking the rolled-up belt from her handbag, she performed a few contortions to get it under her coat around her waist and draw it tight.

Miss Distraught Innocence, she thought with a last glance in the mirror. She raised the sun-visor. The beginnings of my Reformation Period – and every Reformation needs its front man. She recalled her college French lessons. A *chevalier sans reproche.* Lexa giggled. Since President Talbot had already found one, why shouldn't his daughter share the *chevalier*? Why not, indeed? Perfect protection, a paternally prepared package, she alliterated mentally, still giggling. She started the engine and drove toward Cleveland Park.

Russ Hatch arrived at his apartment shortly after six. A

scalding hot, then icy cold, shower was called for, he decided. It would counteract the brain-fuzzing effects of the numerous scotches he drank at Suzanne's, shape him up for the visit to Lady Norworth's and then the showdown he intended having with Dan Madigan.

Twenty minutes or so later, he was in his stall shower, the water temperature raised to the level he wanted, scrubbing himself vigorously with a loofah. His lean body responded gradually to the spray and friction, ridding itself of tensions along with liquor residues through open and tingling pores. Some day I'll have one of those bathroom-sized saunas installed, he promised himself and grinned, thinking how much fun he and Suzanne could have squeezing into it together.

He barely heard his doorbell above the sound of the gushing water. Grumbling annoyance, he turned off the taps, got out of the shower stall and wrapped a large white bath towel around his waist. He left wet footprints as he hurried to the door and glared resentment when he jerked it open.

Russ's jaw dropped.

'Miss Tal – I mean, Lexa!' His bewilderment and confusion complete, he instinctively reached for the towel that girdled him. The movement was clumsy, loosening the tucked-in corner that held the towel around his waist. It flopped open. He grabbed wildly at the edge and secured it again – but not before Lexa caught a glimpse of his sexual organs. He's beautifully built, she thought, magnificent equipment – an unexpected bonus.

She mimed abashment. 'Please forgive me, Russ. I – I should've phoned, but I'm terribly upset and wanted to see you.' She made as if to turn and go off. 'I'll leave, though . . .'

'Uh – look, no. Don't,' Russ gabbled. 'Come on in. Living room over there. Bar's in the corner. Make yourself at home. I'll hurry it up.'

'Well, if I won't be too much of a nuisance . . .'

She was already inside. He swung the door shut, dashed down the corridor leading to his bedroom and bath. He broke all records drying himself and putting on the clothes he would wear later to the House on the Hill.

He went to join Lexa in the living room. She had taken her coat off and sat drinkless, disconsolately wringing her hands.

'Holy smoke! What's wrong? You . . .'

'It's not me, Russ.' She shook her head, blond hair shimmering. 'It's Daddy – I came to you because he likes and trusts you.' Her lips formed into a wan but sincere smile. 'I do, too – I have, ever since we went to Wilmington together . . .'

'Hey, take it easy, Lexa.' His tone and smile were those of the sympathetic, protective male. 'Suppose I mix you a drink . . .'

'No, I'd rather not have one.' She gazed up at him. He saw that she must have been crying.

'All right – then take it slow. You started to say that the President – your father . . .'

'He's had a terrible shock of some kind.'

'I'm afraid he's had several, Lexa. We all have. The news from Africa . . .'

Hatch's voice trailed off. Talbot had a 'terrible shock'? If what Lexa said was true – and he didn't doubt it for an instant for she was clearly very much wrought up herself – it lent additional credence to Suzanne's theory that Talbot really was a victim, not a perpetrator.

'It's the fault of those God-awful men,' Lexa said, as though reading his thoughts. 'They tear him to bits!'

'Who in particular?' Russ asked. He was momentarily in an ambivalent dilemma. On the one hand, he wanted to comfort Lexa. On the other, he desired to draw what information he could from her.

'They're so many.' She searched for a name. 'MacDonald Pearce for one.' She detested Pearce. 'He and the others! You'd never believe Talbot was a President when he came upstairs this afternoon. He was a nervous wreck.' She dabbed at her eyes with a handkerchief. 'I – I gave him something so he'd sleep and came over here to ask your help.'

'Lexa,' Russ said with kindly patience. 'You picked the wrong person. I'm a nobody in Washington. I'll be even less after I repudiate that speech I made yesterday. There isn't much – if anything – I can do to help President Talbot.'

'But there *is*! Kenneth Ramsey and I are the only people near him who are loyal. He can't trust the rest – but he does trust you. If you come to the White House more often, cheer him up, tell him what the others won't . . .'

'Good Lord, Lexa! I can't go barging in on the President – or even into the White House – without going through the red tape of making appointments and . . .'

'I live there, too, Russ. I can invite anyone I want.'

'But . . .'

'Whenever you come, I'll see that you and Daddy can talk together.' She stood up, held both his hands. Her eyes were pleading. 'Stay tomorrow night. We'll have dinner – the three of us. It'll work wonders for him.' And for me. You're going to be my increasingly frequent escort, Senator. The media and public will flip over Charles Talbot's White Knight doubling as my *chevalier blanc* – my Reformation front-man. 'Please, Russ. I'm inviting you – officially, personally, however you want – but please say you'll come.'

'Sure, Lexa. Of course. I'm – well, honored.' What else can I say?

He was totally unprepared for what followed.

Lexa flung her arms around him. 'Oh, I'm so glad – so grateful.' There were tears in her eyes and her lips were open as they covered his mouth. She held him tightly – then broke away. 'You're a great person, Russ.' She forced a smile. 'I'll go now. I want to look in on Daddy.'

The smile was endearing – and arousing. Russ fought to gain control over glands that had been activated by her kiss and the manner in which she held him to her.

'Eight tomorrow?' Lexa asked throatily, holding his eyes – and Russ's glands operated even more strongly.

'Eight'll be fine.' He had difficulty bringing the words up through his constricted throat, which closed almost completely a moment later. She kissed him again – and the press of her pelvis against his thigh was unmistakable. She released him, picked up her fake-fur.

He held her coat. She turned suddenly, her firm breasts rubbing against the backs of his hands. 'Thank you again, Russ.' Then she slid her arms into the coat-sleeves.

Lexa refused to let him accompany her any further than the elevator. The doors were open. The car was empty. She stepped inside, grinned, touched his face. 'You know, freckles always did get to me.' She withdrew her hand as the elevator door slid shut. Russ stood staring at it for several seconds before retracing his steps to his apartment.

25

The House on the Hill: Saturday, February 27. Evening and Night.

Marjorie Norworth welcomed Russell Hatch in her Green Room, kissing his cheek. Her plain, dark-gray Thai silk shift designed exclusively for her by Bungaro, would have looked drab on any other woman. On Majorie, it was an exquisite understatement of high fashion. And only she could have carried off the single piece of jewelry she chose to wear this evening: an enormous, intricately carved white jade medallion – early T'ang Dynasty – it had been given to her by Aristotle Onassis as a princely gesture of gratitude.

Many years before, a cartel of American shipowners had mounted a campaign to ruin Onassis. Buying up legislators, Executive Branch officials and members of the judiciary, the cartel was certain it would succeed. The Federal Government brought criminal and civil actions against Onassis for alleged violations of U.S. maritime laws and promptly seized five of his tankers then in American ports or waters.

Although the charges were based on fine-print technicalities (or trumped-up), the Greek shipping magnate's attorneys despaired. Aware of the overwhelming forces deployed against their client, they predicted that – at best – he faced loss of the seized tankers, a two-year suspended sentence, and a multimillion-dollar fine.

Marjorie and Onassis were old acquaintances. She liked him, enjoyed his bawdy songs and humor, admired the panache with which he confronted his adversaries. She recognized his predicament as an opportunity to demonstrate her own powers and stepped in, pulling strings and mounting pressures at the upper levels of Federal official-dom. The charges against Onassis were dropped. He asked what she would like as a token of his appreciation.

'Oh, I don't know, Ari,' she told him, laughing. 'It should be something no one else has – like a recording of you singing "The Buggering Bishop". In stereo, of course. I wouldn't want to miss any of your *basso profundo* or *tenor castrato* cadenzas when I play it.'

The ribald song consisted of several dozen limerick-like verses and described the good bishop's sexual organ as:

> 'A staff beyond measure, Rome's greatest treasure,
> Exceeding in chunk an elephant's trunk,
> No anus on Earth could swallow its girth.
> He had to call upon God and rip open the pod
> Before he could insert it for pleasure.'

Ari Onassis embellished the verses that followed with interpolations of deep bass grunts and groans – of the Bishop as he went about his buggeries and high-pitched cries and squeals – of altar and choir boys being sodomized by the mitered cleric:

> 'To whose sanctified ear no hymn was so dear
> As the melodious twang of the sphincters he sprang
> In making the path for his Bishopric clear.'

Onassis did make a recording of 'The Buggering Bishop' and gave it to Marjorie – along with the jade gorget that no-one else could have, either. There was not another like it in the world.

All Washington knew of the gift and the story behind it. Marjorie flaunted the magnificent ornament only on occasions when she wanted to remind guests – or some particular individual among them – how far her influence reached and what it could accomplish. She was wearing it now as part of a craftily orchestrated design aimed at demoralizing a guest who would not arrive until later.

*

Russell Hatch was acquainted with Bradford Cooley, but had not before met the outwardly bland FBI Director Emmett Hopper. Marjorie introduced them and blithely – if, to Russ's mind, cryptically – eliminated conversational preliminaries.

'Russ, one night about two weeks after JFK's assassination, Lyndon Johnson and his cronies had a long session in the Red Room. Lyndon called it a political surgery-seminar. He and his Texas Rangers dissected Kennedy's Irish mafia leftovers – *in absentia*, needless to say – and did exploratory autopsies on each other. We're doing much the same.'

Hatch took the cognac Holcomb served him. 'To stay with metaphors I don't quite follow, is this my anesthetic?'

'It's truth serum, the deadliest of all poisons for a politician,' Brad Cooley said wryly and drank some of his bourbon.

'Brad and Emmett are inveterate skeptics,' Marjorie said to Russ. 'Even about my intuitions, which *I* consider infallible. I believe you to be completely trustworthy. They want to satisfy themselves that you are.'

Russ felt his hackles rising. 'Did you invite me here to taken an old-fashioned FBI loyalty oath?' he asked testily.

'Depends on where your loyalties lie,' Emmett Hopper said.

'I often wonder about that myself.'

'We all do at times,' Cooley murmured. His tone sharpened. 'You spoke on the Senate extolling the Administration's African policy.'

'To my regret, I have to plead guilty.'

'You said on the floor that you'd disown Talbot if there was any evidence of escalation or intervention.'

'I did, and I will.'

'But not before consulting your mentor, Madigan?' Hopper asked.

'The word "consult" isn't applicable. I want his version of why everything suddenly broke loose. I don't want to go off half-cock and harm . . .'

'The Administration?' Hopper broke in.

'The national interest, corny as that may sound.'

'Do you hold Charles Talbot responsible for recent events?'

Damned if I enjoy being grilled like this, Russ thought. *It's like some sort of star-chamber proceeding. However, I'll ride along – then start asking my own questions.*

'*De jure* – the final responsibility is his. He's the President, the Chief Executive. *De facto* – I'm not so sure. I've begun to have doubts and form theories which may or may not be valid . . .'

'They probably are,' Cooley said. 'Politicians survive by creating illusions. Madigan gave you the illusion he was obeying Talbot, following his orders. The truth is otherwise. Madigan, Pearce – God knows how many others in Washington – take their orders from Jordan B. Rickhoven III. And so, to a degree, does Charles Talbot.'

It ties in with what Lexa was so wrought up about, Hatch reflected . . . and what Suzy suspected.

'Worse yet, Talbot's supposed subordinates make major decisions without his knowledge, often in direct conflict with his wishes,' Emmett Hopper said.

'Wait, Emmett,' Marjorie interrupted. 'Charlie Talbot is neither an iron man nor an intellectual giant, but I assure you Presidents who were both had very similar problems. Take FDR for example. He loathed Chiang Kai-shek and despised all Chinese. Yet he supported Chiang. Why? Because the major oil companies told him he *must*. Chiang had organized them oil concessions in China. Franklin couldn't afford to antagonize the oil companies.'

Hatch savored the superb Otard he was served. 'In short, you're telling me that President Talbot is a dupe?'

'Not entirely blameless or unwitting – but yes,' Cooley nodded. 'He has been duped and is being duped even more.'

The conversation continued for half an hour, steadily becoming less of an interrogation, more of an exchange of thoughts, opinions, evaluations. Russ sensed that he was being accepted by Cooley and Hopper. But for what reason or purpose were they testing him? The explanations came soon.

Brad Cooley plucked at one of his many chins. 'Bear with me while I deliver a lecture, Russ.' He swallowed bourbon as if to lubricate his vocal cords. 'The men we've been talking about have formed themselves into what is little short of being a civilian junta. Until today, Charles Talbot tried – albeit feebly – to exercise some restraint over them. This afternoon, he was forced into becoming their silenced and submissive partner. As matters now stand, this country is headed hell-bent for war and, preposterous as it may sound to you, beyond war. Into a form of what – for want of a better term – I will call dictatorship.' He glanced at Hopper. 'Care to take over?'

Hopper nodded and spoke for fifteen minutes, giving a bare-bones précis of the backstage and offstage events that had begun with the Weidener murder and culminated in the Oval Office that afternoon.

'Kenneth Ramsey took the precaution of secretly tape-recording the conversation between Talbot and the quad-rumvirate headed by MacDonald Pearce, who is apparently Jordan Rickhoven's Washington mouthpiece. Ramsey brought me a copy of the tapes early this evening. You may hear it if you wish, or accept my word. The last spark of authority – of ability to resist – has been crushed out of Charles Talbot.'

That coincides almost exactly with the description Lexa gave of her father's reactions, Russ thought, but he was wary, very much on his guard. 'I'll accept that Dan Madigan dragged me into a conspiracy,' he said. 'But now you're obviously trying to involve me in what has all the hallmarks of another. Why – and why me?'

'For much the same reasons as Madigan,' Cooley replied. 'You're young, which means you have energy and resiliency. You haven't been in politics long enough to lose all ideals and integrity. You possess – God I detest the word – charisma, an invaluable asset if we are forced to go to the public. Then, you've already established some degree of rapport with Talbot and have access to him . . .'

'I'm supposed to have dinner with him at the White House tomorrow night,' Russ blurted.

Marjorie registered surprise. 'Did Charlie invite you?'

'No. It was his daughter, Lexa.' Hatch did not elaborate.

Lexa Talbot! Marjorie's eyes narrowed, mind operating at top speed. How did I – how *could* I – fail to think of her? Lexa could be a major – even a decisive – piece in my private chess game.

Marjorie had tuned herself out of the men's talk; now she tuned back in as Cooley was saying . . .

'. . . we're not asking for a total commitment until you're absolutely certain, Russ. What we ask now is that you delay disclaiming your Senate speech. You'll begin to understand why before the evening is over.'

Russ spluttered protest. 'You're not making sense. The hawks . . .'

'. . . will be lulled and gulled,' Hopper said calmly. 'Which is not vital but would certainly be helpful to our overall strategy.'

'Which is?'

'I'll give details when you've made a final decision to join the cause,' Cooley grinned. 'The key points – why not? One, we build a hasty defensive wall around Talbot – who, with all his faults, *is* the President. Two, we neutralize the civilian junta – beginning tonight with Dan Madigan. Three, with the cabal defanged, we prop up Talbot and polish his image until he fairly blinds one and all with the light of his statesmanship. I hardly need add that the illumination will be artificial. *Son et lumière* provided by the Charles Pendleton Talbot Protective Society.'

That's not a strategy, Russ Hatch thought. It's a long-odds gamble. On the other hand, even limited war would tear the country apart; so would the removal of a President under the Twenty-Fifth Amendment. Totally brainless, totally unprincipled Alvin Dunlap in the Presidental chair – unthinkable! Even more unthinkable was the prospect of what Brad Cooley had called 'rule by civilian junta'.

Automobile tires crunched on the gravel drive outside.

'It's Dan Madigan,' Marjorie warned and underwent instant transformation into her famed-but-garrulous-Washington-hostess role. 'Did I ever tell you what was positively the most harrowing aspect of the Carter administration?' she chattered. 'Well! During his first year, it was *de rigueur* for everyone to devour peanuts. Naturally, I had to have bowls of the nauseating things everywhere. Guests scooped them up by the handfuls – it was considered practically an act of treason if they didn't – and invariably some dropped on the carpets, where they were stepped on and crushed into greasy globs. My carpet-cleaning bills were astronomical . . .'

Holcomb announced Senator Daniel Madigan. Russ did a double take. Madigan was resplendent in dinner jacket, ruffle-fronted shirt, and colorful rough-woven cummerbund – imported from Basanda and the latest rage among capital hawks. His face blazed scarlet. He was under the impression Majorie had invited him to a Saturday night black-tie party. The only guests in the Green Room were Cooley, Emmett Hopper, and Hatch – all in ordinary street clothes.

Marjorie smirked inwardly. When she had spoken to Madigan her invitation was carefully worded. Without saying so, she led him to think many guests would be present and dinner jackets worn. The psychological ploy was effective. Madigan, obsessive about being appropriately garbed, saw that he was outlandishly overdressed and felt like a fool.

'Uh – I'm sorry,' he stammered, already on the defensive – and thus at a start-off disadvantage. 'I must have misunderstood . . .'

'Everyone makes mistakes, Dan,' Marjorie smiled, toying with her white jade medallion. 'Take off your tie if that will make you any less conspicuous.' The suggestion was a thrust calling added attention to his gaffe. The business of stroking her jade gorget further increased his discomfiture.

Madigan had done yeoman work for the shipping cartel that sought to ruin Aristotle Onassis. In the Senate, he called for a special investigating committee to probe into Onassis's business affairs and private life. Protected by the immunity enjoyed by Senators who speak from the floor, he denounced the Greek shipowner in numerous speeches, openly accusing him of every imaginable crime and perfidy.

When the Federal actions against Onassis were suddenly dropped, Dan Madigan had suffered shocks at several levels. He had believed the cartel was omnipotent. He was certain the outcome would be cut-and-dried, with Onassis crushed and bankrupt. Worst of all, he lost the whole payoff (which he had considered as good as in his pocket) that he was to have earned from the cartel for his services.

Now Marjorie Norworth was waving the jade medallion in his face, reminding him of how she had managed to turn the tables.

Madigan manufactured a smile, asked Holcomb for straight rye whiskey, sat down. The atmosphere's all wrong, he thought. The vibes aren't bad – they're hostile.

'Hear you had a big confab with the President, Dan,' Cooley said lazily. 'You, Pearce, Kurtz, and cloak-and-dagger Kirby.'

'Charlie – President Talbot called us in . . .'

'For an ass-chewing session, only he's the one who got mauled.'

'Afraid you're off the beam, Brad.' *You fucking fag bastard.*

'I'm not, Dan. You are. You think every angle is covered and the machinery can't be stopped . . .'

Madigan unconsciously tugged at his collar.

'. . . and maybe it can't be. Might be that you hawks'll get your war. It'll finish you personally in politics, though. Ever stop to think of that? Sure, you're safe in the Senate until the next election – when war-mongering Dan Madigan won't collect enough votes to be elected Cook County Sewer Commissioner.'

The Senate Majority Leader slammed down his glass. 'I'm leaving.'

'Stay for the parlor games,' Marjorie said, again running fingers over the jade gorget. 'I'm thinking of a number. Seven thousand, seven hundred and ninety-two . . .'

Madigan stiffened, turned white.

'. . . Your account number at the Bauer Kreditbank in Zurich. You drank too much at a party I gave three years ago, took me off in a corner and boasted about it. I *do* have a phenomenal memory, Dan.'

Hopper leaned forward. 'The FBI isn't what it used to be, Senator, but it's maintained connections with various agencies in foreign countries. We could have photostats of all pertinent records en route by courier within thirty-six hours.'

'They'll show all those generous deposits made by Rickhoven and God knows who else,' Brad Cooley leered. 'Jack Anderson would find them fascinating. Or would you prefer Woodward and Bernstein to have first option?'

'You're blackmailing me!' was all Madigan could think to say, and he yelped the words.

'So we are,' Hopper said amiably. 'Not with the Twenty-Fifth Amendment, however.'

Madigan's eyes popped. How did Hopper know? How could he possibly know? Had Talbot talked? Or Pearce or Kurtz or Denby? No. It couldn't be any of them. He wilted as four pairs of eyes stared at him fixedly, mercilessly. He felt as though they were nailing him into his chair. Or my political coffin, he thought.

'What the hell are you people after?' he croaked. 'What do you want from me?'

'Very little,' Cooley replied. 'In fact, we want you to do nothing, absolutely nothing until, say, Friday. Make no speeches or statements. Keep a low profile. If Rickhoven or anyone else asks why you've been struck dumb and paralyzed, you have a plausible excuse. It's your stand-aside tactic to prevent suspicions of plot or conspiracy. You're showing the world that the Legislative Branch doesn't meddle in Executive Branch affairs.'

'Look at it in another light, Dan,' Marjorie murmured. 'You're a hard-nosed, pragmatic pol. By now, it should be clear to you that countermoves will be made against Jordan Rickhoven's trouble-sewing-circle – mmm, I'm proud of myself for that. Anyway, between tonight and Friday, you'll be able to judge in which direction the scales are tipping and join the winning side with fanfares and flourishes.'

No question in my mind who'll win, Madigan thought. *The Rickhoven State-Defense combination is unbeatable*. Then his eyes.

went to Marjorie's carved jade ornament. He was struck with sudden doubt – but only for a split second. *There was no one Marjorie could squeeze at the top because everyone at the top was either in on the deal or powerless. She can't do a God-damned thing to stop what's been started – and neither can Cooley, Hopper, or that double-crossing snot, Hatch. Not that he can guess what he's doing – or thinks he's doing – in this. But they could hurt me personally – hurt me bad – if I don't play ball with them in it, it's only till Friday – or so they say – and much as I hate to admit it, Cooley is right. The excuses will not only stick, but I could get a pat on the back for being so shrewd.*

'Let's get this straight – what you've asked is really all you want?' Madigan asked.

'Except for a minor favor, yes,' Marjorie smiled. 'Keep next Wednesday night free. I'm giving one of my theme-parties. It starts at ten – yes, dinner-jackets. You *must* come.'

'You've made me an invitation I can't refuse,' Dan Madigan said sourly.

'He'll behave,' Emmett Hopper predicted after Madigan left.

'Certainly until Wednesday night,' Marjorie agreed.

'After which, the die shall have been cast,' Brad Cooley intoned, not quite managing to achieve the humorous effect he sought. 'The Rubicon crossed.'

A late supper was served in Lady Norworth's non-facsimile *petite salle à manger* down the corridor from her Red Room. She asked Russell Hatch to sit on her right at the round table that could have easily accommodated eight people. they were starting on their *homard* – which Brad Cooley attacked with gusto and Emmett Hopper savoured with a gourmet's delight – when Marjorie smiled at Russ and made a wholly unexpected and incongruous observation.

'You know, strange as it may seem, I'm acquainted with almost everyone who matters in Washington, but I haven't met one of our leading celebrities, Suzanne Loring.' She saw his startled expression. Then her smile deepened, 'Russ, no relationship has lasted two weeks, much less two years – in this city without my hearing about it.'

'Suzy and I have never hidden behind the bushes,' Russ laughed, recovering from his surprise. 'It's that you mentioned her out of the blue . . .'

'With ulterior purpose. I'd like to meet her – and very quickly. Could you do me a great favor and bring her over for tea on Monday?'

Russ bridled, recalling how Madigan had prevailed upon him to use Suzanne. There would be no repeat performances, not even for Lady Marjorie Norworth.

'I need her professional advice and want to offer her a most unique opportunity to further her career.'

'A bit indefinite – even nebulous . . .'

'It has to be, until I speak with her personally.'

Russ stared at his lobster. 'Afraid I'll have to decline, Marjorie. I stuck my nose into Suzy's professional life once. Never again . . . We almost split up . . .'

'Miss Loring will be free to make her own decisions,' Lady Norworth said. 'I simply thought you would like to escort her. If not, I can always find another intermediary – or get in touch with her myself.'

True, Russ thought. He said, 'You have me, Marjorie. I'll tell Suzy what you said. It'll be up to her whether she wants to come or not. I won't urge . . .'

'Good Lord! I never intended that you should.' Marjorie was satisfied. *Suzanne Loring will leap at the chance to visit the House on the Hill and satisfy her curiosity about it – and about me. She'll leap faster still to accept my proposals.* 'Go on, Russ,' she said with maternal chuckle. 'Eat your *homard* before it melts.'

The men talked. Marjorie Norworth did not listen. She felt supremely confident she would be adding not one, but two, pieces to her private chess set – both of them queens, capable of sweeping the board in any direction. Her mind was occupied with contriving permutations of the moves she could make with them.

26

Washington, D.C.: Sunday, February 28.

Talk continued at the House on the Hill until almost 3:00 A.M. Seasoned veterans of countless intrigues, Lady Norworth, Cooley, and Hopper spoke guardedly, but were frank in telling Russell Hatch that they did. Specifics would be withheld until he finally cast his own die – which he would have to do on Monday, Lady Norworth stressed, for time was short. Even so, they fleshed out the skeleton of their grand design sufficiently for Russ to comprehend that they had potent resources at their disposal and were determined to use them all.

Although bursting to tell Suzanne what he had heard and learned, Russ returned to his own apartment and did not telephone her. It was, he told himself, too late and she would be fast asleep, but this was a rationalization. The Byzantine conspiracies into which he had been – and was being – drawn dismayed him. Their implications overloaded his brain circuits. He wanted to be alone, review the input, appraise it on his own.

Russ sat in his kitchen, drinking coffee laced with Remy-Martin cognac, engrossed with his mental jigsaw puzzle. It defied him, there were either too many fragments or not enough, and very few interlocking contours. *I'm only a hick lawyer*, he thought dismally, sloshing more coffee and Remy into his cup. He downed the mixture, repeated the process – this time increasing the cognac ration. *I'm so far out of my league that I shouldn't even be allowed into the ballpark.*

Horseshit!

I wasn't allowed in, I was dragged. He emptied his cup, reached for coffeepot, then brandy bottle.

Horseshit again!

Innate honesty prevailed.

I wasn't dragged. I sure as hell didn't dig in my heels and kick or scream. Your Honor, we stipulate that the accused went along quietly and offered no resistance.

If I've been suckered – and am being suckered again – then what Brad Cooley said about Charles Talbot applies to me, too. 'Not entirely blameless or unwitting.' Only I'm even less blameless and unwitting than Talbot.

I'm also drunk and getting drunker.

My cup runneth dry. He squinted at the residue of dark fluid. *Maybe I could get some answers by reading coffee dregs. Like reading tea leaves. Oh, balls. What I need is a cross-reading from Suzy. If there are any answers, she'll have them.*

Russ scoured fingers through his tangle of red hair, reached for the Remy bottle. He ruefully conceded that Suzanne Loring was better equipped to interpret and interpolate, assay, and evaluate.

Woman's intuition. Nope, it's more than that. Suzy has her finger on the Washington pulse as they say – whoeverthefuck they are and whereverthefuck the pulse is located. I'll have to ask Suzy to tell me. I should've asked Marjorie.

His silent, cognac-fueled soliloquy took a sharp, abrupt turn.

Suzanne Loring-Lady Marjorie Norworth.

It had suddenly dawned on him that, despite the great difference in their ages and backgrounds, the two women had much in common. Both were motivated – driven – by an obsessive desire to be in on and part of whatever transpired at power levels in Washington.

That's where the pulse is located – where else? Hatch mused. *Who gives a diarrheic crap if stenographers or hall porters – if any of the jerks who pull voting-booth levers – even have a pulse? Nobody. In fact, no body. If they're not breathing, vote 'em dead. Resurrection men. Take the names off the gravestones and put 'em on the registration rolls – and three cheers for the Red, White and Blue.*

Suzy knows it. Marjorie knows it. They make the most of it, counting every pulse-throb, picking up on every offbeat beat and fibrillation.

The cup was empty. So was the Remy bottle. Russ debated whether to fetch a fresh bottle from his liquor cabinet, put the question to a vote. *The Nays carry. I'm smashed as it is, and I have a big day ahead. Suzy – then off to 1600 Pennsylvania Avenue.*

Hey! Lexa Talbot. I must be slipping. He peered at the kitchen clock; it read 4:45. *I've been sitting here more than an hour and a half and never even thought of her.* Buoyed by alcoholic updrafts, his ego soared. *Lexa wasn't just cock-teasing – it went beyond that. Way beyond.* The macho balloon burst. *How do you make it with a President's daughter? Do the Secret Service men tie blindfolds around their heads or stand by holding candles while they watch?*

He grimaced.

While I'm at it, I wonder if Lexa is a pulse taker and power player, too? I suppose she is – in her own way. She admitted she liked being in the driver's seat. I think she meant it. But I can't compare her to Suzy or Lady Norworth. Lexa sits at the right hand of her father who art in the Oval Office and while he sure isn't omniscient and omnipotent, she can relax and bask in the reflected power and glory, Amen.

His bleary mind much amused by the idiotic line, Russ laughed aloud and lurched from kitchen to bathroom. He was clumsily brushing his teeth when a new thought struck him. There were now three women in his life. Suzanne, Lady Marjorie Norworth and Lexa Talbot. *Suzy's Number One,* he assured himself. *Marjorie's on a far-removed plane. As for, Lexa – she's yet another part of my jigsaw puzzle that doesn't fit, and I can't see how she ever will.*

Nevertheless, when he went to sleep, Russ dreamed of Lexa Talbot. The dreams were erotic and, despite the amount of liquor he had drunk and although he was not aware of it, his penis grew rock-hard.

President Charles Talbot started his day at 9:00 A.M., ended it after a fifteen-minute conversation with Kenneth Ramsey.

Ramsey was stunned by the overnight change in the President. Talbot smiled broadly, had a breezy air, acted as though he did not have a single care in the world.

'Chief, the press corps is in an uproar, demanding a statement.'

'Rehash old ones and let it go at that, Ken.'

'But the latest news bulletins . . .'

'Fuck 'em. Refer all questions to the appropriate Cabinet Departments – and, oh, yeah, cancel all my appointments. Say I've gone fishing or ran off with an upstairs maid.'

'I can't fathom your attitude, Chief. It doesn't add.'

'Does for me. I've been skinned alive, and my hide's nailed to the wall. I woke up this morning after sleeping fourteen–fifteen hours, took a good healthy shit and a hot bath and made a major decision. I'll serve out my term coasting and not give a damn what the history books say about me.'

'You won't fight those bastards?'

'And be booted out of office on the grounds that I'm mentally incompetent? Ken, there's a lesson every politician learns. When you've been licked – fair or dirty – shake hands with the cocksuckers who licked you. Otherwise, you can't salvage anything.' Talbot shrugged. 'From here on in, I'll play golf like Eisenhower, screw around like JFK and Johnson, and go skiing like Ford.'

Ken Ramsey swallowed, wet his lips. 'You have almost a dozen appointments scheduled. Sure you don't want to see the people?'

'What, on a Sunday?' Talbot exclaimed with mock indignation. 'I refuse to profane the Sabbath.' He grinned. 'I'll be socializing tonight, though. Lexa stopped me when I was coming downstairs. She's invited Russ Hatch to dinner. I'll enjoy being with Lexa and Hatch. They're young, lively, and won't do any hatchet jobs on Good Old Charlie Talbot, the skinless wonder.'

Suzanne Loring had brunch ready when Russ arrived at one. Hangover and inefficient sleep made him more receptive to the spicy, double-strength bullshots than the creamed chipped beef-and-mushrooms on toast but did not hinder him from talking rapidly and nonstop.

Suzanne listened intently while he told her about the long evening at Lady Norworth's. Her right eyebrow climbed high early on in the monologue and remained there. Her large, deep brown eyes gleamed increasingly brighter as he continued. Visions of Emmy and Pulitzer awards were dancing furiously in her head. She had already retrieved discarded plans for the big inside-story network special that Noah Sturdevant had wanted her to do, dusted them off – and was mentally expanding them. The show would be infinitely bigger and more sensational than he – or she – had dreamed possible.

'. . . call it a cabal, but I prefer Cooley's tag, a "civilian junta". They gave Talbot an ultimatum. If he tries to make waves, they'll kick him out, using the Twenty-Fifth Amendment . . .'

God, I wish I could take notes, Suzanne thought, but that might distract Russ, break the flow.

'. . . Hopper says he has a tape of the meeting, offered to let me hear it . . .'

He took a long swallow of his third bullshot, went on, describing the scene with Dan Madigan and what followed. He was finishing the fourth when he neared the windup – and remembered.

'Oh, I promised to pass a message on to you, honey . . .'

'To me?' Suzy blinked surprise. 'From whom?'

'Marjorie Norworth. She asked me to find out if you'd like to come over for tea tomorrow – wants me to bring you. She said she valued your professional advice – and to make you a proposal that would help your career. She didn't elaborate . . .'

'What did you say?' Suzanne asked eagerly.

'I wasn't about to foul up like I did with the Madigan interview, so I kind of hedged. I agreed to play messenger boy – and leave it up to you whether you wanted to go or not.'

'Thank God!'

Russ grinned knowingly, as though she had confirmed his original opinion. 'I'm glad I did hedge and make it clear. I had a hunch you'd refuse . . .'

'Refuse? You lunatic! I meant thank God you didn't turn the invitation down and didn't forget to mention it to me. You couldn't keep me away if I was in labor . . .'

She guillotined the rest of the sentence, remembering that Russ Hatch's wife had died in agony as a result of an ectopic pregnancy. 'I – I'm sorry, Russ,' she murmured, reaching across the table and taking his hand.

He held and squeezed it. 'Funny, until you apologized, I never even got the connection.' He smiled. There was no trace of remembered loss in his eyes.

Suzanne's heart did a dance competing with that being performed by the visions in her head. *He's getting over it at last*, she thought. Even so, she sensed it best to exercise caution. *Don't push your luck, kiddo*, she warned herself – *and for Christ's sake, don't push him. Let the 'I-love-you/I-love-you-too' moment of truth arrive naturally.*

'So you really want to go?' Russ asked.

'Think I'd miss the chance to be presented to Her Majesty, Washington's greatest living legend? What time?'

'Five. I'll pick you up at like four-thirty.' He tickled her palm with his forefinger. 'Unless you have objections to riding around town with vulgar and obscene characters.'

It being Sunday and the maid's day off, she stood up and began to clear the table.

Russ had saved the news that he was having dinner at the White House for last, tossed it off with an overdone nonchalance that triggered Suzanne's suspicions.

'Talbot ask you to drop over and spoon-feed him?'

Russ felt his face flush, could not lie. 'No. Lexa . . .'

'*Oh?* Is Miss Twitchy-twat baking a cake?'

The flush deepened. 'She thinks Talbot needs to relax, talk to somebody who isn't stabbing him in the back – and damn it, honey, you've got her all wrong. Lexa is . . .'

He broke off, lost for a word or term that wouldn't make matters worse.

'Go on, Sir Galahad,' Suzanne urged. 'Lexa Talbot is *what*?'

He took a deep breath, plunged ahead. 'She's a kid who worries about her father.' He should have stopped there but blundered on. 'Why, she even broke down and cried yesterday . . .'

'You were at the White House?'

Ouch, now I am up to my ears and beyond, Russ groaned silently. 'No. She – uh, came over to my place.'

Goddamnit, you think you've advanced a foot and find you've lost a mile, Suzanne thought angrily and snapped, 'Naturally, you fucked.'

'We did not!'

Suzy knew him well enough to realize he was telling her the truth. *But you will*, she mused with bitter resignation, *and somehow or other, you'll be royally fucked in the process*. She dumped dishes into the sink with such force that two broke.

She regretted the show of jealousy immediately. *Men had their convoluted sense of sportsmanship and gallantry. They sprang to the defence of the object of a jealous outburst – siding with the underbitch, as it were*, she reflected, and worked at repairing the damage.

She soothed Russ, made a joke of the flareup, coaxed him into light banter that led to kisses and fondlings – and finally into her bedroom. There, she gave a virtuoso performance – but, for the first time in their relationship, found it necessary to feign her orgasms.

Why can't I make it! she brooded. *Is it because I'm really jealous, afraid of Lexa Talbot who's seven years younger than I am, the President's daughter, and – my instincts tell me – an oversexed broad who already has Russ hot and eager? Or am I too hot and eager about the special I'm going to get – and I will – to concentrate on making love?*

Either way, I'm the one who's a bitch, she berated herself. *I'm faking orgasm with the man I love. That's a worse form of cheating than screwing somebody behind his back.*

The West Sitting Room adjoins the Presidential bedroom suite in the White House Family Quarters. Under Lexa Talbot's aegis as her father's hostess, it had been redecorated with heavy emphasis on art deco and Tiffany lamps. It was there that Charles Talbot personally mixed the pre-dinner martinis. He made them extremely strong, dry, and cold in a quart-size pitcher, poured three drinks, held up his own glass and grinned broadly at Russell Hatch.

'How do the spicks say it? *Mi casa es su casa* or something like that. Anyway, you get the idea – even if *mi casa* is the White *Casa*.' Talbot's tone and manner showed it was by no means his first drink of the day.

'Dangerous thing to tell a Senator.' Lexa laughed. 'He may take you literally.'

'And move into the Oval Office? You're welcome to it, Russ – after I move out, that is.' Talbot downed his martini, immediately poured himself another. 'That won't be for a while, though.'

Russell Hatch drank slowly, thoughtfully. The President may have had a few, but he was jovial, giving no evidence of the depression Lexa had described.

'Play golf, Russ?'

'A little – and badly.'

'Then it'd be an even match. How about a round when the weather warms up?'

'Be delighted, Mr President.'

'Damn it, Man. You're an upstairs guest, a friend of the family. Stop the Mr President stuff. Try Charlie.'

In the midst of swallowing some of Talbot's sixteen-to-one gin-and-vermouth mixture, Russ waited for the process to complete itself before speaking. 'You put together a great martini – Charlie.'

'Can't get ahead in politics unless you're a good bartender.' Talbot chortled and began mixing another pitcherful. 'I pocketed the Philadelphia Machine with martinis the second time I ran for the Senate. Remember, Puss?'

Lexa nodded. 'How could I forget? Timberlake – that was his name. The boss wound up yelling "We're with you, Charlie!" and peed out through an open window screaming "Piss on everybody else."'

'Damn near fell out of the window, too. Would have, if I hadn't grabbed him.'

'He slobbered all over you. Claimed you'd saved his life.'

'Got us almost eighty thousand votes.' Talbot patted the pitcher, grasped its handle, refilled the glasses. 'Here's to my martini and votes – got any extras lying around, Russ?'

'Only mine. You won that on the first drink.'

'I must be improving. You didn't piss out the window.'

'Thank God!' Lexa said. 'There's probably a guard standing underneath.'

The Family Dining Room connects with the West Sitting Room. Talbot led the way after yet another round of cocktails. He sat at the head of the oblong table, Lexa on his right, Russ on his left facing each other. Dinner, served by white-jacketed Navy mess-waiters assigned to White House duty, began with pâté de foie gras, followed by rack of lamb, tiny roast potatoes, and a variety of vegetables. Lexa and Russ drank wine with their food and had little opportunity to speak. Talbot, staying with martinis, built himself up into a manic-drunk state and monopolized all conversation. He delivered one monologue after another, recounting anecdotes from his long political career, giving Russ practical (and largely cynical) advice on how to win votes and how, once in office, to retain the loyalty of constituents.

'. . . the rural vote's swung many an election. Every rural count has a Courthouse Gang. Promise the guys in it whatever they ask – then deliver about half. That keeps 'em happy and on your side . . .'

'. . . study up on farming, Russ. Forget big issues when you're campaigning in the sticks. Talk acreage yields and fertilizers – farmers have more respect for a man who knows his fertilizers than for the guy who's an expert on trade deficits, believe me . . .'

'. . . when you hit a big town, concentrate on the ethnics. Blacks, Jews, Spicks, Wops, Polacks – milk 'em for all they're worth, and they're worth plenty.' He looked at Lexa. 'Puss used to travel around with me carrying a suitcase full of costumes. We'd get on a platform in a Polack neighbourhood, and she'd be wearing a Polack blouse. Then we'd move on to an Eytie section and she'd switch to a Wop blouse and skirt – changing in the back of a car . . .'

Talbot knitted his brows. 'Hey, you're single, aren't you, Russ?'

'My wife died four years ago.'

'Damn, you should do something about that, son. Public likes to see a female, it doesn't trust candidates who don't have one around. Starts whispers that they're queer. I guess Lexa's won me more elections than my martinis – hey, Puss?'

Talbot's voice was furry, thick. When coffee was served, he refused it with a lax headshake, asked the mess-boy to bring him another martini. 'The boys make 'em almost as good as mine. They should – I taught 'em how myself.'

The drink arrived. He drained half and grinned.

'You gotta come around more often, Russ. Seeing you at the table bucks me up. Reminds me of when I was young.' He finished the martini, gagging on it slightly. 'Oh-oh. That must've been the one too many. Better hit the sack before *I* start pissing out windows.' He stood up unsteadily. Russ leaped to his feet.

'Sit, son. You kids stay. Finish your coffee. Have a nightcap.' Talbot walked around the table, kissed Lexa's forehead, patted Russ clumsily on the shoulders. 'Drop by again real soon, son. You see he does, huh, Puss.' He staggered off toward his suite.

Russ waited a moment, said, 'Lexa, he's . . .'

'Ssh, not here,' she silenced him. 'The mess-boys might hear.' She stood up, took his hand. 'We'll go to my suite. We can talk there.'

Lexa's suite was next to the Queen's Bedroom. She asked Russ to sit beside her on a couch in the parlor of her suite.

'He's given up,' she said without any preface.

Understandable, Russ thought. *Talbot hasn't any alternative if he wants to stay in office. One move that displeases the 'junta' and he's out – for mental disability under the Twenty-Fifth Amendment. Unless the North-Cooley-Hopper scheme – whatever its operative details – works, I only have until tomorrow to make up my mind whether I want to join up with them,* he reminded himself. *But it's not anything to discuss with Lexa Talbot.*

'I wish there was something I could do.' He could think of nothing else to say.

'Russ!' There were tears in Lexa's eyes – more than on the previous evening – and she flung her arms around him. 'You did a lot tonight. You made him feel better. He needs you.' Her arms tightened around him. 'I – I need you, too.' *In more ways than one, Senator.* 'Please hold me and kiss me, Russ!'

Her mouth engulfed his, her tongue stabbing deep. Her right hand moved frantically to loosen his tie, open his collar. Her fingers slid under his shirt, clutched at his flesh.

'Lexa,' Russ stammered against her lips. 'Your father – servants – the Secret Service guards . . .'

She was fully, wildly aroused, but his mind was a crazy jumble. *I'm an all-American yokel at heart. I'm intimidated. By being in the White House. By the President of the United States. Who's passed out cold a few doors down the hall. That's why the role-reversal, with me playing the reluctant maiden.*

Rise up, you damned fool. If she isn't worried, why should I be? He remembered the stories of Warren G. Harding impregnating his mistress in a White House closet and of JFK's threesomes in the Lincoln Bedroom. *Anyway, we're not in a linen closet and it's not a three-way play,* he thought.

'I've wanted you ever since Wilmington,' Lexa murmured hoarsely. She released him for a moment, pulled down the front zipper fastening her two-piece black Régine evening pajamas, shrugged herself free of the top. Seizing his hands, she drew them to her breasts. 'There – feel as much!' Perfect breasts throbbed at his touch, distended nipples were sharp against his palms.

Lexa gripped his right wrist, thrust his hand between her thighs. She was soaked, burning. 'I've been like that all night!' Her hands went to his trousers, held and kneaded the hard bulge straining against the cloth.

Nobody in his right mind would fight this, Russ capitulated mentally. His fingers began a slow stroking movement, caressing her swollen clitoris.

'Aaah – faster!' Lexa begged. 'Make me come once before we get undressed!'

She buried her face against his neck, her mouth sucking, hands tightening on his penis. She bit into his neck, all her muscles cording. Her moan was long, ecstatic. Then she went limp.

'Jesus – Russ!' she panted, stood up, kicked off evening sandals, rid herself of the pajamas. Her body was perfectly proportioned, flawless. Her skin was amazingly smooth, demanding the touch of hands and lips. Whipped cream, Russ thought. Pure whipped cream. 'Hurry, Russ. I want to feel you up inside me!'

She was in a frenzy as she helped him undress.

27

Washington, D.C.: Monday, March 1. Morning Through Evening.

Kenneth Ramsey despondently performed his first morning chore: reading press summaries. Columnists and commentators were – for the most part – lambasting Charles Talbot. Peace groups were calling for protest marches and demonstrations. An NBC telephone survey showed 52 percent of those queried as disapproving the latest U.S. moves in Basanda. An ominous 31 percent thought the nation was being led into another endless, bloody debacle like the Vietnamese War. An even more ominous 42 percent placed the blame for developments squarely on the President.

Talbot came down to the Oval Office a little after nine with obviously very much of a hangover. This did not surprise Ramsey. He had glanced at the Visitors' Log. It recorded that Senator Russell Hatch of Oregon had left the White House at 4:17 A.M.

'Big night with Hatch, Chief?'

'I had some laughs and fun for a change.'

'Glad to hear it. Care to see the press summaries?'

'No thanks. They're bound to be lousy – or worse.'

'They are. How about your appointments for today?'

'Post a quarantine sign. Don't delete the expletives. Tell everybody I said they can take a flying fuck to Mars or Pluto – they're farther than the moon.'

Russ arrived home drained, fell into bed, failed to set his alarm. At ten-fiteen his telephone rang. He fumbled for it, mumbled a hello, recognized Suzanne Loring's voice. It was irked, peevish.

'What did Talbot feed you – knockout drops? You were

supposed to clock with Lady Norworth at ten and call me. Remember?'

'Oh, shit! I overslept. I was up late. Uh – Talbot talked on and on.' *Lexa balled on and on. God, she was fantastic!* 'I'll phone Marjorie right away and get back to you, honey.'

Marjorie Norworth was also annoyed. 'I expected to hear from you by ten.'

Russ apologized, repeating his expurgated explanation. Marjorie relented. 'When Charlie drinks and wants to talk, there's no stopping him,' she said. 'What was his underlying mood?'

'Defeat and resignation, according to what Lexa told me after he went off to bed.'

Marjorie Norworth's supersensitive antennae picked up faint signals, amplified them. Lexa again. She's fast becoming ubiquitous in Russell Hatch's life, confiding more and more family secrets to him. After her father goes off to bed. Marjorie was visualizing new possibilities and permutations She deliberated over them even as she spoke.

'It *is* Monday, Russ. Your D – for decision – Day.'

'I made it last night. I'm in – for better or worse.'

'Good. What did Miss Loring decide?'

'She'd love to come over for tea.'

'I'm delighted. I'll expect you both at five.'

Marjorie had met Lexa Talbot at numerous receptions and parites over the year. She mentally inventoried the impressions Lexa had made on her. Beauty, charm, and poise – obvious qualities but superficial in the present context. Beneath the veneer? A love of adulation, a driving desire to be the center of attraction and attention. A layer of the purely selfish and self-centered – most useful, Marjorie reflected. More useful yet, Lexa's deep-seated insecurity. It was to be expected in anyone whose entire existence was linked to the fortunes of a professional politician. Charles Talbot's fortunes – and thus those of his daughter – depended on the whims of party bosses and the electorate, ample excuse for anxiety and insecurity.

Lady Norworth was viewing herself as a choreographer and casting director. Yes, she thought, there was always room for improvement in any ballet, and if there were two contenders for a newly created leading part, they should be auditioned separately, but in very rapid succession if at all possible.

Marjorie telephoned the White House, gave her name and asked for Lexa Talbot. A minute's delay, and she was through. Although surprised by the call, Lexa accepted it without hesitation. Lady Norworth was one of her father's friends and supporters and had influence and power that Lexa respected and envied.

'It's unpardonably short notice, Lexa, but I'd like to talk with you about your father. Are you free for lunch?'

People in this town don't turn down her invitations, even if they get one at the last minute, Lexa reflected. Marjorie Norworth must know about her father's problems; she was famous – and feared – for learning about whatever occurred in official Washington almost as soon as it did. She might even be able to offer some help.

'Yes, I'm free, Lady Norworth,' she lied, making plans to cancel her lunch-date. 'Where and when should we meet?'

'Here – and I am aware of your bodyguard difficulties. They don't follow you while you remain within the White House complex, though. Walk through the underground corridor to the Executive Office Building, then slip out on the 17th Street side. My chauffeur will be waiting at quarter to twelve. The car's a Rolls, license number one hundred and . . .'

The old girl knows everything and has everything, Lexa thought. In Washington, any license number under 1250 is a major status symbol. For a private citizen to have a one-hundred-and-something plate – Jesus . . .

Marjorie Norworth greeted Lexa in the entrance foyer. Lexa had already concluded that she would be in for far more than a talk about her father. Now, she instantly sensed that Marjorie was subjecting her to X-ray scrutiny. *Why?*

I'll find out soon enough, she thought. *Play it cool and careful*, she warned herself, while maintaining an affable, winsome façade.

Clever young lady, Marjorie complimented Lexa silently as they went upstairs to her suite. *Your intuition is sharp. It's put you on your guard. Yet you're able to operate at two — perhaps more — levels simultaneously. I like that. Now let's see how well you hold up, react to successes, suggestions — and shocks — and if you're willing to take directions when they're to your advantage.*

The parlor bar-panel was open, a luncheon table set. Holcomb served Lexa the Bloody Mary she requested, Marjorie her customary fresh orange juice and withdrew.

'We'll eat after you've had your drink, so please sit over there so we can look at each other,' Marjorie said, smiled — and fired her first exploratory shot. 'Lexa, your father is in very serious trouble.'

Lexa absorbed the statement without changing her expression. 'Yes, I'm afraid he is.' *Why try to deny it?*

'I'm concerned about his predicament — more so about his mental and emotional state. Russell Hatch tells me that you are, too.'

Marjorie was watching Lexa closely, saw the blond girl's eyes narrow almost imperceptibly at the mention of Hatch's name. *I can still rely on my instincts*, Marjorie thought contentedly.

How much more did that bastard tell her, Lexa wondered.

Marjorie was reading her mind practically verbatim. 'Russ has a very high regard for you and Charlie,' she smiled disarmingly to ease the pressure for a moment even while testing for response.

'We think a lot of him, too,' Lexa said. 'Russ is one of the few trustworthy people in this town.'

Nimble return, but you're boiling with anger because you don't have a monopoly on Hatch. Marjorie said, 'Mmm. The young senator's fan-club has been growing fast of late.' She added a throw-away line. 'Of course, he's always had Suzanne Loring on his side.'

'I've heard they had a big thing going.' *Not so big that I didn't manage to dent it last night. There'll be more dents — until*

Hatch is my private property to tow around and show everyone what a good one-man woman I am. Then Emmett Hopper can shove his photographs and statements up his ass. He won't dare show them to Charles P. Talbot – not when I'm snug and cozy with the President's favourite bosom-friend.

'It's not difficult to become fond of Russ – and he does have many credentials,' Marjorie said. Instinct and experience kept her squarely on Lexa's ESP band, and her tone purposely implied a double entendre. She was pleased that Lexa took it in her easy stride.

'That makes it a consensus.' *Interpret the line any way you want. It's all you'll get out of me until I hear a hell of a lot more from you.* 'But we were going to talk about Daddy, weren't we?'

'Forgive me for going off on tangents, Lexa. Yes, we were.' Marjorie's violet eyes hooded. *I'll probe deeper to determine what is – or isn't – at your core.* 'You do want Charlie to complete his term as President, don't you?'

'My God – yes.' Lexa's eyes showed a flash of fear.

More fear for herself and her position than for her father, Marjorie reflected approvingly. Lexa was passing her examination – so far. 'You'd also like him to snap back, be more than just a figurehead?'

'Yes!'

Never has an affirmative reply been more definite – and never has so much been said in a single word, Marjorie mused. *I detect in you what I have in myself – or, rather, what you will have with a little guidance. The Adlerians call it the will to prevail, the urge to power. The will to prevail over men in particular.*

'Lexa, do you know about Freud's theory of penis-envy?'

The President's daughter blinked, laughed. 'Who doesn't?'

Marjorie laughed, too, nodding. 'It is a cliché. But did you ever read what a female psychiatrist, Dr Sofie Lazarsfeld, said about it?' She paused. Lexa shook her head. Marjorie went on, quoting from memory. ' "Actually what women desire is not the possession of a penis in their own organism, but the power and privileges which the possessors of a penis have secured for themselves." '

287

Lexa thought that over for a few seconds and her eyes lit up. 'God how true!' she exclaimed. She stared at Lady Norworth. 'I'm beginning to get your message.'

'That we may have much to offer each other?'

'Yes – we probably do.'

Marjorie stood up. 'I see you've finished your drink. I won't offer you another. We have too much to talk about over lunch.' She rang for Holcomb.

The two women were seated at the luncheon table and Holcomb had served the first course and left the suite when Marjorie Norworth began to speak again.

'Lexa, there are many things you don't know but should if we hope to salvage Charlie's career – and Charlie himself.'

For the next hour, Lexa Talbot listened – with sharply varying emotional reactions which she no longer made any attempt to conceal.

Secretary of State MacDonald Pearce leaned forward, arms on his desk.

'What's the progress report?' he asked Defense Secretary John Kurtz.

'We're carrying all the sail we can,' Kurtz replied. 'The two divisions we're airlifting go on Red Alert tomorrow. Wednesday, they begin to movement to designated airfields. They'll board transport planes Thursday night – Friday morning at the latest. It's impossible to mount an operation this size any sooner.'

Pearce's thin lips tightened. 'Have any qualms, John?'

Kurtz packed tobacco into his pipe, shrugged. 'There's always a chance something might foul our lines.'

'A calculated risk in any endeavor,' Pearce said. 'Minimal in this instance. On the one hand, Talbot has been made impotent, and he's aware of it. On the other, we've made certain that he carries all the blame, no matter what happens.'

She's incredible, Suzanne Loring thought, watching Marjorie

288

Norworth pouring tea. Marjorie was wearing a pheasant-feather tunic-smock. *On me, it'd be garish – on her, it's sensational. My God, the woman must be into – but like deep into – her sixties, but who'd ever guess seeing her? I won't bitch or moan if I look as good when I reach forty!*

Suzanne took sugar only, Russ sugar and cream. Marjorie had her tea plain and touched none of the tiny, wedge-shaped sandwiches or luscious pastries.

'I'm allergic to calories,' she said. 'They make me break out in lumps – huge ones in all the wrong places.'

'Me, too,' Suzanne nodded, but helped herself. 'Takes me an hour of yoga a day to keep the swellings away.'

'You're still young, my dear – thirty, perhaps . . .'

'Thank you, kind lady,' she says blushing. Thirty-three, come August fifth.'

'Ah, a Leo.'

'Don't tell me you believe in astrology, Lady Norworth?'

'Do you?'

'Afraid not.'

'Neither do I.' *A point in your favor. You're frank and forthright, Suzanne. I gave you an opening, hinted that I was an astrology nut. See if you'd pick up on it to ingratiate yourself.* 'Having established that, I insist you call me Marjorie.'

Russell Hatch looked at the two women and felt strangely extraneous. They were on a wave band that seemed to exclude him.

Marjorie had made her initial appraisals of Suzanne, and found them favorable. *The girl is every bit as bright and attractive in the flesh as she is on a television screen,* Marjorie thought. *She's self-possessed, and there's strength – possibly even steel underneath the delightful feminine wrapper.* Sensing Russ's discomfiture, she smiled at him.

'You have to understand that Suzanne and I are natural allies, Russ. *Au fond,* we're of the same breed.' Marjorie saw Suzanne's right eyebrow slant up questioningly and grinned. 'We both have' – *yes, use the Austrian term again, it fits* – 'a very strong urge to prevail.' Suzanne's eyebrow lowered and her expression became one of agreement. *Another point for you, Miss Loring,* Marjorie thought.

'Hasn't everybody?' Russ asked.

'To some degree, but . . .'

'There's no lack of it in Russ,' Suzanne interjected.

You jumped to his defense much too fast, Marjorie mused. *But then, you're hopelessly in love with him.* She subtracted points from Suzanne's score-sheet. *Women that much in love with a man were vulnerable, likely to be adversely affected on the cerebral level if wounded at the emotional. However . . .*

'I'm sure there isn't,' she said. 'With men, it's conditioning. They're trained from birth to strive, play the traditional male role. Women like you are still in the minority, Suzanne. You're self-made, independent. You have a brilliant career. You couldn't have accomplished what you have without a powerful drive.'

'Compensation,' Suzanne said uneasily. *All I need to have Marjorie Norworth plant the idea that I'm a career-mad ball-breaker into Russ's head.* 'I got tired of being stepped on.'

'Isn't that a rationalization? I can't picture you worrying about waxy buildup on your kitchen floors after having twenty million people hang on your every word each week.'

'Believe it or not, Marjorie, that doesn't turn me on.'

'*Something* must, otherwise you wouldn't be a success.'

Suzanne's laugh was a hearty chuckle. 'I'm nosey. My mother claimed I was a born *yenta*. I always wanted to know what was going on – and why. That's where it all started, I think. Then I learned I could take stuffed shirts and hypocrites apart and make them look like the God-damned fools they really are – and get paid for doing it. That adds up to motivation, no matter how you look at it.'

I must award you several points there, Marjorie said silently. *You're really saying that you do have a strong will to power and enjoy manipulating people. You simply haven't realized it – or admitted it to yourself yet. You will, though. Your appetite will increase – eventually, it might become insatiable, like mine.*

'I'm puzzled about one thing,' Marjorie said aloud. 'The interview with Dan Madigan . . .'

She saw the quick, embarrassed looks that passed between Suzanne and Russ, and the explanation became clear. Russ had done the prevailing, and Suzanne had submitted. *You are vulnerable, Suzanne, and I'm subtracting points.*

'. . . but never mind. Unless I get down to business, I'll be dashing off on tangents forever.' Marjorie Norworth grew very serious. Very serious. 'Suzanne, you have your own television show, but how much do you know about the technical side of broadcasting?'

'Depends on what you mean by "technical". If you mean how shows are planned, put together, produced, and either filmed or taped or shown live, quite a lot. After all, I did start from the bottom.'

'Then perhaps you'll answer a great many questions I have to ask.'

'I'll do my best.'

'Sure you want me in on this?' Russ asked.

'Absolutely,' Marjorie assured him. 'Brad, Emmett, and I kept the details of our save-Talbot scheme from you night before last. As I ask Suzanne my questions, I'll be filling you both in.'

Russ settled back in his chair, lit a Pall Mall.

'Before we've finished, you'll know everything,' Marjorie went on. 'Unless I'm more mistaken than I've ever been in my life, you'll understand why we're so confident. And Suzanne – to use your phrase – you'll be turned on more than you've ever been in *your* life.'

Three hours later when Suzanne and Russ left the House on the Hill, they agreed that Marjorie Norworth's promises had been the understatements of the century.

'Where to?' Russ asked as they piled into his Pontiac.

'My apartment first – we'll start there,' Suzy was breathless. 'We've got work to do – Christ, but we've got work to do!'

Marjorie Norworth was supremely satisfied and telephoned Bradford Cooley at his home. She made no mention of having lunched with Lexa Talbot.

'Russ is with us,' she told Cooley. 'So is the Loring girl.'

'I take it you trust her.'

'In regard to our project – implicitly.'

'What of the technical aspects?'

'Suzanne says there are no obstacles – in fact, it's all much simpler than I had imagined. She's taken it upon herself to make all the necessary arrangements through her network.' *As I anticipated she would.* 'She is, I might add, beside herself with enthusiasm.'

'I would have preferred CBS or NBC to Continental,' Cooley said with a disgruntled note in his voice. 'They're larger and have more local outlets throughout the country.'

'Stop niggling, Brad. CBN is big enough, and we have the extra safety margin of being able to control Suzanne Loring through Russell Hatch.'

'Perhaps you're right, Marjorie.'

'I'm seldom wrong, Brad. Very seldom.'

When she had ended her conversation with Cooley, Marjorie sat back and totted up the mental scorecards she had kept during the day. It wasn't much of a contest, she thought, and chose the queen who was certain to sweep the board in her private chess game.

28

Washington, D.C.: Monday, March 1. Night.

Lexa Talbot had agreed with Marjorie that she should make no mention of their meeting to her father. His mental state being what it was – and since Talbot was often subject to extreme mood-swings – common sense dictated that he be told nothing of what was planned until the last possible moment. On the other hand, the planning itself demanded that she find a pretext to insure that Charles Talbot would be at the House on the Hill Wednesday evening. For reasons of her own, Lexa also wanted to see Russell Hatch alone, and she contrived a logical means to accomplish both ends. The dual-purpose ploy would have to wait until she and her father had dinner, though.

The day had been long, hectic and nerve-wracking for Kenneth Ramsey. It was late before he felt he could escape and go home. He was locking up his desk when an Associated Press correspondent – a personal friend – telephoned. 'He says it's urgent,' Ramsey's exhausted secretary declared.

'Put him on,' Ramsey told her wearily.

'I'm passing along a tip, Ken,' the AP man said. 'A group calling itself the "Emergency Committee to Prevent Talbot's War" is going to stage a no-warning protest march down Pennsylvania Avenue tonight.'

Ramsey groaned. 'Got any specifics?'

'No. My guess is that they'll carry placards, yell slogans . . .'

'And do their Goddamndest to make us overreact so they'll be given just that much more publicity.'

'Yeah, it follows. I don't envy you people the head-aches.'

'Thanks. I appreciate the tipoff.'

So much for going home, Ramsey thought, telephoning his wife. 'I'm stuck here, haven't any idea how long,' he told her. It could be a very long night.

That done, Ken Ramsey focused his mind on the prob-lem of the protest march. *Shit, I'll have to take charge*, he realized. There was no use consulting – or even informing – the President. Talbot had spent most of the day upstairs – 'repairing today's hangover and laying the groundwork for the one I'll have tomorrow,' as he put it to Ramsey.

He'll have to take security precautions, Ramsey thought. Low-keyed, kept to a minimum. It was imperative that any provocations be avoided. The faltering Talbot Administra-tion couldn't afford a bloody riot literally on the President's front doorstep.

Ramsey conferred with the White House Security Chief, a case-hardened law-and-order fanatic who had different views.

'A cinch. We seal off Penn Avenue and all the side streets for blocks around. If the motherfuckers try to bust through, they'll be smothered with tear and vomit gas . . .'

'Forget that kind of crap!' Ramsey barked. He was stern, tough – the nightclub bouncer flexing muscle. 'This thing's been organized on the spur of the moment – there won't be much of a turnout. So we stay cool. We *play* it cool, under-stand?'

'What – and let 'em run loose?'

'Long as they keep it peaceful, we allow them to march. Put in a call for a hundred District cops in regular uniform. No riot gear. They're to stay in clear sight lining the side-walks, keep their hands off their nightsticks and hold onto their tempers.'

'I'm against it. Suppose those protesting bastards turn into a mob and start trashing – or worse?'

'Then we'll use one of the nine million and six contingency plans crammed into your filing cabinets.'

'Mr Ramsey, who's taking the final responsibility?'

'I am.' *Who else is there?* 'I'll put it in writing – as a Presidential directive.'

'You're the producer – where do we start?' Russell Hatch asked when he and Suzanne were in her apartment.

She glanced at her wristwatch: eight forty. The longest – and by far most fascinating – afternoon tea on record, she reflected.

'We start by getting organized, friend. One, I beat my IBM – to hell making notes while things are still fresh in mind. You order the food – double-thick steaks, rare, huh – because we'll be hungry before long. Two, you answer questions, give me every scrap of information you have.'

'That's all?'

'God, no! Three, I follow the spoor of CBN's two-headed dragon and lie – or tangle – with him. Four, we dig through the background and research material I keep here.'

'Five – bed, maybe?' Russ leered.

'Not a chance, buster, so button your fly. Five, we put what we have to that point together until it spells mother – and scheme, probably all through the night.'

'I always thought big TV show producers just sat on their butts smoking fat cigars. At least, that's what you've told me.'

'Fuck off, Senator, so I can work – or you'll have a big, fat kick planted right amidst your balls.'

Suzanne worked feverishly, wolfed down steak and potatoes, completed her notes, interrogated Russ and, at ten fifty-five, gleefully announced. 'We're got enough to make the dragon drool.'

Noah Sturdevant, Continental Broadcasting Network board chairman, lived on New York's Park Avenue. Suzanne had his home telephone number and gambled that he might be in. Using the living room phone, she pushed the 212 area code and seven more digits. A maid answered on the second ring-back. Suzanne identified herself. The maid asked her to wait – which meant Suzanne was in luck. The dragon was at home, and he eventually came on the line, much annoyed.

'Miss Loring, I am having a small party. I hope whatever you have to say justifies my leaving my guests.'

'Mr Sturdevant, what I have to say will justify your leaving your wife, children and mistress, if you've got one.' Speaking rapidly and tersely, Suzanne sketched out what she had learned from Lady Marjorie Norworth and Russ Hatch and told him what would take place Wednesday night. 'If that doesn't blow your mind, Mr Sturdevant, you're a basket case,' she concluded.

Sturdevant absorbed her smart-ass coda without a trace of indecision. He was in raptures.

'Fantastic, Miss Loring! A magnificent coup! My mind boggles – absolutely boggles – at the thought of what this will mean to CBN – and to you, of course . . .'

He's peeing his pants, Suzanne chortled silently.

'. . . Now, how can CBN and I assist you?'

'By making me Queen for a Day – or rather, two days. Cancel my tomorrow-night show. I won't have time to tape an interview. Next, I need a no-limit shooting license with the station here. I give orders, nobody asks questions. Tomorrow, you fly the special equipment I mentioned and the net's best technicians down from New York. Warn them all in the crews to keep their mouths shut and follow instructions. For the moment, that's my shopping-list.'

'Consider it filled, Miss Loring.' A pause, then grudgingly: 'My previous bonus arrangement will be in effect again.'

'I assumed it would be, Mr Sturdevant. Indeed, I did.'

She hung up, laughed – but she was tired. Excitement and the day's pressures made her – and Russ – feel as though they were running down, and it was only eleven twenty-five.

'Coffee's the answer,' Russ said. 'I'll make it.' Going into the kitchen, he push-buttoned the coffee machine, programming it to produce a full quart of TRIPLE-STRENGTH ESPRESSO. After minutes he returned to the living room with a thermos jug and two mugs.

Suzanne peered into the mug Russ gave her, right eyebrow elevating. 'You weren't gone long enough to drain a crankcase, and nobody chews tobacco anymore. It *has* to be something else.'

Russ gagged as he drank from his own mug. 'Pure caffeine and half a pound of energy-giving sugar. Delicious. Taste it.'

She took a tentative sip. 'My God! Who gave you the recipe – Lucretia Borgia?'

'A frail Chinese herb doctor I saved from death at the hands of the American Medical Association. Chairman Mao lived on it.'

'Balls! It's what killed him. Okay, let's drink it down and go to work.'

Charles Talbot and his daughter had dinner alone. It was latish, for he had delayed coming into the Family Dining Room until a few minutes before nine. He picked at his food, drank martinis. I'd better get to it before he slides over the edge and stops registering, Lexa thought.

'You and I have a date Wednesday night, Daddy,' she announced. 'We're going out – to a party.'

'Who's giving it and why, Puss?'

'I promised I wouldn't tell. It's supposed to be a surprise.'

'Give me a raincheck. I'm not in a partying mood these days.'

'Silly! I already accepted for both of us.' She gave him her fondest, most compelling smile. *Now the bait that'll give me an excuse to see Russ.* 'Besides, you should *want* to go in the worst way. You'll have a ball. Russ Hatch will be there, along with a lot of your friends.' *And a lot more of your enemies, but that's going to be the biggest – and wildest – surprise.*

Talbot, although not yet ossified, was far from sober. He picked up on the mention of Hatch, furrowed his brows.

'Oh, you mean you and Russ're going together and taking me along.' The frown erased. He grinned lopsidedly. 'A deal, Puss. Anyplace kinda like you go is bound to be fun.'

He bit, faster than I could have hoped, Lexa thought. *He's given me the excuse. Russ wasn't supposed to go with us – he was to be there when we arrived. I can tell him Daddy won't come unless he stops by here and the three of us go to the party together. It's a little thin, but I'll thicken it up.*

Talbot's frown returned. 'Hey, you kind of go for Russ Hatch, don't you, Baby?'

'He's awfully nice and good company.'

'I second the motion.' The frown started to fade, then went into reverse, deepening as Talbot cocked his head. 'Hey, what's that noise?' Although the Family Dining Room was fairly well soundproofed, a faint muffled chanting came from outside the building. Talbot stepped on a call-button under the table. A Secret Service man entered immediately. 'Who's making that racket?' he demanded. It was growing louder.

'Mr President, I think Mr Ramsey should tell you about it.'

'Ken still here? Tell him to come up, son.'

Ramsey appeared in moments. 'Some peace marchers coming up Penn Avenue,' he explained, hiding the truth. They were more anti-Talbot than antiwar, led by a flatbed truck on which a makeshift gallows had been mounted. A dummy dangled from the noose – President Charles Talbot hung in effigy. 'It's not a big crowd – less than a thousand people.' Which was accurate.

'Notify Security!'

'I did, Chief. Ordered up some District police to keep the marchers calm and moving.'

'Have 'em baton-charge the bastards!'

'Bad move, Daddy,' Lexa warned, her mind working along the same lines that Ramsey's had earlier. 'You'd be asking for trouble. Pretend they're not even out there.'

Ramsey shot her a grateful look. 'Wiser to ignore them, Chief. If the cops crack so much as a single skull the media will scream it's police brutality, you're a fascist and the country's going Nazi.'

The marchers were passing directly in front of the White House; their shouted slogans were clearly audible.

'No more guns! No more men! No more Vietnams ever again!'

'Ship Talbot, not troops, to Africa!'

'Fuck Basanda! Fuck War! Fuck you, Charlie!'

Lexa and Ramsey were silent as the shouting slowly faded. Talbot appeared to have sunk into sodden depression.

'Must be Ku-Kluxers,' he muttered at last. 'Racists.'

'Wrong,' Ramsey said. 'Roughly speaking, they're two-thirds black.' He felt immense relief at having guessed correctly. The demonstration was hastily organized – the unimaginative slogans alone proved it – and violence had been avoided. The marchers would trudge on a few more blocks and disperse. He told Talbot as much.

The President gave no sign of listening. He stared across the table at Lexa in a rapidly gathering stupor. 'Must be ten-thirty, huh?'

'Closer to midnight, I'm afraid, Daddy.'

'Be damned. G'night, Puss, Ken. I'm heading for bed.' A comforting thought formed in his liquor-numbed brain. *One Quaalude on top of all the booze and I'll sleep, forget Basanda, Pearces, Kurtzes, Twenty-Fifth Amendments, even all those shit-headed people yelling and screaming . . .*

'. . . we'll use the same footage both times, with one voiceover commentary for Wednesday night, another for the special show Thursday,' Suzanne Loring was saying. 'I'm not in love with the idea, but it's part of the deal I made with Lady N. and . . .'

She stopped as her telephone rang.

'Must be Sturdevant having a stroke of genius – or just a plain stroke.' She picked up the phone, said 'Hello,' listened a moment and held the handset out to Russ. 'Your answering service.'

Russ had informed the service he would be at Suzanne's number, with instructions that it was not to be given out, but that he be notified if there any calls that seemed important.

'Senator, someone might be playing joke, but a lady identifying herself as Miss Lexa Talbot says she *must* talk to you. She did leave the White House number. It's . . .'

'I know it – and thanks.' Russ disconnected by pressing a finger down on the handset hook. His face flushed uncomfortably when he told Suzanne of the message, avoiding her eyes as he did.

You did lay her after all, she accused him silently. *When, where and, for God's sake, why?*

'Don't keep the Princess waiting,' Suzanne said unnecessarily, for he was already punch dialing.

'Oh, yes, Senator Hatch,' the White House operator said. 'Miss Talbot left word you were to be put right through to her.'

A second's silence, a muted click, then: 'Russ! I'm so glad you called. I've got something to ask you – privately. Are you home?'

'No.' His flush deepened. 'I'm at Suzanne Loring's apartment.'

'Oh.' *That screws things up for me – or wait, does it? It could be a pure-gold chance to put that other dent or two in their Big Thing.* 'Are you very busy?' Her tone clearly indicated she meant 'Are you in bed together?'

'We're working.'

'Do you think she'd mind if I came over in fifteen minutes?'

Russ was dumbstruck by the request. Lexa *here*? His consternation eased only slightly as he remembered she wanted to talk to him urgently, privately, and he stammered when he spoke.

'Uh – I don't know – I'll ask.' He covered the mouthpiece with his left hand. 'Suzy, it doesn't make sense – it's crazy – but Lexa Talbot wants to come here, like right away. Do you – would you – mind if she does?'

Suzanne was no less stunned. Her large eyes grew huge. 'Why?' – *Why not? There's an advantage to meeting the competition on my own home grounds* – 'Invite her. She's welcome. I'll roll out the red carpet.'

Using the protest march as an excuse, Lexa asked for a doubled security escort. Arriving at Potomac Plaza, she had two of the four Secret Service men accompany her inside. She reasoned they would serve to underscore her position, help cut Suzanne Loring down to size.

Suzanne opened her apartment door. She and Lexa Talbot were face-to-face. Their preset smiles shaded from the counterfeit charming to patently bogus under the impact of an instant mutual antipathy transcending sexual jealousy.

'Hello, Miss Talbot – I'd recognize you anywhere.' *For what you are. A cunt.* Suzy glanced at the bodyguards flanking Lexa. 'Oh, Gee! I only baked a small cake.'

'They'll stay in the corridor,' Lexa said. *Oh, hell, wasted effort.* Obviously, the Secret Service men failed to intimidate Suzanne Loring or even impress her. Lexa consoled herself by ascribing the nonreaction to television-celebrity swollen ego. 'I'm *so* glad to meet you. I've heard so much about you from Russ.'

'I've heard a lot about you, too, Miss Talbot,' Suzanne said dryly.

'Please call me Lexa – and may I call you Suzanne?'

'Be my guest, *Lexa* – oh, but then you are. Come in.' She stepped aside, winked at the security men. 'Don't get worried if you hear strange noises – there's nothing duller than a quiet orgy.'

She closed the door, took Lexa's coat, led her into the living room. Russ was standing, clearly ill-at-ease. He shook hands with Lexa. She held his a little too long, making certain that Suzanne noticed, released it, turned, observed that papers were piled and spread almost everywhere around the room.

'What a *charming* place you have, Suzanne,' Lexa smiled – her voice conveying: *You've sure managed to turn a plush penthouse into a cluttered dump.*

Suzanne was clearing papers from a chair to provide Lexa a place to sit. 'It does have a lived-in look,' she riposted nonchalantly. 'Care for a drink, Lexa?'

'No, but I'd love a cup of coffee.'

Suzy's face lit up. 'We have some – freshly made . . .'

Russ was about to protest, clamped his jaws shut.

'. . . Russ and I use mugs instead of cups, but if you prefer a cup . . .' Translation: *I'm not going to any trouble for you.*

'No, *please* don't bother. A mug will do fine.' Translation: *I don't mind slumming.*

Suzanne filled a mug from the thermos jug. Lexa took it.

'Mm, looks strong. Just what I need.' One swallow and she choked. *You bitch.* 'A new blend?'

'Russ's own secret formula.' Suzanne gave Hatch a mischievous grin. 'He dotes on it.'

Lexa ostentatiously moved file folders aside to make space on the glass-topped table next to her. She sat the mug down.

Russ observed the byplay silently – at once uncomfortable, feeling cornered and flattered and intrigued. He found himself making comparisons between the two women. Both were attractive, desirable, famous. Being male, he assumed himself to be the sole cause of the patent antagonism between them. Odd. Lexa was twenty-five, bandbox groomed and composed, perfectly poised. Although nearing thirty-three, Suzy – with tousled short hair, sloppy blue jeans, and faded shirt – seemed younger. Suzanne Loring was the self-sufficient, fiercely independent career girl. Yet, paradoxically, he felt the stir of unfamiliar protective feelings towards her.

Lexa's voice cut short his reverie.

'I'm terribly embarrassed, Suzanne. What I have to ask Russ is – well, confidential. But it'll only take a few minutes.'

'Don't apologize. I'll go putter around in the bathroom.'

Bullshit, Russ thought. *Lexa was being the high and mighty President's daughter, telling Suzanne to make herself scarce.* 'Hold on, Suzy,' he said, and turned to Lexa. 'Lexa, what I know Suzy knows.' *Unless you want to talk about our balling in the White House, which I doubt.* 'If she doesn't hear it now, she will never from me.'

Thanks for that, my love, Suzanne thought as she blew him a mental kiss. *You're not pure prick and may be I don't have so much to worry about, after all. Could be that at some level you see through Miss Utterly Ravishing-Wonderful and realize she's pure poison.*

'But it's about Daddy!' Lexa exclaimed.

Daddy, yet, Suzanne thought. *Too cutesie-pootsie for words. I may have to go to the bathroom – and puke.*

'Same difference,' Russ shrugged. 'Suzy's clued in.'

She really does have her claws into him, Lexa conceded.

'All right, I'll have to trust you both,' Lexa said. 'Daddy's terribly insecure – afraid of almost everyone. He's leaning on you more and more, Russ. He refuses to go Wednesday night unless you and I take him together.'

She paused, looked to be pleading.

'Would you come over to the White House a bit early Wednesday night, have a drink with him and reassure him before we go?'

'Sure.' Russ scrubbed at his brick-red hair. 'What else would you have me to do?'

'Only that.'

Russ frowned puzzlement. *Why the hell couldn't she ask me over the phone?*

Lexa read the unspoken question, had an answer ready. 'I know it seems strange that I came all the way over here – but I didn't want anyone overhear me tell you that Daddy's wrought up, shaky.' She abruptly changed tack, addressed Suzanne. 'You don't object to Russ seeing Daddy and me, do you?'

Suzanne boiled inwardly. *The two-bit little schemer is patronizing me – what's she going to pull next, a switchblade?* She parodied Lexa's treacly-sweet tones when she replied.

'Heavens to Betsy!' – *that tops 'Daddy' on the Shirley Temple scale, sister* – 'Why on earth should I object? I'll even get the Senator dressed, straighten his bow tie, and make sure he arrives on time.'

I give up, it's too much for me, Russ thought wearily. *Who can figure women?*

Lexa left very soon afterward. She was effusive in her apologies for having intruded and her thanks to Suzanne for her hospitality. Then she hugged Suzanne and kissed the air next to her cheek.

'I don't want to smear your makeup,' she said.

'What makeup?' Russ laughed. He reached out, gently pinched Suzanne's cheek. 'That's nature's own genuine organic skin. Except for the moisturizer Suzy hunts for in the medicine cabinet every morning.'

Suzanne melted.

'You're so lucky,' Lexa tried to recover her fumble. 'You can save the makeup for the cameras once a week. I have to be on stage all the time.'

When the door finally closed and they were alone Suzanne took Russ by the arm and propelled him toward the bedroom.

'Senator, you've just turned me into the hottest, horniest organic female this side of the equator,' she said.

'I thought we were going to work . . .'

'All through the night. And we are. After.'

This night, Suzanne Loring had no need to feign her orgasms. Not her first – or even her second . . . or third . . .

29

Washington, D.C.: Tuesday, March 2.

Bottles, jars, plastic containers clattered as Suzanne rooted through her medicine cabinet. Russ, haggard and bleary-eyed leaned against the bathroom doorframe. 'Lost that moisturizer again?' he asked, yawning. Neither hot bath nor hot coffee had done much to relieve his tiredness.

'Uh-uh,' Suzanne replied, continuing her search. 'Dexis. I know there's a full bottle – whee, here it is!' She opened the bottle, tipped two spansules into her palm. 'One apiece for starters.'

Russ took a spansule gratefully, dry-swallowed it. Dexidrene was the only aid that could keep them going through the day.

'My car, yours, or shall I call for a limo?' Suzy washed her dexi down with water.

'Mine.'

At 8:00 A.M., they, a bulging Vuitton carryall (and the bottle containing twenty-three Dexidrene spansules) were at CBN's Washington studios. To Suzanne's amused surprise, the station manager (who seldom if ever arrived before nine-thirty) was there ahead of them. His manner was respectful, even servile. As might be expected of any CBN local-outlet station manager who had been awakened at midnight and given his orders by Noah Sturdevant.

'All our facilities are at your disposal, Miss Loring,' he said, practically standing at attention.

Suzanne dumped the papers cramming the carryall on her desk. 'That's the good news. Now for the bad. Where's my secretary? Where's the rest of day-staff?'

'I notified everyone to be here early. They should start coming in at any moment.' Nervous face-twitches accompanied the reply.

Russ planted himself in a leather-upholstered armchair. The dexis had cut in; he felt wide awake and was enjoying the spectacle.

'Until they do – you're the facilities, buster.' Suzy rummaged through the papers, pulled out a sheet on which she had typed a long list of items and instructions. She handed it to the station manager. 'Get started – but like right now.'

He scuttled off, clutching the paper and reading it as he went.

Suzy glanced at Russ. 'Haul your ass out of the bleachers, Sergeant – this isn't a spectator sport.' She jabbed a finger toward a straight-backed chair in front of her desk. 'Sit there. When meat-head starts bringing stuff in, we go over it together – fast and furious.'

'*Ja wohl*, boss-person.' And eight or nine hours ago I was feeling protective. I must have been out of my head.

The protest march along Pennsylvania Avenue made the front pages of *Time* and *Post* – but just barely. Other stories took precedence.

'. . . U.S. Air Force fighter-bombers have attacked Basandan rebel forces near Gidanu . . .'

'. . . A carrier task force detached from the Navy's Mediterranean Sixth Fleet has arrived in the port of Kinsolo. The carrier is the 100,000-ton nuclear-powered *Martin Luther King*, the newest and most powerful warship . . .'

'. . . The Basandan Military Grand Council, formed as the country's internal governing body after Prime Minister Kwida's death, has declared a state of siege and imposed martial law . . .'

'. . . Cuban troops are reportedly en route to aid Basandan rebel forces . . .'

'. . . A Kremlin announcement states that the Soviet Union will seek United Nations condemnation of American military action . . .'

*

The President's hangover was worse than it had been the day before.

'I'll get the doc to give you a shot of something,' Ken Ramsey said when Talbot came down to the Oval Office.

'Nah. I'll suffer.'

'Damn it, Chief, you can't . . .'

'I can't what? Suffer through a hangover? Crap.'

'Whatever you say.' Ramsey produced the news summaries.

'Toss 'em in the wastebasket, Ken.'

'You've *got* to know what's going on.'

'Oh, hell. Read me a quick skim.' Talbot slouched back in the Presidential chair, closed his eyes. 'Quietly, huh? There's a bottle factory going full blast inside my skull.'

It took Ramsey five minutes to run over the highlights.

Talbot's eyes remained shut. His headache had intensified.

'Now I know,' he muttered. 'I still can't do anything about any of it.'

'Yes, you can.'

'Tell me.'

'Let the doc work on you – knock you out for the day. Keep off the booze until tomorrow night . . .'

'Tomorrow night. That's Wednesday. What the fuck is all this about Wednesday night?' Talbot forced his eyes open. 'Lexa was at me last night – she and Russ Hatch have something cooked up. Now you.'

'Who do you figure you can trust, Chief?'

'Trust? Shit. You, I guess. Lexa. Hatch, maybe.' *Avery Braithwaite, but he doesn't count anymore. Marjorie? No. I don't know where she shops of late.* 'Short roster, Ken.'

'It's a lot longer than you think – but I won't go into that. Leave it at Lexa, Hatch – even with the maybe – and me. Hang on until Wednesday night. The whole picture might change.'

'How? Why all the mystery?'

'Just because. Take my word for it – and Lexa's.'

Talbot would have pressed further, but a wave of nausea swept over him. He dry-heaved, his complexion turning greenish.

'Uh – Ken.' He dry-heaved again. 'I'll see the doc.'

Thank God, Ramsey thought. The physician would shoot Talbot full of sedatives to keep him under until five or so the following day, then jolt him back. By then, it would be safe to brief Charles Talbot about what would happen that night.

Lady Marjorie Norworth started telephoning a highly selective list of men at 10:00 A.M. Senator Early Frobase, President Pro Tempore of the Senate, was the first.

'Early, I've had a fabulous inspiration for an up-to-the-minute theme party,' she gushed. 'I'm calling it the "Back Basanda's Battle for Freedom" party, and inviting only those who are *for* our Basanda policy. It starts at ten tomorrow night. I suppose all Washington will say I'm turning my home into a hawk's nest – but what do I care?' Marjorie's laugh indicated she was sharing a secret. 'I've always been a hawk at heart – ever since FDR and Lend-Lease.'

She paused to listen a moment.

'Oh, yes, Early,' she assured him. '*All* the extra serving maids will be black – and I'll have Miss Quigley drop in later.'

MacDonald Pearce was next.

'. . . a show of solidarity. Imagine how it will disconcert all the peace-at-any-pricers!'

Pearce accepted eagerly. As did John Kurtz, G. Howard Denby, Senator Pace . . .

The number of definite acceptances grew steadily as Marjorie telephoned and bubbled her way down the list. There were no refusals, only a few uncertains – comparatively minor functionaries who said they had previous engagements but solemnly (and sincerely) promised they would make every effort to cancel them.

Shortly after one o'clock, Marjorie received a call from Suzanne Loring.

'I'm doing beautifully,' Marjorie said. 'I still have a few more people to phone, but we're already sure of a full house for tomorrow night.'

'You'll have a full house inside an hour,' Suzanne told

her. 'The technical crews and specialists arrived from New York. They'll be seething all over your place.'

'I'll be delighted. I absolutely *draw* energy from a bustle of humanity around me!'

'You should be here – we have so many people rushing and running you'd have more energy than if you were wired into the full TVA output. Being a grounded-out pair, Russ and I are getting ours from Dexis – oops – I'm told they're ready in the projection room. Have to rush, Marjorie – we have miles of film to screen and edit. Talk to you later.'

It wasn't possible to ignore White House press corps demands any longer. With Charles Talbot in bed – and in another, Sodium Pentothal-induced slumber-world – Ken Ramsey took the initiative and composed a statement. He gave it – and strict instructions – to the Presidential Press Secretary, Michael Harris.

'Any deviations, and I'll have your balls, Mike.'

'That's no threat,' Harris said sourly. 'Those media bastards have already torn off my balls, cock, and pubic hairs.' He held up the typed statement. 'This won't make the mothers give 'em back either, I guarantee you.'

'Tell them they can have both of mine.'

'Balls?'

'Pricks. The small one I carry slung in front – and the giant-sized reamer that's been shoved up my ass ever since I took this job.'

'Yeah, you've got it rough, too, Ken.' Harris grinned sympathetically. 'I'll do my best to horseshit the troops.'

The press lobby was jammed. Michael Harris bravely stepped up on a small platform and read the statement prepared by Ramsey.

'The President has no immediate plans to hold a press conference as he does not believe it would serve any constructive purpose. His recently announced domestic program is familiar to all of you. Measures to implement it are before Congress. Questions involving the developing situation in Africa should be directed to the appropriate Cabinet

309

Departments – State in regard to diplomatic matters, Defense in regard to military matters.' He took a deep breath. 'That, folks, is the end of the statement.'

'Is this a news blackout?' a voice shouted above the ensuing angry din.

'Not at all. The President simply believes that accurate information may be best obtained from sources directly . . .'

'The President is Commander-in-Chief of the armed forces . . .'

'Among his countless other duties. He cannot possibly have every detail constantly at his fingertips.'

'Details? Since when is the start of a shooting war a detail?'

'Military questions should be referred to the Defense Department.'

'Does Talbot at least admit there *is* a shooting war?'

'To my knowledge, he has made no statement on the subject.'

'Will he?'

'That is up to the President.'

Harris parried the barrage of increasingly angry and bitterly phrased questions for half an hour – then gave up and fled.

'Add another of those oversized bunghole reamers to the White House inventory,' he said, reporting on the session to Ken Ramsey.

'They shove it up you, Mike?'

'No, but they'll ram it up Talbot's – so far that it'll rupture his tonsils, if he's got any.'

'No room. He had the world's biggest shaft hammered into his a few days ago – the Washington Monument's a toothpick by comparison, take it from me.'

'Christ, he's the *President*. Why doesn't he make like one and pull it out?'

'A hint to cheer you, Mike. Experts in the delicate art of shaft-extraction are working overtime.'

Marjorie gloated over her list of definite acceptances. One person remained to be called. She left him until last because assurance that the others would be present is what could guarantee his presence. Since crews of men with tools and esoteric gadgets were what Suzanne Loring had forecast – swarming through the downstairs rooms and another crew with even more complex gear had invaded her suite – Marjorie retreated to her social secretary's office. There she set about the complicated, time-consuming task of locating Jordan B. Rickhoven III.

After nearly an hour – and fifteen telephone calls – she learned that Rickhoven was in San Clemente, California. He was paying a 'purely social visit' to the former President he privately disparaged as 'the blue-jawed baboon', but who continued to wield influence with several foreign Heads of State.

There were long delays as both the ex-President's and the billionaire's aides screened the call and passed it up their organizational chains of authority.

Rickhoven and his host had retired to confer in the small study which the former President, noted for his obsessive use of football terms, called 'The Locker Room'. It was there that Rickhoven was finally informed: 'A call for you from Washington, sir. Lady Marjorie Norworth.'

'Yes, I'll speak with her.' Jordan Rickhoven did not bother to ask his blue-jawed baboon friend if he might use the Locker Room extension telephone. Such niceties were extraneous. Rickhoven money – 'black satchel cash' – had paid for the sprawling San Clemente estate.

Marjorie told Rickhoven about her Wednesday night party.

'You positively *must* fly in for it, Jordan.' She reeled off the names of the more important officials who would be attending. 'They'll be delighted to see you – and you'll have an *utterly* unique opportunity to talk with them in the most *favorable* atmosphere.'

She's right, the billionaire thought, admiring Marjorie Norworth's unfailing intuition. She invariably sensed the right moment to ingratiate herself with the winning side. And the party would enable him to update himself, refine plans, prevent blunders, and apply pressures. He had but a single question.

'Marjorie, will Talbot . . . ?'

'Jordan!' Her tone was reproachful. 'How could you *possibly* think I would make the hideous *faux pas* of asking *him* to mix with guests who are behind the Basandan Loyalist cause?'

Rickhoven grinned. It was a ridiculous question. Marjorie was fine-tuned to every Washington undercurrent and nuance.

'My apologies, Marjorie. I'll be there.'

Suzanne and Russ left the CBN studios a little after 10:00 P.M. They had not stopped working since their arrival fourteen hours earlier. Both were exhausted. Not even Dexidrene could keep them going any longer.

Suzanne settled into the seat of Russ's car, leaned her head on his shoulder. 'Tired, too?' she asked.

'Barely breathing.' He started the engine.

'Too tired to, too?'

'You'd go great as a locomotive whistle. The answer is yes, I am.'

'Me, too. We're two who're too tired to, too.' She yawned, her eyelids drooping. 'Console yourself with the thought that we'll make history.'

Russ activated his windshield wipers against the light, drizzling rain. 'Or make the obituary columns – like General Weidener.'

Two other minds ran in similar tracks.

Bradford Cooley and Emmett Hopper lolled in Cooley's *atrium*.

'Ten-twenty,' Cooley said, looking at his wristwatch. 'Another twenty-seven hours – more or less – and we'll have the returns in on Phase One. Say forty-eight hours, and they'll start coming in on Phase Two. Care to estimate the odds, Emmett?'

'Even, Brad. Either we hang them – or they hang us, perhaps in the literal sense of the word.'

Marjorie Norworth harbored no misgivings. Still in her

social secretary's office because men continued to work in her suite, she sat at her desk, writing. The words came easily. Tomorrow night, they would be spoken by her guest of honor.

30

Washington, D.C.: Wednesday, March 3. Day and Evening.

As Press Secretary Michael Harris predicted, the news media attacks on Talbot ran the gamut from vitriolic to vicious. Several columnists hinted broadly that impeachment proceedings might be in order. Nationally syndicated pundit Abel Shaneycroft vented his spleen by openly accusing Talbot of premeditated fraud on a global scale:

'Hoodwinking the American public with sham liberal talk, President Charles Pendleton Talbot stands revealed as an amoral swindler. Diverting attention from his real aims, he pretended to take courageous steps that would end civil unrest and revive the domestic economy. But his master plan was nothing less than one of rape – rape of the American public, rape of the Republic of Basanda and, by extension, rape of the world . . .'

Ken Ramsey stopped reading.

Fortunately, Talbot remained deep in sedated sleep. His physician had told Ramsey that it would be simple to awaken him at five o'clock and, within half an hour, restore him to fully functioning consciousness.

'He'll be in fine condition – only for God's sake, don't let him hear any news reports or he'll grab for the nearest bottle and empty it,' the Naval medical officer said.

'All right for him to have a couple of drinks?'

'Yes – provided what he hears is upbeat.'

'It will be, Admiral. It will be.'

Suzanne and Russ, refreshed by sleep, returned to the CBN studios. Much remained to be done – and Suzanne was harassed by hourly telephoned demands for 'progress reports' from Noah Sturdevant.

At noon, she lost patience and temper.

'Look, Mr Sturdevant. We're splicing footage, dubbing voiceovers, drafting scripts, pulling together sixty-two thousand loose ends. I'm not wearing pants because I put a bedpan on top of my chair so I don't have to run to the john when I have to micturate – that's piss in basic English . . .'

'Miss Loring . . .'

'Hold on, Caligula. My water's running. There, good to the last pop. If you want this special, *you* go to the john, lock the door and squat on the seat. Do anything. But stop bugging me!'

'Tsk,' Russ Hatch remonstrated, glancing up from the final draft of a voiceover commentary he had been reading. 'You're a liar. You are wearing pants. I felt 'em when I slipped my hand up your skirt.'

'Fun-nee!' Suzy giggled. 'You know, that monster probably believes that I *am* sitting on a bedpan.'

Russ turned serious, tapped the sheaf of papers. 'Lousy paragraph on page two. The writer plugs CBN twice – overdoing it for the private-showing version, no?'

'Sure is. Delete one – or both. Dumb-assed writers don't realize that the hard-sell CBN rah-rah goes in the second version.' She reached for her telephone. 'Hungry? Sent-up lunch?'

'Great – anything I can eat with one hand. Heavy on the carbohydrates, though, honey. Starting at three when I'm supposed to check in with Marjorie, I'll be dashing all over town.'

The four FBI agents were experienced, tough, intelligent – and black. Emmett Hopper had asked them to sign a special secrecy-oath before he briefed them. The men complied – and the briefing, which began at ten was continuing, even though it was twelve-thirty.

Oddly enough, none of the agents betrayed any sign of boredom. On the contrary, all were alert, eager, enthusiastic – despite the candid warnings Hopper gave them at the beginning and which he reiterated as a windup.

'There *is* a chance we'll all lose our jobs, perhaps even be arrested, tried, and sent to prison. If any of you want to change your minds, refuse the detail, you may do so. It won't count against you on your bureau records. Naturally, if you do, the secrecy oath remains binding.' Hopper paused, looked at the varied-shade black faces. 'Well?'

Silence.

'Nichols?' Hopper started with the man farthest on his left.

'I want the assignment, Mr Hopper.'

The next agent. 'Kidderly?'

'Yes, sir. I do, too.'

The other two men gave like replies. Agent Kidderly wanted to add that he wouldn't trade the assignment for anything in the world but thought better of it. Director Hopper liked brevity.

'Report to me at two-thirty,' Hopper said. 'I'll drive over with you.'

The final horde of men Suzanne and CBN sent to the House on the Hill finished their work at 3:00 A.M. and departed. A half dozen specialists had to return in midafternoon. But the peace and quiet that ensued lasted only until eight-thirty on Wednesday morning, when the decorators', florists', and caterers' trucks began to arrive.

Lady Norworth was downstairs, personally supervising the chaos. Although she had slept only five hours, she was in top form – and radiant.

'I can't remember when you looked better, Lady Norworth,' Holcomb told her.

'Thank you, Holcomb. To tell you the truth, I can't remember when I felt better – or more excited.' She saw several men carrying a heavy cumbersome crate toward the Red Room. 'No!' she called to them. 'That must be the Fertility Goddess statue – it goes into the State Dining Room. Holcomb, please show them where it is – and don't forget when the orchids arrive, they're to be banked around the foot of the statue . . .'

'Lady Norworth.' It was the footman. 'The people with the masks are here.'

'They weren't to be delivered until eleven! Oh, well, I'll have to tell them where each one is to be hung – and please bring me some orange juice.'

The footman hurried off. Can't understand it, he shook his head. She looks and acts like she's twenty this morning.

Russ arrived at the House on the Hill at three on the dot. He was astounded by the effects the decorators had created – and were still creating.

Marjorie Norworth had spent yet another fortune to provide a prime setting for one of her theme-parties. Examples of African art and artifacts (presumably Basandan) were everywhere. Carved wooden masks were hung on the walls. Primitively wrought gold, silver and copper jewelry was casually – but artistically – displayed. Two life-sized carved figures stood in the entrance foyer – each worth twenty thousand dollars or more if genuine and, Russ guessed correctly, they were. He glimpsed other, more magnificent statues through open doorways.

Holcomb led Russ upstairs, not to Marjorie's suite, but to her social secretary's office.

'I'm sure the Senator would like a large Scotch, Holcomb,' Marjorie said, kissing Russ.

'You and Suzanne must have worked like slaves,' she said when he was settled in a chair, drink in hand.

'Suzy did most of it – and she's still at it. I feel guilty sitting here with a drink, doing nothing.'

'She *is* a fabulous young woman, Russ.' The violet eyes hooded. 'Are you in love with her?'

Russ almost dropped his glass.

'Don't look as though I've hit you with a brick. Are you – or aren't you?'

'I – damn it, maybe. I don't know – we haven't talked in being-in-love terms. We've been together and close . . .'

'You've already talked too much. It shows you're really not. A pity, but perhaps it's just as well.'

Russ was totally confused. 'Why?'

'Because of your political future. I want to discuss it with you briefly this afternoon. It's the reason I asked you to come here at three, during the lull before the storm.'

'Marjorie, I don't have a political future!'

'Can anyone be so naïve? After tonight – and more particularly tomorrow night – you will be established as an important figure. Your political career will be assured – and you can make of it whatever you wish. It you were in love with Suzanne you'd doubtless end up marrying her . . .'

'For argument's sake, what would be wrong with that?' Russ gulped Scotch.

'Any number of things. She's devoted to her own career – a clash right there. Then, voters aren't overly happy with candidates whose wives are independent and have their own careers. The ballot-casters prefer men whose wives are loving helpmates. And don't forget the obvious conflict of interest. You, a politician, with a wife who delights in tearing politics and politicians apart. You'd both be suspect – Suzanne of parroting what you tell her, you of . . .'

'All academic, Marjorie. I've barely gotten into my third year as a Senator. I wouldn't be up for reelection – even *if* I decided to run again – until . . .'

'There's a Presidential campaign next year.'

'WHAT?'

'Pay attention to me, Russ. Two years from now you'll be forty-one. Charlie Talbot won't run again, I warrant you. The country will be ready for another young, charismatic President. Given sufficient financial backing – by me – and building on the reputation you'll have after tomorrow night, a nomination is certain. As for your election – well, I'm willing to wager many millions on it.'

Russell Hatch gaped. If Marjorie Norworth were serious, the prospect wasn't as insanely far-fetched as it sounded. My God! To be President!

Marjorie could almost look directly into his brain, and her smile would have done credit to a *Madame* de Maintenon – or a Medici.

'We not only have two big nights ahead of us, but two big years,' she murmured – and the 'we' was proprietary. Then four more after that, she added to herself. What I've started will grow – to be the ultimate success of *my* political career.

'When are you going over to the White House?' she asked.

'At seven – and if you'll excuse me, Marjorie, I think I should leave. I've got a lot to do – and then dress . . .'

'Shoo – off with you.' Marjorie smiled, made exaggerated go-away gestures with her graceful hands.

'Oh, I forgot. I'll be back here at six-thirty. Suzanne has to check the installations and talk to the men in the main technical crew. I promised to drive her over.'

'Until six-thirty, then.' She stood up and kissed him. 'If you have a moment to spare in all your to-ings and fro-ings, give a thought to your future – as the future President Russell Hatch. President Hatch. It has a nice sound, Russ.'

Emmett Hopper came minutes after Russ departed. He was accompanied by the four black FBI agents wearing the bureau 'uniform' – dark, monochromatic, conservative business suits. Each carried a small suitcase. Holcomb said Lady Norworth was upstairs.

'Shall I tell her you're here, Mr Hopper?'

'No need to disturb her, Holcomb. These gentlemen will be your extra barmen and waiters tonight. They'll spend the rest of the afternoon familiarizing themselves with the house. Their wigs and dashikis are in the suitcases.'

Having delivered the agents, Hopper returned to the J. Edgar Hoover Building.

Russ, already attired in dinner jacket, brought Suzanne to Lady Norworth's. She was casually dressed, but brought with her the clothes into which she would change later.

The decorators and florists had completed their work. The staff, both regular and special, was garbed in keeping with the party theme. Even Holcomb wore an overdone Afro wig and dashiki. Too much, Russ thought. However, as Marjorie says, Washington goes for the gauche.

'I'm surprised there aren't any prowling lions and you're

not wearing a bone in your nose,' he grinned wryly to Holcomb.

'Can't have everything, Senator,' the majordomo grinned back. 'But the staff will be addressing the guests as *bwana* tonight.'

'They'll freak out,' Suzanne giggled. 'Maybe we can build a slow fire and shrink their heads.'

Marjorie Norworth came down the broad staircase. She had not yet changed for the evening and was, by her standards, simply dressed.

'Suzanne, my dear.' She embraced Suzy. 'Please come upstairs.' A glance at Russ. 'Run along, young man. We mustn't have you receiving demerits for being tardy at the White House.'

'He won't be,' Suzanne smiled at Russ. 'I swore to Lexa Talbot that he'd be on time. With his tie straight – which it is. Run along *bwana* – I'll see you later.'

Lexa Talbot was waiting for Russ in the West Sitting Room.

'You're gorgeous in a dinner jacket, Russ,' she said after they exchanged greetings. 'Makes you look even taller and more broad-shouldered.'

'I'll find a job as a headwaiter someplace.'

'You'll have me as a steady customer. I'll be there every night to ogle.'

Russ noticed that she was wearing the same dress she had Saturday evening, when she came to his apartment. It surprised him. *I never expected Lexa Talbot to wear the same dress twice*, he mused. *Especially one like that – casual and what is it women call them, basic black – for a big night. I thought for sure she'd be sleek and sequined or some damned thing.*

Lexa gave herself a mental pat on the back. It was child's play to read what he was thinking. The double effect she sought was achieved. The dress reminded him of Saturday – and by process of association, he would think of Sunday night. Then, Suzanne Loring was certain to be dressed to the teeth. The contrast would have an impact on Russ, make him defensive and protective – toward little me.

'Observant man,' she drove the point home. 'You recognize my dress. It's the most practical thing I could think of—considering that Daddy and I will be roosting in Lady Norworth's attic for hours.'

'Not quite in her attic,' Russ said, because he did not quite know what else to say. 'All the same' – *oh, hell, drop it* – 'Uh, how is your father?'

'Daddy's a bundle of clichés, Russ. He's walking on air, ready to jump out of his skin with joy, on top of the world. Ken Ramsey and I've told him as much as he needs to hear for the present. Ken is helping him dress and watching him like a hawk – hey, that's a great word, considering – anyway, watching that he doesn't talk to anyone and accidentally say the wrong thing. Let's have a drink while we wait for his grand entrance.'

She mixed two martinis, gave Russ one. They had barely started on their drinks when Charles Talbot joined them. He was a new man, a swashbuckler resplendent in shawl-collared dinner-jacket, self-assured and ebullient. The lines in his athlete's face, which had become deep furrows recently, were miraculously ironed down to shallow crinkles.

'Hi, Puss.' He kissed Lexa, pumped Russ's hand. 'How's my daughter's beau this evening – and where's my drink?'

Lexa quickly mixed a weak martini. Talbot tasted it, made a face. 'We run out of gin?'

'You need a clear head, Daddy. You'll have a lot of studying and practicing to do while we're hiding in what Russ claims isn't quite Lady N's attic.'

Talbot made another face. 'And we really have to sneak up the back way?' He saw Russ and Lexa nod. 'Hell.' He emptied his glass. 'Well, let's start rolling.'

31

The House on the Hill: Wednesday, March 3. Night.

Two beautiful black girls clad only in short African skirts knotted low on their hips stood in the entrance foyer. African necklaces served to accentuate the beauty of their bare breasts. They gave each arriving guest a gaudy lapel badge: 'I'm Backing Basanda.' Senator Daniel Aloysius Madigan pinned his on with foreboding, unable to fathom what lay behind Marjorie Norworth's hawkish extravaganza. He roamed from room to room, hoping to obtain some clue.

Early Frobase was no help. Clutching a liquor glass, he stood near the laden buffet tables in the facsimile State Dining Room, staring mesmerized at the topless black female servants and in no mood to make conversation. MacDonald Pearce was more talkative and subjected Madigan to a characteristic pedantic lecture. Its gist: Lady Norworth was a reliable bellwether of opinion, always – but always – aligning herself with the victorious faction. Her hawkish stand was 'an indicator infinitely more valid than the findings of all the poll-takers in the country'.

Madigan said he agreed and moved on, encountering Russell Hatch, who was friendly and affable. 'What's the payoff going to be?' Madigan asked.

Having delivered Charles Talbot and his daughter safely at seven forty-five, Russ left them with Marjorie. He and Suzanne spent the next two hours tidying loose ends. All being in order, he could afford to relax, to mingle with the guests who began to arrive at ten and to be pleasant with everyone. Even Daniel Madigan.

'Far as I can see, it's just a party, Dan,' he said, smiling. 'Loosen up, have fun.' He gave Madigan a good-natured pat on the shoulder, ambled away.

Madigan found John Kurtz and G. Howard Denby in a two-man huddle. They welcomed him into it.

'This blowout is going to shiver the doves' timbers when they hear about it tomorrow,' Kurtz beamed.

'Flocks of them will rush to change sides,' Denby predicted. 'Marjorie's the pace-setter – the bastards'll realize they'd better get in step or else.' It was a long and vehement speech for the normally taciturn and emotionless CIA Director.

Emmett Hopper's arrival caused no stir. It was assumed that the FBI Chief had decided to protect himself by climbing on the Basanda bandwagon. But there was considerable surprise minutes later when Congressman Bradford Cooley appeared. North Dakota Senator Atherton Pace intercepted Cooley as he waddled toward the nearest bar.

'Didn't expect you here, Brad.' Pace's laugh was a whinny. 'You've been the noisiest and plumpest dove in the House.'

'Take my advice, Atherton, give up ornithology,' Cooley said ambiguously and continued on to the bar.

Jordan B. Rickhoven III came at ten-thirty. Marjorie Norworth herself led him into the facsimile State Dining Room. Men crowded to make their obeisances. To most he was 'Mr Rickhoven' – said with the respect due the man who held long-term leases on half the politicians in Washington. Pearce preened as he called the billionaire 'Jordan'. Madigan flaunted the degree of familiarity he enjoyed by addressing Rickhoven as 'JB'.

Rickhoven accepted the homages with his customary insouciance, but Marjorie sensed his impatience to exploit the part for his own purposes. Giving a plausible excuse, she left his side and seemed to float from the room in her exotically embroidered Zandra Rhodes gown. She literally sparkled as she went. It was, in her shrewdly accurate opinion, most definitely an all-diamonds night – and she had chosen to wear her largest and finest.

*

Jordan Rickhoven preempted the Blue Room as a private conference chamber where he, Pearce, Madigan, Kurtz, Denby and Frobase could talk behind closed doors.

'Talbot under control?' Rickhoven asked.

'Gagged and trussed,' Denby said.

'Alvin Dunlap coming tonight?'

'He was invited and he accepted,' Kurtz said. 'We told him not to show. If we have to use the Twenty-Fifth on Talbot, it'll be more effective for Dunlap to come on the scene as an innocent neutral bravely shouldering the load thrust on him.'

Dan Madigan saw his opening. The presence of Frobase would make his alibi insurance more binding. 'Early and I should keep a low profile, too, for a few days,' he said. 'With him being President Pro Tem and me Majority Leader in the Senate – well, hell, why risk having people add things up in case we're pushed into hanging the Twenty-Fifth frame around Charlie Talbot's neck.'

'Nonsense,' MacDonald Pearce sniffed. 'Talbot is helpless.'

Kurtz sucked his cold pipe. 'He *might* have second thoughts and try sailing against the wind. I tend to agree with Dan.'

'So do I,' Rickhoven nodded – to Madigan's immense relief. The billionaire looked at Kurtz. 'What's the latest at your end, John?'

'The two divisions go off tomorrow or the next day. They'll be in action as soon as they land.'

'Good – and you, Mac. Anything new?'

'Ah – our Ambassador reports anti-Government riots in Kinsolo. They've been quelled, however. The Military Grand Council acted swiftly – using force, naturally. Some two hundred rioters were killed.'

'Mac, I haven't heard from Dollinger – my man in Basanda – for almost two days.' It was a statement demanding reply. Pearce cleared his throat uneasily.

'I – ah – would have preferred to tell you privately.' He saw Rickhoven scowl and shriveled. 'Jordan – a mob in Kinsolo attacked his car and burned it . . .'

'With Dollinger inside?' Rickhoven's aquiline face purpled. 'Goddamnit, it takes years – decades – to make a top executive like Dollinger, only minutes to break a politician! Get this through your heads. If any more of my upper-echelon people over there are so much as scratched, I'll hold the three of you – Pearce, Kurtz, Denby – personally responsible.' He regained his composure and a few minutes later declared the impromptu conference ended.

Lady Marjorie Norworth entered the State Dining Room again – with Suzanne Loring, boldly dramatic in St Laurent paisley chiffon, her dark hair wrapped in a crepe de chine turban. The men's conversation ceased. A female guest? It shattered all House on the Hill theme-party traditions. That the female guest was Suzanne Loring, the television personality who delighted in bedeviling politicians multiplied the men's consternation. Marjorie took Suzanne from one group to another, explaining why she was there.

'The public should *know* about this party,' Lady Norworth bubbled. 'People should realize how many leading figures in our Government attended to demonstrate their sympathy for the Basandan Loyalists – and we *do* want it all reported by someone trustworthy. Need I remind you how wonderfully *fair* Miss Loring was to Senator Madigan?'

Fears were allayed. Marjorie Norworth would never cause her guests embarrassment – or risk harming her own position, and publicity of the right kind *was* highly desirable. The men thawed. Their talk resumed, as free and unguarded as before.

Marjorie and Suzanne went into the Red Room. Jordan Rickhoven was chatting with the new Treasury Secretary. Marjorie made the introductions. Suzanne gave Rickhoven a winsome smile.

'At last, I meet my most favorite tycoon.'

'And I my most favorite television celebrity. May I get you a drink?'

'Yes, thanks.' A dashiki-clad black servant was passing with a huge tray of fresh drinks. 'Could you snare a glass of champagne from our trusty tray-bearer?'

Rickhoven signaled. The servant said, 'Yes, *bwana*,' offered the tray. Rickhoven took two glasses of champagne, passed one to Suzanne with a courtly gesture. 'Wonder how they "here's to you" in Basandan,' he said, smiling.

'I've heard most tribes speak Swahili' – *I haven't, but who cares?* – 'and the only two Swahili words I know are *piga* and *chunga kali*. The first means shoot – as in shoot a rifle – and the second means danger. So *piga* and *chunga kali*, Mr Rickhoven.'

His slow-forming smile was uncertain, but they touched glasses and drank.

Marjorie asked the eight or ten men who had gravitated to the Green Room if they would mind leaving it for a few minutes. 'We'll have some entertainment. The servants will shift furniture and bring in folding chairs.'

The men trooped out obediently. Once beyond Marjorie's earshot, some grumbled.

'Shit, we'll probably have to watch a bunch of fucking jigs prance around waving spears.'

'Beating drums while they yowl their heads off.'

'If we're lucky, it won't last long.'

'If we're luckier, the nigra chicks'll do the dancing, make those bare tits bounce.'

The last remark stimulated the Minnesota Congressman Boyd Sorenson – a nationally known figure. Sorenson was famed for his large family – nine children – his unrelenting crusades against pornography, permissive sex, abortion, and for his adherence to the strict Calvinist doctrines of the religion to which he belonged.

'Ever have a nigger whore give you head?' he asked his companions. 'A black bitch will suck your spine out through the head of your cock. Jesus, it's great!'

Navy Undersecretary Peebles leered agreement. 'Black broads may hate our white guts, but they sure love to work over a white prick!'

As might have been anticipated, even the folding chairs Marjorie rented for the evening were luxurious. Seats and backs were thickly padded and upholstered in a zebra-skin patterned fabric – befitting the evening's African theme. Arrayed in rows, they transformed the Green Room into a miniature theater – a cinema theater, apparently, for the huge metallic screen at one end of the room had been lowered.

The complex projection machine, which could show television programs as they were broadcast, videotapes or motion picture films, was set up, precisely positioned. Holcomb, not at all self-conscious in his Afro wig and dashiki, stood beside the apparatus.

The several dozen guests, each carrying a brimful glass of his favorite liquor, took their seats quickly. Whatever the entertainment would be, they wanted it done and over with so they could return to their gossip-and-rumor tradings and deal makings.

Jordan Rickhoven took a chair in a row midway between projector and screen. His three acolytes – Pearce, Kurtz, and Denby – automatically chose the same row. They still smarted from Rickhoven's outburst and were vying with each other to regain favor.

Dan Madigan and Early Frobase sat together, well apart from Rickhoven and the fawning trio. Sorenson and Peebles carelessly planted themselves in the front row. They had no interest in viewing any films. They were immersed in a continuing discussion on the merits of fellatio as performed by black prostitutes and comparing their personal experiences in clinical detail.

The audience seats were filled. Some folding seats had been grouped around the projection machine. These were taken by Marjorie, Suzanne Loring, Emmett Hopper, Bradford Cooley and Russell Hatch. Four black males – in Afro wigs and dashikis – did not sit. They remained standing, ranged along the left-hand wall. The guests assumed they were there to retrieve empty glasses and serve more drinks.

'I think we're about ready,' Marjorie murmured. She rose to her feet, a regal figure, her diamonds blazing.

'My dear friends,' she said raising her voice. The hum of

talk among the guests subsided. Men craned their heads around to look at her. 'I am at a loss – *truly* at a loss – for words to describe my joy and gratification at seeing so many of you here tonight because I cannot remember ever giving a party that had so much significance.'

She paused for a split second, glanced down at Brad Cooley, who lovingly nursed a large Baccarat tumbler filled with bourbon. He winked at her, and she continued.

'I feel that my home is simply *filled* with positive vibrations – and that each and every one of you feels gratified, too. This is the final proof that you, who govern our country, wholeheartedly support those who are determined to bring *true* democracy to Basanda.'

Men holding liquor glasses are hard put to clap their hands, even when they wish to applaud statements praising them. Marjorie's guests had to content themselves with loud murmurs of approval.

'The assholes think they're heroes,' Suzanne whispered to Russ, who was seated beside her.

'What else would they think?' he whispered back. 'They probably expect Jordan B. to give them medals as party favors later.'

'More likely they expect wads of cash.'

'Two-thirds of 'em get those anyway.'

The murmurs faded. Marjorie resumed.

'You are all backing the Basandan Loyalist cause, but I'm afraid very few of us have *actually been* to Basanda. Perhaps that is an advntage. I remember what Harry Truman said when Ike Eisenhower announced that he would go to Korea. "The dumb s.o.b. isn't smart enough to know that politicians should stay away from places where people are shooting at each other. There's plenty of sniping going on right here in Washington." '

A ripple of laughter from the audience.

'But we really *should* learn something about the country and its people.'

Marjorie paused again, inclined her lovely head toward Suzanne, went on. 'Thanks to Miss Loring, we have a film – she calls it "a patch-job of film-clips" – made in Basanda by

Continental Broadcasting Network camera teams. None of what we'll see tonight has been shown publicly. I *do* hope you will find it as fascinating – and as educational – as I did when Miss Loring gave me a preview earlier today.'

Lady Norworth sat down.

'A fucking travelog,' an anonymous – and drunken – voice commented.

MacDonald Pearce shifted restlessly. 'Not like Marjorie Norworth – not at all,' he muttered. 'It's totally out of character. I detect a false note . . .'

'Stop being paranoid,' Rickhoven told him curtly – but he, too, felt vague misgivings.

Frobase nudged Madigan. 'She gone nuts? This blowout must be costing her a fortune – and for what? To show us a half-assed movie?'

'Relax, Early,' Madigan said in a drawl intended to hide his own growing sense of apprehension. 'Marjorie got where she is by doing things that were different.' He drank down half the contents of his full glass.

Cooley's chair was beside one occupied by Hopper. 'I can't help but think of bullfights,' Cooley said.

'The moment of truth?' Hopper's lowered voice was taut. 'Exactly.'

Holcomb manipulated switches. The lights in the Green Room dimmed down to a bare glow.

A blinding cone of light shot out from the projector lens, splashed against the metallic screen and formed into an image of the Kinsolo waterfront. Blood-red color seeped down, swirled, formed into the superimposed words:

WELCOME TO BASANDA

32

The House on the Hill: Wednesday, March 3. Midnight.

The WELCOME TO BASANDA title wiped to a long shot of a jungle clearing. At its far end, blacks in oddments of military uniform held longish implements and flailed and jabbed at shapeless bundles on the ground.

VOICEOVER: 'K'tu, an upland village, early this January.'

The camera lens zoomed in. The bundles were hideously mutilated corpses – one that of a young woman, her belly slit open. Black hands thrust a bayonet-tipped rifle into the open belly. The rifle swung upward. An almost fully formed baby was skewered on the bayonet.

Jumpcut to the exterior of the Prime Ministerial Palace in Kinsolo.

VOICEOVER: 'A few days after this incident, Prime Minister Odu Mwandi made a statement to our correspondents.'

Cut to Mwandi's audience chamber, Mwandi, wearing a flamboyant uniform encrusted with medals, glared into the camera, spoke:

'The rebel beasts must be eliminated, annihilated.'

The first sequence stunned Marjorie's guests into breathless silence. Now there were approving murmurs. Yes, rebels guilty of such atrocities deserved to be exterminated.

The camera held on a frozen-frame of Mwandi with his mouth open.

VOICEOVER: 'The Prime Minister neglected to mention that the butchers were his troops and the victims were K'tu villagers. Their crime: they failed to observe his birthday with sufficient pomp.'

A new scene. An open square in Kinsolo. Twenty wooden stakes were driven into the earth. A man or woman was tied to each. Loyalist soldiers were dousing the bound figures with fluid poured from five-gallon jerry-cans. A crowd ringed the square, held at bay by more soldiers brandishing rifles and submachine guns.

VOICEOVER: 'These victims were guilty of absolutely nothing. They were selected at random to serve as examples. The film is silent, made with hand-held cameras smuggled past Basandan guards and secret police. The cameramen concealed themselves in nearby buildings.'

The jerry-cans were emptied. The soldiers stepped away from the stakes, lit matches. The twenty men and women exploded into flame.

VOICEOVER: 'The human beings you see being burned alive were drenched in gasoline provided by the United States Government.'

MacDonald Pearce leaped from his chair. 'I demand the film be stopped?' he shouted, his voice shrill. There were other loud protests.

Act One, Marjorie thought and then said, 'All right, Holcomb.'

The projector went dark. The Green Room lights came on full. Guests were cursing, leaving their chairs, starting for the doors. Emmett Hopper stood up, waved a hand. The black FBI agents masquerading as servants drew .357 Magnum revolvers from under their dashikis. Agent Nichols aimed at the ceiling, fired. The deafening blast halted the milling guests in their tracks.

G. Howard Denby gasped and his complexion turned greenish-yellow. Hopper. An FBI coup. A spasm contorted Denby's bowels. Hopper and the FBI would never dare – unless they had orders. That meant Talbot. Denby found himself staring into the muzzle of a Magnum and was wracked by a second spasm. The CIA Director who could blandly order assassinations and countenance massacres was a pitiful physical coward.

'You're insane!' Rickhoven barked at Marjorie Norworth. He seized Pearce's arm, pulled him toward the doors.

FBI agent Kidderley stepped forward, delivered a short karate-chop that slammed Rickhoven to the floor.

'Call the police!' Pearce shrieked hysterically.

'Go back to your seats – all of you!' Hopper commanded.

Kurtz sneered. 'Hopper, when the President hears . . .'

'He heard what he needed to hear from you Saturday, Kurtz.'

The explanation, Kurtz thought, was that Talbot had chosen Hopper and the FBI as his last-ditch retaliatory weapons.

'Let these fools play out their hand,' Rickhoven said, getting to his feet with Pearce's help. 'We'll invoke the Twenty-Fifth in the morning.'

Pearce saw Dan Madigan, motioned to him. Madigan looked away hastily. Instinct told him to edge to a straddling position, poise himself to jump the fence.

Urged on by Hopper's men, the guests returned to their folding chairs. Only Denby remained standing. He could not bring himself to sit in his own befoulment The lights dimmed – only slightly The projector started again. The voiceover picked up in midsentence.

'. . . by no means the only manifestations of American largesse. Basandan Prime Ministers enjoy the use of more than fifty custom-built Cadillac limousines – all armored, six also gold-plated.'

On the screen, a long row of glittering limousines in the courtyard of the Prime Ministerial Palace. Jump-cut to a huge white yacht.

VOICEOVER: 'Built secretly at a cost of fifty-four million dollars to the U.S. taxpayer, this yacht was presented to Odu Mwandi as a gift.'

Wipe to a long shot of opulent villas on a hillside.

VOICEOVER: 'Each of these houses cost the American people over two hundred thousand dollars. They were given free to Basanda government officials.'

Flip to a view of an obscene slum. Lean-tos and tar-paper shacks. Children with hunger-swollen bellies. Emaciated adults with empty eyes.

VOICEOVER: 'The Tsomba quarter, scarcely a mile

332

from the Prime Ministerial Palace, where twenty people die of hunger daily.'

Closeshot of carrion birds tearing at a human body.

VOICEOVER: 'Mwandi's successor, Percival Kwida, continued to wage war against so-called rebels – people like these Bima tribesmen who protested confiscation of their crops and livestock.'

On the screen, three hundred or more Basandans of both sexes and all ages were penned inside a barbed wire enclosure. Loyalist troops squatting behind machine guns opened fire, mowed them down.

VOICEOVER: 'Kwida's rule was brief, but no less bloody than that of his predecessor. In Kinsolo, he ordered thousands murdered.'

Jumpcut to a hundred corpses dangling from gibbets.

VOICEOVER: 'The Military Grand Council that took power after Kwida's death operates under the direction of the American Central Intelligence Agency, but the terror and massacres continue.'

More scenes of carnage and horror, then WELCOME TO BASANDA and the CBN logo.

VOICEOVER: 'These films were made in violation of Basandan and U.S. Government censorship regulations. They have not been shown publicly because of pressures exerted by Federal agencies. These have threatened CBN and all other news media with reprisals if they released information injurious to the Loyalist image. Noah Sturdevant, CBN board chairman, believes the truth must at last be told. He and all other CBN executives are prepared to accept the consequences.'

The screen went black. Holcomb switched off the projector, turned the room lights up.

G. Howard Denby, ignoring the sticky wetness and stench of his own excrement, regained the bluster he confused with courage.

'The film violates section one-fifty-nine of the National Security Act,' he declared loudly. 'As CIA Director, I am authorized to seize it and detain all persons involved in its dissemination.'

Hopper spoke. 'Denby, the act authorizes seizure by *either* CIA or FBI. I officially confiscated the film this afternoon. I have also placed all persons involved under protective house arrest. You will have to obtain a Presidential order before I transfer the film to your custody or lift the protective arrest order.'

Rickhoven also resorted to bluster. 'Hopper, you've unlawfully detained all of us here – at gunpoint. We have been deprived of our civil liberties . . .'

'Swear a warrant for my arrest,' Hopper shrugged. 'Or complain to President Talbot.'

'Talbot!' Kurtz exclaimed. 'That son of a bitch is finished!'

'Where's a phone?' Frobase demanded. 'I'm still President Pro Tem of the Senate, by God. You can't stop me from calling . . .'

'Who, Senator?' Russell Hatch asked, standing up, 'Alvin Dunlap, so you can start Führer Rickhoven's *putsch*?'

'Talbot's mentally incompetent!' Frobase bellowed, falling into the trap. He charged toward Hatch. A dashiki-clad FBI man grabbed him.

'Take your fucking hands off me, nigger!'

Lady Norworth nodded to her majordomo. 'We have more films, gentlemen,' she said. 'Home movies. Mine.'

Holcomb had replaced the film reel with a videotape. The projector beam flared.

VIDEO: Senator Early Frobase and a black woman lay on a bed. Both were naked. He pawed at her huge, pendulous breasts.

AUDIO: The woman's voice (bored): 'Get with it. Do what you want.' Frobase's voice (hoarse, ragged): 'Hold your tits together.'

VIDEO: The woman turned on her side, hands pressing breasts into what seemed one great lump of flesh. Frobase, in juxtaposition, his tongue lapping at her massive thighs, gripped his erect penis in one hand and slapped and pounded it against her breasts.

AUDIO: Frobase made grunting animal noises.

'That should do,' Marjorie said. Holcomb switched off the machine. The Green Room shook with obscene laughter. Early Frobase broke away from the FBI agent, and wailing, flung himself to the floor, clawed at the carpet.

'Scratch one Mississippi Senator,' Russ said to Suzanne. 'He'll be resigning – but fast.'

'Uh-huh,' she grinned. 'Due to urgent personal considerations.'

'Ahm plum dee-stroyed!' Cooley declared loudly in his bogus Alabama backwoods dialect. 'Ouah distinguished Senatuh performin' preee-verted sexual acts with a nigra-woman.' He chortled, dropped the accent. 'Shouldn't we come to order – *gentlemen*?'

The tumult died away. Marjorie, violet eyes glowing with triumph, said: 'I have literally *hundreds* of home movies starring *many* different performers. Shall we show more?'

Dead silence. Almost every guest had been 'upstairs' at one time or another in the past. None ever dreamed his words and actions were under closed-circuit television surveillance and being registered on videotapes. Fear hung heavy in the room.

MacDonald Pearce thought of the young girls – 'Ride me!' – and clutched a chairback as his knees threatened to buckle. Rickhoven could almost hear the jeering yelps that could greet images of him crawling on his hands and knees, begging to be whipped and kicked. His facial muscles sagged: he seemed to age thirty years.

Kurtz dropped his pipe, made no effort to retrieve it. Denby was doubled up, holding both hands to his stomach, vainly trying to ease the pain that ripped and tore at it. Senator Pace sweated profusely.

Dan Madigan alone remained cool, composed. Marjorie and her coterie were certain to have more than 'home movies' to back their play, whatever they were after. They hadn't made that clear yet, but they would – and very soon, he guessed. Now or never, Madigan reflected, deciding that safety lay in switching allegiances. Adjusting his butterfly bow tie which had somehow been twisted askew in the jostlings and turmoil, he assumed the manner of a minor miscreant willing to admit guilt.

'Gentlemen, *I* believe we owe Lady Norworth a vote of thanks,' he declared, loud enough to be heard by everyone. 'The Basanda film opened my eyes. It should have opened yours.'

Rickhoven moved close to Madigan, glared pure hate. 'You slimy, two-faced . . .'

'Easy, JB. I'm an old-time pro, remember? If you can't lick 'em, join 'em – the First Commandment in politics.'

'I'll break you!'

'Fuck you will. Tomorrow, I'll start cranking up a committee investigation of your bank. I hear it might not be solvent. We'll bust you wide open.'

'That won't be necessary, Dan.'

Heads snapped up in stupefied astonishment. It was Talbot's voice, booming from a concealed loudspeaker.

'I fibbed, Jordan,' Marjorie said. 'The *President* is here. He and his daughter are in my suite with the technicians.' She turned to Suzanne. 'You explain it, my dear.'

'The fiendish delight is mine,' Suzanne grinned. 'Gents, Big Brother has been with you all tonight. CBN crews installed thirty-six invisible microphones in the rooms where you've been boozing and babbling – with a tape recorder linked to each mike. Your every whisper has been electrically immortalized up in Lady Norworth's suite – which is the control booth and monitoring center.' She paused, and then added. 'Okay, guys. Let's treat the lovely folks to some samples.'

Marjorie's suite was crammed with electronic gear. Charles Talbot, Lexa, six Secret Service men, and a dozen technicians found it difficult to move around. But all grinned as the sound men began operating their playback equipment.

Clearly identifiable voices came over the hidden speaker in the Green Room.

'I want those divisions committed to action – in so deep that they can't be pulled out, no matter what.' Jordan Rickhoven.

Amplified clicking sounds.

'We have all been following your instructions to the letter, Jordan.' MacDonald Pearce.

More clicks.

'I say if we have too much static from the public, we force Talbot to declare a National Emergency. If he balks, we boot him out, put Dunlap in. He'll do it.' G. Howard Denby.

'We should, I agree.' John Kurtz.

Again clicks.

'. . . a nigger whore go down on you?' Congressman Boyd Sorenson.

A click and a pause.

'Talbot's mentally incompetent!' Senator Early Frobase.

'Time for a station break.' Suzanne said for the benefit of the sound men, who stopped the playbacks. She leered at the men in the Green Room. 'And now, all of you out there on the verge of cardiac arrest, a message from our sponsor. Take it away, Mr President!'

Charles Talbot leaned toward the microphone that had been placed on a small table for his use, looked at a paper Marjorie had given him earlier and read the lines he had spent an hour rehearsing.

'This is President Charles Talbot – the President of the United States. Your President, elected by the American people and sworn to preserve, protect and defend the Constitution.' A two-beat pause. 'I shall be coming downstairs shortly. The following men will remain in the Green Room until I am ready to meet with them: Pearce, Kurtz, Madigan, Denby, Rickhoven. The others may leave, but not before they have this firmly in mind. I, the President, now have all the material I need to insure your unquestioning obedience to my lawful orders, your full cooperation in governing this country through democratic processes – and your absolute silence about what transpired here tonight. I, as a citizen, hope that you will return to your homes, read the Constitution – and then pray for your country. Good night.'

A soundman switched off the mike. Talbot turned to Lexa. 'How did I sound?'

'Like Lincoln at Gettysburg.'

Talbot and his companions gathered in the Blue Room.

'I'm grateful,' he said simply.

'We both are,' Lexa said, tears glistening in her eyes. She embraced Marjorie Norworth, then Suzanne, and, in turn, Russ, Bradford Cooley, and Emmett Hopper.

Talbot shook hands with the men, sought to read their minds. Favors of the magnitude they had done him were not given free in Washington. What to offer as rewards? Cooley had gone to Columbia Law School. Braithwaite would have to be removed as Chief Justice by one means or another. An Associate Justice could be kicked upstairs to replace him – and Cooley offered the resulting vacancy. Hopper? Easy, Talbot thought. I'll give him the jackpot he's always wanted. As for Hatch – big assignments, much public exposure and more White House invitations.

Marjorie watched the tableaux closely. Talbot owed her the largest debt of all, and she intended to collect – with usurious interest. He left them, went into the Green Room. Four Secret Service men accompanied him. Two remained with Lexa. Cooley, Hopper, and Hatch followed behind the President's bodyguards.

The Green Room had the surreal air of a funeral parlor from which most of the mourners had fled in panic, leaving behind a litter of dirty ashtrays, glasses – and a tiny group of men so bereft by grief they could not bring themselves to leave.

Rickhoven sat at one end of the room with Pearce and Kurtz, the most bereft of the bitter-end grievers huddled together, giving each other wordless comfort. Madigan lolled in a chair well apart from them, calmly smoking a panatela – the relative certain he was the chief beneficiary of the yet unread will. Denby, ashen and expressionless, leaned against a wall – a coffinless corpse propped on display. The ultimate surreal touch was added by Hopper's quartet of black FBI agents – who might have been gaudily costumed requiem singers waiting for the mortician to arrive and pay them their fee.

The door opened. A Secret Service man announced: 'Gentlemen, the President of the United States.' The seated men started to rise.

'Never mind the formalities.' Talbot came into the room, gave the FBI men a friendly nod, went to the chairs near the projection machine, took one, crossed his legs, indicated that Cooley, Hopper and Russ were to sit near him. The Secret Service men stood.

'Should my men leave, Mr President?' Hopper asked.

'No, they've earned their tickets.' Talbot opened a small loose-leaf memo book. It contained more of Marjorie Norworth's compositions. 'Secretary Kurtz.'

'Yes, Mr President.' The response was faint, shaky.

'Upon leaving here, you will go to the Pentagon and issue orders canceling all troop and supply movements to Basanda. Units earmarked for shipment will immediately return to their permanent bases. All aircraft being used in the Basandan airlift are to be grounded. Have I made myself clear so far?'

'Yes, sir.' Barely more than a whisper.

'Next, you will radio our commanders in Basanda to effect an immediate and total cease-fire. They are to evacuate all American civilians without delay and prepare to withdraw all military personnel.'

'They – they may have to shot their way out.'

'I doubt it. Secretary Pearce, no sleep for you tonight. Go to your office, rout your people out of bed. Establish contact with Basandan rebel leaders. Inform them of our new policy of complete withdrawal. Request – do *not* demand, request – they release the Americans they took prisoner at Gidanu. Notify the British, French and Soviet Ambassadors . . .'

'We'll tell the world we're weak, afraid!' Pearce croaked.

'Wrong. We'll be telling the world we have the sense to dump lost causes.'

'We have treaty obligations!'

'There are loopholes in every treaty – find them!' Talbot rasped. 'Or I'll find myself another Secretary of State.'

Pearce felt a flicker of hope. He had anticipated a demand for his resignation. Talbot was hinting he might retain his post. *If so, I can quietly start to rebuild*, he thought.

Charles Talbot read aloud from the memo book. 'Our position is this. Basandan Governments have consistently proven to be corrupt, tyrannical, savagely cruel, and merciless. We refuse to repeat the ghastly mistakes of the Johnson and Nixon Administrations. America must not become embroiled in – and torn apart internally – by a war to keep thieves, torturers, and mass-murderers in power.'

Dan Madigan spoke up. 'Mr President, with your permission, I'd like to repeat those words and endorse them in the Senate.'

Nimble footwork, Russ thought, not without admiration. I'm getting a cram-course in survival training.

Cooley chuckled. *The Instant Transmogrification of Daniel Madigan from Brutus into Marc Antony*, he mused.

Rickhoven was unable to remain silent longer. 'Talbot, you're selling out our friends and allies . . .'

'Bullshit!' Talbot snorted. 'But if you'll show me the courtesy of addressing me as "Mr President", I'll ease your mind. You've done a lot for the party in the past. That makes *you* a friend and ally. We won't be selling you out.' *We can't afford to.*

'My apologies, Mr President.' Rickhoven sensed there was to be a trade-off.

'I want you all in the Oval Office at eleven in the morning.' Talbot said. 'We have a scenario to study.' He stood up. The Secret Service men closed in around him.

'Mr President.' Denby's voice was a thin quaver. 'Do you have any instructions for me?'

'I will have – at eleven. There's a big part in the scenario for you, Denby. A very big part.'

Hopper and Cooley exchanged knowing looks. Hopper's eyes gleamed.

33

Washington, D.C.: Thursday, March 4. Morning and Early Afternoon.

Kenneth Ramsey ushered the group into the Oval Office at precisely 11:00 A.M. The President made quick appraisals of the men as they entered.

Pearce and Kurtz were hollow-eyed, bedraggled. Obviously, neither had slept. Madigan was dapper, collected. Rickhoven's nonchalance was a bit overdone this morning. Next came Hopper – brisk and businesslike – and Cooley, his clothes rumpled as usual, his expression faintly sardonic. Denby looked sickly. Hatch appeared crisp, fresh, eager.

Talbot activated the doorlock, neutralized his intercom. He told Hatch and the FBI Director to take the chairs nearest his desk, the others to sit where they chose. He nodded to Kurtz. 'You start, John' – wisest to get back on a first-name basis – 'Make it fast. We have exactly one hour for this confab.'

'Your orders have been carried out, Mr President,' Kurtz reported. 'To the letter,' he added.

'Any leaks to the press?'

'Not yet.'

'Much static from the generals and admirals?'

'A little.' They had screamed their heads off.

'What from Foggy Bottom, Mac?' Talbot asked Pearce, bracing for the pedantic monolog certain to follow.

'The State Department implemented your directives, Mr President. Direct communication was established with the rebel side. The insurgents admit holding ninety-seven American civilians taken captive when they overran Gidanu . . .'

'There were supposed to be over a hundred.'

'Ah – the rebels claim the others were killed by our raiding aircraft. I don't believe it, of course . . .'

'I do,' Talbot growled. 'They wouldn't admit having live prisoners who can tell us what really happened if it wasn't so. Go on.'

'The rebel high command promises to release all the prisoners when our troops advancing on Gidanu begin their withdrawal toward Kinsolo.' Pearce clearly loathed every word he uttered.

'They can't be trusted to keep their word,' Denby protested.

'Shut up, Denby!' Talbot snapped, addressed Pearce again. 'The notifications to foreign governments?' Pearce hesitated. Talbot grew angry. 'Goddamnit, Mac, eat your crow and be done with it!'

MacDonald Pearce swallowed, shards of his shattered ego going down with the bile-soured saliva. 'The British and French Ambassadors applaud our decision. The – ah – Soviet Ambassador declares his government will use its good offices with the rebels to prevent incidents which might impede our withdrawal.'

'Looks like we're batting a thousand,' Talbot grinned, glanced at Madigan. 'Anything to contribute, Dan?'

'Uh-huh. I mean, yes, Mr President. Early Frobase is resigning – due to bad health. If it's okay, I'll say my piece in the Senate this afternoon.'

'Be fine. I'll be making my policy-change announcement to the press right after this meeting.' *If those asshole speechwriters have it ready by then. I still can't understand why Jim Zander suddenly quit and disappeared. I could use him.* 'Your speech should mesh in perfectly, Dan.' He turned to Jordan Rickhoven. 'JB, while I can't say you're my favorite person as of this point in time . . .'

'I don't run in popularity contests,' Rickhoven grated. 'I run corporations – and do my share of financing political careers.'

'That's what I'm getting at. My being personally pissed off at you doesn't matter. Uncle Sam needs you – to coin a phrase. We can't let you go down the drain. Your companies are too big.' *A collapse of the Rickhoven Empire would be a body blow to the ailing national economy.* 'In round figures, what'll the Basanda pullout cost you, JB?'

'Our holdings there are valued at over four billion . . . '

'Balls. A paper-figure. Pure fiction. Your companies have earned back their original investments a dozen times.'

'Asset values . . .'

'Look, we're trying to help. The Federal Government has statutory authority to reimburse American companies whose overseas properties are seized or nationalized.' Talbot looked at Brad Cooley. 'How much will your committee sit still for, Brad?'

'A shade under a billion, I guess. Provided we break it up into chunks so no one will choke on the amounts. Can you push it through in the Senate, Dan?'

'For JB? Sure,' Madigan nodded.

'Next, your bank,' Talbot said to Rickhoven. 'Previous Administrations bailed out aircraft, utilities, and other companies. No reason we can't bail out a bank.'

'Under Title Nine of the Classen Act,' Cooley offered.

'A hundred million injection will take Rickhoven National off the critical list,' Madigan said. 'I checked with the Fed.'

'What are the mechanics of Title Nine?' Talbot asked.

Cooley puffed his fat, pink cheeks. 'In effect, all it takes is an Executive Branch nod to the Federal Reserve System. In other words, it's up to you, Mr President.'

'Nope. It's up to *you*, JB,' Talbot said. 'The package offer is about a billion for loss of your Basanda holdings, a hundred million to shore up your bank. Does that bring you back into the fold?'

With tax write-offs added in, passable – but no better, Rickhoven thought. He shrugged. 'Yes, I'm back in the fold – but I'd like to remind you people of something. The Basanda operation would have revived industry, given the economy a boost . . .'

'Which brings us to the scenario I mentioned at Marjorie's,' Talbot grinned. He did not need her notes. He .

had memorized the details. 'My policy announcement today is a replay of the pitch I made a couple of weeks ago. Basically, an open confession of errors. We inherited the Basanda treaty, sent aid in good faith, believing that we were helping a democracy. We admit we were suckered into supporting ruthless dictatorships. Having learned the truth we're pulling out.' The President expanded his chest.

'Hereafter, we will stand by our allies only if they are truly free and democratic. We will not spend American lives or money to sustain tyranny – anywhere, at any time . . .'

FDR updated, plus soupçons of LBJ and Dick Nixon, Brad Cooley mused. Talbot's being controlled by the Marjorie Norworth guidance system.

' . . . we have no quarrel with other nations,' Talbot went on, unconsciously shifting into campaign-speech delivery. 'We are committed to peace. As proof, we shall reduce our armed forces . . .'

'You can't be serious!' Kurtz exclaimed.

'John, we'll reduce militaty *personnel* strength – in stages, by five per cent annually, starting with the next fiscal year.'

Beautiful! Madigan cheered silently, the light dawning.

Talbot resumed his campaign-style oratory. 'But we are determined to guarantee our national security. I shall ask Congress for funds to reequip our armed forces with the new material required to maintain their defensive capability despite manpower reductions.' He stepped down from the soapbox, smiled broadly. 'We'll buy new trucks, tanks, uniforms, messkits, missiles – the works. The pump gets primed and the affluence starts flowing – without a war.'

MacDonald Pearce spluttered. 'The Russians and Chinese . . . '

'Will recognize the gimmick. They've been using it for years, same as we have – modernizing the military every now and then to keep people working.' Talbot laughed. 'I'll even visit Moscow and Peking like Nixon, let 'em know it *is* a gimmick.' His gray eyes narrowed, grew serious. 'Brad, Dan, how much can we get?'

'Congress always heaves a sigh of relief when a war scare

ends,' Cooley said. 'Probably twenty–thirty billion in emergency appropriations if we make a big hoopla.'

'We'll hard sell it as the Talbot Doctrine!' Madigan enthused. 'Christ, the Senate will approve twenty billion.'

'Make it thirty,' Talbot said.

They're haggling like Armenian rug-peddlers, Russ Hatch laughed inwardly. A few weeks ago, he would have been shocked and enraged.

'Thirty,' Brad Cooley nodded. 'Course, we'll have to promise my distinguished colleagues that industries in their home states will receive fat slices of the defense contracts.'

'What the hell, I'll deliver thirty in the Senate,' Madigan said.

John Kurtz was frowning. 'Two questions, Mr President. First, how do we make the Basanda story stick?'

'With razzle-dazzle glue. G-Man Hopper and Senator Hatch go public. Tonight. On Suzanne Loring's show – which incidentally, is her bonus for helping me out of the shitpot you guys built.' A reminder that Kurtz and his fellows had yet to redeem themselves fully. 'The public will see the film shown at Marjorie's – only with a different commentary. Then Emmett and Russ confirm what I'll tell the press. The pitch is worked out to have a hell of an impact.'

Could be, Kurtz granted. 'My second question. The scenario holds that the Administration was deceived, kept in the dark – but by whom? How can we convince . . . ?'

'A cinch. Remember the CIA scandals under Kennedy, Johnson, Nixon, and Ford? The Bay of Pigs, assassinations of foreign political leaders, the overthrowing of foreign governments and the rest?'

'Of course, but . . .'

'No buts. Basanda was another dirty CIA stew. The agency hid the facts, duped everyone. If it hadn't been for FBI Director Hopper and Cabinet Secretaries Pearce and Kurtz, the CIA would have dragged us into another Vietnam catastrophe. A version a grateful nation will gladly buy.'

G. Howard Denby paled, choked. 'You mean . . . ?'

'I said there's a big part in the scenario for you, Denby,' Talbot said in a gelid tone. 'You can carry the can.'

Denby's initial impulse was to take the offensive, threaten to make disclosures, release classified documents implicating everyone from Talbot on down. Then he looked at the tightly shut faces of the other men in the Oval Office.

'If you're thinking of a secret-papers blitz, forget it,' Charles Talbot said. 'I've ordered all your files sealed and placed under FBI custody – and, oh, yes, you've been dismissed. Fired.'

Denby was seized by an excruciating abdominal cramp. He doubled over, groaned loudly. Madigan, who was seated nearest him, leaned closer – and straightened up hastily, grimacing disgust.

'My God!' Madigan exclaimed. 'He's shit his pants!'

'I don't wonder,' President Talbot said. 'I don't wonder at all.'

The speechwriters had done an excellent piece of work. The three-page script was concise, pithy, covered all the points Talbot wished to make. At thirty minutes past noon, Talbot faced the White House press corps. There was a determined jut to his jaw when he spoke.

'I will read a statement. There are to be no questions afterward. Save them for a normal press conference I plan to hold later this week.' He glanced at the papers on his lectern and began to read.

'Many American Presidents have regretted their failure to heed the warning contained in Mark Twain's epigram: "It is easier to stay out than it is to get out." We should have stayed out of Basanda. We did not – and, until early this morning, we were becoming more and more deeply enmeshed in the bloody conflict there. At 2 A.M. this morning, I issued orders that we get *out* – without delay. There are sound – and I fear shocking – reasons behind the sudden policy-reversal.'

The rest of the statement reiterated what Talbot had said in the Oval Office and concluded: 'It is for the American people to judge whether my decision was right or wrong, and for their elected representatives to approve or disapprove the program I have outlined.' Talbot gathered up the three sheets of paper as the press corps broke into an ovation.

'He's making noises like a statesman!' one correspondent yelled into the ear of another.

'Shit, man. I already thought of that as my lead. "President Charles Talbot today seemed to gain the stature of a world statesman as he" – et cetera.'

Denby was in no physical condition to go anywhere by himself. Two Secret Service agents helped him leave the Oval Office and took him to a West Wing bathroom, where he managed to clean himself up a little. When he emerged, two other men were waiting and offered to drive him home. He assumed they, too, were members of the White House Secret Service detail and accepted thankfully.

They escorted him outside, one holding each arm, for Denby could scarcely stand. 'Kinda chilly,' one man said. Both paused, took gloves from their pockets, put them on. The taller of the pair helped Denby into the right-hand front seat of his parked Chrysler Imperial, then got behind the wheel. His partner got in the back and said, 'We'll have a car follow.'

They drove out of the White House gates, a black Ford sedan trailing behind. Five minutes later, Denby dimly realized that they were going in the wrong direction. He reached out to tap the driver on the shoulder – and the man in the back seat plunged a hypodermic needle into Denby's arm, pressed the syringe-plunger. G. Howard Denby gasped, slumped back in the seat – and died.

The two cars continued into Prince George County, Maryland. When in open country, they turned off on a secluded dirt road that was screened on both sides by thick bushes. Denby's car pulled over, stopped. The Ford halted a few yards behind.

'Nobody around?' the man driving the Chrysler asked. 'Nope.'

Both left-side doors opened. The two men got out, pulled

Denby's limp body over to the driver's seat. The taller man produced a 38-caliber automatic, held it at the correct angle against Denby's right temple, fired one shot. The bullet tore into the skull. The man raised Denby's right hand, pressing and smearing the lifeless fingers against the pistol butt, trigger and muzzle.

'Ought to do it,' he grunted, dropping the weapon on the front seat. The two men closed the Chrysler's doors, hurried to the Ford, climbed inside. The driver of the Ford eased past the Chrysler.

'We'll be seeing him again,' he remarked in a bored tone.

'Probably before the day is out,' the man who had wielded the hypo said, pulling off his gloves.

Once the corpse was found and identified as being that of Central Intelligence Agency Director G. Howard Denby, the FBI would be called in to assist local authorities in their investigations of the suicide. The three men in the Ford sedan were the agents whom FBI Director Emmett Hopper would then assign to the case. It had all been settled that morning before Hopper and the trio left the J. Edgar Hoover Building for the White House.

Lexa Talbot was punctual for the one o'clock luncheon date she had made with Marjorie the night before. The House on the Hill had undergone retransformation. The African masks, statuary and artifacts were gone, the State Dining Room cleaned and returned to its normal pristine elegance.

'Holcomb will serve us in my suite,' Marjorie said. 'The CBN people were very good about moving their paraphernalia out.'

She led Lexa upstairs.

'Has your father made his statement to the press?' Marjorie asked when they reached the door of her suite and went inside.

'He had it scheduled for twelve-thirty. There's been nothing on the radio yet, though – I kept my set on driving over.'

'Then the bulletins should start coming over at any minute.' Marjorie switched on the FM band of her parlor

348

radio. Lexa saw that a luncheon table was set – just as it had been before.

'A drink first, Lexa?'

'Please. A Bloody Mary.'

'We're having consommé à la Madriléne – it might be too much tomato, don't you think?' She rang for Holcomb.

'It would be,' Lexa nodded. 'A martini, then.'

Holcomb entered, began mixing the drink in a pitcher.

' . . . A special bulletin . . .'

'Ah! Must be about Charlie's press statement.' Marjorie went to the radio, turned up the volume.

'Only minutes ago, President Charles P. Talbot stunned members of the White House press corps with a series of announcements . . .'

Marjorie and Lexa sat in armchairs and listened. Marjorie smiled as she heard quotes from Talbot's statement. They paraphrased sentences she had carefully written out for him. Lexa sipped at her martini and also smiled. When the announcer concluded the long bulletin, Marjorie turned off the radio.

'Charlie's on the comeback trail once more,' she said.

'Because of you.'

'True. But then, I'm fond of your father. He and I had a delightful affair years ago – did you know? Ah, you're surprised – you didn't. Of course, I've had more affairs than I could ever begin to count – more than one President among them – as I imagine you've heard from the gossips.'

Marjorie laughed.

'And so, my dear, having known Presidents – even unto the Biblical sense – I'm quick to recognize their flaws . . .'

'Everyone has weaknesses, Marjorie.'

'Naturally. But our concern – yours and mine – is with Charles Talbot's flaws. We have to protect him from his own weaknesses. He's a good hail-fellow-well-met politician. As a leader – be honest, Lexa – he falls short . . .'

Not even I can argue that, Lexa thought.

' . . . he wants to be liked, see everyone around him content and happy. Charlie simply cannot bring himself to abide by what I always think of as Truman's Law.'

349

'Afraid you've lost me.'

'Harry Truman used to say, "The only way to run a country is by making sure forty-nine percent of the people hate your guts – then the other fifty-one percent will be on your side."' Marjorie chuckled. 'It was FDR's technique, too, but he only used it on politicians. He always maintained his public appeal.'

Lady Norworth allowed herself a moment or two for remembering, sighed, returned to the here and now.

'You and I will have to watch over Charles Talbot like a pair of mother hens for the rest of his term, Lexa.'

'After his reelection, too.'

'My dear, Charlie mustn't be allowed to run again!'

Lexa's eyes blazed. 'You just said you were fond of him...'

'I am. I am also able to face facts. We can make Charles Talbot look and act like a President, appear to be a leader, for the next twenty-two months. At the end of that time, he'll leave office in a blaze of glory – a heroic figure.'

'A heroic figure is certain to be renominated.'

'Unless we use every wile and guile to prevent him from accepting the renomination, yes.'

'I'd be insane to discourage him.'

'Lexa, you'd be insane if you didn't. Think of Charlie – of your father – objectively. Once renominated, he would *believe* himself to be the image we create for him, become convinced he's infallible. He'd take no advice, be totally unmanageable and destroy himself. We could never hope to wet-nurse him through another four years.'

'You asked me to lunch – why? Because you wanted to tell me you intend to dump Daddy and support the opposition in the next election?' Lexa felt suddenly empty, abandoned. She did not want to relinquish the prestige and privileges she enjoyed as the President's daughter. 'Marjorie...'

'You leap to conclusions too soon, my dear. I invited you to lunch today because tonight Senator Russell Hatch will abruptly emerge from his state of anonymity and become a national figure. A very prominent national figure. Come, we'll have our lunch and talk about him...'

34

Washington, D.C.: Thursday, March 4. Evening and Night.

The camera was on Suzanne Loring.

'Washington was really turned inside out today, and CBN is devoting an hour and a half to this special show as a public service. Normally, I tape my interviews in advance. Tonight, they will be live – with Mr Emmett Hopper, Director of the Federal Bureau of Investigation, and Senator Russell Hatch of Oregon.'

Camera to Hopper and Hatch, back to Suzanne.

'Before I begin the interviews, you will see a film – but first a quick recap of the sensational stories that have been breaking in the capital since early afternoon. At twelve-thirty, President Charles Talbot announced an end to all American involvement in Basanda – and made a revelation that has shocked the nation.

'The President bluntly declared that United States policy in Basanda stemmed from a sinister, ongoing plot organized by the Central Intelligence Agency. He bluntly charged CIA Director G. Howard Denby with attempting to push America into a shooting war and with planning a coup that would – and I quote – "turn the United States into a police state".

'A few hours later, Denby was found dead in his automobile. According to law enforcement authorities, he had committed suicide. The consensus along the Potomac is Denby's act was tantamount to a full confession of guilt.'

Suzanne turned her head to the left, where Emmett Hopper sat beside her. The camera pulled back, panned, showed them both.

'Is that your opinion, too, Mr Hopper?'

'To my great regret, I must say yes, it is.'

Suzanne's voice: 'Any comment, Senator Hatch?'

Camera on Russ: 'Extremely damaging evidence has been uncovered against Denby and the CIA.'

Suzanne: 'Much is contained in the film we will show now.'

Across the nation, viewers saw a long shot of the Kinsolo waterfront and a blood-red title: WELCOME TO BASANDA fill their screens.

VOICEOVER: 'The motion pictures you are about to see will horrify you. Until today, CBN was banned from showing them by orders from the Central Intelligence Agency. Officials of the CIA represented themselves to be acting on Presidential instructions. We now know the claims were false – outright lies.'

The WELCOME TO BASANDA title wiped to a long-shot of a jungle clearing. At its far end, blacks in oddments of military uniform held longish implements and flailed and jabbed at shapeless bundles on the ground. The camera lens zoomed in. The bundles were hideously mutilated corpses – one that of a young woman, her belly slit open. Black hands thrust a bayonet-tipped rifle into the open belly. The rifle swung upward. An almost fully formed baby was skewered on the bayonet.

VOICEOVER: 'Working hand in glove with vicious dictatorships, a super-powerful organization such as the CIA easily keeps atrocities such as these secret.'

Jumpcut to the exterior of the Prime Ministerial Palace in Kinsolo.

VOICEOVER: 'Using enormous sums for which it did not have to account, the CIA built this palace for its stooge, the late Prime Minister Odu Mwandi . . .'

The ensuing scenes were identical to those in the version shown at Marjorie Norworth's party, but the soundtrack commentary was entirely different. Odu Mwandi, Percival Kwida, and the Military Grand Council remained villains. However there were no criticisms of the Talbot Administration, Cabinet Departments, or U.S. armed forces and their

352

commanders. Blame was placed squarely – and entirely – on the CIA. Minutes before the film ended, an assistant producer gave Suzanne Loring a scrawled memo.

'All outlets report switchboards clogged. Calls fifty-to-one favorable. God' – CBN-ese for Noah Sturdevant – 'phoned from New York. Says if rest of show holds up, your bonus doubled.'

It'll hold up, Suzanne thought exuberantly.

A light flashed. Suzanne set her features in a grim expression. Another light. She was back on camera.

'Horrible, ghastly,' she said. A one-beat pause. 'Mr Hopper, I'd like to ask you how *you* feel after seeing those motion pictures.'

Hopper, also grim: 'Sickened and ashamed, Miss Loring.'

Suzanne: 'Our audience doubtless wonders why the FBI had no information about any of this.'

Hopper, his expression rueful, bitter: 'The FBI has no investigative authority outside the continental limits of the United States.'

Suzanne: 'Surely there is an exchange of information between our two leading intelligence agencies?'

Hopper: 'A widespread misconception. Although the FBI has regularly passed data to the CIA, there has been no reciprocal flow for several years.'

Suzanne: 'Senator Hatch, you volunteered to appear tonight as a supporter and friend of President Talbot. Would you care to tell us something about his views?'

Tom Sawyer was serious, earnest: 'The one-way policy was set by previous Presidential Administrations. President Talbot has assured me he will change it – and make changes in the CIA.'

Suzanne: 'Does he intend to dismantle the Agency?'

Hatch: 'He will make the CIA accountable.'

Suzanne: 'Accountable to whom, Senator?'

Hatch: 'The President, Congress – and the American people.'

Suzanne: 'Gentlemen, it's difficult for me to imagine how the facts about Basanda were kept from the President and his

Cabinet officers. Is there an explanation?'

Russ was scheduled to field that question.

Hatch: 'There certainly is. The CIA fed whole rivers of reports to the Executive Branch. The reports appeared legitimate and accurate. In actual fact, they were grossly distorted or wholly fabricated.'

He ran fingers through his hair. It was becoming a conscious gesture, done for effect.

Hatch: 'The President and Cabinet members receive countless reports daily. They must rely on their subordinates. Were they to investigate each and every report personally, Government would grind to a halt. Howard Denby knew this and took full advantage.'

A message flashed on Suzanne's monitor-set, which was hidden from the cameras: 'CALLS NOW 100 TO 1 FAVORABLE. GOD TELEXES YOUR BONUS DOUBLED. SAYS YOU MUST BE CAUSING APOPLEXY EPIDEMICS IN NBC, CBS, AND ABC EXECUTIVE SUITES.'

Suzanne kept her face straight for the cameras. If Noah Sturdevant is making funnies over the Telex, we *must* be a smash-hit. She readied the question Marjorie Norworth had urged her to ask.

Suzanne: 'Gentlemen, do you believe that Howard Denby and the CIA actually planned a *coup d'état* here, in the United States?'

Hopper: 'No comment.' (Said in a manner that left no doubt he believed it without reservation.)

Hatch: 'President Talbot made the charge while Denby was alive and could have refuted it. Denby killed himself. I'm an attorney and refuse to pass judgment on a man who is no longer able to speak in his own defense or offer mitigating pleas.'

Beautiful, Suzanne thought sourly. *Rest in peace, G. Howard Denby – hung, drawn, and quartered posthumously. Red-blooded Americans will hereafter stand in line to shit on your grave.*

Suzanne: 'Senator, you and Mr Hopper were instrumental in bringing the truth about Basanda and Denby to

354

the President's attention. Won't you tell us how you learned . . .'

Hatch: 'Sorry, I can't compromise my sources.'

Hopper: 'The means Senator Hatch and I employed must remain under the classified heading for the time being, Miss Loring.'

Suzanne: 'Well, in that case, let's turn to President Talbot's startling new defense proposals.'

Russ gave his hair another tousling.

Hatch: 'Oh, yes. The Talbot Doctrine . . .'

Suzanne (registering surprise): 'Did you say "Talbot Doctrine?"'

Hatch: 'Yep' – the 'yep' went with the candid, boyish grin – 'It's what they're calling it in the Senate. I predict the program will sail through Congress.'

Deliver me from the temptation to blow the hole can of worms wide open, Suzy reflected. *There, I'm delivered. Pull a stunt like that and good-bye bonus, contract, career – the professional works. Stick to the script, don't buck the System. History isn't made, it's manufactured. Truth is wherever the dollars lie.*

Suzanne: 'Do you foresee any weakening of our military power?'

Hatch: 'None. In fact, President Talbot's program will make us stronger, more able to guarantee our security, maintain peace . . .'

When the show ended, someone rushed to tell Suzanne that Noah Sturdevant was *holding* on the telephone – an unheard-of concesssion. 'He wants to talk to you, Miss Loring. He's in Seventh Heaven!'

'Where else should God be?' Suzy cracked, turned to Russ. 'I'll talk to him – then *I'm* taking *you* to dinner. We'll celebrate.'

His face reddened. 'I – I can't, honey. Have to rush.'

'Rush? Where?'

He squirmed. 'Lexa and President Talbot asked me over to the White House for dinner.'

'Oh. We'll have our celebration tomorrow night, then.'

355

She was managing to keep up a brave front.

'Christ, I'm sorry – but we're – Lexa, Talbot and I – are going to a Kennedy Center concert. He wants to be seen in public and . . .'

'Sure, Russ.' *The elevator cables have snapped. I'm dropping.*

'I'll phone you in the morning, honey.' Hatch was edging away.

'Do that – and have fun tonight.'

Suzanne took the telephone receiver an assistant producer thrust at her. 'Mr Sturdevant, I presume?'

'Miss Loring! My congratulations?'

She glanced over her shoulder. Emmett Hopper was still in the studio, signing autographs for station employees. But Russ had gone.

'. . . imagine how much you gained tonight, Miss Loring!'

'I'm trying not to think of what I've lost.'

'*Lost?* I don't understand.'

'You wouldn't, Mr Sturdevant. You couldn't. Good night.'

Noah Sturevant heard the line go dead as Suzanne hung up. He scowled indignantly. Temperamental bitch, he thought – or maybe she's menstruating again.

No one on the White House staff could remember a day like it. Telephone, Telex, and telegram traffic soared to all-time peaks in early afternoon, and remained there. Streams of couriers brought letters, reports, dispatches from Cabinet Departments, Federal bureaus and agencies, Congressmen and Senators. Delivery trucks lined up at the service-entrance gates. They brought the homage-gifts that sincere well-wishers, self-seeking opportunists and nut-fringe types customarily send Presidents on momentous occasions.

These, coming as they did in such huge quantities, required assembly-line processing. Secret Service agents ran parcels and packages through X-ray scanning devices, then opened them for closer inspection, after which secretaries logged the gifts on PG (Presidential Gift) Form 102 sheets. Names and addresses of senders were noted down, cards accompanying gifts were stapled to the forms. (Later, each sender would receive a thank-you note bearing a mass-produced forgery of Charles Talbot's signature.)

The gifts were next sorted by category. Flowers were sent on to veterans' hospitals (for the public relations value). Edibles – whether home-baked cakes or costly gourmet-shop food-hampers – went into the incinerators (against the possibility they might be poisoned). Durable items – ranging from Argyll socks to Steuben glass pseudo-art sculptures – were consigned to the limbo of warehouse storage. 'Live-stock' – today, two toy poodles, a Corgi puppy and a Siamese kitten – became the property of the press section. Temporarily. Until human-appeal photos of the President fondling the animals could be taken – after which the creatures were sent to the Army Chemical Warfare Center for use in biological warfare experiments.

President Charles Talbot spent the afternoon and evening in the Oval Office, a benign monarch occupying his Presidential chair as though it were a throne. He conferred with aides and assistants (whose behavior toward him now far transcended normal respect), spoke on the telephone, read documents (using a felt-tipped pen to make check marks on those he approved, drawing X's on those he did not). He was most engrossed by the news-media summaries that were being updated for him every half hour. Acclaim was snowballing.

At five twenty-five, Ken Ramsey brought what he thought was bad news.

'Chief, Bethesda Naval just reported that Avery Braithwaite tore up a bedsheet and hung himself.'

Talbot did not even blink.

'Too bad.' *Like hell! Another problem solved.* 'Okay, Ken, you know the routine. A statement expressing my shock and grief – dear friend, great jurist – blah-blah. Personal telegrams to his family. Big funeral. Flags at half-mast – all the trimmings. Put some people on it. By the way, when's the next media-summary due?'

Talbot and Lexa watched Suzanne Loring's special broadcast in the Oval Office. He swaggered self-confidence when it was over.

'It's the capper, Puss,' he declared. 'I'm in – solid. Anybody tries to screw me around again, I'll crack down – with a Goddamned sledgehammer.'

Marjorie does have him measured, Lexa thought. *He's already ego-tripping, and he'll get worse and worse. It's going to be a constant struggle to hold him down, protect him from himself.*

'Baby, when Hatch gets here for dinner, you and he go upstairs and eat. I'd rather not be away from my desk while things are still popping.'

'Look – you should cultivate Hatch. He'll be more and more valuable to you after tonight. He came across like Sir Lancelot and helped convert twenty million people into true believers that you're King Arthur defending them with your magic sword.'

She grinned, snapped her fingers.

'Your daughter is a genius, *mon cher père*. We'll have dinner served right here.'

'In the Oval Office? I never heard of any President . . .'

'So what? You can stay near your desk and butter up Russell Hatch while you're buttering your rolls.'

'Ummm. Not bad. Puss. Hatch'll figure it's a special honor.'

Lexa met Russ in the Reception Foyer.

'You were wonderful,' she said as they walked down corridors to the Oval Office. 'I'm only sorry we can't offer you a private upstairs dinner, but Daddy's still busy . . .'

'I'm not surprised. Lexa, if he'd rather cancel . . .'

'Oh, no! He insists we have dinner together – even though it might be hectic.'

The sofas flanking the Oval Office fireplace had been moved aside, a table placed in the open area. It was set with the White House gold service usually reserved for visiting royalty or ultra-important State dinners.

'Daddy wanted to go all out – to suit the occasion,' Lexa

said after Talbot pumped Russ's hand and pounded his shoulder.

Talbot gave Russ sheafs of messages and news-media summaries to skim over and busied himself mixing martinis.

Russ, holding the papers, glanced around, looking for a chair. *I am operating at the genius-level tonight*, Lexa thought. 'Sit at Daddy's desk, Russ,' she said quickly.

He hesitated.

'Go on, son,' Talbot said over his shoulder. 'You can spread out the papers there.'

Hatch seated himself in the Presidential chair – and an instant later experienced what he could describe to himself only as sort of electric shock, a surge of energy. He pretended to read the papers Talbot had given him, but the words blurred together. His fingers unconsciously stroked the desk top. *Truman and Carter were full of shit*, he mused. *The buck doesn't stop here. This is the peak, the apex from which it can be passed – or hurled – in any direction.*

His thoughts were reflected by his facial expressions and Lexa Talbot read them and her smile was cryptic.

Charles Talbot completed his barman's chores, carried filled glasses to Lexa and Russ.

'The returns seem to indicate a pretty clean sweep, don't they?' he grinned, putting a glass on the desk blotter. He went to get his own.

An administrative assistant entered with more documents.

'Pile 'em over there next to the Senator,' Talbot said. 'We'll be having dinner in a few minutes – see to it there aren't any calls and no more business for an hour or so, okay?'

'Of course, Mr President.'

The assistant left. Talbot raised his glass high. 'Here's to our victory banquet coming up . . .'

Russ rose from the Presidential chair – to his surprise, he felt a twinge of reluctance as he did – and lifted his glass.

'. . . that's what politics are all about, Russ,' Talbot chuckled. 'Tough – sometimes gutter-dirty – fights, victories and then the fun of celebrating.' He drank some of his martini. 'I remember once when I was campaigning in

Springfield – running for my second term in the House – and the local bosses ganged up . . .'

A purring sound intruded, interrupted him.

'Damn, I told that guy we wanted peace and quiet – oh, it's my personal line.' Talbot went to the Presidential desk, picked up his private-line phone. 'Yes?' he said into the transmitter.

'Marjorie – Mr President and lord of all you survey.'

'Hi, Marjorie . . .'

'Do you have a radio on?'

'Nope. Lexa, Russ, and I are having a drink – why do you ask?'

'There's been a news flash from Beirut. The Lebanese have started shooting at each other again.'

'Penny ante stuff for Mac Pearce and his crew to worry about.'

'Charlie, as FDR once said, in politics always do a big encore when the applause is loud. You're riding high – ride even higher. Get on the hotline to the Kremlin. Suggest a joint U.S.-Russian peace-keeping force for Lebanon.'

'We're not even out of Basanda yet,' Talbot protested, 'won't be clear of that mess for weeks . . .'

'Exactly. Calling the Kremlin will be an earnest of your peaceful intentions toward everyone, including the Russians. Play cooperative, and they won't raise any fuss over the new defense program.' Her tone became patronizing, but Talbot failed to detect the change. 'Breathe deeply, Charlie – let the concept penetrate and sink in.'

Talbot's forehead wrinkled in thought. 'By God, you've got something there, Marjorie, I'll do it!'

'Smart decision, Charlie. Very smart. Give Lexa and Russ my love – and, oh, yes. Tell Lexa we should hold another mother-hen meeting very soon. Good night, Charlie.'

Talbot replaced the receiver, looked at Lexa. 'Puss, what the hell is a mother-hen meeting – Marjorie says you and she should hold one again.'

'It's a new club we've formed, Daddy,' Lexa replied. 'Come, finish your drink with Russ and me.'

'In a minute.' He started pushing call buttons. 'I have to find somebody who can work the hotline and a Russian interpreter. You two stay and hear this. I'm going to knock the world for a loop – and tonight's just the beginning!'

It most certainly is, Lexa thought. *The beginning of a great many things.*

Epilogue

Washington, D.C. Twenty-two Months Later. January 20.

The NBC television commentator was rhapsodic.

'. . . even Mother Nature appears pleased and happy. The skies are clear, the temperature an unseasonably warm fifty-seven degrees. The huge masses of spectators are in a holiday mood – perhaps they take the benign weather as yet another promising augury for the future.

'There are, of course, the usual numbers of notables waiting on the Inaugural platform – Cabinet officers, Senate and House leaders and other important officials. Among them is Lady Marjorie Norworth, the famed Washington hostess. Her presence is something of a surprise to capital observers. Although Lady Norworth enjoyed close friendships with several Presidents, this is the first time she has been accorded the coveted honor of a place on the Inaugural stand itself.

'But this *is* a precedent-shattering Inauguration. Never before in American history has an incumbent President been succeeded by his own son-in-law – sorry to break off this commentary, ladies and gentlemen. The Marine band has sounded ruffles and flourishes – you can hear it in the background – and there, now it has begun to play *Hail to the Chief* . . .'

The ceremony was – as always – dignified and impressive. The Inaugural Address gave – as always – hope and inspiration.

'. . . all of us, regardless of race, creed, or color united to keep America strong, free, and prosperous. Thank you – and may whatever God you worship bless you – my fellow citizens.'

President Russell Hatch turned away from the forest of microphones arrayed before him.

'Lexa,' he said – but his wife had stepped a few feet to the right and was embracing her father.

'Mr President.' Hatch recognized Lady Marjorie Norworth's voice, whirled, and practically leaped to her side. She took both his hands, squeezed them, smiled. 'I want to be the first to congratulate you.'

'Marjorie, if it hadn't been for you and all you did . . .'

'Idiot.' She lowered her voice. 'I'm not talking about the Presidency. Lexa told me the big news yesterday – that she's pregnant.'

President Russell Hatch beamed, nodded.

'Lexa, my dear!' Marjorie called out over his shoulder. Like her husband, Lexa Hatch responded instantly, hurried to join them.

'Yes, Marjorie?'

'I'll be over this evening to help you dress for the Inaugural Ball – and I'm bringing a little gift for you.'

Official Washington was stunned. Lexa Hatch appeared at the Inaugural Ball wearing the famed T'ang Dynasty jade gorget that Aristotle Onassis had given to Lady Marjorie Norworth. The nation's new First Lady and the longtime queen of the House on the Hill were now allied. Henceforth, they would be the behind-scenes makers and breakers, the decisive manipulative forces in power-struggles – the invincible and final arbiters.

Only United States Supreme Court Associate Justice Bradford Cooley showed no surprise. His eyes gleamed with saturnine amusement when he drew Marjorie Norworth aside at the ball.

'Yet another brilliant stroke, Marjorie,' he laughed. 'A potential adversary is firmly on your side, and she has been publicly designated as your eventual successor.' His expression shaded to the quizzical. 'But don't you fear that your Crown Princess might become impatient and want the throne entirely to herself?'

'I fear nothing of the sort, Brad,' Marjorie said. 'Lexa

will be content to wait, I can guarantee that.' *And if I can't, I have an envelope in my safe that will*. During the last six months of Charles Talbot's term, she had prevailed on him to set in motion the machinery that consolidated the FBI and CIA into a single super-intelligence agency, with Emmett Hopper as its Director. Hopper showed his gratitude by giving her a large, thick envelope containing his files on Lexa and on James Zander. They included the photographs his agents had taken of Lexa at the orgy in the house on A Street.

Marjorie is sure of her ground, Cooley thought, *and she's never been one to make dangerous miscalculations*. He raised his glass of bourbon. 'To you, Marjorie – the true victor,' he said, his smile fond, his tone sincere.

'Thank you, Brad.'

Under their half-hooded lids, Lady Marjorie Norworth's violet eyes were aglow with the sense of power at last fully realized.

Bestsellers available in paperback from Grafton Books

Emmanuelle Arsan

Emmanuelle	£2.50 ☐
Emmanuelle 2	£2.50 ☐
Laure	£1.95 ☐
Nea	£1.95 ☐
Vanna	£2.50 ☐

Jonathan Black

Ride the Golden Tiger	£2.95 ☐
Oil	£2.50 ☐
The World Rapers	£2.50 ☐
The House on the Hill	£2.50 ☐
Megacorp	£2.50 ☐
The Plunderers	£2.50 ☐

Herbert Kastle

Cross-Country	£2.50 ☐
Little Love	£2.50 ☐
Millionaires	£2.50 ☐
Miami Golden Boy	£2.50 ☐
The Movie Maker	£2.95 ☐
The Gang	£2.50 ☐
Hit Squad	£1.95 ☐
Dirty Movies	£2.95 ☐
Hot Prowl	£1.95 ☐
Sunset People	£2.50 ☐
David's War	£1.95 ☐

To order direct from the publisher just tick the titles you want
and fill in the order form.

The world's greatest novelists now available in paperback from Grafton Books

Eric van Lustbader

Jian	£3.50	☐
The Miko	£2.95	☐
The Ninja	£3.50	☐
Sirens	£3.50	☐
Beneath An Opal Moon	£2.95	☐
Black Heart	£3.50	☐

Nelson de Mille

By the Rivers of Babylon	£2.50	☐
Cathedral	£1.95	☐
The Talbot Odyssey	£3.50	☐

Justin Scott

The Shipkiller	£2.50	☐
The Man Who Loved the Normandie	£2.50	☐
A Pride of Kings	£2.95	☐

Leslie Waller

Trocadero	£2.50	☐
The Swiss Account	£2.50	☐
The American	£2.50	☐
The Family	£1.95	☐
The Banker	£2.50	☐
The Brave and the Free	£1.95	☐
Gameplan	£1.95	☐

David Charney

Sensei	£2.50	☐
Sensei II: The Swordmaster	£2.50	☐

Paul-Loup Sulitzer

The Green King	£2.95	☐

To order direct from the publisher just tick the titles you want
and fill in the order form.

GF781

All these books are available at your local bookshop or newsagent, or can be ordered direct from the publisher.

To order direct from the publishers just tick the titles you want and fill in the form below.

Name _____

Address _____

_____

Send to:
Grafton Cash Sales
PO Box 11, Falmouth, Cornwall TR10 9EN.

Please enclose remittance to the value of the cover price plus:

UK 60p for the first book, 25p for the second book plus 15p per copy for each additional book ordered to a maximum charge of £1.90.

BFPO 60p for the first book, 25p for the second book plus 15p per copy for the next 7 books, thereafter 9p per book.

Overseas including Eire £1.25 for the first book, 75p for second book and 28p for each additional book.

Grafton Books reserve the right to show new retail prices on covers, which may differ from those previously advertised in the text or elsewhere.